NAMELESS

JULIE COOPER

Quills & Quartos
PUBLISHING

Edited by Jan Ashton and Regina McCaughey-Silvia

Cover Design by Holly Perret

ISBN: 978-1-951033-85-9 (ebook) and 978-1-951033-86-6 (paperback)

To Merry: Not just my sister but my very first friend.
Thank you for always having my back.

PROLOGUE

L ast night, I dreamt of Pemberley again.

The park was very large, containing a great variety of ground. I entered it in one of its lowest points, and drove for some time through a beautiful wood, stretching over a wide extent, up and up, and further up still.

I saw and admired every remarkable spot and point of view. After rapidly ascending for half a mile, I found myself at the top of a considerable eminence, where the wood ceased, and my eye was instantly caught by Pemberley House, situated upon the cliff's apex, into which the road, with some abruptness, wound. It was a large, handsome, stone building, standing well on rising ground, fronted by a ridge of high woody hills; in the rear, a wing had been constructed upon a precipice of some natural importance, jutting out over the valley below.

I have since seen many great estates in England and Europe, but never a place for which nature had done more, or where natural beauty had been so little counteracted by an awkward taste, as Pemberley. But even as I watched, delighted, the wood encircling its winding roads changed from idyllic flora and fauna to haggard, witchy crones, clawing at me—grasping and pointing, darkening as an unearthly night sky cloaked the sun.

Startled, I gasped and ran for the great house; in the manner of dreams, however, I slogged through bogs, unable to gain purchase, incapable of moving forward. I was caught, trapped, held firmly in place by branched talons. Suddenly and without warning, in the way of the most fearsome dreams, I found myself at the centre of Pemberley's massive ballroom. The spires of a thousand candles glittered from its crystal chandeliers; the music of fifty instruments played a waltz to which no one danced. And then the choking smoke began to fill my lungs as Pemberley began to burn. I could not even scream; there was no air, my voice strangling upon the bitter, beautiful flames.

CHAPTER ONE

December 1, 1819

T he Dowager Countess of Matlock rang her silver bell, a sound I had grown to hate. Clearly never having had any idea of restraint, the countess slept little and demanded much. I had learned a good deal of her sufferings in the twelve months I had been in her service; too, she cherished a rather selfish pride which would not allow her to admit to imperfections, aches, pains, or loneliness. The only worse position in the house than mine was Lady Matlock's personal maid, Dawson, with whom I often exchanged grim looks of mutual sympathy.

"My vinaigrette," she demanded, when I scurried into the room like a trained mouse. "And at once, you lazy girl. My nephew is to visit. Where is Dawson? She must arrange my hair. I should like to wear the pale pink pelisse. Mademoiselle says that no one would ever guess me to have reached the half-century mark when I wear pink."

I forbore pointing out that as her son was in his mid-forties, she must have seen her half-century mark decades' past. When one is in service, one quickly learns to mind one's tongue.

It had not been an easy lesson. I had been raised a daughter of Longbourn, accustomed to saying whatever my tongue demanded. It was providential, really, that Mama and Papa had died together—Mama *never* would have learnt discretion, or how to gracefully undertake the role of impoverished relation. It was helpful, too, that I had spent six of the seven years since my parents' deaths with my uncle and aunt Gardiner. I was much more adjusted to a less indulged existence by the time my brother-in-law found the position with Lady Matlock for me, and I was fortunate to live in comfort. While thoughts of those early happy, melancholy years could sadden me, I had also learnt another important lesson—to remember the past only as it gave me wisdom and pleasure to do so. There were tears enough locked within me to drown myself, were I to indulge them. I never did.

If Lady Matlock seldom remembered past pleasures, she had no trouble recalling current difficulties. She had only the one child, the current earl, who, to my way of seeing it, paid her to stay away. She spoke of her grandchildren only in terms of their many failings, and of her other relations, I heard little. I had met a niece and one of Lady Matlock's two sisters during my year in her service. She had never mentioned *any* of her nephews individually except to complain of their selfishness and neglect—collectively—so I would wager this nephew's visit a surprise to us both. Suddenly, however, he had become a treasure, a favourite, and her dearest relation.

"Willsy is a grieving widower," she warned me.

I hid my smile at a grown man called 'Willsy'. Very unsympathetic of me.

"He lost his wife only three months' past, and it is said he *cannot* recover. They had no children to be of comfort to him now. They were *such* a couple, leaders of the highest circles. His estate is Pemberley, you know—I am certain even *you* have heard of it. The parties they once held! They were written up in all the London papers. Everyone who was *anyone* coveted an invitation to a party at Pemberley—it was a sign of social success, even more so than vouchers at Almack's."

Pemberley... The name did sound familiar, but I could not place it in that moment. I ought to have, of course—many years before, I had heard it discussed at Netherfield, and even the hated Wickham mentioned it once or twice. But after losing Papa and the idyllic life at Longbourn, I had firmly consigned any thoughts of 'higher circles' to my past, accepting my present circumstances with hope, and seldom bothering to read of the doings of society in the papers. I paid little attention to 'the Quality', as Dawson termed England's elite.

I had wanted, of course, to marry, and there had been a few encouraging prospects. Mama would call me too fastidious, had she lived. I did not think I was; I had utterly given up on the idea of love. But I had wished for respect, good character, and intelligence. Somehow, all those things together had been too much to ask for from those few whose interest I attracted. Nevertheless, Lady Matlock's comparison of Pemberley to Almack's sounded a bit ridiculous; she was a master of hyperbole.

Of course, I could have remained at Longbourn after my parents' deaths—Charlotte generously offered. But my pride interfered. Mary stayed, and had found her place as Charlotte's helpful companion. She did not complain and was, I think, content. However, *Mary* had never refused the marriage proposal of Longbourn's master, and thus *he* did not feel compelled to continually remind her of her lost status and all that could have been hers, had she not been so stubborn. Neither the years nor my position in life had taught me to regret my refusal; my cousin was even more repellent as the Master of Longbourn than he had been as Lady Matlock's loathsome vicar. Charlotte ignored him, for the most part—a heroic act of blindness I could not emulate.

I had visited Charlotte once at the parsonage at Matlock Court shortly after her marriage to Mr Collins, before my parents' deaths and before the current earl inherited. It had been a pleasant visit, except for any time spent in the company of Lady Matlock or my cousin. I had never dreamt I would visit the countess again after Papa died and Mr Collins vacated the living she had granted him. Of course, she was at Matlock Court no longer. She had brought Rosings Park with her into marriage, and the earl paid her quite generously to remain here—in Kent—and as far away from himself as was possible.

I opened my mouth to ask where in the country Pemberley was to be found, when Dawson entered, curtseyed, and handed over a card to my mistress. She looked at it.

"Willsy is here! How delightful! He is early, even! I did not expect him before tea. What do you wait for, girl? Bring him to me. Dawson, we will have an early tea here in the pink parlour. Do not forget the lobster cakes! Ensure Cook serves it with the good china! And if the silver is not polished to perfection, I shall know why!"

I shall always be grateful that the countess sent me on the errand to fetch her long-lost nephew; had I not, our first meeting in the eight years since last I saw him might have taken place under her watchful eye. Lady Matlock was arrogant, self-absorbed, and callous; she was not stupid, however. She would have seen at once that there was *something* there.

He stood in the front parlour where Dawson had left him, a broad-shouldered man in an elegantly cut coat, his back to me, staring out the window at the grey skies. It was only as I entered that I realised her ladyship had never uttered his surname, and so I stumbled a bit with my greeting.

"Excuse me, um, sir," I began, and then he turned to face me.

I was so astonished, I spoke aloud my first foolish thought. "Mr Darcy? *You* cannot be her favourite nephew!"

I am not sure how it was that I recognised him so quickly. His hair, worn short, was already silvering, though he was not yet forty, and deep creases cut where once had been only dimples. His skin looked browner, as though he spent a good deal of time out of doors. But his eyes still held those dark, unfathomable depths. There were no laugh lines around them, but then, I had not expected there would be.

Fleetingly, I wished that I had understood sooner that it was he who visited; I was not as delusional as Lady Matlock in believing that if I wore a certain colour, I could discard the years since I had seen him last. Still, my pride would have demanded I make at least some attempt at looking my best. But what, really, did it matter? At closer to thirty years than twenty, employed as companion to his aunt, it would not have mattered had I been as stout as Mr Collins and dressed in rags.

"I apologise," I added hastily. "'Tis only that I was surprised. Please come with me, sir, and I shall take you to your aunt."

He just stood, looking at me, and I was reminded of the time I had rushed in a downpour to visit Jane, arriving unexpectedly at Netherfield with my hems six inches deep in mud. In a way, it eased my chagrin at seeing him again after all these years in my role of impoverished gentlewoman. He had not approved of me at my best; there was no use acting self-conscious now.

He did not move. "You know me, then?" he asked.

Did I? That brief period of time near the end of my old life was so very long ago. So much of what I thought I understood had turned out to be nonsense. I remembered the man I *thought* I had known—and hated, even, in the way of overly dramatic, foolish young girls. It did not matter.

"Of course, sir. If you will follow me," I repeated.

For a moment he looked as though he might argue the point—although what he wished to argue about was beyond my comprehension. But then he nodded and did as I requested. Once we were in his aunt's parlour, I ceased to exist—a state which, I am sorry to say, had become most comfortable for me. My ideas and opinions were no longer necessary or welcome, a difficulty in the beginning. But I had finally accepted the encumbrances of servitude, and now wore them as a second skin.

There were compensations, however. The countess's supercilious nature guaranteed that I was not obliged to listen, particularly, to her effusions and criticisms. She could be amusing in her conceit because she believed her own lies, laughed at her own jests, and revealed her own secrets—she required nothing of one's real self.

To his credit, Mr Darcy tried to include me in the insipid, fractured conversation. But that only led Lady Matlock to send me away in order to fetch letters—supposedly to be found in her room—from her son, Mr Darcy's cousin. Since I knew for a fact that the earl had written to her only twice in the year I had been in residence, I did not feel overly confident that they would be easily found.

A cursory look inside the bureau drawer she had indicated revealed letters from some of her London friends, and one dressmaker's bill from Madame Marchand, but nothing from the earl. However, atop her bureau there stood a miniature I had never seen before; I was certain it had not been there yesterday, or any of the many other times she had required me to fetch and carry. The frame was silver and needed polish.

Mr Darcy's solemn eyes bored into me; beside him posed a lavishly dressed golden-haired beauty, the sleeves little puffs at her slim shoulders, her forehead noble, her nose slim, her mouth a rosebud, her unusually coloured bluish-green eyes sparkling. I picked it up, staring. On the back was engraved 'September 2, 1812, Our Wedding Day, Mr and Mrs Fitzwilliam Darcy'.

It was almost impossible to think that the vibrant female in the portrait should be dead. Mr Darcy appeared exactly as I remembered him from Netherfield Park—unflappable, distinguished, handsome, staid. Yet, the artist had caught a hint of puzzlement in his eyes. *What am I doing with this diamond of the first water?* his eyes asked. *She is much too alive for me!* And yet, she was dead, and he was in the parlour enduring Lady Matlock.

Life was beyond strange, at times.

The only other letter in the drawer was written in the firm, masculine scrawl that I instinctively knew was his. I remembered suddenly, the time that Caroline Bingley had remarked upon his handwriting with such excessive flattery. Caroline Bingley! I had not thought of that name for so many years! Obviously, she had not succeeded in capturing her prize, and idly I wondered what had ever happened to her. I unfolded it—for if I was wrong about the author, and it was, indeed, from the earl, I should never hear the end of it.

My Lady Aunt,

I shall be in the area the first of December, and perhaps you will agree to a visit of a fortnight or so at Rosings Park. Write to me at Darcy House in London if it will be an inconvenience.

Yours&c,
F.D.

And that was all. Evidently, the gentleman no longer believed in long letters to his relatives. I smiled to myself at the thought.

In the absence of any letters from the earl, I happily considered myself dismissed, retiring to my room to enjoy a bit of time to myself with a book—a wonderful luxury, because Lady Matlock hated for anyone to be reading while she talked aloud to herself. But the words would not right themselves on the page, insisting upon blurring, coaxing my thoughts towards a past that ought to be dead and buried like my parents.

Why was he here? I wondered. I knew, of course, that Mr Darcy was related to the earl through his maternal line; I would never forget my cousin Collins introducing himself so boldly and embarrassingly at the Netherfield ball. But I had not heard his name mentioned in so many years, he had faded into the past. I had paid little enough attention to the countess's rambling outpourings upon receiving his letter, but I doubt any clues had emerged. That he was grieving, I was certain—his visage was a study in mourning. Perhaps he was making the rounds of all his relations, avoiding his own company, getting through the first year of loneliness by passing time with his family. But after my year with Lady Matlock, I would think the earl's company to be a good deal more favourable.

I peered up at the clock, noting the time. It had been half an hour since I left aunt and nephew. I would try to escape for a walk before it grew any later, I decided. I dared not leave the house without permission, but if the countess was attempting to keep all his attention upon herself, she would not hesitate to grant it. I paused by my looking glass, trying to see what Mr Darcy would see: no longer a girl, a woman past her first blush of youth, a too-determined chin, dark-eyed, in an old-maid's lace cap. Defiantly, I tugged it off and exchanged it for my Sunday best. Not that it would impress him—nor was I trying to. The alteration was for myself. My hair was both the bane of my existence and my greatest pride. It was heavy, full and thick, and even with an iron, would never behave in such smooth fashionableness as the dead Mrs Darcy's, instead curling madly when the weather was wet or sultry. It fell almost to my waist when unrestrained, with not a hint of grey in it.

I am eight and twenty, and in my heart—if not to the world—a girl yet. I do not care what he thinks. Even so, I tugged a few curls down at my ears, and they obligingly coiled flatteringly, framing my chin—which was still thankfully firm, if too sharp in other ways—and donned my wrap.

As I approached the parlour, all was quiet; perhaps they had both retired to their rooms. I peeked in.

The countess was snoring, her chins compressed against her ample bosom. Mr Darcy was, once again, staring out the window. But I had not been as quiet as I supposed, for he turned suddenly and looked at me. I opened my mouth to say something, but he held his hand up peremptorily and strode towards me, his eyes fixed upon me. *Rather like a predator,* I thought fancifully.

I fell into step beside him as he motioned me out the door in his somewhat imperious way. However, I could not blame him for making his escape, and as soon as we were well away, I attempted to make mine.

"I will take you to Mrs Jenkinson, and she will show you to your rooms," I said. "We usually dine at eight, if it suits."

"Where are you going? Out of doors? I was watching at the window—I thought I might see you leave," he said. "I remember you liked to roam the countryside."

Was this a criticism? It seemed an odd thing to mention or even remember, but of course, he had endured an hour of Lady Matlock and her stuffy parlour. It made memories of roaming extremely attractive; I bolted whenever I could.

"Yes, that is—my hours of wandering are few, but I wish to stroll in the garden before nightfall," I said with some hesitation. "It is walled and quite safe. I shall see you at dinner, then?"

"May I walk with you?" he persisted.

Internally I sighed; I had no wish to be rude to a guest, much less someone in mourning. If he wanted company, I ought to be a good enough person to provide some for him. But I could summon no enthusiasm.

"Very well," I replied, and walked briskly to another parlour overlooking the terrace. He hurried to unlatch the door before I could reach for it, and then, finally I was out. It had not rained for a few days, but it probably would again, soon. For now, the air was fresh and clear and felt delicious in my lungs.

For some time, we walked silently together amongst the plantings. Mr Darcy had not much changed, it seemed; as I recalled, he had never been overly fond of conversation. I mostly ignored him, pretending he was only a large, gloomy shadow, and fixed my attention upon the greenery, inhaling deeply of the evening breezes, trying to centre myself within their refreshment.

"I am sorry about your parents," he said at last, startling me.

"Oh...thank you. It has been many years. I am surprised you heard."

"My aunt mentioned it. How do your sisters fare?"

Lady Matlock had probably prattled off what she knew of them as well; hopefully, she had not said *everything* she knew. "My sister, Jane, is married to the earl...er, your cousin's vicar, Mr Tilney. They have three children with a fourth on the way. Her life suits her very well." I could believe he did not know this, since he had never been interested in those of less importance than himself. Because he had been at least partially responsible for crushing Jane's long-ago hopes for Mr Bingley, revealing to him of her current happiness was a matter of pride and I would probably have said the same thing no matter its accuracy. Fortunately, it was very true. "It was Mr Tilney who kindly arranged this position for me after my uncle Gardiner died, and my aunt removed to her elderly mother's home with her three youngest."

He did not contribute any useless platitudes, or worse, any congratulatory ones—only nodding—which I appreciated. "Kitty resides with my aunt and uncle Philips, with her husband, who is my uncle's law clerk, in Meryton. They have one son. My sister, Mary, is yet at Longbourn with my cousin Collins and his wife and their two children."

He nodded. I waited, tensely, for him to ask after my youngest sister, thinking it too much to hope that he would fail to remember her. I glanced sideways at him. But he said nothing, fortunately. Because, of course, I had no idea what to say.

I quickly thought of questions of my own, hoping they would forestall any I dreaded. "What do you hear from our old friends, Mr and Miss Bingley?"

He stiffened. I was not mistaken in it, for I watched him carefully. His answers, however, were smoothly enough given. "Miss Bingley eloped to the Continent eighteen months ago, and Mr Bingley does not hear from her often."

This, I admit, surprised me mightily. Of all people I knew or had ever known, Caroline Bingley seemed the least likely to commit such an indiscretion.

"Mr Bingley is married to my sister, Georgiana," he said, after a small hesitation. "They have been married two and a half years now. No children as yet." He added nothing more, but seemed as though he could have.

He is waiting, I realised. Waiting for me to say something about…old times. Ancient history, really. Of Mr Bingley's abrupt departure, with him, from our neighbourhood, just before the Christmas of 1811. Perhaps Mr Darcy had even known, as Miss Bingley had, that Jane had been in London after, and kept the knowledge from his friend. Regardless, we had never seen either of them again, and after my parents' deaths in August of the following year, neither had I given them much thought. It all seemed so insignificant now.

"I wish them very happy," I murmured perfunctorily. Truthfully, I did not much care whether any of them were happy or not, but I certainly wished none ill. I was sadly deceived—we all had been—in Lieutenant Wickham's character, and had long ago decided that nothing the scoundrel had said against Mr Darcy could be trusted. The happiness or unhappiness of the Bingleys was irrelevant.

But now it seemed unmannerly not to offer my own condolences.

"I was very sorry to hear of your wife's death, when the countess told me of it today," I said dutifully.

He answered not another word. In fact, the remainder of the walk was accomplished in utter and complete silence.

CHAPTER TWO

The next day I was not so fortunate in escaping Lady Matlock. She was at her worst, wanting a certain necklace, and then her ear bobs, a particular 'favourite' book—which I had certainly never seen her read—and then, that it be exchanged for a different one. She alternated between boasting to Mr Darcy of her various illnesses and claiming herself in the pink of health, and offering him the various potions and plasters which were responsible for the latter. One moment, she was excessively flattering; the next, she berated him for his neglect. She was such an ugly mixture of neediness and disapproval, I wondered how he endured it.

Of course, this was my life now. I forced myself to remember that she was a human being who grieved her husband's loss and possessed not an ounce of charm with which to fill it. She only had me, and that because I required a roof over my head and meals to eat and a bit of money besides. In one way she was generous; upon her husband's death, she had discarded most of her dresses in favour of black bombazine and crape. She had given me trunks full of discards to make over for myself, and even if in the most frightful colours, I could do *something* with them—all of my mother's daughters were skilled with a needle. But I wondered why *he* put up with *her*, needing neither her home nor her clothing. He said little, but as the days crept by, I made a few little discoveries of his feelings.

When Lady Matlock uttered something mildly foolish, he flicked an imaginary speck of dust off his waistcoat or trousers. When her words were utterly, embarrassingly ridiculous, he smoothed his left brow with his left forefinger, as if preventing his eye from rolling upwards. Yet, he was polite; he gamely agreed with her nonsense, whether or not she deserved such consideration. But if she mentioned his dead wife, he turned to stone.

Even the oblivious dowager countess soon learned that unless she wished for her favoured guest to disappear or in some way turn his coveted attention away from her, the late Mrs Darcy was never to be mentioned.

I wondered how long he would bear with his aunt. I could admit that it was mildly embarrassing, knowing he watched me scampering about fulfilling her ladyship's demands, especially when she was critical or accused me of disremembering when she reversed her instruction. Lady Matlock was only related to him by marriage, and it was kind of him to visit her. But I selfishly wished he might not stay a good deal longer; he saw too much.

A week after he had arrived, I entered the breakfast parlour to see him alone in it. This was unusual—Lady Matlock very much looked forward to her kippers each morning and was seldom late to the table.

I glanced at him—I suppose my surprise showed—for he said, "Apparently, my aunt is indisposed. The apothecary has been called, but she will not be down."

"Oh. Perhaps I should order a tray be brought to me in her room, then."

His brow furrowed in something like annoyance. "You are not her nurse, and she has her woman. Do have your breakfast."

There was nothing wrong in his words, but I wondered at the irritation in them as I took a plate and studied the selection of food at the sideboard. Still, he had always been somewhat ill tempered, had he not? Unexpectedly I remembered that long-ago assembly, our first meeting, when Mr Bingley had begged him to dance with me. To this day, I do not know what made me say it.

"The hash is tolerable, I suppose, but not handsome enough to tempt me." I put a poached egg on my plate and, suddenly embarrassed, seated myself as far away from him as possible. What might have been a humorous set-down had I still been a daughter of Longbourn was a ridiculous mortification from his aunt's companion.

He did not acknowledge my silly remark, and I hoped he had not heard—I had spoken only in a murmur. It did not take me long to finish my egg.

"I suppose I will see whether Dawson has any news of her ladyship's health, if you will excuse me," I said, standing.

He stood as well, offering a shallow bow. Quickly I escaped the room.

Dawson relayed unfortunate news—the countess was genuinely sick, and not simply in an ill humour. Mr Burns gave it as his opinion that it was the grippe, though Dawson was not so sure. She, evidently, had nursed her sister's family through the grippe and two children died from it; her ladyship did not seem nearly so sick as they.

"More than likely caught a chill from sleeping with the window open, though I've told her time and again it will be the death of her," Dawson grumbled. "But the Quality cannot be brought low by so humble a complaint. It all must be life-threatening, or it will not do."

I smiled. "We shall hope so. Were you up in the night with her? Have you had your breakfast?"

"Hetty brung me a tray. The mistress be too poorly to bother about me unless she wants her barley water. I'm dozing by her fire, as comfortable as may be, with sewing enough to last the week."

"When shall I take my turn? I can sew and bring her barley water as needed."

"You shan't," she replied with finality. "When she's truly ill, she only wants me. There's no help for it."

"Oh, you cannot do it all yourself!"

Dawson only shrugged. "Dora will do the nights. Mistress been running us off our feet of late, and we could all use a rest. You more than some others, I'm thinking."

I hesitated, torn between wanting to accept the proffered break in routine, and guilt at how *much* I wanted it. "You will tell me if I can do anything to assist you?"

"Go on with you," she said, turning back to the countess's chamber, and shutting me out of it. I stared only a moment at the solid oak in front of me and then hurried away.

I went to my room and fetched wrap and parasol, deciding upon the garden again as my destination. There was a village only a mile away, but then I would be required to make conversation and—since the apothecary had, no doubt, reported to all and sundry news of the illness—talk about it, and the countess, all morning. Rosings's grounds were extensive, with a pretty little wilderness and hermitage, and plenty of quiet. I almost took my sewing with me, for the weather was clear, but decided that for today I would give myself up to the pleasures of idleness.

I had not been walking above a quarter hour, when, unexpectedly, I met Mr Darcy. I paused for an awkward greeting, but to my surprise, he fell into step beside me.

"You need not feel obliged to accompany me," I said. "I have no direction to my ramble, and shall probably stay out of doors all morning."

He only nodded solemnly, matching his steps to my shorter ones. After a few moments, he said, "It was untrue, and I ought not to have said it. I apologise, most sincerely, if belatedly."

For a moment, I was confused as to his meaning. And then I felt a flush spread over my cheeks. "Please, sir, forgive my ungoverned tongue. It is all to be forgotten."

For a long minute, he said nothing, and I hoped the subject closed. But it was not.

"I, however, have remembered that moment often over the years," he said, much to my surprise. "It was badly done. It must have given you a poor opinion of my character."

Had it? Perhaps it had set the stage, so to speak, for my ill opinion of him at the time. But most of the seeds of that opinion had been sown by George Wickham. *That* blackguard had managed to secure my hatred in its entirety, with none left over for any other.

"I suppose I was not overfond of your remark at the time, but I can assure you—truthfully—I had not even remembered, not for many years, not until the very moment I said it, and 'twas only my absurd idea of a joke."

This time, he seemed to accept my reassurance, and the

silence stretched between us. More as a wish to show that I took no thought for past insults than for any desire to continue conversing, I thought of a neutral subject. "The countess speaks highly of Pemberley. It is in the Peaks, I think she said? We—that is, my aunt and uncle and I— always wished to tour the area, but were never able, although my aunt lives in a village—Lambton—in Derbyshire now. Perhaps someday yet I will visit."

This turned out to be a brilliant conversational gambit. On the subject of the beauty of the Peaks and his home estate, he was never at a loss. In fact, he made great word-pictures of them, so that I could almost see snow-tipped mountains scraping indigo skies and a white-stoned, sparkling Pemberley majestically placed at the jewelled tip of its woods and fields. I peered sideways at his face, and it was almost startling, the transformation. Instead of the grim gentleman I was accustomed to seeing, he wore an almost lightness of expression, enthusiasm, even reverence within it.

This is the face of a man in love, I thought to myself. Too bad it was for a place, and a pile of stones.

The countess was still indisposed the following day, and it went very much as the previous one. Mr Darcy greeted me sombrely over the breakfast table; we ate in silence, and then separated. Despite inclement weather, I had no intention of remaining within the house. I took my basket of threads with me—and an umbrella—as I went out of doors, heading this time for the little hermitage.

It was a round stone building with a narrow door, but largish windows let in the sun—had there been any—from every side. It boasted padded benches and I meant to sort my threads and look upon the beauty of the garden while I did so. It might grow too chilly to stay long, but I was warmly dressed and hoped for at least an hour of fresh air.

To my near-dismay, Mr Darcy joined me as soon as I was within the garden walls—almost as if he had waited for me. I stifled my sigh, reminding myself of the need to be gracious.

"I intended to sit in the hermitage for a bit—it appears as though it may be a wet morning," I said, somewhat unnecessarily, for he, too, carried an umbrella. He only nodded.

We walked in silence, and I sped up as the hermitage came within sight along with the first drops of rain. He followed me inside, and suddenly, the building seemed *excessively* small. I seated myself on one bench, and he placed himself upon the opposite one, although he still seemed quite close, his long legs stretched in front of him, nearly to my toes.

But he did nothing at all alarming, only stared out into the garden. The rain showered and splashed beyond the doorway, which he had left ajar—a nod to propriety, I supposed, but which left a frosty breeze to inhabit the room with us. I opened my basket and sorted amongst my threads for a time, organising them into the colours I wanted.

"You are sewing something?"

"I have already sewn it—a dress for the advent of a new niece or nephew. But I will add something pretty to the hems. Leaves, I think. Of course, Jane has plenty of clothing what with the three who preceded it, but I think a new baby ought to have some new things."

He nodded. "What are their names—her children?"

I smiled, because I adored—and was adored by—my nephews. "Harry, John—whom we call Jack—and James."

"Three boys. I wonder that Tilney can write his sermons, with such a troop underfoot."

I glanced at him sharply, but his face held a hint of something close to a smile, and I wondered, suddenly—did he know Mr Tilney? I had not thought of it before, that if the earl was his cousin, it was likely he had visited. Jane surely would have mentioned it though, had the Tilneys dined with Mr Darcy. Would she not? The earl, who was, evidently, a perfectly jovial fellow when not coping with his maternal parent, had them up to the Court often when there were guests.

"Do you know Mr Tilney?" I asked, curious.

It was like watching a curtain fall, a shuttered expression closing his face. "I was at school with him. Long ago."

"Really," I said, fascinated. I could not imagine Mr Darcy as a schoolboy, any more than I could imagine calling him 'Willsy'. "We met him while living with my relations in Gracechurch Street. He held the curacy in their parish at the time, and apparently had a *tendre* for Janey rather quickly, though he was so proper, we did not know it, and of course she was in mourning in the beginning. There was no chance for marriage, due to his circumstance. But once he discovered he was to get the living at Matlock Court, he began wooing her in earnest."

I did not tell him of the weeks of uncertainty Jane experienced—the fear that if she gave her heart, it would be broken again. Still, it is a very different thing to be courted properly than to rely upon a few dances or the opinions of a neighbourhood, and especially by one of such good character as Mr Tilney. Jane, too, had learned to show more of her feelings than was comfortable for her. They had managed the business rather well, and what was better, Mr Tilney had no sisters. I did not say that, either.

"He was always a good man," Mr Darcy said. "Steady."

It seemed we had exhausted the topic, but my hands were busy and I felt no need to chatter. If he wished to speak, he was welcome to do so, but I would not make an effort to draw him out. Several minutes passed with only the sound of the rain on the roof between us.

"I am sorry," he said suddenly, "that Lady Matlock is so demanding upon you."

I was immediately embarrassed. "It is hardly your fault if she is," I said stiffly.

"She is my aunt."

"She is also your cousin's mother, but rather than cope with her temper, he doubles her allowance if she stays in this property, as far from himself as he can send her." It was none of my business, and most of the time I could not blame anyone for not wanting the countess nearby on a daily basis. But let him take his apologies to the earl, if he had any.

He had no reply to this, and once again, I regretted my hasty tongue. In a gentler voice, I added, "One evening, when I had been here a few months, Lady Matlock overindulged in her sherry. It was the anniversary of her marriage, fifty years to the day, she said. She told me of the old earl's final illness, and of the other children she had buried. And that there was no one alive who cared enough to notice or remember any longer." I hesitated. "I try to remember that night, on days that are hard."

"When I was young, I used to spend summers at Matlock Court with my mother," he said, after a long pause. "While the countess did not come much into the nursery, she was never unkind, and was patient with my shyness. One could never tell whether she and the earl had a…close connexion, but I suppose they must have. There is little to be learnt from outward appearances, I know."

Once again, the idea of him as a child in the nursery was a foreign concept. In outward appearances, *he* was ever the prosperous, prideful gentleman from Derbyshire, unchanged —excepting the silvering hair—from the Mr Darcy of my memories of eight years ago. But we were none of us our exterior, were we? Inside of me still lived the proud twenty-year-old girl, the grief-stricken daughter, the hopeful young woman of Gracechurch Street, and so forth.

Suddenly, I realised that to all *outward* appearances, I was an unchaperoned, unwed female in a darkened hermitage with a handsome, eligible widower. "You are so very correct," I replied, laughing aloud.

He glanced at me curiously, but I did not explain the joke.

CHAPTER THREE

On the third day of Lady Matlock's indisposition, the weather improved slightly and I almost expected that Mr Darcy would join me on my wanderings about the park; I had even brought a handkerchief with me to embroider, should we sit together in the hermitage once again. He was nowhere to be seen, and I told myself I was not disappointed. Neither did I allow my mind to dwell on his whereabouts. After all, it was not as though we had talked much. The only conversations we truly managed concerned Derbyshire and his ancestral home. I needed no help in longing for a holiday in the Peaks.

Uncle had meant to take us touring—we had often planned to visit Lambton—and I truly believe that, had he not died, we would have done the thing by now. How odd it was, to consider that I might have visited Pemberley on that trip; had we done so, I might have asked Mr Darcy's housekeeper for a tour. I might have happened by just as Mr Darcy and his beautiful, elegant wife strolled through their beautiful, elegant home, laughing and smiling at each other, noticing no one else. For some reason, the thought soured me on my pleasant day of freedom.

It was envy, of course. I had lived, I had been happy, even; but it was not the life or the happiness I had anticipated. And then my uncle died; Uncle Gardiner, who had been almost more of a father to me than my own. I did not want to dwell on my loss, but today was the sort of day that brought losses to one's mind. Grey skies, cold and comfortless, with nothing blooming.

Earlier today I had received a letter from Aunt Gardiner, and it was wonderful to finally discern the beginnings of happiness within its lines. Her eldest daughter, happily wed just before her father's death, expected to give her a first grandchild. The three who remained with her had adjusted to country living, and she explained her ailing mother's health had actually improved since their arrival. The neighbourhood was welcoming, and several difficulties had been overcome; the vicar had agreed to educate the boys, and a retired drawing master of uncommon ability had volunteered to work with Ellen and help cultivate her artistic passions. Her mother's roof had been replaced for the *most* reasonable sum, and they were, at last, cosy and comfortable. It made sense, I suppose, that at the very point when my aunt was recovering her spirits, I should be overcome by a wave of longing—for my uncle and aunt, for the home we once shared, for the company of my young cousins.

But then, worse, came a stabbing misery: I yearned for my parents and Longbourn—or at least, what Longbourn had represented. Safety. Status. Youth. Unfairly, I blamed Mr Darcy for the onslaught of despair—seeing him again had harrowed up my feelings from their neatly aligned rows, disturbing my peace by poking at parts of the past I had chosen to forget.

I walked faster, trying to outpace my emotions. I knew several methods in achieving control, but it had been a long while since I had to use them. *Remember how fortunate you are that your health is exceptional, that you can walk these grounds with strong limbs and lungs. Remember the comfort of your chambers, the excellence of your meals, even the small savings you are accumulating. Remember that you are not without family, that you are loved.*

My breath hitched. *No! I will not allow it! No self-pity! No stupid, useless tears!*

And then I heard a voice calling, though some distance away.

I did not wish to see Mr Darcy *now*, when I was so near to losing my composure. And perhaps he had not yet spotted me.

And so, with an impulsive loss of dignity so complete I blush to remember it, I hitched up my skirts and ran.

I must have run a half mile or so, and while I was an avid walker, I do not believe I had run so far in a stretch since I was a girl. Collapsing at the foot of a large oak, hardly able to catch my breath, I tore at the fastenings of my now mud-splashed coat, sweating, gasping, heart pounding wildly. My cap slipped and hung askew, my hair almost combusting at the loss of pins and fabric securing it.

And so of course, that is where he found me, obviously alarmed by my flight, as well as my current unkempt and disordered condition. I might have even laughed at his expression, were I not so embarrassed.

I yanked off the hated cap, uncaring of the wrenching pins still clinging to my hair. At least now the breeze could reach my scalp. With a deep sigh, I leant back upon the oak, closing my eyes and hoping that a stray bolt of lightning might end my mortification.

I expected his remonstrances, but his question, when it came, surprised me.

"Does my presence distress you?"

I opened my eyes. Heedless of his clothing, he knelt beside me on the ground. He looked concerned and yet... there was a penetrating keenness in his gaze, as if he asked more than his words implied.

"Your presence at Rosings, or your presence now, in particular?" I replied with my own question.

"Is there a difference?"

I sighed, closing my eyes again. A distant bird trilled its song. A breeze fluttered leaves in a raspy rustling. He simply waited.

"No," I said. "It is not you. I...I do not like to remember what I cannot always forget. It was a moment of...homesickness, for a home long gone. I ran from it."

"Does that work?" he asked, as if he really wondered.

I considered. I no longer was in any danger of sobbing, so... "Yes. Sometimes."

He settled in beside me at the base of the huge oak tree. We were in a more densely forested section of the park, and it was colder here in the gloom, now that my sweat was drying. I tried to think of something to say, but nothing occurred to me. My deepest thoughts were too close to the surface, my tenderest emotions too exposed. 'How do you find the weather?' was the only question that seemed safe, and it was a stupid one since we were sitting out of doors in it. So I sat in silence, close enough to hear his intake of breath and soft exhale.

And then, in the most casual tone one could imagine, he asked, "I wonder whether you would do me the honour of marrying me?"

I turned to stare at him. Had he suddenly sprouted a second head, I could not have been more astonished.

"Is this a joke?"

He frowned. "It would be a terrible one. No, of course not."

"Mr Darcy...I am nearly nine and twenty." I am not quite certain why I felt the need to clarify that—he must have had some idea.

"And I am nearly seven and thirty," he replied. "It does not signify."

But it did. He and the first Mrs Darcy were childless, and so it made sense that he would want to marry again, so quickly even, to fill his nursery. Surely a female at the peak of her youth and beauty would be a better choice.

"Why?" My mother was probably rolling in her grave at my hesitation, but it made no sense why he would wish it, other than the fact that I was here, obviously available, and the whole thing could likely be accomplished at very little trouble to himself.

"Because it is my dearest wish," he said politely, stiltedly, and completely unbelievably.

My pride, that prickly wench, revolted, but I was accustomed to bridling her. This was my fourth proposal of marriage. Mr Collins had been the first; Mr Plimpton—of extremely good fortune and noxious breath—was the second. While I might have overcome his odours, he spoke to me as if I were a not-overbright child. Mr MacAdam was handsome, prosperous, charming, and, to use the slang term, a rakehell. I was, at first, delighted with his courtship, but when Uncle discovered several flaws of an alarming nature in his character, I broke it off immediately. Heaven only knew our family had suffered enough with one of those.

Of the four, Mr Darcy was far and away the best of the lot.

I was not desperate. While the countess would not live forever, by the time she departed this mortal coil and Jane must take me in, the children would be older and I, hopefully, would be more accustomed to the idea of living as my sister's impoverished relation. I did not *need* to marry.

I wanted to. I wanted my own home, my own life. Not at any cost, as Charlotte had. Was marriage, to *him*, a price worth paying?

I had been staring at him while these thoughts blundered and plundered through my mind, my mouth open in shock, when without warning, he leant in.

Is he going to kiss me? I barely had time to think the question before his lips were upon mine. I had been kissed before, as well—once by John Lucas in my fourteenth year, and thrice by the nefarious Mr MacAdam. This was not anything like those. His lips were firm, with nothing tentative about his intent, but neither did he loot and pillage, such as Mr MacAdam was wont to do. This was a man who knew what he wanted to discover, but did not mind searching for it.

He wanted me. It was in the seeking pressure, the restrained hunger, the intensity of purpose, the coaxing pleasure. Within it, I was taken by yet another surprise: I wanted him, as well. I wanted to wrap my arms around his neck, be held close, to return his seeking with my own. I wanted to know what he thought, and I wanted his thoughts to be of me. I was young again, pretty and proud and powerful.

He drew back; he had never touched me, except with his lips, and yet my whole being felt as if he had.

I was speechless, although I managed one word: "Yes."

He blinked, as if I had surprised him. Had he thought I

would say no? I was not stupid; the life he could offer me was far better than my current one. I had decided upon my three requisites, of intelligence, respect, and character. He met them all, and then some. Love was not a part of it, but there *was* feeling. It was not a cold transaction, as I first feared. I might have agreed regardless, but that kiss soothed my pride and encouraged...happiness. Or at least its cousin, contentment.

I pulled my disordered senses into some sort of regulation. "I suppose you will wish to wait until your year of mourning is completed."

"No. Absolutely not. No banns. I will get a licence."

Again, I was surprised—by his vehemence, if not his words. It was not quite the thing, to remarry so quickly...but most would understand, if not approve. He was childless at close enough to forty. Brows would raise at his choice of bride, however.

"We must find someone for your aunt," I said. "I cannot leave her in the lurch."

His expression turned incredulous. "She treats you as a drudge. Your quick departure is the least of what she deserves."

This was true enough. "But it is not the least of what Dawson, her longsuffering maid, deserves."

He shook his head, his feelings about Dawson's plight obvious. "I must go and make arrangements. Your settlement. Will Tilney act for you?"

I had not thought of practicalities. "I am sure he will."

Nodding crisply, he stood, and held out his hands to help me up. "I shall go to him then, and whilst there, I will order my cousin to find someone for his mother, and do it expeditiously. I shall also make it clear to my aunt how you are to be treated until I return for you."

I accepted his assistance in standing, noticing how quickly he dropped my hands when I was steady on my feet, astounded at how little he thought of issuing edicts to earls. "I wish you would not do that. In fact, I wish you would say nothing to her."

He frowned his disapproval.

"I must live in her house for what may become weeks while you settle things. It will be awkward. She will not like it." Of that, I was certain.

"I will return before Yuletide. This, I promise you."

"Even so." I fell into step beside him, wondering why he did not take my arm, while noting that he did not argue the point of his aunt's displeasure. I understood, and even appreciated that he did not try for more kisses. Mr MacAdam had constantly pushed at boundaries, making me feel as though I must be always on my guard, telling me time and again that he loved me beyond reason...and thus leaving all responsibility for good judgment upon my shoulders. Truly, I ought to have been warned long before Uncle Gardiner's discoveries that the man was careless at best and dangerous, at worst. His good looks had, briefly, eclipsed my good sense.

Mr Darcy was not the same sort of prettiness. There was nothing angelic or golden about him. He was all hardness— hard muscle, hard expression, hard lines upon his face. His gaze was direct and piercing, his jaw chiselled from tenacity and fortitude. And yet, he took my breath away, and I was glad that he was taking responsibility for my sanity. I was not sure *I* was to be trusted.

What would he do, I wondered, if I reached for his hand? But it was the sort of thing lovers did. I was too old not to know the difference between desire and affection.

Still, there was every chance affection might grow someday. I was certain my uncle would have approved the match. I only hoped that Pemberley would, eventually, approve of me.

Mr Darcy used the excuse of his aunt's illness to make a speedy departure before noon. There was no one to think a thing about it when I walked out with him upon his leave-taking. We strolled together out the entry, down the brick steps, and along the vast lawn. At a place just to the east of the walkway that was neither in view of the house nor of his coach, he halted, turning to look down at me.

I wondered what he saw; I had repaired my appearance, but in my high-necked grey gown and lace cap, I supposed I appeared as the Maiden Spinster, sprinkled in shelf dust. He gently clasped one of my front curls, rubbing the lock between his thumb and finger, studying it as if it were words written in a strange tongue. I hoped he would kiss me again, but was also attacked by an unusual shyness.

"Will you remove this?" he asked, lightly touching the frilled edge of my cap, his expression almost indifferent.

It was a strange request, but I obeyed as if in a dream, plucking pins and pulling off the thing. It seemed wicked, somehow, to be discarding even so innocuous a piece of my wardrobe in the light of day, in a place where really, anyone might round the bend and see us. It made me self-conscious, and I wondered whether he would be so dispassionate if I demanded the removal of his cravat. I handed my cap to him, and he took it with some surprise, as if he did not know what to do with it.

I flushed; for some reason, I had thought he wanted the ugly thing as a sort of keepsake, and I snatched it back.

"Well, goodbye, then," I said, studying the high polish of his boots, my cheeks on fire.

A large hand clasped my chin and tilted it upwards. Unable to avoid his direct gaze, I saw his amusement. Suddenly, I was exasperated. "How am I to understand what odd freaks a gentleman might take into his head?" I said, sounding every bit the Maiden Spinster. "I have never been engaged."

A peculiarly intense expression filtered into his eyes, his hand tightening on my chin. "No," he said. "No, you have not."

And then he did what seemed to me at the time an odd thing; he pulled off his gloves, dropping them heedlessly to the ground. His fingers threaded in my hair, dislodging pins, pulling a little painfully, even, where the pins tried to restrain his searching hands. When they were buried in the masses of my hair, he simply stood there, looking at what he'd done, clenching them briefly. I thought he might kiss me again; our faces were very close—I could feel the heat of his breath—happily nothing like Mr Plimpton's. But after a few fraught moments, he extricated his fingers, more carefully this time, though I was certain my hair now looked a fright. He stepped back, bent down, picked up his gloves.

"I will return as soon as possible," he said. "Be well."

We were back to formalities, so I gave a little curtsey. He bowed.

Nodding curtly, he turned on his heel and strode towards the carriage. I plunged my hands in my pockets, following more slowly to watch him drive away. My right hand touched my embroidery scissors, enclosed in a leather case, and the handkerchief I had meant to finish stitching today. Without letting myself think about it, I withdrew them and hastily clipped one of my curls, wrapping it in the linen.

"Wait," I called, hurrying forward. "Wait, please."

He stopped, nearly to his carriage, and slowly turned, his countenance inexplicably fierce. "Yes?"

His coachman and his man stood nearby, openly curious, gawking.

"I only..." I trailed off, back to blushing again in the face of his apparent anger. Awkwardly, I stuck out my hand, as if to shake his.

Slowly, he held out his in return, and I placed my gloved hand against his palm, dropping the handkerchief onto it. He stared at it for a moment before fisting his hand around it.

"Goodbye, Mr Darcy."

"Thank you," he said, his anger muted though not completely disappeared, but his voice less harsh. He bowed again. I stood stiffly, feeling as though I had made a fool of myself and thus back to being annoyed with him—but it was a familiar emotion, and easily borne.

He strode to his carriage; I watched to see if he would drop my offering onto the ground, but he had the courtesy to keep it, at least until I was out of sight. We were off to a grand start.

CHAPTER FOUR

The following ten days were distinctly odd. The countess was indisposed for two more of them, but no longer required Dawson to remain strictly at her bedside; in fact, she rather seemed to wish for a cavalcade of servants to adjust the curtains, freshen her teacup, plump her pillows, and listen to her complaints. Thankfully, none of them were me.

When she did return to the breakfast room, she favoured me with her considered opinion that her beloved nephew had departed because I was too dull to entertain such an impressive gentleman in her absence. Had I any conversation, wit, or intellect, he would have remained until she could take up her duties as hostess again.

I did not respond, of course, to her foolish allegations, but I pondered them. For all she knew, she was correct—the person I displayed to her was a ghost of myself, a shadow girl who had all the cleverness of wall papers or a piece of furniture adorning her parlour, and who could occasionally be useful in fetching her things and nodding agreement.

Was that who Mr Darcy had seen? As I re-examined our conversations, I had not revealed overmuch. I was too accustomed to hiding everything that was important. Had he proposed marriage to the Maiden Spinster or to the Shadow Girl? Or had he remembered—fondly, perhaps—the girl from Longbourn, and this was an attempt at recapturing his youth? I smiled to myself at that thought, for he had not much cared for the 'tolerable' old me, even if he now regretted stating those feelings publicly.

For that matter, who had *I* agreed to wed? Was I marrying the tall, handsome, wealthy Londoner, the novelty of Hertfordshire? I covered another smile; in those days, I had not much cared for him, either. But how was he changed, really? I barely knew him.

As one day turned into another, the whole interlude seemed ever more fantastic. I wondered, even, whether it had really happened, or if I had finally slipped from sanity beneath the weight of my boredom and loneliness, fabricating the whole proposal in my mind.

And yet, there *had* been that kiss. I could not have manufactured it, for I had never experienced anything like it. In that moment, I had understood him, and he had understood me. But nothing else was at all clear, and after a week of nearly crippling uncertainty, I managed to thrust most thoughts of him and marriage and the future from my mind.

Which was why I was almost surprised when he was announced on the eleventh day after his departure. And he had brought a guest with him—my brother Tilney.

Mr Tilney was a tall bear of a man, almost Mr Darcy's height, with a pleasing countenance and intelligent, lively nature. He had chestnut hair—thinning a bit at the top now—and a genuine, kindly smile. I rushed to him and he hugged me, lifting me off the ground. When he set me back upon my feet, he promptly picked me up again. "The first was from Janey, and this is from me," he exclaimed, as I laughed. "Now, please tell me—what is this I hear about weddings? And to this great oaf—" he smiled at a dour-looking Mr Darcy. "If you are not happy in Kent, come to us, darling girl. We shall stack a couple of children atop each other and clear a path for you. No need for desperate measures, what?"

As his voice was a booming one, there was no question that half the household heard his words. Especially the half containing the countess.

"Fitzwilliam Darcy," she said, in awful tones. "What is this? This *person*—" she looked disapprovingly at my brother —"cannot be serious."

"He is very serious, my lady," Mr Darcy said immediately. "We are to be wed, and at once. Your son will ensure the quick replacement of your companion. I have his word on it."

The dowager countess was not pacified. "While a capable female and not utterly stupid, she is overreaching," she said frostily. And then she added, though it came out in a hiss that I hoped Mr Tilney did not hear, "Make use of her if you will, but there is no need to throw yourself away. Your grief makes you foolish!"

I had done my best to look upon her as a fellow sufferer, though a wealthier one. Of course, I had never allowed her to see me in the same way—but that, too, was her fault. She wanted only the Shadow Girl, or even less. I ceased feeling guilt for abandoning her without notice.

Mr Darcy leant close to her and spoke in a low tone. I could not hear what he said, but two spots of colour flared bright enough to burn through her face powder.

"Are you packed?" he asked, straightening to look directly at me, dismissing the countess as if she had left the room.

"I am not. I did not know when I would be leaving."

Mr Tilney was looking between the two of us, clearly a little confused. Possibly having missed the slur delivered by the countess, he wondered why we spoke so quickly of departure. Perhaps they had planned upon staying at least overnight.

"I shall take care of it quickly," I said with some urgency, for I would not happily stay another minute. With a quick curtsey, I hurried up the stairs, hearing Mr Darcy's low-voiced murmurs, probably explaining to Mr Tilney, and the higher pitched ones of the countess, probably protesting.

When I was in my own room, I pulled out my trunk and began hastily tossing things into it. But moments later, Dawson joined me. She did not say a word, only began efficiently folding and rolling my gowns and shawls in far better style than I ever had. I slowed my own pace, checking my wild hurry. Mr Darcy would not leave me here if I took an extra thirty minutes to do the job correctly.

After a few minutes of work, I said, "I am sorry, Dawson, to leave without any notice. If you ever wish a position at Pemberley, in Derbyshire, I hope you will remember me. And I would always give you a character, no matter how long in the future you asked for one."

She gave me her grim smile. "I'd think you a fool if you spurned an offer from *him*. I heard what she said, madam, but I do not believe she would have allowed it. She let her temper get the best of her, is all it was. You're the best of the women she's had here. I know she hates to lose you."

Dawson had never called me 'madam' before this; my new status had merited something already. "I thank you," was my only reply, and we returned to packing.

The trunk was almost full when the countess entered, unannounced. She had never entered my room before, and looked fully annoyed at seeing her woman helping me. "My plum-coloured day-dress needs pressing, Dawson," she ordered frigidly. Dawson departed hastily, not daring another word.

"Well," she said, in a voice full of disgust and displeasure. "You are a sly one. Play host to a fellow who is grieving, allow you freedom to run about unchecked on my property, and you take full advantage. Clever."

I found it unnecessary to answer her accusations, remaining silent.

"It was a lucky thing for you I had the grippe, I suppose. I might, perhaps, wish to be informed why you should betray my hospitality with your arts and allurements, even while I lay nearly dying."

"I do not pretend to possess equal frankness with your ladyship. You may ask questions which I shall not choose to answer," I retorted.

Her eyes narrowed. "You ought to know already that I am not to be trifled with. But however insincere you may choose to be, you shall not find me so. His grief has disordered his mind! You have drawn him in! How can you be so lost to every feeling of propriety and delicacy, giving him no time to mourn?"

She had hit upon *my* deepest concern, of course. But it was none of hers. I continued to fold the last of my garments.

"I am almost the nearest relation he has in the world. You believe I am unkind. I am not. I wish you no ill. But *Pemberley?* How do you imagine your father's tiny country estate prepared you for Pemberley? He is accustomed to the very best—he has already *had* the best, while you have done nothing more important than fancywork in your entire life! You can scarcely hold a conversation, much less entertain!

The Pemberley parties were famous when his wife was alive, but I have told you that. You believe you can step into her place, when she made the place all her own."

Lady Matlock strode away from me, towards the small window in my chamber. There was no view from there, but she had begun speaking absently, as if looking only at the past. "We went to his wedding, the earl and I. I had never seen Fitzwilliam look so happy. The wedding breakfast was for a hundred-fifty. I know you believe yourself to be an accomplished woman; you have a thorough knowledge, I suppose, of music, singing, drawing, and dancing." The countess turned back around to face me, angry, still—but it was not *all* anger. "Yet she was something *more*. Mrs Darcy found time to speak to each of us on her wedding day—she possessed a certain something in her air and manner of walking, the tone of her voice, her address and expressions, which enchanted. She was the *pinnacle* of accomplishment. My husband turned to me after talking to her and said, 'By Jove, she makes a man feel young again'."

She pinned me with her stare. "I never saw such capacity and taste, application and elegance, as was united in his first wife—Mrs Anne Darcy. That she should be replaced by an elderly spinster is ridiculous and insupportable. What advantage can it be to you to try it?"

I could not remain silent. "How far your nephew might approve of your interference in his affairs, I cannot tell, but you have certainly no right to concern yourself in mine. I must beg, therefore, to be importuned no farther on the subject."

"You are resolved to have him, then?"

"I am only resolved to act in that manner, which will, in my own opinion, constitute my happiness and his."

"You are determined to ruin him in the opinion of all his friends, and make him the contempt of the world."

"The world in general would have too much sense to join in such scorn," I replied, latching my trunk.

She shook her head in disgust. "It only shows," she said, "how little you know of the world. Unfeeling, selfish girl."

It was not until we were in the coach that I took a full breath. I sat beside my betrothed, while Mr Tilney watched me with concern.

"Were you not safe in that house, my sister?"

So he *had* heard. "I was safe, to the best of my knowledge. We had few visitors, and those, respectable ones."

Mr Darcy stiffened, and I could only imagine his thoughts, the indignity of being forced to defend his silly aunt's honour.

Mr Tilney took my hand, and in his usual kind way, sought to lighten the mood. "I taught her how to throw a punch, Darcy, and no mere flourishing—she can defend herself."

I grinned at him. I had indeed asked him questions on the science of pugilism, which he expertly demonstrated in a most un-vicar-like manner, and much to Jane's chagrin. But then he surprised me.

"I ask you to come home to us," Mr Tilney continued. "If you wish to marry Darcy, surely there is no hurry. He can visit you from our home." He fixed a stern gaze upon my betrothed. "Darcy, what is thirty miles of good road? You have had a bad year. Time to come to know each other would surely give this marriage a better foundation."

"I do not wish to wait," he said, his voice low and even. He turned to me. "Do you wish it?"

I noticed that he did not phrase his question, '*Unless* you wish it?' A picture entered my mind of him pulling from his pocket a list titled 'Female Acquaintances Previous to Marrying Anne Darcy', crossing off my name, and moving on to the next woman who still had only one chin and all her teeth. I smiled reassuringly at Mr Tilney.

I had stayed with the Tilneys on many occasions, and I loved them dearly. After my uncle's death, when Aunt Gardiner determined she must live with her mother, I *planned* to live with them permanently. I simply did not *want* to. It was not only that their home was rather full; I did not mind the lack of privacy so very much. When I had first asked Mr Tilney whether a position as companion or governess might be found for me, he and Jane had protested, and, I think, were rather hurt. I was sorry for it. But I hated the thought of being a burden, a charge on their income when they needed it for their own brood. I suppose, if I were being brutally honest, it was easier living with the critical countess, who had no power to touch my feelings, than to watch everything Jane had—love, children, family—and know I had no opportunities for the same. My accursed pride!

"You have, evidently, known Mr Darcy for many years. Do you know of any reason why, beyond the brevity of our courtship, I should *not* marry him?"

Mr Tilney furrowed his brow. "No, of course not. He is all that is respectable. But we would have you happy, my sister. I feel as though the home the countess provided for you was not as good a home as you deserved, and you might have made this decision in haste to escape it. It is not your only recourse."

Mr Darcy appeared to take no notice, as though our

conversation could not have meant less to him; and why should it, really? If I did not marry him, he would have no trouble finding another. The carriage slowed as we entered the town of Hunsford, the sounds of other vehicles and people calling to one another floating on the dusty air. I had been here several times, to Madame Marchand's shop and a few other places when the countess was in a mood for commerce. To my surprise, however, the carriage drew to a halt before a church of red sandstone. I looked at Mr Darcy, who withdrew his pocket watch.

"Now?" I asked, almost incredulously.

"We are here somewhat earlier than I arranged," he said brusquely. "What shall it be? I am to take the carriage on to Pemberley. Your brother was to return to Matlock on the post. You are, of course, free to accompany him. Or we may wed today, and you may accompany me to Pemberley. The choice is yours."

I suppose I had assumed that Mr Tilney had come to travel with me to Pemberley. But of course, if we were married, there was no reason for it, and I was certain he hated being away from Jane at any time, much less while she was increasing. Mr Darcy's terseness was off-putting, I admit. But this was my chance, one I had longed for on lonely nights and long, tedious days. I knew I would regret losing it.

I took a deep breath. "I suppose we should see whether there is someone available to marry us, though we are early. You will witness?" I asked Mr Tilney.

I thought I felt Mr Darcy's body beside me easing just a bit—as if he had truly cared more for the answer than he had let on—but it was likely my imagination.

"Darcy," Mr Tilney tried, seeing he was having no success in convincing me, "come to Matlock, and let us host a grand wedding breakfast, with all your family. Do not you wish to present your bride to the world with proper ceremony?"

"I did that once," he replied—coldly, I thought.

Mr Tilney evidently heard the warning as well, and gave it up with a sigh. He went into the church to see what authority he could summon while Mr Darcy helped me out of the carriage. I looked up at him—while he looked at anything *except* me. He hardly appeared the eager groom.

"Is this difficult for you?" I asked. "Marrying again? You insist you do not wish to wait, but if this is some sort of debt to your honour, because you asked me on impulse and you are determined to follow through with it no matter what concerns have since occurred to you, I beg—"

"Foolish woman," he interrupted, stopping further speech with a hard kiss that, I supposed, was his answer. It was only later that I wondered if the kiss was more defence than passion, designed to prevent me from further questioning.

If so, his technique was flawless.

Less than half an hour later, I was Mrs Darcy. Signing the register one last time with the name I had carried since birth, I was struck by a sudden pang. For a moment, my fingers froze, unable to form the necessary curves and strokes. It felt like the end of who I was, who I had always been.

No, I thought. *I am adding to, not subtracting.* I signed with a flourish, the largest signature on the page.

We accompanied Mr Tilney to arrange his return journey to Matlock Court. I heard my husband offer to rent a coach, but the affable Mr Tilney insisted that the post, leaving within the hour, would be quick and comfortable.

"You will write to us soon, and reassure your sister you

are well?" he implored me. "She will be angry with me for not convincing you to delay this madness. Ah, well, I was a would-be groom once, and remember the impatience, even if she cannot."

"My sister's anger is very easily tolerated, since it never lasts beyond the posy you will bring her from her own garden," I replied, grinning.

"I may have to raid the earl's garden for this one," he said, grinning back. He turned to Mr Darcy, holding out his hand. "I owe you much, my friend, but you have called in a great favour. You must bring your bride to Matlock, if you care for me at all," he said, as Mr Darcy shook it. "After the babe arrives. In the summer."

Mr Darcy made a noncommittal sound, and moved to withdraw his hand, but Mr Tilney gripped it more tightly. "Come summer," he repeated, with more gravity than I had ever before heard from him.

Mr Darcy nodded curtly. The men separated.

I hugged my brother, treasuring the simplicity of his concern, his connexion to Jane, his offer of family. Like my sister, he was all that was good.

And then we entered our carriage and left him, standing alone in the street watching after us until he was only a tiny speck.

We had driven but a few hours when we stopped at the Green Dragon to change horses. Needless to say, we were not overwhelming each other with brilliant conversation. I was, to put it mildly, a bit nervous, frantically trying to dredge forth information I had heard over the years regarding the intimate details of wifehood. It was difficult to come up with much, because shortly after Jane's marriage, I made a conscientious effort to not dwell upon love, lovers, or anything in between. There had been fancies, though, over the years, and longings and secret wishes. Perhaps the turmoil showed upon my face, because he took my hand—the first time he had touched me since our wedding.

"I am dashed sick of travelling," he said. "I feel as though I am wearing more road dust than the road. I wish to stop here for the day. And night."

I nodded, inhaling deeply, trying for a calm appearance.

"Would you prefer I take one room or two?" he asked, as if questioning how much sugar I preferred in my tea.

My face flamed. But I wanted…a connexion. A good memory.

"May I see where they will put us before I decide?"

He looked at me curiously and perhaps with a bit of wariness. "I abandoned the idea of a wedding breakfast easily enough," I confided, "because I have never particularly dreamt of having one. It does not mean I have no preferences, and that I shall look to you to decide what they are. I realise you probably care little for romance. Nevertheless." His brow furrowed, as if he might protest—but whether it was my independence or his lack of romantic intention, I could not tell, and hurried on.

"I have no mother to explain what will happen between us, but I have a husband who has, presumably, managed the business before. I want you to explain it to me, but not if the room is ugly, fusty, with noisy neighbours rattling the walls with their snores. I want you to be kind, and careful with me."

I expelled this speech all in one breath, almost, and felt nearly dizzy at the end of saying it.

He stared at me—and my bright red cheeks—for what felt like a solid minute.

"I have stayed here before," he said, his voice so low, it shivered up my spine. "The owners are fastidious, they know the Darcy name, and will give us the best of what accommodation is available. The walls are thick. I shall take one room, but if it is not to your liking, nothing will happen between us except sleep. I give you my word—I will always be careful with you. For as long as we both shall live."

It was a promise made as solemnly as our wedding vows. He only mentioned care, not kindness. I tried not to think about what the difference might be.

CHAPTER FIVE

Despite Mr Darcy's desire to wed quickly, he showed a strange reluctance to return to Pemberley. We had a journey of one hundred-ninety miles, a distance we could have travelled in three or four days, even at a snail's pace.

He stretched it into two weeks.

I did not argue the delay.

It was a happy journey. Mr Darcy loved the country through which we passed and could point out the many places nature had formed for our amusement and awe. We walked the fields of Dovedale, and he spoke of fishing—a favourite sport he much enjoyed—and seemed to find tramping about the countryside as great a diversion as I. We both hated oysters and loved early mornings. We did not speak of the past nor of the future, only relished the present. The weather cooperated with our ramblings for the most part, although my gown hems suffered. I did not care, and laughed when his man made a great fuss over the state of his boots.

And the nights. The first one was not comfortable, and I

am afraid I giggled when the full expectation of what was to happen was explained to me. It was over very quickly—which I realised later must have been on purpose—but he held me close afterward and expressed his gratitude for my sufferings, such as they were. The next two nights were spent in sleep only, but he shared a bed with me, and I began to grow accustomed to his light snore, to expecting his large body beside me when I rolled over in the night. And the fourth night…he took his time. He worshipped every inch of me with reverence and dedication; and though it might be blasphemous to say so, it was a holy experience.

Every day thereafter was tinged with anticipation. A light touch on my elbow or the small of my back was fraught with meaning. We walked aimlessly and laughed at nothing in particular and looked at each other and imagined the night to come. We were aligned, in those heady days. I thought I was falling in love, but of course, love does not come as a result of bed pleasure and novelty. Still, when we woke Christmas morning to the sound of rain beating on the roof of The Ostrich, and Mr Darcy sent word to his coach and man that we would remain until the weather cleared and we stayed two days in our room…I was utterly, blissfully happy for what felt like the first time in years.

But the bridal trip could not last forever, of course. "We will reach Pemberley today," he announced one morning as I called for the inn's maid to help me dress. He left me to it, and I was suddenly overwhelmed with an anxiety unusual to my nature. I had the wardrobe of a lady's impoverished companion, with absolutely nothing to wear that was suitable for presenting myself as mistress of a great estate, especially one which had suffered such a recent loss. I was the replacement mistress, the second choice. I decided upon a walking dress which, although in an ugly shade of brown, was of quality jaconet muslin, richly trimmed, showing my figure to advantage.

My hair was another problem. I was at the mercy of inn servants, and not all of them had experience with hair that had a life of its own. It was necessary to be very firm with its management, to show it just who was in charge. Unfortunately, many inn maids, by nature, were timid creatures, afraid to offend or cause pain.

Sadly, the maid *du jour* was the worst of the lot, until finally I dismissed her with a sigh, and then undid all her efforts. I re-braided my hair as I did every night, and then pinned it tightly into a severe spinster's bun, leaving side curls to frame my face; truly, it was the only coiffure I could manage on my own. It was not particularly flattering but it was tidy. I refused to greet Pemberley wearing a lace cap, so I donned the Sunday bonnet, which was growing rather shabby since lately it had been my Monday through Saturday bonnet as well. Wistfully, I imagined a better trimmed affair with ribbons and gauze, a matching silk scarf thrown carelessly over my shoulders complementing the ensemble and softening the dreadful brown into a winsome amber.

I had been brought up to run a house the size of Longbourn, and Jane and I had, in our flights of fancy so long ago, discussed the challenges of being mistress to Netherfield Park, which was easily twice its size, with its twenty-five servants. I had lived at Rosings Park and visited Matlock Court, with their forty. Pemberley was, from Mr Darcy's description, larger still.

We had not been travelling long before we turned off the main road, driving past high iron gates. Through the carriage window I saw the gatekeeper nodding solemnly, stone-faced, at our coachman, as though he allowed a funeral procession to pass instead of his master of many weeks' absence.

Neither was it the drive I had imagined, with wide lawns, raked and brushed, fields and gardens and manicured perfections. Instead, Pemberley Woods barricaded its master's home, the tree branches meeting overhead like clenched fists in the twisting, turning drive, barely wide enough, in places, for the horses to pass. And then, the trees gave way to boulders on one side, the road following a rocky cliff's edge; if I peered out the window, I felt I would be looking over its rim. Each bend revealed only endless curves and frightening periphery.

"Inefficient," I murmured, finally leaning back in my seat, my voice sounding loud within the quiet coach, and only then did I realise that my husband had not spoken more than a word or two in our entire morning. Mr Darcy was not, and never would be a talkative man, but I had become accustomed to his murmured asides, his occasional remark upon some passing carriage, town, or vista. I had been too caught up in my own nerves to notice his silence.

He glanced sharply at me, as though he had forgotten I sat beside him. "The road," I said. "Have you never considered simply tunnelling a hole through the mountainside?"

He gave a half-smile, and that, too, was the first of the day. "It was cut by my great-grandfather who wished to preserve as many trees as possible, and, I suppose, begrudged the road the removal of any. He *was* a bit stingy with its width."

I nodded in agreement, for I love trees and nature's beauties more than man's in most cases. "But how much longer until the house?"

He nodded, gesturing out my window, at the same time sunlight flooded the carriage.

It was exquisite, more beautiful than anything he could have described, or I could have imagined. "Oh," I murmured, and for the first time that day, he took my hand, touching me.

I already knew he wanted no one's pity, but one could not help but feel sympathy. I had only been married for two weeks, but if I lost him now, I would surely mourn. This homecoming must be difficult. Sure enough, even as we lurched forward, I noticed his expression growing distant. His hand grew limp around mine, as if his mind and spirit resided elsewhere.

The road widened, a sea of lawn swelling from the house and rolling out towards the woods, reclaiming space from them in civilised carpeted surfaces. The horses sped up, sensing their stables were near. As we drew closer, the broad face of Pemberley, in all its sky-backed majesty, filled my view. One woman, alone, all clad in black, stood waiting.

"Devil take it," he snarled. "I told Mrs de Bourgh to have the household waiting to greet you. And there she stands alone, as if no one expected us—" He broke off, seeming to recall himself then, adding, "I do beg your pardon."

"De Bourgh?" I questioned. "Is that our housekeeper?"

"No, no," he said, impatiently, still obviously annoyed. "Mrs Reynolds is the housekeeper. Mrs de Bourgh is Anne's mother. Do not mind if she does not seem over-warm in the beginning. She will grow accustomed, eventually."

And with those words, we drew to a halt, a footman let down the steps, and he leapt out of the carriage. He held out his hand, and for a moment, I simply stared at it. I was to be mistress of Pemberley, of this country house larger than Rosings Park and Netherfield combined, while his dead wife's mother looked on. Oh, and she would hate me.

Perfect.

I can still remember her, if I try; she was a tall, large woman, with strongly marked features which could never have been handsome. Her air was not conciliating, nor was her manner of receiving me such as to make me forget my inferior rank. It seemed impossible that she be parent to the woman in Lady Matlock's miniature. Even supposing Mrs Anne Darcy's portrait to be a flattering pose, she had been...sparkling. Golden. Vivacious. A woman who knew her own worth and felt it a high one, while dispensing charm and a certain fascination to us lesser mortals. I tried to imagine Mrs de Bourgh as her mother and failed utterly. And yet I knew, without being told, that this grave creature with the claw-like hands stretched towards Mr Darcy *must* be she. Her scorn for me in my made-over dress was transparent, to me at least; and I knew that somehow, in some way, my humble personal circumstances were public knowledge.

It was not uncommon for servants to make a display of greeting a new mistress, especially of a home as grand as Pemberley, but I took her meaning—I was not worthy of attention, even from the upper servants, much less the notice of the whole household.

"Mrs Darcy, Mrs de Bourgh. Mrs de Bourgh, Mrs Darcy," my husband said, performing the barest of introductions. One might suppose he did not much care for either of us.

It did not matter. I was Mrs Darcy now; I could sympathise with this woman, but Pemberley was to be my home. She gave the shallowest of curtseys, barely polite. I returned her a curtsey perfectly appropriate to a guest of no particular moment—not disrespectful by any means, but definitely not above me in rank. I saw the flash of surprise in her eyes as she recognised it.

So, she knew my recent circumstances, but not my roots.

"Where is Reynolds? Morton?" Mr Darcy asked.

How she would have answered, I could not say, for at that moment a respectable-looking woman in her late fifties hurried from the house and proceeded quickly towards us; a man, obviously another upper servant, was at her side. He was likely the butler, and she could be no one but the missing housekeeper. "You must be Mrs Reynolds," I said, holding out my hand. "So good of you to come out to greet us, and on such a cold winter day."

It was my acknowledgement of her slight, with an offer of an olive branch in one gesture. Mrs Reynolds was more adept at hiding her astonishment, in the way of the best servants, but nevertheless, her eyes flitted to Mrs de Bourgh, however briefly. She took my hand, though, which was the recognition I required.

"Of course, madam. Please forgive us, as we did not know exactly when you would arrive. I will, of course, bring the household out for inspection any time you wish."

Mrs de Bourgh's eyes narrowed. She did not like this acceptance of my role, so easily won.

Mr Darcy said a few words to Morton so quietly I could not hear, but the tips of the butler's ears reddened and not, I think, with the chill. "Mrs Darcy, this is our butler, Morton. Thank you both for your attendance upon us. Let us go in out of the weather," he finished, offering me his arm.

I did not truly blame Mrs Reynolds or Morton. They were accustomed to taking their tone and their orders from the first Mrs Darcy, and, plainly, her mother. I knew that two mistresses in a house was a recipe for disaster. Mama had spoken often about the trouble she had when Papa's mother was alive and living at Longbourn; I could only imagine how *that* must have been and was certain Mama had made the situation worse, if she possibly could. But while Mama would never have stood for open insult, neither would she recognise subtle or even obvious disrespect in so many aspects of mannerly behaviours. In fact, she might have handed Mrs de Bourgh her cloak and parasol, as if she were a footman. The thought made me smile. I took my husband's arm, and followed the servants into the house.

A few moments later, we entered a majestic drawing room, lined floor to ceiling with windows. Plush sofas flanked two fireplaces, one at either end of the long room. A globe stood on a nearby table, and I gently set it spinning. Mr Darcy went directly to a desk piled high with letters and began sorting through them. I realised how little I knew about him, about what kind of a landowner he was and his daily concerns and routine. It would not, certainly, include lying about in bedchambers and paying passionate attentions to his wife, even had he been wildly in love with me.

Mrs de Bourgh entered, followed by Mrs Reynolds and a maid with a tray. I approached Mrs Reynolds, stopping her from following Mrs de Bourgh to the fireplace nearest Mr Darcy. "Mrs Reynolds, so good of you to know how much in need of refreshments we would be after our long drive," I said.

It was almost comical; she froze in place, uncertain. "Mrs de Bourgh said Mr Darcy would want his tea," she said in a gentle attempt to manoeuvre the situation back towards the woman she was so accustomed to obeying.

"I would prefer to have the tea over here, if you would be so kind." I walked towards the opposite side of the room, knowing that it was best if I asserted authority early. There was no way for Mrs de Bourgh to outstrip me, and gain the table before I could; likewise, I doubted Mrs Reynolds had any wish to present defiance. I was taking my place as mistress, as was proper. Difficulties between two mistresses were hardest on those who served them both.

Mrs de Bourgh had no choice but to follow us to the opposite side of the room, with no opportunity to take control of the chessboard—er, the tea tray. I directed Mrs Reynolds to set it before me, and went about preparing to serve it as she made her escape. "Would you care for weak tea, or strong?" I politely asked Mrs de Bourgh.

"Strong," she replied, a pinched expression upon her face. At that moment Mr Darcy looked up, mild annoyance crossing his features as he saw this collapse of Pemberley tradition in progress, with a tea tray so far from its accustomed placement.

"Mr Darcy, she did not understand that we never have our tea on this side of the room in the afternoon," Mrs de Bourgh explained. "The windows face full west."

"I am certain Mr Darcy has more important worries, after his long absence from Pemberley," I said smilingly. "Milk? Sugar?"

"It does not matter where we drink it," Mr Darcy said, bringing his mail with him so as to retain ample ammunition for ignoring the battle in progress.

Mrs de Bourgh haughtily accepted the proffered cup, drinking it in silent indignation.

I already knew how Mr Darcy took his, from our brief honeymoon, and served him as well. He muttered his thanks. After a few moments something occurred to him. "Are the new accommodations ready?"

"They are ready for you, Mr Darcy," Mrs de Bourgh said. "Though the views are nothing to the cliffside chambers."

"Have you been making alterations?" I asked him politely.

"I thought we would be more comfortable in the other

wing," he said in an impassive voice I had not heard from him since the dowager countess's teas. "I prefer the views of the woods."

"Pemberley's family wing was built upon the cliffside. The view from the mistress's chamber makes one feel as though one were enthroned in the clouds. The eastern side of the house has only lodged guests, up until now," Mrs de Bourgh said, with an emphasis on the word *guests*.

I forbore pointing out that of the two of us, she was more guest than I. And why was it that Mr Darcy had failed to mention her presence? It was awkward, of course, but I deserved more notice than a quick word as we were arriving, and I was deeply irritated with him.

On the other hand, most men were oblivious to subtleties. And while I did not consider her manoeuvrings particularly subtle, perhaps he, like my father, only saw what he wished—although at least my father had noticed enough to laugh. Even if he likely *would* have laughed at Mrs de Bourgh and embarrassed me.

She was to be pitied; she had lost her daughter and now, clearly, the authority of her place in the household, far sooner than she should have had to lose it. It was not my fault and yet I was to blame. Like the countess, Mrs de Bourgh could not hurt me, but I had very much wished for peace, and it might be some time before it could be established.

"I have to meet with Mr Williams—my steward," Mr Darcy said, still absorbed in his letters. "I shall ask Mrs Reynolds to show you to your rooms."

"Oh, no need," Mrs de Bourgh announced. "I shall be happy to show her the way."

And that is how I found myself viewing my bedchamber

for the first time with my husband's first wife's mother. *Awkward, thy name is Darcy,* I thought.

I had followed her up the impressive staircase, her feet somehow making no noise on the marble floors. She flung the doors open to a cosy sitting room, beautifully furnished, and from thence to a bedchamber, its wide windows overlooking a carpet of lawn edged by the forests we'd driven through to get here.

"'Tis a beautiful view," I assured her, although she had not asked how I liked it.

"It will have to do, I suppose," she replied grimly. She walked to a door that was nearly hidden by the panelling. "Mr Darcy's rooms are through here. You can lock it if you wish." She pointed this out with little inflection, yet somehow, I knew she relished saying it. Perhaps she did not simply hate me, but Mr Darcy as well?

I noticed my things had been unpacked and my brushes laid out. "I shall need to see Mrs Reynolds about a maid," I commented, wishing the older woman would go away instead of standing about like a great beady-eyed vulture, staring at me.

"I have lived here since the day my dear Anne came as his bride," she announced, as if I had asked her a question regarding her length of residence. "She did not call me 'Mama', for she always said we were more like sisters than mother and daughter. We were ever celebrated for our entertainments. Anne always said that no one could match me for organising the best affairs."

Idly, I wondered how Mr Darcy had looked upon the news that not only had he wed a diamond of the first water, but the diamond's mother as well. Perhaps *that* was my main attraction—my orphan status. And she stood there and stood and stood, long past the point of awkwardness, for I had ceased speaking.

I probably ought not to have asked, but Mrs de Bourgh was waiting, her arms folded, the minutes ticking by. It seems silly now, to believe that I *knew* she wanted me to ask her, but somehow, I did, or thought I did. At the time, it simply seemed she would never go away unless I asked her the stupidly obvious question.

"How did your daughter die, Mrs de Bourgh?"

She glared at me sombrely, those narrowed eyes staring and staring, her querulous expression filled with malice, scorn, and pity. "As to that, madam, you will have to ask Mr Darcy. He is the only one who knows the answer." And with that, she turned on her heel and left the room at last.

CHAPTER SIX

Once she was gone, I breathed a sigh of relief. Some people, I believe, have gifts of darkness, just as some are charming or pretty. Their darkness pervades the rooms they inhabit, the people they associate with, and, even the air they breathe. Mrs de Bourgh had polluted my rooms and, it seemed likely, all of Pemberley. Had it begun with her grief? Or had she always been melancholy?

I went to the nearest window, unlatching it so that the breezes might sweep my chamber, and took a deep breath, drawing in its cleansing chill. This room did, indeed, give one the feeling of living in a forest glade—if a rather gloomy one. Unlike the sitting room, this chamber was decorated in a spare style, very masculine, with dark drapery and heavy furniture, but I did not mind. I was perfectly capable of decorating my own rooms.

I contemplated the problem of Mrs de Bourgh. Mrs Reynolds was afraid of her, and yet clearly respected her as well. I wondered who, truly, had been mistress of Pemberley. Had it been Anne Darcy? Or her mother? Or, perhaps it was as she claimed—they had done it together, a perfect, united front. I heard sounds coming from the next chamber, the murmured voices of Mr Darcy and his man. It had been only an hour or so since we last parted, so his business with the steward had not been lengthy. Or had it only been an excuse? I waited until I was sure Mr Darcy was alone, and then tapped on the connecting door. He opened it immediately, as if he had been standing just beyond it. Waiting.

I opened my mouth to tell him that it would not do—that Mrs de Bourgh and I could never happily share a house, that it was a recipe for disaster and a mistake of monumental proportions to even try. But he dove for my mouth, stopping me, stopping my words, an impatient, greedy kiss that caught me completely unprepared.

I might have ended it as he walked me backwards towards my bed. Though he gave me little chance to take a breath, he never used his greater strength to overpower me, and there was always a choice. But there was something desperate, even reckless about him now. Why was his homecoming not a happy one? What ghosts did he confront here? Were the wounds of his wife's death gnawing at him? I had no answers, but one thing was certain—this was a man in urgent need of relief from some burden.

He had come to me, to his wife, hoping to find it.

I gave, withholding nothing, while birdsong floated in upon the draughts of weak sunlight. I clutched him to me, feeling the hard muscles of his back and arms, the vitality of his man's body, the might and potency of his loving, marvelling at his need for me despite his power. It was as mystifying as it was exhilarating. But I wondered at it, too, and at his need. He held all the cards—to use a gambling metaphor which Lady Matlock would have despised—and yet, he could not have all to be as he wished; no amount of command would return his wife to him. How much had he convinced himself that coming back here with me would make a difference?

We lay sprawled in the aftermath in a patch of sunlight while our breath returned to normal. We had not even fully undressed, nor were we beneath the coverlet, and the room was cold. I could almost feel when he came back to himself— and his desire to escape, now that he had his release. But I was not a receptacle for unwanted feelings, to be discarded once they were discharged.

I propped myself up on one elbow, playing with the fabric edge of his ruined cravat. "Dare leave me now, and I shall order Cook to serve us naught but oysters for a month. You shall waste away to nothing."

He relaxed a little onto the pillows, meeting my eyes. "But you would suffer as well in such a punishment."

"You forget, I have a detailed knowledge of your aunt's potions and possets. I am certain there are curatives, even for starvation."

"I have heard that oysters increase one's, er, manly stamina," he pointed out, a slight grin lightening his expression.

"Do they really? Well, you certainly do not miss them in your diet." I touched his face. "You need not stay long. Just… long enough."

He pulled me close, loosening the restrictions of clothing that he could reach. And then he held me while the sunlight faded, not talking, both of us taking comfort in the touch.

After much consideration, I decided *not* to mention my troubles with Mrs de Bourgh to my husband. At least not as a first step. For one thing, he could—and reasonably so—

accuse me of failing to put any effort into a peaceful resolution. Secondly, until I put in such effort, expelling her could make acceptance into the community difficult, giving me a reputation for pettiness and jealousy. I had no idea how popular she was, but I must give the neighbourhood an opportunity to know me without a cloud of hostility preceding my introduction. It was possible that she would try and ruin my standing, but it was equally possible that she would decide further battle ill-considered. Thirdly, my pride protested, as though I required Mr Darcy to conquer all my difficulties for me.

Compassion for her sorrows was in there somewhere; I am too self-sufficient to completely empathise, but I am not cold. I understand grief. I have never lost a child, but I have lost both parents, a sister, my uncle, and everything I have ever known and called home, twice. Especially do I understand the anger that comes with loss, the temptation to shake a fist at God, the contempt for well-meaning platitudes and envy of others whose miracles *I* was never granted. Oh, yes, I do understand those sentiments. But when one encounters stinging nettles, one does not roll naked amongst them. Relief is seldom found by drowning in bitterness.

In her position, I should *not* have begun a confrontation on my first day, although I might have privately mocked the new Mrs Darcy's taste in fabrics—especially since I presented such a perfect target for derision. Of course, in her position, *I* would have demanded Mr Darcy find me a house elsewhere. And she still might. One could only hope.

I began the very next morning after breakfast by asking Mrs Reynolds to show me the house. Mr Darcy would have done it, and I certainly would have preferred his company. But it was important to begin building a connexion with the housekeeper. Mrs Reynolds, he said, had been with the family since he was a small child. Her deepest loyalties ought to be with my husband. Despite her discomfort at being caught amidst the friction between me and Mrs de Bourgh, and unless the family had treated her ill, she would possess a moral code requiring her first loyalty to be to him and thus, me.

I followed her into a magnificent dining-parlour—we had dined in a much smaller one the night before. It was a large, well-proportioned room, handsomely fitted up, with beautiful prospects from every window. "This is the cliffside wing," she explained.

The house was built in a sort of modified 'L' shape, or perhaps a backwards-block style 'J'. The cliffside wing to the west took up one half of the long, straight edge; the eastern wing, extending nearly to Pemberley Woods, held most of the home's square footage, the new family apartments being located within the annexe of the 'J'. I had walked through that section of the house, simply taking its measure—a dizzying number of rooms. But I was eager to see the rest.

From here I could see the cliff's edge, from which we had ascended yesterday, receiving increased abruptness from the distance. The windows showed a magnificent vista of mountain peaks, rugged boulders, and trees clinging perilously to their serrated edges. As I passed into other rooms, these objects were taking different positions—but from every window there were beauties to be seen. The ballroom was the *pièce de résistance*, its windows large and staring out into the vastness of a mountain valley. I think I even gasped, because Mrs Reynolds smiled knowingly.

"It is something, isn't it?" she said. "Mrs Darcy wished to add a terrace on that side, and change the window sashes so they could be raised from the bottom, creating doors leading onto it. The master refused, because balls are always at night, aren't they? Not much of a view, and a danger, it being so close to the cliff's rim—though there is a small hidden door leading out onto its edge, for he let her have the view, at least for herself. He seldom denied her much." She sighed, obvious sorrow in her tone. "'Tis cool in the evenings up here, even in summer. So, the upper and lower sashes are fixed, but the middle *can* be raised to allow breezes in by these levers. And of course, there is a full terrace on the other side, more inland and facing the gardens, if not connected directly to the ballroom."

I could only stare. Besides the immense windows, the ballroom was all whites and golds, with three enormous, magnificent crystal chandeliers. Even though the space was frigid now, I could well imagine it lit brightly, instruments playing, dancing in the arms of Mr Darcy. The one dance we had shared, so many years ago at Netherfield, was spoiled by the memory of my stupid anger. Of course, the next time I would insist upon a waltz, and...

My reverie was spoiled by a sudden blast of wind, so violent that the chandelier directly above me rocked wildly, the pendeloques and prisms crashing against each other in a glassy scream. My sudden harsh intake of breath was covered, however, by Mrs Reynolds's remarks.

"Goodness me, I wonder who lowered the sash on this one! Well, it's a good thing we looked in today. It's a miracle no rain got in." She walked to a set of levers and set about closing it, while I wondered how we had avoided a drenching. The rain beat against its panes now that it was closed.

The other rooms were lofty and handsome, and their furniture suitable to the fortune of the Darcys. But I saw, with admiration of its tastefulness, that it was neither gaudy nor uselessly fine—with less of splendour and more real elegance than the décor of Matlock Court. Was this the work of Anne Darcy? Or of prior generations? I asked one who was certain to know the answer.

Mrs Reynolds appeared startled by my easy introduction of the topic of my predecessor. She was cautiously willing to speak.

"Many of the rooms are just as they were in old Mr Darcy's time, ma'am," she answered. "The hall, the gallery, and all the rooms we show are just as they have always been. Young Mrs Darcy redecorated the cliffside wing—her rooms, its dining parlours and the ballroom. Much of the furniture she recovered from the attics and had refurbished. She had a wonderful eye, and could tell just how the place would look when she was finished. 'Reynolds,' she would say, 'you do not believe me now, since I have caused such destruction in your realm, but you will see I was right to do it. And you will, at some future date, admit it is so. See if you do not.' And she always was...I always did." Mrs Reynolds stopped talking suddenly, as if fearing she had said too much, too enthusiastically. I hastened to reassure her, though the 'young Mrs Darcy' was a bit of a sting. Surely we could not be *too* far apart in age.

"How wonderful," I said, truthfully enough. "And Mr Darcy's parents? Were you here when they were alive?"

And in this question, Mrs Reynolds unbent fully as she spoke of what, to her, were glorious years with old Mr Darcy and his wife at Pemberley's helm. We walked through the gallery and she showed me their portraits, talking of her early days as a younger servant and her rise through the ranks to her current exalted position.

"Mr Darcy looks much like his father," I commented. "They are both very handsome."

"Yes," she said, almost wistfully. We walked a bit further, and there was a portrait of Mr Darcy himself, looking very much as I remembered him from those days in Meryton. But his hung alone on the wall.

"Is there a portrait of Anne de Bourgh Darcy?"

"There are, three of them. But Mr Darcy had them moved to one of the closed rooms after her death—he was distraught, and said he was having difficulties bearing the memories. It was so unexpected, you understand." And then she added something very odd, speaking fast, as if needing to get the words out before prevented. "Mr Darcy is a good man. I say no more than the truth. I would not listen to the gossip, nor will I let anyone repeat it in my hearing. *I* have never had a cross word from him in my life, and I have known him ever since he was four years old."

"Repeat what in your hearing?" I asked.

But she stiffened, clearly regretting her phrasing. "Just... gossip, ma'am. Of folks with nothing better to do."

Her confidences were ended, and I knew better than to push. Another portrait caught my eye. "Oh, there is Mr Bingley."

"Do you know him?" she said, her voice lightening. "Yes, that was painted upon the occasion of his betrothal to Miss Darcy."

I stared at the picture for a moment. Mr Bingley looked much the same as I remembered, perhaps a bit less ebullient. Miss Darcy was tall, and on a larger scale than Jane, her appearance womanly and graceful. She was less handsome than her brother, but there was intelligence and sweetness in her face. I recalled what Mr Wickham had said of her arrogance, but of course, if *he* was speaking, *he* was lying. "I knew him many years ago. I will look forward to renewing our acquaintance, and meeting Mrs Bingley."

"They always visit in the summer months, but perhaps they will come sooner," she replied.

I made one or two remarks upon other pictures—there were many, very grand, our footsteps echoing upon the marble floors as we walked, and since she gave tours nearly every week that included this room, she was very knowledgeable regarding its contents, naming great artists and the staggering sums paid for most. It was a gallery worthy of kings; I was dutifully impressed. She showed me to a 'morning parlour' where the first Mrs Darcy had attended to her daily correspondence. It was a pretty, graceful, almost fragile room, the furniture delicate, perfectly matched. I admired especially a writing desk that was the envy of all writing desks, placed at an angle to catch the morning sun for which the room was named. As for the rest, Anne Darcy had carefully selected every piece, and I could applaud her taste—but it was not mine. It was a showpiece of a room; I would spend no time here. It could be added to the tour, for all I cared.

And then, she brought me to the library.

I recalled Miss Bingley speaking of Mr Darcy's library in terms of respect, but she had accorded the same adulation to his penmanship. This...this was a dream. Shelves crept up the sides of every wall, all the way to lofty ceilings. There were wheeled ladders built in, running along a brass railing, so one could access even the most distant shelf. The furniture was leather and designed for comfort rather than for show. A few paintings hung within the limited wall space available, although they all seemed to memorialise favoured hunting dogs.

And the books! I had never seen so many in one place—they overflowed even the abundant shelving, and were stacked in piles beside the desk and tables. Surely there was more knowledge in this one room than could be absorbed by an entire university. The answers to a million questions, the

accumulated wisdom of generations assembled in one place
—and at my fingertips.

I moved aside a curtain to peer out the window; this
room, evidently was the point at which the rest of the house
met the cliffside wing, and from this view, Pemberley was a
different place than appeared from the dining parlour. Every
disposition of the ground was mild and idyllic; I looked on
the whole scene—the lawns, the trees scattered upon its
surfaces and winding into the forest like an enchanted path—
with delight. A smell permeated the thick draperies, a secret,
dark scent of leather, musty books, heavy velvet and soft
carpets too worn to show the neighbourhood and too thick
and serviceable to toss. The large fireplace was cold, the
room icy, but the kindling was set and ready to light, the
whole atmosphere calling, "Enter and welcome! Come and
stay!"

"Oh, my," I murmured. "I have never seen anything so
wonderful in all my life."

Mrs Reynolds smiled fondly. "I believe those to be the
master's sentiments. He never allows this room to be redecorated, unless it is to add more books—and even more
volumes are stored in two smaller book rooms. Many were
the times I heard Mrs Darcy complain of the shabby furniture, but he wouldn't hear a word of it."

Shabby! The sofas were abnormally large and of the
softest leather, made for curling up within. Perhaps one or
two cushions required restuffing and a bit of stitching, but
they were still impressive and obviously designed for the
space.

"Oh, how my father would have adored this room," I said,
the sudden emotion so surprising me with its power that I
had to fumble for a handkerchief.

"When did you lose him?" she asked gently, kindly.

"It has been almost eight years now," I replied, quickly composing myself. "A carriage accident. I apologise. He was a great reader, and I love books as well. This library is a dream to me, and I anticipate many happy hours. In fact, I must have the fire lit now and begin it warming."

"'Tis early in the day for the library fire. Would you not prefer the morning parlour?"

But I insisted, smiling to myself at her efforts to control her alarm at this new evidence of irreverence for tradition. Heedless of draughts, I threw open the drapes cloaking the other large floor-to-ceiling windows, delighted to have the green and mysterious views of Pemberley Woods brought within.

"Shall I leave you here, then?"

I looked at her curiously. "But we have yet to see the upper floor of this wing, I believe. We have only explored the lower."

Stiffening, her face assumed an impassive mien. "No, ma'am. It was closed up after the mistress's death. I am sorry he did not explain—Mr Darcy keeps the keys to that floor himself."

She left me alone, then, with my thoughts churning. Still, there were only simple conclusions to draw. Mrs de Bourgh had not accused my husband of having anything to do with her daughter's death, and yet she had said that 'only *he* knew how Anne died', while Mrs Reynolds urged me to disbelieve gossip surrounding him. Had whatever happened to her, occurred upstairs?

What gossip? Gossip having to do with his wife's death? As if *he* were responsible for it?

I tried to imagine Mr Darcy having *anything* to do with murder and malice aforethought. I failed. What of an accident? An argument, perhaps...an angry shove, a head colliding with hearthstone. And then I laughed at myself. Mr Darcy did *not* lose control of his temper; in fact, I would wager that it was a point of pride with him. George Wickham —a name I hated recalling—had spread vitriol about him everywhere in Hertfordshire. I would never forget the first time they met in Meryton—Wickham had gone very white in the face. He was afraid, I knew he was afraid—but at the time, I did not realise what I knew, and it seemed so impossible that such a charming man had anything to fear. Mr Darcy had turned red with anger and, of course, I had thought him a naturally unpleasant man who dwelt in pessimism and vexation. He had made a *terrible* first impression upon me; I smiled to recall it now.

Mr Darcy had remembered that little insult towards me from that Meryton assembly, all these years later. I even knew *why* he remembered it—because it had been so out of character. Day in and day out, my husband was every bit the gentleman. He was polite, even kindly, to the bootblack, stablemen, inn servants, and his housekeeper, just as he was to his crass, boring relations. Knowing what I know of him now, I realise that only the most intense provocation *could* have incited his unpleasant response to George Wickham.

And what *had* he done in response? Acknowledged the greeting with...unfriendliness. And that was all. Since I full well knew Wickham's capacity to cause suffering, I could only imagine what offenses he might have offered my husband. I was certain they were awful, and that Mr Darcy had not murdered him or even punched him in the nose in retribution. I, personally, would support either of those actions. I would help him bury the body.

His wife's death had affected him deeply, deeply enough that he hated hearing her name mentioned and had shut up the rooms they had shared together. I could not imagine

Pemberley's Mr Darcy being subjected to a coroner's inquest. But why did her own mother not know how she died? Or *did* she know more than she said, only wishing to cause me distress? Distressing me would never bring her daughter back, but people were often irrational in grief.

Mr Darcy and I *must* discuss this. It was ridiculous to shut up an entire floor, in effect, throwing away the key, thus causing talk for the rest of his life about it. Why carry such a burden? Pemberley was huge; he could live in the rest of the house without ever entering those rooms again—why not let it rest in peace quietly? I was selfish enough to not desire, particularly, to hear him sing praises to his lost love; he had certainly never said he loved me, and I doubt such effusions came easily to him regardless. But if he was hurting, or troubled, or upset, I was here to be hurt, troubled, and upset with him. For him. The only thing worse than suffering, was suffering alone.

And yet, I, too, disliked putting my grief on public display. If it were possible, I might have preferred Longbourn shut up, covered in sheets and packed away rather than so abruptly having a new master chortling over his good fortune, making changes that seemed stupid to me while calling them improvements. I must have more patience with Mrs de Bourgh *and* my husband, both. I had resided at Pemberley all of two days. Perhaps I ought to wait a few more before deciding I knew best.

CHAPTER SEVEN

If it had not been for the writing desk debacle, I might have ignored the cliffside wing's upper floor for years.

My preference for the library was immediate; for reading, the room was perfection. However, for writing letters, it was less so for me. There was a desk, of course, but built for generations of Darcy men; Mr Darcy fit it comfortably and often occupied it. The tables were the wrong height. My mind latched upon the writing desk in the morning parlour as ideal—there was enough room in the library's spaces to set up my own within it.

But when I gave orders to a sturdy footman to have it moved, the look of unease upon his face was obvious. I imagined him speeding away to Mrs Reynolds to report another blow to Pemberley's established customs. I did understand; it was an estate which thrived upon tradition. It did not change easily or lightly. However, Mrs Reynolds had been the one to tell me that the morning parlour had been *redone* by Anne Darcy. Therefore, *its* desk had not stood in place for a century, but for less than a decade. Mrs Reynolds had also pointed out that much of the furniture she had placed throughout the house had come from the attics; who was to say that some previous Darcy scion had not preferred the writing desk reside in the library?

It was not Mrs Reynolds who appeared before me, however, but the bombazine-clad Mrs de Bourgh. I had not understood, she said. I did not realise that the morning parlour had been flawlessly decorated in a period style, and every stick of furniture, the vases, the wallpapers, each piece of bric-a-brac selected for a cohesive whole. To remove the writing desk from its pride of place was akin to slashing the portraits, sloshing mud upon the carpets, and storing dead bodies in its place.

Well, perhaps she did not use those exact words. But it was clearly what she meant, all delivered with a sort of imperious condescension, as if I were too stupid to have realised my error unless she pointed it out.

"I appreciate that," I said, with what I hoped was kindness. "I promise you, I do not plan any major redecorations to the house as a whole. I see the work your daughter has done here, and I appreciate it. It is beautiful, and I know you must be proud of her efforts."

She gave an irksome, regal nod, as if I were finally seeing reason.

"I do, however, require the writing desk to be moved at present. If Mr Darcy wishes, another can be commissioned for me, that the original desk might be restored to its former placement. But for the nonce, it will have a new home in the library."

I thought it magnanimous of me, really. I had no desire to force Mr Darcy to buy new furniture.

"You will not understand, madam," the lady repeated herself. "It is a mishmash of style and décor to wreck the morning parlour thus. Pemberley House will be poorer for the change."

"I noted several other pieces of the same period throughout the house—in the green parlour, the gold parlour, the hall, and even in Mr Darcy's bedchamber," I replied evenly. "Perhaps one of those furnishings could be placed in the desk's current position while it is in use elsewhere."

She liked even less that I had knowledge enough of style to see the weakness of her argument, and grew less civil in her exchange. "I can see you are the obstinate sort who intends to push herself upon others, to force her decided, uninformed opinions, and ignore the work of generations. I wonder at you. Pemberley will be ruined."

I sighed. "I believe, of the two of us, there is only one attempting to force an opinion. When your daughter came here as Pemberley's mistress, she made changes. Some of them were large, some small. Her influence will be felt for decades. I, too, will make changes, beginning with the library. Future mistresses will do the same. We all will leave our mark, and it is hoped that Pemberley will be the richer for it."

The gleam in her eye should have warned me, but I was more naïve then. I had been most reasonable; I thought that whether or not she conceded my point, she must at least accept my right to make it. I remember wondering whether I would have to have such an argument about every tiny change I wished, and thinking that I would have to proceed slowly so that our home would not become a battlefield. It was fortunate, I thought, that the first Mrs Darcy had had excellent taste. Even if it was not my own, most changes could certainly wait.

Foolishly, I waited in the library so I could direct the

desk's placement. When the door opened, however, it admitted not burly desk-carting footmen, but my husband. He was very upset. He did not, of course, raise his voice or betray it physically, but it was in him nonetheless. Mrs de Bourgh followed him inside, her aspect solemn but her small eyes sharpened, the triumphant vulture circling.

"The library is not to be changed," he ordered, low-voiced but intent. "Not a stick of it. Am I understood?"

Of course, this command—given as if I were a ridiculous child and without any discussion—put my back up. I had many, many things I wished to say—but I refused to give Mrs de Bourgh the conflict she craved. She wanted me to react poorly, which would only drive Mr Darcy to further entrench his position. I had no idea what she had told him, but I could imagine my plan had been presented in as inciting a way as possible.

I wondered what she would do if I threw my arms around my husband and exclaimed my joy in seeing him in the middle of the day, utterly ignoring his temper. I was too angry to manage the pretence, however, as much as I might have enjoyed the expression upon her face.

My marriage was not a tool for her manipulation. She was not allowed to create arguments between us for her amusement and pleasure.

Instead, I took three deep breaths—something my aunt used to do when the children were naughty, before she reprimanded them. I looked at my husband, really looked at him. His eyes were a little wild—whatever she had said to him stirred emotions far deeper than this discussion deserved. In that moment, I hated her, not only for what she had done, but to be completely frank, that she knew so well how to do it. I could not imagine what could have caused a resentment so deep at such an innocent provocation.

I stood, went to him, and placed my hand upon his cheek. He stiffened; thus I was happy I had not chosen any deeper expression of affection. "I can see the arrangement of this room means a great deal to you. I understand. I believe it to be my favourite room in the house," I said. "Please, excuse me."

Thankfully, he only nodded, allowing me to exit gracefully. I had not missed his quick confusion at my response; it was not one he had expected.

I discovered the maids had chosen this moment to freshen my chambers; they looked at me with veiled annoyance when I entered my sitting room. Well, they should not have expected me to understand their daily schedule so soon. I greeted them, asking their names.

"Nora, ma'am," said the elder.

"Alice, ma'am," murmured the younger.

"Have you finished my bedchamber?"

"No ma'am," Nora answered. "We always start in here."

"Usually that would be fine, Nora, and now that I know your routine, I shall not disturb it in the future. But for today, the bedchamber will be first. Thank you," I said, dismissal in my tone.

There is little worse for a servant than a mistress with unclear expectations. With the possible exception of Mrs Hill, who had the patience of Job, Longbourn's had suffered under my mother's rule. After she rid the home of anyone loyal to my grandmother, Mama proceeded to constantly change her priorities, issuing criticism when the servants performed in a way that had been requisite only the week before and then forgetting the new demands a week after. While living with my aunt and uncle, I saw how important adherence to routine was in the smooth administration of a household. In my own home, although I intended to respect the maids' customary schedule, it would not rule me or my decisions. As expected, they retreated apologetically, their annoyance at disruption fading.

I walked to the window overlooking the woods. To another, it might be bleak and forbidding, but I relished it, for it matched my mood.

"Marriage is difficult," I murmured. I must begin introducing myself to the neighbourhood, creating friendships. I could not rely upon Mr Darcy to be my only one, and if ugly gossip was circulating regarding his first wife's death, it was doubly important that I establish my place in the community to spread an equally strong and opposite point of view.

It would take much time, however. Mr Darcy had already explained that most of the families were in London for the Season; the Derbyshire weather kept many from the county for the winter months. Of the few remaining, I could expect them to leave cards, after which I would leave mine, before actual visits occurred. Even as I watched, raindrops angrily spattered against the glass, flung there by a stiff wind; as the shadows lengthened, it would turn to sleet, and then snow would overtake the moisture and one would have to be mad to venture out in it, especially along Pemberley's insanely curving drive. There had been no callers today, and tomorrow was not looking much better.

I sighed, deciding I would walk through the rooms containing furniture I believed would look well in a matching style of the morning parlour. If Mrs de Bourgh thought this subject was closed and her battle won, she would soon learn differently.

From the largest dining parlour in the cliffside wing, I spotted an inconspicuous door which would lead, I believed, to another route to the kitchens I had visited this morning. I opened it to be certain, and noted a staircase leading to its upper levels. Fully expecting that I would reach some sort of a locked door barring my way, I nevertheless climbed them. When I reached the landing, however, the door opened easily.

I found myself at the head of another marble-floored corridor. I noticed quickly that it did not smell nor resemble a boarded-up place with musty shadows. Rather, every surface gleamed as if it were scrubbed and scoured regularly; empty crystalline vases, sparkling clean, were set in niches along the panelled passageway, awaiting their floral arrangements.

Curious, I strolled along the empty passage until I came to a set of double doors. I am unsure, even now, why I chose to enter these rooms after passing by so many others. It was a sitting room, done in green and gold; a portrait of a hunter, beside another of a spaniel, hung over a bare marble mantel. The masculine style told me this must have been Mr Darcy's sitting room. I wandered through it, finding it spotless but almost impersonal. Of course, they would have moved every-thing that meant something to him to the new rooms in the east wing.

I wandered through his dressing room, the wardrobe empty, to his bedchamber. Rather than being cloaked in holland covers, it was made up as if ready for its next occu-pant. I walked through it, my footsteps hushed upon the thick carpet, and put my hand out to enter the next room, half expecting Mrs de Bourgh to be guarding the entrance on the other side. For of course, I was now trespassing into the previous Mrs Darcy's lair.

Her rooms were enormous, each one easily thrice the size of the current mistress's chambers. I even snickered, imagining the journey Mr Darcy would have had to make in order to join her in her bedroom. I could not imagine how much money must have gone into the marbled columns, chaise longues, pier glasses, goddesses and gilt, marquetry and damask. Her sitting room could easily accommodate a party of thirty.

It was fascinating. The morning parlour was cloaked in restraint, in comparison.

Another door led to a vast dressing room—filled with wardrobes, clothes presses and mirrors. A huge dressing table with an immense looking-glass took up a good deal of space. I opened a wardrobe door, unsurprised to see it filled floor to ceiling with shelves of shoes and slippers. Another contained hats of every sort and style. An evening dress hung by the mirror, as if newly pressed and only awaiting its owner to slip into it.

It was a stylish round gown, in an exotic shade of plum satin. I was certain there would be matching slippers, coordinating bonnet, and possibly matching underclothing somewhere about. She was shorter than I, and very slender; judging by her clothing, hers was the type of figure that wore all the latest fashions with modish perfection. I was rather fuller at the bust and hips, and had to choose styles more carefully. I replaced the gown with a sigh.

I wondered why her clothing remained; although I understood his remarriage a hasty one, if Mr Darcy was recovered enough from his grief to remarry, he ought to be recovered enough to put away his dead wife's belongings. Even had I been the same size, style, and shape, I would never have worn any of it.

I hugged myself a little, shivering, my remade gown not

warm enough for this exploration. Nevertheless, I entered Anne's bedchamber.

And I gasped. I had never seen such a sight; it reminded me a little of the 'state' bedchamber at Haye-Park, but that had been much smaller, designed to be a fashionable, modern version of an ancient style.

William and Mary could not have been more royally received. Her bed was on a raised dais, with steps leading up to it. The walls were decorated in pink *ciselé* velvet and gold draperies, with coordinated damask swaths hanging from a gilded dome affixed to the high, lavishly decorated ceiling. The bed coverings were gold satin and fur. A nearly translucent pale pink négligée lay draped across the end of it, again, as if its wearer was expected at any moment. The fireplace was lit, casting its warmth across the immense space. Vases were scattered around the room, each containing delicate, blood-red roses, with extra petals strewn across the bed. Another massive dressing table, identical to the one in the sitting room, displayed a brush set and various pots and jars of cosmetics, some of the lids off, as if the owner had only recently left it during the act of dressing.

Mrs Reynolds had lied to me; Mr Darcy probably had, indeed, ordered these rooms closed, but she kept this one ready for occupancy. Pemberley's conservatory was supplying its flowers, and Pemberley's servants were dusting, mopping, and polishing, just as they always had. Just as if someone used the room regularly, just as one person always had.

This was not simply a bedchamber; it was a shrine to a ghost.

"Well," I said aloud, just to hear a living voice. "This *is* something." I knew nothing of the de Bourgh family lineage, but Anne Darcy had pronouncedly royal taste, akin to pictures I'd seen of the grandiose Brighton pavilion. Had Mr Darcy approached her bed as a supplicant each evening?

"Stop," I ordered myself. If I began imagining their intimacy, I would grow jealous and perhaps even anxious. I knew he enjoyed what we did together, and...she was dead. Whatever they had shared was gone the way of all the earth.

To clear my head, I walked out onto an extensive terrace-balcony running along nearly the whole of this side of the wing—one could enter through the mistress's or master's chambers or sitting rooms—and walked its length. It had been built out far enough beyond the lower level to create a devastating view, looking over peaks and boulders and sky, perched along the cliff's rim. One had the feeling, almost, of floating alongside the clouds, exactly as Mrs de Bourgh had claimed, and though the wind was freezing, the sensation was incredible. I walked to the edge to enjoy it, noticing that the terrace wall was low, frighteningly so. Perhaps the same Darcy forebear who built the cliff-edged road enjoyed such risks. I understood it, however. The impression of being one with the sky might have been ruined by too large a barrier, although looking down upon the perilous four-hundred-foot cliff, or even the thirty-foot drop-off to the foundation footers spoiled most of it for me regardless.

The nearest door leading back into the sitting room was locked, forcing me to re-enter via the mistress's chamber with its atmosphere of melancholy anticipation. I must have been in too great a hurry to leave it, however. As I passed a commode on my way out, my hand brushed against a small porcelain figurine. It hit on the furniture's edge and broke into several sharp pieces.

"Blast it," I swore, completely annoyed. I fumbled for my handkerchief and scraped the fragments into it. One of them cut my hand, and it bled rather badly. In the end, I had to use one of Anne's handkerchiefs to bind the wound.

All told, my explorations of the afternoon were rather too eventful. I did not mind leaving that floor, and retiring instead to my plainer, smaller chambers with their living forest views.

Dinner was at eight o'clock; I had not seen Mr Darcy since leaving him in the library, and I wondered if he would avoid me all evening. I had tried to find him, had even asked Mrs Reynolds whether he was in the house. No, she said, he was with his steward, Mr Williams. I could just imagine him sending over a note, something polite and formal. *I have business to attend,* it would say. *I shall dine with Mr Williams tonight.*

So when we met in the green parlour just before dinner, I greeted him with some relief, rather than my earlier displeasure. After a moment of what I thought might be surprise, he smiled and spoke of the gruesome weather. I was not finished with our argument, of course; still, it could wait until other appetites were sated.

I had just taken his arm when Mrs Reynolds entered, a worried frown upon her face. "Excuse me, sir," she said. "Mrs de Bourgh is too upset to come down. She has had a small altercation with Nora. Mrs de Bourgh has accused her of stealing something, a figurine, or else breaking it and disposing of or hiding the evidence. Nora swears she did not and is very distressed."

"Doubtless she did not, then. Nora has been with us an age. We must look for another perpetrator."

Mrs Reynolds bit her lip, her cheeks flushing. "That is just it, sir. Mrs de Bourgh sent her to fetch some possession of hers from the old mistress's chambers. She is the only one who has been in it, excepting Mrs de Bourgh herself."

Mr Darcy's expression grew thunderous, and although he spoke very calmly, we both heard the disapproval in his voice. "I remember giving orders for that floor to be shut up. I believe I asked you for the keys."

To her credit, Mrs Reynolds did not flinch, though she was very red-faced. "Yes, sir. Mrs de Bourgh refused to give me her keys, sir. She said my orders did not include hers. I ought to have told you, but she was so very distressed about Mrs Darcy's death. She wished to spend time in her old rooms. I thought it was the grief, sir. I do apologise."

He opened his mouth to respond, but I interrupted. "As to the figurine, Mrs Reynolds, it was I who broke it." I held up my hand; I had removed the bandage for dinner, but an angry red scratch remained. "I entered via the stairs from the dining parlour. The door off the landing was unlocked, and I looked around. As I was leaving, I brushed against a porcelain and it fell and broke. I put the pieces in a box on Mr Darcy's bureau, along with a note to him explaining the accident and its cause, as he was not at home and thus, I could not explain. I had no idea another would be accused, and so quickly. You will please convey my apologies to Nora?"

Mrs Reynolds opened her mouth, then closed it again. Her expression lightened, and I knew she would not tell Mr Darcy that she had warned me against entering the upper floor of the cliffside wing. It was very good of her, though I had already admitted that she had in my note. I did not much care for secrets.

"I will, madam. I will tell her, and inform Mrs de Bourgh

the truth of the matter. I am certain she will be relieved that it was not a case of theft. Thank you, madam."

Mr Darcy's jaw remained clenched after she hurried away.

"Will you ask Mrs de Bourgh for her keys?"

He did not answer me but stiffly held out his arm. I placed my hand upon his sleeve; I could feel his tension. I began walking with him towards the dining parlour.

"She knew Nora had done nothing wrong," I said, conversationally. "Perhaps she did not realise I would tell you of the accident. I have seen her twice in passing this afternoon. I am certain she saw the bandage on my hand. I am also certain that she spends most of her time on that closed floor, maintaining the rooms just as they were in Mrs Darcy's lifetime, and noticed the figurine's absence immediately. Doubtlessly she checked the dustbins for the shards. The vases in her daughter's former bedchamber are filled with fresh flowers, and she has a négligée laid out upon the bed. *That* was the most alarming touch, at least to me. It is as if she expects Anne to return."

If he could have grown stiffer, he would have. I know he would have recoiled from my words, from *me*, had politeness not been ingrained. "Her grief is exacerbated by my presence, and I wonder that she would not like to live elsewhere," I finished.

I said nothing more. I was not sorry that I had made my feelings on the situation clear. Mrs de Bourgh was actively trying to cause dissension between us. And whether it was grief or a jealous hatred or both, I could not stand by as her victim.

Mr Darcy said nothing the entire meal. I, conscious of the footmen listening, had nothing to say either. As soon as I could, I excused myself. I was nearly to the door when he spoke; I turned to face him.

"Your hand," he said. "Is it painful? Should I call someone to look at it?"

"No," I replied. "I barely notice it now. Just a scratch."

And that was all.

For the first time since our marriage, he did not come to me that night.

CHAPTER EIGHT

I slept poorly.

My first instinct had been to go to him regardless of the closed door between our rooms, but his desire to be left to himself was obvious. If our concerns had only involved furniture rearrangements, I would have. But I remembered, only too well, my own times of overarching grief, clouding my every thought. In those moments, I did not want Jane or my aunt; I did not want to have to *be* something for someone else. Not very often, or even for very long, but I had needed times of respite from the company of others.

Still, it was astonishing how quickly I had learned to expect him beside me as I slept. It did not occur to me until the morning that he might believe that if he was not in the mood for intimacies, he should not come. Well, *that* would be an awkward conversation.

I hoped, however, to speak to him a little at breakfast —*not* regarding bed-sport schedules—and urged Clara, the maid Mrs Reynolds had assigned me, to hurry.

Alas, I was disappointed, for he was not alone. The

gentlemen stood when I entered the breakfast parlour, and he soberly introduced me to his steward—and second cousin —Richard Williams. Mr Williams was a paler version of Mr Darcy—thinner, with sideburns I thought overwhelmed his slender face, but of a similar height.

The men talked to each other like the old friends they plainly were. Mr Williams was a bit shy with me, clearly more comfortable in conversation with my husband. Still, I did my best to draw him out, until he finally eased his manner a little, asking after my family and Hertfordshire. He was perfectly pleasant, but I believed him happiest when the conversation veered back to plantings, orchards, and sheep.

"I have had a letter from Georgiana," Mr Darcy announced as the meal concluded. "She and Mr Bingley will arrive this afternoon."

"Oh," I said, surprised. "Do they live nearby? The weather looks to be awful again."

"Bingley purchased Haddon Hall two years ago. 'Tis but thirty miles of easy road."

"Except for your drive," I smiled.

Mr Williams frowned. "The drive should be in excellent condition. If you noticed anything amiss, that ought to be attended to—"

"My wife is teasing," Mr Darcy said, for the first time looking at me directly with none of yesterday's travail in his expression. "She does not care for the slope of the road, and suggested a tunnel be built through the hillside instead." And he gave his small half-smile, one that meant he was remembering my little joke, perhaps with fondness. One that meant he was trying to re-establish our connexion. I returned it in full. We were both weary of distress and difficulty, I believed. We had come together to leave the past behind and start anew. I took heart in his farewell as he departed, for he bent to kiss my cheek. I did not need to be told that affectionate displays were unusual for him. Even Mr Williams looked a bit surprised, and then…affronted?

Mrs de Bourgh did not come down to breakfast, though I waited. I did not wish to put off a confrontation; as much as I sympathised with her grief, she could not be allowed to bully me or my servants. But it appeared she would hide from me, for now.

I noticed with pleasure that the library fire was already lit when I entered, as if in anticipation of my arrival there…and then was astonished to see that a desk—*the* writing desk— had been installed in a spot near the larger desk, a bit closer to the fireplace. When Mrs Reynolds entered with the tea I had requested, I asked her about it. She appeared a bit uncomfortable.

"We, all of us, have been too long accustomed to putting most decisions for the household before Mrs de Bourgh. When you asked Robert for the writing desk, he mentioned it to her, and she was distressed. I heard a fuss was made. Mr Darcy asked me last night if I knew what, exactly, you wanted done to the library, and I told him that, to the best of my knowledge, you only wanted this desk placed within it."

Of course, servants always heard everything there was to hear; I had no doubt that Mrs Reynolds had discovered every word of Mr Darcy's reprimand to me, which was a bit embarrassing. But there was nothing to be done about it.

"Did Mrs de Bourgh take charge of the house while Mrs Darcy was alive?" I asked. It would be helpful to know just how much authority the older woman habitually exercised. Yesterday, I think Mrs Reynolds might have evaded the question. But Mrs de Bourgh had made a tactical error in blaming one of her people for my mishap, and especially one of her most dependable ones.

"It is difficult to answer, Mrs Darcy. Not exactly, no. But Mrs de Bourgh was Mrs Darcy's...voice, so to speak. She was always more fastidious, more exacting than Mrs Darcy, and dealt with details too insignificant to demand the mistress's attention. I promise you, she has never before behaved in such a manner as yesterday." She straightened. "But we have all been reminded that you are mistress of Pemberley now. It is to be hoped she will be able to quickly adapt to the changes."

It was not precisely an apology, but then, Mrs Reynolds had not precisely done anything wrong. To her, *Pemberley* was mistress, and she had always done the best she could for her. Interesting too, that she had referred to Mrs de Bourgh as Anne Darcy's 'voice'. One could surmise that all plans and preferences, simple and affirming, came from the mistress, while her mother was responsible for the less desirable duties involving discipline and corrections. Clever, really. Without ever receiving a harsh word from Mrs Darcy, a strict order was maintained—and none would really blame Mrs de Bourgh for acting in her daughter's place.

When Mrs Reynolds departed, I went to the writing desk, envisioning Mr Darcy here, directing the arrangement of the furniture. I opened the drawers, finding writing materials of excellent quality. There was also a piece of paper, folded in half. I picked it up, read it.

Forgive me.

It was unsigned, but the writing was unmistakeable. An apology from my husband.

I awaited the arrival of Mr and Mrs Bingley with anticipation, curiosity, and some nostalgia. Anticipation, because I remembered Mr Bingley as being sweet-tempered and amiable, and of course, I was anxious to meet my new sister. Curiosity, because naturally I wondered about the kind of man he had become, and I only had Mr Wickham's word on the character of Mrs Bingley (which word was certainly unreliable). He had described her as proud and disagreeable, so she was likely humble and kindly. And nostalgia, oh yes. In many ways, Mr Bingley represented the close of a very happy chapter of my life—even my youth.

He had raised my sister's hopes and then disappeared; she had suffered. But it was impossible to imagine her with any other than my brother Tilney, now. Looking back, we were *all* very young then. Even Mr Darcy, whom I was accustomed to believing so much my senior, had only been eight and twenty—my current age. It did not seem so very elderly and mature to me now.

Mr Darcy met me in the green parlour just as Robert gave word that the Bingley carriage was at the top of the drive. I hoped he had not been avoiding me, but since his hair was damp and curling at the ends, it was more likely he had arrived home from his engagement with Mr Williams only just in time to ready himself for the Bingley arrival. I reached my hand towards him, and he took mine in his, squeezing reassuringly. Together we walked out onto the portico; the rain was coming down in sheets. A footman held a large umbrella over the lady, and they dashed up the steps. She was laughing as they neared us, and she threw herself into her brother's arms, heedless of the damp.

"Fitzwilliam! I know I should have waited, as it was a terrible drive and I am sure our coachman will not forgive me for ever so long if he takes a chill, but I was so happy to hear your news!"

While she spoke, Mr Bingley approached. "Mr and Mrs Darcy! Ho-ho!" he said, laughing also, while my husband herded us all indoors before we allowed in any more of the damp and wind. Then there was a flurry of coat-taking and more greetings and moving into the welcome warmth of the green parlour.

But once we were seated, there was an uncomfortable pause while Mr Darcy had a word with the butler. Mrs Bingley looked flushed and rather helpless—as I would later learn, conversation with unfamiliar persons was difficult for her. Mr Bingley simply stared at me for a few moments before finally seeming to realise the gap. And then he put his foot in it.

"How is all your family?" he cried, with that familiar good-natured cheer. "And Longbourn, such a pretty property, as I remember it. All are well?"

Mr Darcy joined us in time to hear his question. "Her parents died nearly eight years ago, Bingley. Lady Matlock's idiot vicar—do you remember the one? Collins?—inherited." He spoke, not coldly, but in a controlled way that suggested some annoyance. "I believe I mentioned it at the time."

Mr Bingley flushed. "Did you? My deepest condolences, Mrs Darcy."

I was a little slow to respond—I was so astonished that Mr Darcy had known of the death of my parents when it happened, and that it meant at least enough, in the moment, to repeat the news. He had told me he'd heard it from Lady Matlock; he had not mentioned just *when* she had told him. But of course, Mr Collins held the Matlock living when my father died, and she *would* have known.

But it was all beside the point. If Mr Bingley had known

back then of Jane's loss, did that not mean he had never, truly, been in love with her? He might have called upon her with a friend's concern, or, even if not willing to raise her hopes at such a time...he might have, at least, remembered it happened at all. Jane, of course, no longer felt anything towards him—but she could always recall when she had.

"I am so sorry, too," Mrs Bingley put in, gamely trying to cover his blunder. "I lost my parents when I was young. It was very difficult."

I smiled at her with genuine warmth. "It was long ago now." As I drew her out with gentle questioning, she shed some of her shyness, telling me of a redecorating project she had undertaken, of a play in London they attended, and of horses they were breeding.

Mr Darcy and Mr Bingley discussed plantings and fields, crops and yields, with all the enthusiasm my father once showed for such subjects. I stole occasional looks at them, cataloguing their differences.

Mr Bingley was not much changed, except his waist had thickened, while the rest of him remained slender, giving his limbs a stick-like appearance. Mr Tilney was not at all slim, but he was...proportional, strong and fit. Mr Darcy was of an athletic build, with not an ounce of extra flesh. I did not, usually, dwell upon his appearance; when I looked at him, it was not to enumerate his flaws or perfections, but at certain moments, his beauty struck me.

Mrs Bingley might have caught my glances, for she smiled wistfully. "I ought not to have come so soon, when you have been home only a few days. I knew I should have waited. But I was so eager to see my brother happy again, as if a new marriage could—" She stopped suddenly, looking stricken, as if she had spoken out of turn.

"All is well, Mrs Bingley," I reassured her. "I know he has

had a terrible loss, and it will take time to recover from it. I also know that there is no cure for grief, and I cannot and do not expect his feelings for his first wife to be subsumed by feelings for his new one."

She reached out and took my hand. "Please, call me Georgiana. We are sisters now," she said. "And I am certain to grow wiser in marriage just by listening to you."

"Oh, yes, most certainly you should come to me for advice. After all, I have been married for almost three weeks," I said, laughing gaily. "I believe you are the expert in the room, my dear, for all my great age."

I expected her to laugh too, but she did not. Instead, she glanced over at her husband, and there was both sorrow and bitterness in her look. "I am afraid I have none to give," she said, her voice small.

A terrible sorrow filled me, and I was not even sure why. I did not know her at all, and barely knew her husband. But I had esteemed him once, and had no wish for his unhappiness despite the pain Jane had suffered. And, as Georgiana had pointed out, we were to be sisters. It seemed to me a tragedy almost, as if a cherished memory became only a pretence. The men continued talking about farming; Mr Darcy made a remark and Mr Bingley laughed at it, neither paying any attention to the sudden seriousness of our conversation.

"You will give me your opinions regardless," I urged, "and I will try and heed them. And although I *am* so inexperienced, I will tell you what I think, too. We will be friends as well as sisters, shall we not? I have never been married, but I watched my parents, who seldom understood each other, and I watched my aunt and uncle, who had a wonderful accord. Neither marriage was 'easy' because such a connexion never is, though one was much happier than the other. It takes courage to be a wife."

She dropped her gaze. "Perhaps it takes more courage to refuse to be one."

Had she never loved Mr Bingley, then? How sad—to choose a path as Charlotte had done, without the strength of will to endure the consequences. However, Mr Bingley was no Collins. There must be *something* that could be made of him.

And so, to make her laugh, I told her of my ridiculous cousin, and his ridiculous opinions and finally, his ridiculous marriage proposal. And she did laugh aloud; I saw both men's gazes swing sharply towards her, as if it were not a usual sound. And I laughed, too—the memory had long since lost its power to mortify—and I knew we would be friends. As we talked and grew to know one another a bit, I discovered her birthday was the same month as Lydia's. They were—or would have been—so close in age. *I will look after you, my sister,* I silently vowed, as I had never managed to do for the one I had lost.

Our guests easily agreed to stay the night and then the rest of the week, or at least until the weather improved. Mrs de Bourgh joined us for dinner, which was somewhat of a damper on the meal, I thought, as she had little to add except disapproving looks. Georgiana, in her shy way, tried to bring her into the conversation, but she answered the polite questions with clipped responses designed to put off the questioner. She did not join us in the parlour after we separated from the men, but excused herself to her rooms, claiming a megrim. The mood improved after her departure, and when the gentlemen re-joined us, we were quite the convivial little group. It was late when we retired at last.

Clara was brushing out my hair—never an easy task—when my husband entered my dressing room. It surprised her into dropping the brush.

"Never mind it," he said. "You may retire for the night, Clara."

"Yes, sir," she murmured, almost scampering out the door.

I sighed. As happy as I was that he had come, I wished it had been fifteen minutes later. I *could* brush out and braid my own hair, had done so for years—but having my own maid to do it for me was a definite source of happiness allotted to Mrs Darcy.

To my astonishment, however, he picked up the brush as I reached for it, and nudged me back to face the mirror. And then, he began brushing my hair. I felt oddly shy, wondering, at first, if this was a task he once performed for his first wife. But his strokes were tentative; of course, her hair had been smooth, and doubtlessly much easier to cope with. The tendrils of my hair reached out wildly, as if to drag the brush from his clutch.

"You will not hurt me. My hair takes on a life of its own if it is not braided at night."

He did not answer, and after a time, I realised the strokes were not from a hairbrush, but from his fingers combing the thick locks. I began to be calmer, easier, as he ran his hands through the masses, as he massaged my scalp; it felt wondrous, blissful. He stopped, finally, and I sighed, leaning back against him.

I tilted my head up to meet his eyes. "I shall braid it now," I said.

"I would prefer you did not," he murmured. "I have wanted to see it like this, touch it like this, for years."

I thought he was joking. "You mean weeks," I teased. "Without assistance, I can only keep it in the severest style, such as I wore at Rosings."

"No," he refuted, looking at my reflection in the glass. "At Netherfield. Almost as soon as I came to know you. I wanted to gather it up in my fists, bury my face within it." He matched word to action, shocking me. And then he swept me up within his arms; he did not bring me to my chamber but to his.

I was overwhelmed—to know he had thought of me with *anything* except contempt, the idea that he had looked upon me with desire, was shocking to me. He laid me on the bed, but I sat up. "I thought you hated me, hated all of us! You left—"

He stopped my words with kisses, frantic ones, but I broke free, putting my hands up to his face, his jaw stubbled and rough underneath them. The dusky firelight cast his face in shadow, but his eyes were haunted. I could almost feel his misery, even. Did he feel guilty for the desire he had now for his new wife?

For one moment, I thought of him in that great stately bed in the cliffside wing, surrounded by gold and white satin and blood-red flowers, a masterful lover with a different woman, a King William with his Mary. I shoved the thoughts from my head.

"I am not that young girl any longer," I whispered, apologetic, trying to smile. "Though she and I do both have unmanageable hair."

For long moments, he said nothing. He made no move to begin kissing me again. I *did* want his passion, almost desperately. If I could not have his love, I wanted this. But he must see *me*; he must give himself to *me*.

"I hope I am different, now, too," he replied, finally.

I felt a measure of relief. "You are my husband, for one thing."

"So I am," he said, and it seemed the shadows lifted just a little.

Earlier, I could not imagine saying this, but now it seemed safe—if still a bit discomfiting. "On those nights when we are bickering, or you need to be alone, I think...I mean, I would wish...that we bid each other a goodnight, even so." He looked a bit startled, so I blurted out the rest. "You need not come to me only when you wish to...that is, I have become accustomed, although we have not been married long, to—" I stumbled with my words, more flustered with the saying of them than I expected, finding myself flushing.

He smiled fully, kissing me again, but in a gentler, slower fashion. "You would like us to sleep together, even when your husband has behaved like an ass?"

"Especially then," I nodded. "Or if I have." I wrapped my arms around his neck, feeling us fit together fully, hard and soft, male and female. "It does not always have to be...this. But if you would not rather, or need time alone, you must say so."

"I have been alone enough," he said, his voice gruff. And when he began the loving again, he was himself, urgent, passionate and wonderful, the despair fading back into the past where it belonged.

CHAPTER NINE

Mr and Mrs Bingley stayed the week. I enjoyed the visit, but it was apparent that husband and wife had a great distance between them. I could not tell, truthfully, whether Mr Bingley made any effort to breach it, but then, men were often less sentimental. Georgiana never mentioned their troubles, beyond her brief remark that first evening. Still, I heard her sometimes making bitter little asides to him that were probably meant to be cutting, but which seemed to float right over his head, all unnoticed. I saw his attempts to converse with her, as if she were not angry or upset, as if those feelings *could* be safely discounted until they disappeared.

I thought then, how grateful I was that Jane had never had the opportunity to marry him. Gentle, kindly Jane would have little understanding of how to stand up for herself to a man like Bingley. He was amiable, truly, but he was not sensitive. What he could not understand, or did not want to understand, he would ignore, for as long as he was allowed to ignore it. She was much better off with Mr Tilney, who paid special attention to her feelings and was devoted to her happiness.

The morning before their departure, I met Mr Bingley in the breakfast parlour. He said that my husband had already gone off with Mr Williams. I took my bread to the fireplace to toast it.

"I say, you should let the boy do that," Mr Bingley said, waving at the footman, Bertie, standing ready to assist.

I smiled politely at Bertie. "He knows I prefer my own way," I said. I hated anyone else to do it, for I was particular —disliking if it was too charred or too light. My mother had understood the trick of it, being something of a toasting expert. Although she was seldom affectionate—at least to me —if a servant put toast before me that was not exactly right, she would snatch it away and deliver me a perfect piece, simply because she knew my preferences, and she wanted me to have it as I wished. It took me some years to realise it, to look upon that perfect toast as another child might remember sweet maternal words and embraces.

"Will Georgiana be down soon?" I asked him, more to make conversation than to obtain a report of her where-abouts. Since their visit began, she had never risen early.

He only shrugged, his attention more on the parlour window where a dreary sky showed through. At least it was not raining.

Suddenly he said, "I *do* remember those days at Nether-field, and with...with your family. I have been remembering them a great deal, since we received the letter from Darcy announcing he'd wed you. I-I had put them out of my mind because—well, to be honest, it was painful to recollect those good days, the good times we all had together. It nearly broke my heart to leave, it truly did."

I hardly knew what to say to this. I think I murmured an apology or something equally nonsensical.

He peered at me intently. "I still wonder...that is, the wondering has been...gnawing at me these weeks, since his announcement. I have tried and tried not to ask it, but my curiosity will not be repressed. Did I make a mistake? Ought I...to have stayed?"

I do not believe I have ever been more astonished. What did the answer matter now? What use was there in dwelling upon what could never be undone? The very act of asking it meant an acknowledgement that he had, indeed, known he had raised Jane's hopes.

I smiled in my kindliest manner. "It was the best possible decision you could have made," I said, with utmost sincerity. "It all worked out perfectly, did it not?"

His eyes widened with something like surprise. It was, perhaps, not at all the answer he had expected. Could he have been replaying those past events in his mind as some sort of youthful, dramatic catastrophe? It had seemed as such to me and Jane back then, of course, when we *were* youthful. But he had been in control of those events, not us, and to recast them as some sort of Shakespearean tragedy now, when he had every opportunity for happiness in his current situation, was simply ridiculous.

"I...I suppose so," he mumbled. Out of the corner of my eye, I saw a glimmer of movement, a black shadow turning away from the breakfast room.

Mrs de Bourgh had been lurking, eavesdropping on our talk. But why she would wish to, I could not say.

Mr Darcy and I stood together on the portico as the Bingley carriage set off. I wanted to tell him about that odd breakfast conversation, but it seemed hurtful towards his sister, that her husband should even *wonder* whether another woman had once loved him. Besides, he seemed distant, perhaps even unhappy.

"Your sister is a perfect combination of sense and good humour," I said. "I enjoyed her visit very much. I hope they will come often."

He looked at me then, as if he had, briefly, forgotten I stood near him. "You were good to her. Thank you."

"She is the easiest person in the world to be good to," I said.

He glanced at the sky, as if judging the weather. "Would you like to go for a drive?"

I was surprised by the offer. "I thought you and Mr Williams had maps to review?" He had spent a good deal of time this week thus occupied, telling Bingley they were yet incomplete.

He shrugged. "It will wait. The roads will be wet, but Mr Frost is the best driver in the country. Or so he informs me."

I laughed. "In that case, I would love to go for a drive. Let me change, and I will be right down." He nodded, and I hurried up to our rooms. But I paused on the stair, looking behind me. Mr Darcy had not followed me back inside—Robert still held the door; instead, he remained on the portico, staring, long after the Bingley carriage rounded the bend and disappeared.

My wardrobe was, sadly, still not to my liking, but of course I had not yet had the time to improve it. When he offered a drive, I assumed we would go to Hopewell, the nearest town of any size, from which I might select such improvements—or at least, note where they might be obtained. To my surprise, however, we trotted right on through it.

I did not mind, particularly. While it was chilly and grey, it was not storming, the roads wet but decently surfaced. Mr Darcy's carriage was well sprung and equipped with blankets and foot warmers; it reminded me of our honeymoon, driving together towards no destination in particular, simply viewing the sights and enjoying our companionship. I curled in closer to my husband, and he put his arm around me.

"Is it too cold for you?"

"No," I said. "Is my hat poking you?"

"Yes," he said. "Take it off."

I grinned up at him, half-tempted to do so. Only the knowledge that if I did, I would emerge from the carriage resembling a hoyden gave me motivation for keeping it in place.

I sighed, leaning back against his shoulder. "Pemberley is beautiful," I said, "but this is so nice, just to be alone together. I am unused to so many servants. Rosings did not have half so many, and, of course, Gracechurch Street fewer still."

"Did you care for living in London?"

"I liked living with my aunt and uncle. Their home was a happy one, always busy, and yet orderly. It was a good place for grieving girls to go. They made a special point to take us to all the sights and entertainments of town, far more than was usual for them, helping us to see that the world was a big place, a bigger place than, perhaps, we were accustomed to viewing it. They brought us to parties and their friends became ours."

"I was surprised to learn you did not marry," he said, after a short period of silence. "I am certain you had opportunity."

It was unexpected, really, how easy he was to talk to, after years of keeping most of my thoughts to myself. "I can admit I had the wrong idea about marriage," I said. "I thought a grand love would pop into my life, fully formed, and he would look a certain way and act a certain way and it would be so easily recognisable that I could point to the hour and minute it struck. Perhaps you would not recall, but when Mr Bingley took Netherfield Park, there was speculation that he and my sister would make a match of it. At that time, I believed it was how love worked—one would recognise one's own true love from across a crowded ballroom, eyes would meet, a certain something would fall into place, with roses blooming and church bells ringing. And when their romance failed to take, everything seemed so very wrong."

I could not interpret Mr Darcy's expression; if I did not know better, I would have guessed remorse or self-reproach. "She is happy, though?" he asked, with some strange intensity.

"Oh, yes. And Jane's connexion with Mr Tilney came about in a much different manner. He regularly dined with us, because of course the curacy in Cheapside paid very little. Dear Mr Tilney used to say that unless Uncle Gardiner filled him up regularly, he would be in danger of blowing away with every stiff wind. Jane and I loved him as a friend, like an elder brother. He was kind, intelligent, and of excellent character, but it never crossed either of our minds to make of him a *romantic* figure. He was only Mr Tilney, the poor curate. And then he learned he was to get the living at Matlock, and suddenly he was calling every day with definite intention." I laughed. "It quickly became quite obvious that he had set his sights upon my sister, and it was so *easy* for her feelings of respect and friendship to become more. By the time he proposed marriage, I understood better what to look for in a husband. Unfortunately, Mr Tilneys were not thick on the ground in Gracechurch Street. Or, fortunately, as the case may be."

I smiled up at him, but he was not smiling. He did not look at me, but at some past memory, his expression one I remembered from the Hertfordshire days, a revulsion, almost. I did not know what I had said that would cause such turmoil. Had he summoned the memory of my family's imperfections, so often on display, and which had given him such a disgust of us? If so, it was past time to forgive them.

I touched his face, recalling him to the present. "I understand all the reasons why a match between Jane and Mr Bingley would not have been ideal," I said gently. "I did not mean to sound critical of him, and I am certain Georgiana is a wonderful wife, even if I will always believe Jane would have been, as well." I repeated what I told Mr Bingley earlier. "Luckily, everything has turned out for the best, has it not?"

To my surprise, he clutched me to him, kissing me deeply, thoroughly, and managing to remove my bonnet, after all.

I fell asleep before we arrived at our intended destination. I had no idea how long we had been travelling, but judging by my sore hip from remaining too long in one position, I thought at least a couple of hours. I wondered if Mr Darcy had simply had his carriage driven up the highways and byways to allow me rest, but I saw an unfamiliar village when I looked out the carriage window. It was colder now, though we had left early enough that it was still morning. Perhaps we were at a higher elevation, further within the peaks Derbyshire was so known for. The foot warmer had lost its warmth, and I began to hope for an inn to appear soon—the horses, no doubt agreed.

Instead, we pulled up in the front of a pretty property, a pleasant, fertile spot, well wooded, and rich in pasture with orchards beyond. A small green court was the whole of its demesne in front, with a neat wicket-gate to pass through for admittance. It was comfortable and compact, perfectly proportioned, recently painted, the roof newly tiled, with light-filled windows shining down at me. I looked at my husband quizzically. He smiled, a little sheepishly.

And then a woman emerged, followed by a lithesome girl and two lanky boys, and I gasped. I turned to my husband. "Mr Darcy! I cannot believe it! How could you know?" I could barely wait for the step to be lowered before I was scrambling out of the carriage in a most unladylike fashion, rushing to my Aunt Gardiner's open arms, heedless of my hatless state.

"Auntie, oh, Auntie," I cried, happy tears falling down my cheeks. Mr Darcy approached in a much more dignified manner, and I happily introduced him.

"Let me look at you," she said, her eyes smiling in that way she always had. "Why, Mrs Darcy, you have grown even more beautiful since I saw you last! It is clear that marriage agrees with you! I was never more surprised to receive your letter announcing the match. And to a Darcy! And now you have come all the way here, and I cannot believe my eyes."

For we had indeed driven all the way to Lambton, a good twenty miles from Pemberley.

And then I hugged Ellen, who looked exactly the same, and Edward and Michael, who had each grown at least a foot. An elderly woman, somewhat bent with age, emerged—my aunt's mama, Mrs Spengler. Introductions were performed, and she welcomed us to her home, inviting us in, where a grand tea was all laid out, and I discovered that we were expected, that my husband had written a week ago, saying we would visit today, when I could not even recall mentioning the place to him—though I *must* have. He sat much more quietly than he ever had with Mr Bingley, but not as stiffly he had been all those years ago at Netherfield, nor even recently while in company with his aunt, Lady Matlock. He was, simply, a quiet man, much more comfortable listening than talking, though able to converse easily upon any number of subjects. He excused himself once, asking Edward and Michael to show him around the property, but really, I supposed, to give my aunt and me the privacy to speak of memories in which he could not share. The boys, who had been growing a bit restless, were unmistakeably anxious to act the part of 'master' and my heart swelled at this sign of my husband's compassion.

When he returned, Ellen brought out her drawings, explaining the many improvements old Mr Duncan, her master, had wrought to her already considerable talent, and all three children spoke of the numerous friends they had made in the village, and the kindliness of the vicar who was supervising the boys' education. They did not appear to miss London at all.

After a lovely two-hour visit, our carriage returned from Lambton's inn, where the horses had been fed, watered and rested. I knew we must say our farewells; it was important to reach Pemberley before darkness fell.

"I hope you both, and your children, will visit us at Pemberley this summer for a long stay," Mr Darcy said, to which they all happily agreed. Only Mrs Gardiner walked us out, and my husband made a point of leaving us alone while he spoke with our coachman.

I hugged her tightly. "It is easier saying goodbye this

time, knowing as I do that we will see each other again in a few months," I said.

She looked at me with an earnest expression. "Are you as happy as you appear, my dear?"

"I am, Auntie," I said. "Mr Darcy is very good to me. I am doubly happy now, to see you so much improved since our last farewell."

A sadness passed between us, a shared grief, and I held her hands tightly.

"It was the best possible decision to come home to Lambton," she said. "I did not think so at first. Everything that *could* go wrong seemed to. There were, as I am certain you recall, so many business matters to settle, so many unfinished schemes that desperately needed Mr Gardiner's attention in order to reach completion. Mr Ferrars was too accustomed to following my husband's direction, and was so at sea without him, that for a time I was unsure if we would see a return on *any* of our investments. I had thought myself lucky to get a good offer on the Gracechurch Street house, but when I arrived here, I was appalled. Although Mama had always enough to live on and to spare, I found that as her health declined, so had her property. The roof was a regular sieve, the garden a wilderness! She had only three servants left, all even older than herself. Her sheep had been sold when her hired man left and she could not find another. She hadn't wanted to complain, you see, and told us nothing of her situation. It was a...a hard time."

I had known nothing of these challenges, except for her struggles with Uncle's former business partner, Mr Ferrars, and the accompanying financial difficulties. How much had it cost her, I wondered, to write to me those cheerful letters describing the prettiness of Lambton and her mother's property and amusing anecdotes of her children? Naturally, I had seen her melancholy; she could not hide it. But I believed my uncle's death its only cause.

"Oh, Auntie. I am so sorry! I had no idea!"

She smiled at me fondly. "I did not *wish* you to know, silly girl. Your burdens were enough without assuming mine. And all's well that ends well. Mama is so much improved, now that her diet is, and since the repairs to the house mean it isn't falling down around her ears. She needed us here, desperately. And children are so resilient. They do miss their father, but between lessons and new friendships and even a future opportunity for young Edward..."

"What is this opportunity?"

"'Tis too soon to count my chickens," my aunt replied, "but I *will* say that the vicar is deeply impressed with him, and we have hope that when the time comes, he will be well placed. Mr Martin, whom I hired to help us with the property, is far better than any hired man I have ever known—he takes care of simply everything! The house is so snug and comfortable now—and Mr Ferrars at last worked everything out with the creditors and the other investors, to everyone's satisfaction. It appears that we shall have more than enough to live comfortably, sheep to shear in June, and orchards to harvest come autumn. In fact, I was just realising I could invite you to live with us again when your letter arrived with the surprising news of your marriage."

"It is like a miracle that so much has fallen into place," I said. "But you, Auntie? Are you well, truly?"

She squeezed my hands, smiling. "Yes, yes I am. I have friends here still, from when I was a girl. The neighbourhood has been most welcoming. I will always miss your uncle, and I have my sorrowful moments. But I am much improved."

"I am so glad," I said. "And you really will come to us this summer?"

"You may count upon it." She gave a last squeeze to my fingers. "My dear girl, *nothing* felt miraculous while we were in the middle of our troubles, but now, on the other side of the worst of it, I can see how it was. Be patient, if you find marriage to be more difficult in the future than it is at present."

"I think it more likely that my husband shall be the one requiring patience, of the two of us," I laughed.

She looked a little troubled then, as if there was something she wished to add. Then she closed her mouth. "Be strong, my dear, and take good care," was all she said.

CHAPTER TEN

After returning from my visit to my aunt, I was in the most optimistic of frames. Mrs de Bourgh, of course, was a gloomy storm cloud, raining criticisms from dawn to dusk, but I attempted patience. Pemberley was a large place, I reasoned, and eventually she would find acceptance of her loss, as my aunt had done. I could not help hoping she might wish to live elsewhere in the near future; I even wondered if Mr Darcy ought perhaps to allow her to set up housekeeping with her own servants in the upper floor of the cliffside wing, once he, too, had achieved his peace with the past.

The morning came, however, that one of her gibes truly hit her mark. I dressed for the day with Clara to help with my hair—she had quite a knack for it—and went into breakfast. Mrs de Bourgh was already there. Her plate was emptied, and with a sigh, I knew she was waiting apurpose to needle me.

Her maid, Parker, a colourless, older woman, entered and brought her a heavy book that she had evidently requested. Mrs de Bourgh accepted it and set it upon the table. Opening it, she began reading aloud. It was an account book, of sorts, having solely to do with entertaining. In her raspy, cultured accents, she read details from the last ball her daughter ever hosted—the sums for flowers and fruit purchased, amounts paid to a certain confectioner for everything from plates and chairs to hundreds of paste stones. Swan ices coloured in gold, musicians from town, new livery to match the theme—all told, she had spent nearly a thousand pounds on it. "She had the place done in gold and hand-cut glass," Mrs de Bourgh continued. "Everything sparkled; everything shone. Anne is the granddaughter of a duke, and I am the daughter of a baron. She brought a fortune of twenty thousand to the marriage, and a fine property in Ramsgate. Pemberley was her stage; that night, in her simple golden gown, with diamonds in her hair, her perfections, her breeding, and her beauty glittered brighter than anyone and anything else on it. Mr Darcy bought those diamonds for her, and she looked so beautiful, she took the breath away from all who gazed upon her. It was the anniversary of their wedding day. Hundreds came."

Her lips stretched into a sneer. "And look at you. You are a nobody! Parker dresses better than you do."

It was, unfortunately, accurate that day. Parker happened to be wearing a dress, probably a castoff from her mistress or even Anne Darcy, with the new lower waist and fashionable sleeves, while I wore another of my remade dresses from the dowager countess, in an unfortunate shade of chartreuse. It did not help that Mr Darcy had never given me anything in the way of jewellery, much less diamonds. She had succeeded, for once, in hurting my feelings.

"I suppose the estate will be the better for not spending thousands on entertainments this year," I forced myself to answer mildly.

She looked at me with pure hatred. "Nothing will be *better* at this estate, this year or any other. But I do agree with Mr Darcy's decision not to entertain." Leaving the account book on the table, she stood and walked towards the door, turning back to me just before exiting. "You are simply not worth the expense."

I had been raised with sisters, so I was no stranger to hurtful insults. Lydia had been the grand master of them, able to strike at the heart of one's most tender feelings with unerring accuracy. She would have met her match in Mrs de Bourgh. If my husband chose not to shower his second wife with gifts, there was not much I could do about it; however, my wardrobe *was* sadly inadequate. I had been married over a month, and in the course of learning the pleasures and responsibilities of being Mrs Darcy, I *had* neglected my appearance. While I had no desire to let her know her cruel words struck home, I determined it as my duty to resupply at least some fashion deficiencies from Hopewell. When I approached Mr Darcy with my request, however, he was surprisingly opposed to the scheme.

"We must go to London. There is little of quality to be found in Hopewell."

"Yes, well, London would be ideal," I said patiently, "but the weather is turned bad again, and who knows when it would be safe to travel? It could be months! And in the meantime, I look like a frump!"

Annoyingly, he only smiled. "You look beautiful, always, no matter what you wear. And there shall not be many visitors until we can go to town. I promise I shall take you the next time the weather clears. I must leave now, as I am meeting with tenants." He kissed me on the cheek somewhat dismissively, it seemed to me, and hurried away.

I was upset, even though it was the first time he had ever

called me 'beautiful'; I felt he did not mean it, that he was offering me a conciliatory pat on the head as though I were a trained dog. I understood how to shop, and what one could or could not procure from a town the size of Hopewell; it seemed about the equal of Meryton. Had he even put me off with, "I will take you some other day, as soon as I have the time," I might have been satisfied. But I was certain that I was hearing his dead wife's opinion of the place. I already knew her taste to be exceedingly different from my own. I would not require satins and furs! And, there was that hurt, simmering below the surface. It was maddening.

But I had my pin money, and I only required a carriage, not his chaperonage. The weather was awful and I did not relish a ride down the winding drive but, I am sorry to admit, my back was up, my temper high.

Mr Williams came in late morning, as he usually did, for Cook always put up enough breakfast to serve a crowd, and his kitchen was not nearly so gifted. I made a point to greet him, and then presented my request.

I could, of course, have simply ordered the carriage brought around. However, the outcome of the morning's two unsuccessful conversations seemed a foreshadowing that somehow, some means would be found to prevent me, whether by de Bourgh's machinations or my husband's—as well as a persistent feeling of being imprisoned at Pemberley, of being thought a despised, unimportant eyesore.

"I wish to go to Hopewell later this morning, but I am sure Mr Darcy took the carriage," I said casually to him. "We have more than one, I assume?"

"Oh. Oh, yes." Mr Williams had always been polite, but he was very shy. He never spoke to me directly if he could avoid it; I was unsurprised he remained a bachelor. "Mr Frost brought him to the Chadwick farm, I believe."

"We have but one coachman?"

"No, no. Perkins is able enough." He hesitated. "Perhaps you would prefer to wait for less er, inclement weather?"

Mr Darcy had overruled me, but his steward could not. "No, thank you. Unless the shops are closed due to rain?"

"Um. No, ma'am. I-I will accompany you, then," he said quietly.

"Why should you? I will take Clara, and John can ride along. I will send Perkins and John both to the pub to wait for me, so they do not take a chill in this wind."

"Yes, ma'am. I feel Mr Darcy would wish me to, ma'am." He left to make arrangements without eating his breakfast.

He had *not* sounded enthusiastic. I felt a bit sorry for him, and a bit guilty for my insistence, but neither did I understand the fuss. How many times had I made similar trips, with only one of my sisters accompanying me, to Meryton? It gave me another pang of the sharpest, bitterest sort of homesickness, a yearning for a home long gone. I grew more determined than ever to reclaim some of *myself*, that girl who had died with my parents. A shopping expedition was a first step.

The journey down the mountain was, as usual, hair-raising, even more so this first time with Clara beside me instead of Mr Darcy. At times it appeared as though the branches of trees would hit us as they whipped wildly in the wind; at other times the drive looked too narrow, the mountainside too close to its edge, or that we would fly off the very side of it. Mr Williams remained unconcerned, if he did not appear very happy.

When the carriage pulled up to a neat, tidy square, I was happy to see the number of shops—it appeared there would be more choices than Meryton had once provided. After arranging to meet up with the carriage in the same place two hours hence, I entered the first shop, a linen draper, with Mr

Williams trailing me like a spaniel, while Clara remained hunched near the door.

The merchants had to realise who I was; the Darcy carriage would hardly go unrecognised, and I had an entourage announcing myself. And yet, the shopkeeper made no move to assist me, and though I smiled at him, he would not meet my eyes. I was puzzled, and then Mr Williams said, "Come now, Davis."

Mr Davis hesitated, and then asked *him* how he could be of assistance. I pointed out three bolts I wished to examine, which instruction Mr Williams dutifully repeated before the draper brought them down. I scrutinised them and found two to my taste, ordering several lengths from each. Mr Williams repeated my order until Davis nodded, after which the steward said to me, "Is there anything else you wish to see here?"

I *did* wish to see more, *much* more, but the sullen attitude of Mr Davis was off-putting, as was filtering all of my requests through Mr Williams. I shook my head, and he ordered Davis to have the fabrics delivered to Pemberley. We were out the door only ten minutes after we entered.

At the haberdashery, I had no luck whatsoever. The shop-keeper turned her back to me, disappeared into a back room and never emerged, though Mr Williams called to her more than once.

As we left, I looked at the steward, but he showed no signs of wishing to explain, and as the wind was blowing fit to turn my umbrella inside out, we marched along to the next shop capturing my attention, Miss Bickford's Fine Dresses.

Probably due to the weather, again, I was the only customer in the shop. But a girl jumped off her stool and looked at us wide-eyed, while a rather magnificent personage turned to greet me. To my mind, she was dressed for a day in Paris rather than Hopewell, wearing blossom-coloured fine muslin and a hat trimmed in a concoction of feathers and frills that would not have been amiss in a London ballroom. The smile she bequeathed me was of a queen welcoming a subject. It was an enormous improvement over the previous shops, and I smiled back.

This was Miss Bickford herself, and *she* did not suffer from unfriendliness or excessive silence. Rather, she greeted me effusively, calling me 'Dear Mrs Darcy', and immediately set out a number of plates for my viewing pleasure. Clara, admiring a selection of Mechlin laces and ribbons with the shop girl, appeared well-occupied. I looked at Mr Williams. "Would you care to wait at the pub with Perkins and John?" I asked. "I shall be some time."

Still appearing forlorn, he shook his head and took a seat upon a wooden bench near the door. I dismissed him from my mind as I indulged in my first *real* shopping trip in many years. My aunt and uncle had provided for me and provided for me well; however, I had always been conscious that the money they expended upon me was their own, for they would not take any of my small inheritance. They were not wealthy, although very comfortable, but my uncle's fortunes sometimes vacillated, when investments failed to produce immediate results. I was accustomed to economising, to looking for bargains, and to choosing the practical over the pretty.

Not today. Miss Bickford was only too eager to assist, and while I did not much care for her personal taste in hats, most of her suggestions were elegant and her pattern books, excellent. Her establishment, though small, held a number of fabrics and trims I found irresistible after my lengthy fashion drought. Periodically, I glanced back at Mr Williams, but after a time, he had grown comfortable enough to doze, his chin to his chest. He was not unhandsome, I considered, but was entirely too thin; I ought not to have said anything to him about shopping until after his breakfast.

Miss Bickford was not at all shy about voicing *her* thoughts. "I am so delighted you came to us today," she said. "Though usually we are so busy, I knew the weather would keep custom from my door. I even thought of closing the shop, but I knew better! I sent Matilda and Selma home, but I told Lucy that someone was bound to see a need and we would be here to fill it!" She prattled incessantly of nothing in particular between tasteful recommendations. After a time, I became so accustomed to this that I almost believed I misheard when she began speaking of Anne Darcy.

"I often dressed the first Mrs Darcy—oh, she had her London *modiste,*" she said, pronouncing the word as though it were *guttersnipe*, "but she knew what she had in me. She would have been foolish to ignore my talents and she was by no means foolish. I never hesitated to be honest, you see. Tell the truth and shame the devil, I always say." Here she paused, giving me a significant look that I could not really comprehend. "Although, of course, one's dressmaker must be able to keep a confidence. Neither I, nor my girls, will ever say a word that ought not to be said, and *that* you can count on."

She paused again. I am sure I looked a bit confused, for I could not imagine what secrets of mine that a dressmaker ought to keep. My taste in fashion? My measurements? Surely they were rather obvious, regardless?

Miss Bickford saw my puzzlement and gave a little laugh. "I told Mrs Darcy that she ought never to wear puce—a fashionable colour, to be sure, but it made her look sallow. I tell the truth to all my customers—I must! If they wear one of my creations and look awful, who will be blamed but me? Her fancy London seamstress would have had her wearing it the day after the queen. No originality, that woman. But if I tell the truth to someone who pays me good money for my opinion, it doesn't mean I'll tell another the same."

This time, I finally understood. She'd couched her words as regarded fabrics and fashions, but Anne Darcy seemingly had shared a secret or two. She was telling me that her loyalty was to *me*, not the Darcys of Pemberley. I glanced back at Mr Williams, but he appeared to be dozing. Evidently, she did not trust it. It was odd, really, that he had accompanied me, but this entire excursion had been odd.

Miss Bickford, meanwhile, prattled on. "Her in puce satin? Ridiculous! Although she is dead, I stick by my word. Like that colour you're wearing now, Mrs Darcy. I hope you don't expect me to sell it to you! Whoever did it, ought to be shot."

I reassured her that I had no love for the shade, and she was comforted; we managed a very good accord, although I had to disabuse her of the notion that frills and furbelows ought to be added to every selection. Clara finally joined Mr Williams on the bench, I took so long at it, but at last we came to good agreement upon a number of frocks.

"Go to the back with Lucy now," Miss Bickford ordered, and I obediently followed Lucy to a dressing room at the rear of the establishment. She helped me disrobe and had me stand upon a low pedestal whilst she took my measurements, laboriously recording them in a small notebook.

After a few moments of silence, Lucy spoke for the first time. "Ain't you scairt?" she mouthed.

I frowned. "Scared of being measured?"

"Cor, no. Of livin' with him who kilt his wife," she said, still whispering. "Everyone says as how he did it, and Lord

Cavendish and Mr Simpson bein' in his pocket and all, there weren't never gonna be an inquest. But I'd be awful scairt he'd do it agin."

As she spoke these extraordinary, preposterous words, a memory emerged: me, asking Mrs de Bourgh how her daughter died, and her, answering, 'As to that, madam, you will have to ask Mr Darcy. He is the only one who knows the answer'.

It took me a moment to find my tongue, but I did. "Miss Bickford would not be pleased to hear you repeat such foolishness," I reprimanded severely. "My husband is an honourable man, a gentleman, in the truest sense of the word. He would never harm me or anyone else, and if you will say such things about him, I will take my custom elsewhere."

Her eyes grew large and round. "Yes, ma'am," she mumbled. "Beg pardon, ma'am."

Lucy was young, and not over-bright. But I had been slow to understand the situation, as well. I ought to have guessed that there was more to Mr Darcy's reluctance—even if I could never have guessed its cause—than simply a desire for a larger fabric selection. He had not wished to expose me, and thus himself, to the rumourmongers of Hopewell.

When I emerged from the back rooms, I was somehow unsurprised to see that Mr Williams was gone. Clara, wide-eyed, stood ramrod straight beside the door. Miss Bickford was quiet, solemn even, her chattering ceased. Mr Darcy, looking like an executioner all in black, stood waiting, his countenance stern, his bearing rigid.

I turned to Miss Bickford. "I thank you for all your time today. You will send a note over to Pemberley when you wish me to come for fittings?"

Mr Darcy spoke after me. "Perhaps you would come to Pemberley for the fittings, ma'am. We will send the carriage."

"Oh—er, oh, yes," she replied. "I would be happy to, of course."

I sighed. "And Miss Bickford...double it, if you please."

She blinked. "Double? Er, that is...would you like to select—"

But I interrupted. "I trust your taste, now that you know mine. Whatever I ordered...make more. And the ribbons Clara was admiring, as well."

Her surprise—and pleasure, I hoped—were certain, but such feelings were impossible to express while the glowering master of Pemberley hovered like a thundercloud.

I sighed again, and took my leave.

Our return to the estate was accomplished in silence. Of course, we could not speak with Clara listening to every word. For once, I did not even notice the perilous Pemberley drive; I looked at my husband, willing him to look back at me, but he did not. He was present in the carriage, but his mind and heart, I felt, were somewhere else entirely.

When we arrived home, young Clara scurried into the house; clearly, she felt the tension swirling between us and wanted no part of it. He took my arm as we exited the carriage, his touch light. *Now*, I thought, *we will talk of this, we will speak, and we will put it behind us.*

I did not care if the entire world believed my husband capable of violence; they were wrong. Mr Darcy, at his angriest, would never so much as lay a hand upon someone he loved. Perhaps I was even jumping to conclusions at the reasons for my poor reception in Hopewell; the idea that he might slay his wife, as Lucy believed, was ludicrous. Could it be that they were angry at his hasty remarriage? Granted, it was swift, but death was, sadly, too common for it to be utterly shocking, and what business was it of theirs?

But at the door, he bowed, turned away and stalked back to the carriage. After climbing into it, the footman put up the steps and gently shut the door. The carriage, with my husband inside, drove away, leaving me to enter the house alone.

He did not come home for dinner, rather, sending a note saying he was unavoidably detained by business. I supposed it could be true; after all, his day *had* been interrupted. I waited up as late as I could, but when the clock struck eleven, I knew I would soon be in danger of falling asleep. I wandered into his chamber; he was the usual visitor to mine. Would he use the excuse of my slumber to avoid me? He could not quite do so if I was in his bed already; it seemed, however, very bold. His man would witness my advances as well.

And yet, what was the difference, truly, whether he came to mine or I came to his? I certainly agreed with the concept of separate dressing rooms, but why did we need separate bedchambers? Did I really wish for the solitude it might afford? Or was a sometimes more painful, less comfortable lack of privacy a better choice? However, should I force him to make it, as well? It could be detrimental to my kindest feelings if he ejected me summarily.

It came down to trust, I decided. I either trusted that he would respect me within my private spaces—and within his —or I did not. I either trusted him to be kind if I overstepped his boundaries, or I did not. The answers were simple, at least to me. And though he might not agree with my decision, I blew out my candle, climbed into his bed, pulled the blankets up over my shoulders, and, eventually, fell asleep.

I awakened to the murmurs of male voices speaking quietly from within Mr Darcy's dressing room. A few minutes later, I saw him entering, clad in a nightshirt, illuminated only by the fire. He normally wore nothing to bed, but his nightshirt meant...something. Doubtless he knew I was here, in his bed, as his man would have mentioned it. He might be sending me a signal not to touch him, not to expect anything from him. Or he might simply consider it gentlemanly, as he was not stupid; he *must* know he ought not to avoid confronting our troubles. He climbed in the opposite side and lay down, sighing, his back to me.

Well, perhaps he was stupid—in this, anyway. Heavens, he had been married for several years; at least under these circumstances, he ought to have recognised my presence for the conciliatory gesture it was, then countered with a gesture of his own.

I was tired, and still hurt. I did not feel like acting the part of a beggar for his affections. At that moment, it would have been easiest to simply go back to sleep.

Instead, I reached across what felt like a vast space between us, took his wrist and, tugging it over to my side of the bed, rolled over so that my back was to him, placing his hand so it rested upon my hip.

For some moments he lay utterly still. And then, I felt the mattress shift as he rolled to face my back; there were still several inches of space between us. With gentle touches, he stroked my shoulder, back, and hip in comforting circles, up and down and over. There was nothing lustful in his touch, but it was deeply intimate, even so. I fell asleep to the rhythm of his easy, soothing caress.

CHAPTER ELEVEN

The next morning, Mr Darcy was gone. I was not particularly concerned, for he always rose early, and I had wakened later than usual. It was not until Mrs de Bourgh gloated at breakfast that I realised what it meant.

"You have driven him away," she announced. "It is as I expected. The only surprising part is how quickly you were able to accomplish it. He tired of you so swiftly, but then, men are like this—they act on impulse and then live with regret. My daughter and I often laughed about their natures. 'Men will do anything to have what they want from a woman, and then spend the rest of their lives whining into their cups that they got it,' she'd often say. I suppose he will live at his house in London, for the most part, from now on."

I was alarmed. Had he truly left the estate for more than just the day? But I knew better than to let her see it. "If that is true," I said easily, "at least I have Pemberley to comfort me."

She turned white—whiter than I could have imagined possible since she was already so pale. Hers was a fury that burned cold. Immediately she stood. "You will never belong here," she said. "Never." She swept out of the room.

I tried not to be anxious, but I returned to my rooms to search for any sign of a note. There was nothing. I looked out of the window; the weather was not so awful as yesterday, but the roads would be slick, and in some places, mud and snow would be a danger. It was dreadfully cold. Had my little defiance been such a terrible thing that he felt he must flee? It seemed ridiculous.

Mr Williams arrived for his breakfast, and this time I waited until he had eaten and was departing before approaching him.

"May I speak with you, sir?"

He was instantly wary. "I...that is, I have an engagement very soon with—"

"I shall not keep you. Allow me to walk you out."

He nodded, and I pulled my shawl more tightly around me as we stepped out into the chill. As soon as we were out of earshot, I asked him my questions.

"Has Mr Darcy left the estate? If so, where did he go?"

His discomfort was obvious. "Er...he had business in London. Unavoidable. Could not be delayed." He flushed, a poor liar.

I stopped, peering at him. "Is he really for London?"

"Oh, yes. To be sure." His expression conveyed an earnestness that would be difficult to pretend.

So at least that much was true. "Do you know when he intends to return?"

"As to that, ma'am, I am sorry. I do not."

"Was this trip planned before yesterday?"

"It...er, that is, I am sure he...it was business that has been urgently awaiting his attention."

Liar. Mr Darcy told me only the day before that we would

go to London the next time the weather cleared, implying a wait of at least a month or two. He had no intention of leaving, yesterday. The only thing that had changed was that I had gone shopping and heard some foolish gossip. *Incredible.*

"Does everyone in town, with the possible exception of Miss Bickford, believe he murdered his first wife?"

Mr Williams actually halted in his tracks, his expression a picture of alarm and dismay as he stared back at me.

"Did you think I would not ask about it? I would have asked him, had he remained long enough. Now I am asking you. Do me the credit of answering truthfully, if you please."

There was something angry in his expression now. At Mr Darcy, or at me, for pressing? "He is the best landlord and the best master," he said grimly.

"That is not an answer to the question I asked," I replied, exasperated. "I will make this simpler. Do *you* believe that he killed Anne Darcy?"

I do not know what I expected him to say—but at a minimum, a vehement denial, followed by, perhaps, an expostulation upon the stupidity of the population of Hopewell. Instead, he opened and closed his mouth several times, started to speak, his cheeks stained so red that I knew he was about to lie again. And then, he turned around and walked away without saying a word.

I stood, staring after him. I felt sick, actually, physically ill. Despite the cold, I set off in the other direction, covering a good distance in ground-eating strides. What could his lack of an answer mean? Why would he not defend Mr Darcy? The path I was on led steadily upwards, for Pemberley was set between two sets of higher, forested peaks. I barely noticed the climb; I was too upset, too appalled. I needed to talk with someone, but whom?

The bare branches of trees mocked me, snatching at my hair, pointing at my distress—reminding me of the claw-like hands of Mrs de Bourgh, always watching and waiting, hoping for my downfall.

My path crested at a lookout, of sorts, and there I stopped, the wind at this higher elevation whipping my skirts around my legs and my hair from its neat coiffure. *Mr Darcy, a murderer.* They might just as easily have accused him of being a leech hunter or a resurrectionist, for all the sense it made.

I wanted, almost desperately, to run to my aunt. It would not be impossible; Perkins could, and probably would take me. And I knew with certainty that Mr Darcy would not come fetch me; he would never defend himself, whether he had done it or not. But would he explain himself if I stayed? *Could* I stay, if he had done this awful thing?

I was conscious of a growing distaste for Anne Darcy. I allowed that it might be based upon resentment that she had held Mr Darcy's heart for so many years, even though their marriage had nothing to do with me. I was revolted by her bedchamber, her extravagance. I was disgusted by her mother's every description of her opinions, her arrogance.

Was this mocking sort of Venus the wife Mr Darcy desired? My imagination grew lurid, picturing the passion that such a woman could inspire. Beautiful, wealthy, blue-blooded and confident, she had fascinated, perhaps captivated many. Had it tempted him to violence? Jealousy?

I looked out over the wild beauty before me. Pemberley sat atop it—unyielding, austere, majestic, and imposing. Much like Mr Darcy himself, for that matter. Those who served her were loyal to my husband. They needn't have been, not really. I had known plenty of servants, and loyalty was not a byword. But it only meant he had treated them well; it did not prove guilt or innocence.

My heart rebelled. He was good to more than those who served him. I remembered his kindness to his sister, who plainly adored him. I thought of the times he had been so caring towards me, such as the journey to visit my aunt, undertaken simply to increase my happiness… Of his great tenderness in those dark and silent nights spent together, of his…love for me, even if he did not say the words or call it that himself. I remembered each of the few times I knew he had been angry; there had been little outward expressions of it—he kept most everything within, walled off, constrained. His control was a part of who he was, a defining characteristic. Perhaps this was why he had hied off to London, to avoid any confrontation? But now that my initial dismay at his sudden absence was past, I even doubted that. A man who was furious with his wife did not rub her back until she drifted off to sleep. He was upset that I had defied him, but I gave it even odds that it was mortification, rather than anger, motivating his feelings. Whatever he did in London now, it made perfect, logical sense in his man's brain that he should do it, and do it immediately.

This was not a man who would explode in a rage, or who would give way to shame or temper. It was ludicrous to imagine him goaded or provoked into an unrestrained wrath. Which meant my choices were simple: either he had killed her in cold blood, or he had not killed her at all.

And I knew which of those choices I believed.

I took a different path down the mountainside than I had going up. I was not in a particular hurry to return indoors, and the exercise kept me warm enough. I was curious when this new path led me to a large cottage within a grove of trees. It had been a pretty thing once, with a spacious appearance—far too grand for a gamekeeper, but not quite large enough to be a dowager house. I could only surmise that it was some sort of hunting lodge, although it seemed oddly placed for such, and practically within sight of Pemberley, except for the trees surrounding it.

Another unusual thing about it was its forlorn appearance. All the outbuildings of Pemberley were in immaculate condition, but not this one. Weeds had taken over its lot, tiles were gone from the roof, a pane of glass was missing in one of the big front windows. Curious, I approached it, cautiously peering through the broken pane.

It was dirty within, with pine needles and other debris having blown inside, and possibly woodland creatures taking up residence as well. There was some furniture, knocked over and jumbled, its upholstery torn, as well as shattered knick-knacks and ruined paintings. I knew I was being fanciful, but it looked as if a madman had broken loose within, and I shivered, backing away from the sight.

And then I nearly jumped out of my skin when I backed into a solid figure behind me.

"Oh, excuse me!" I cried, startled, whirling to discover who else was trespassing upon this eerie scene.

It was Mr Williams, looking as I had never seen him appear before—his face hardened, or perhaps tortured. "You ought not to be here," he said, and there was a coldness in his aspect I could hardly recognise.

"What is this place?"

"It is called Thorncroft," he replied, still not looking at me, but at the wintry exterior of the ruined cottage.

"It is in terrible disrepair, but perhaps it could be refurbished," I offered.

"No," he said in an emotionless voice. "Better it decays in its own time, its own way. Let it die its own death." He said it as though it were a curse he was repeating, a spell recited by firelight to frighten gullible youth.

This cottage—Thorncroft—had something to do with Anne Darcy; I cannot say how I knew this. Perhaps her ghost whispered it in my ear, because if ever a place was haunted, this was it. To test my theory, I said in a low voice, "Did you find her so very handsome, then?"

"Only the most beautiful woman I have ever known," he answered sharply. Suddenly he looked dangerous and cruel, the haunting seeping out of Thorncroft and into his eyes, and I thought, *I am too far away from the house and no one would hear me if I screamed.* And I could not run or move, like a rabbit trapped by a polecat, frozen in place by fear or fate.

But a bird screeched and he blinked, as if awakening. "You should leave this place now, Mrs Darcy," he said, himself again, merely the shy and sad Mr Williams. "It is not kept up, and is unsafe for the curious."

I turned and left, walking rapidly away, forcing myself not to break into a run. I glanced back only once, to see him still standing, staring at Thorncroft. And I wondered if I had the courage to face whatever secrets I had just stumbled onto, all unknowing.

I returned to the house and tried to write to my aunt. I had only written a few meaningless sentences though, when I found my attention wandering. I wanted to ask her whether she had heard of any scandal associated with my husband's first marriage. If I were with her, in person, I certainly would have. But it seemed wrong, somehow, to put onto paper those rumours so upsetting to Mr Darcy; it would be as if I were participating in their spread.

The dignified Mrs Reynolds would never say anything ill of her former mistress; she managed a tightly disciplined household, and had admired the first Mrs Darcy. I could, probably, obtain information from Clara, who was young and artless. I recoiled from the thought of using her in such a way. My mother had exchanged gossip with her servants regularly; my aunt never did. I knew who had the better run establishment.

In the end, I simply wrote to my husband.

Dear Mr Darcy,

I cannot imagine why you departed Pemberley without so much as a farewell. I trust you believe such unkindness justi-fied, for reasons I cannot comprehend.

I would apologise for my unauthorised shopping expedition, had you explained why you hate Hopewell, or why some therein hate you. In my ignorance, it seemed only an arbitrary refusal, having more to do with your own schedule and the demands upon your time, than any edict regarding the utter avoidance of the town. I did disobey, but I hope you do not believe it was a purposeful defiance. Or if it was, perhaps only a minor one. I would be lying if I said I was sorry; at the moment, I am more filled with vexation than gentler feelings.

I miss you. It is difficult for me to write that sentiment upon paper. However, I am determined to be honest.

I do regret our current separation. If you would talk *to me, you would find me ever willing to overcome our differences and reach a mutual understanding and sympathy. I wish you would come home.*

Yours&c.

I knew not where to send it, or even if I should. But in this instance, it seemed unwise to withhold my strongest feelings as was my habit. I sealed it, deciding I would give it to Mr Williams to post. With some bitterness, I expected *he* would know how to reach him.

Lambton was not so very far from Pemberley. It would not be strange if my aunt did, indeed, know more of the situation than I. Neither by word nor deed had she implied anything towards Mr Darcy except a deep respect, even happiness in my situation. There was, however, that moment at our leave-taking, when she had counselled patience, and I had thought there was more she might have said.

I took a long time deciding what to say in my letter to her.

My Dearest Aunt,

I know I have written this before, but let me tell you, again and again, how good it was to see you and know you are thriving. I do not mistake your courage in moving forward for an absence of longing for the past. I honour you for your efforts, and they serve as an example to me. I need your strength now! When the Good Book counsels that the 'two must become one' it does not acknowledge, perhaps, that men can be so difficult to understand. Mr Darcy, plainly, does not think as I do. I do not, plainly, think as he does. Added to these mutual misperceptions are certain vicious rumours prevalent amongst the countryside. It all makes for a perplexity of mind and heart— what is real, and what is not?

To be certain, my husband is a good man, and if you have heard otherwise, believe nothing of it. He is also a confusing one, who shares little of his inner self. Although, come to think of it, I am not sure I have shared much of mine. I am so used to keeping my thoughts safely sheltered within my own head, and it is a difficult habit to break. As I write this, I imagine you nodding sagely. Yes, I suppose Mr Darcy and I have more in common than one might think; you have always teased me for my independence of spirit.

Auntie, he is a man accustomed to great solitude. I have only realised it as I pen this to you, for of course he was married for many years, has a large extended family and a goodly number of servants. I have made assumptions because of those things that may not have been correct. What do we really know of other persons? What struggles, all unseen, hide behind polite smiles? And now I have descended into philosophy, so I will cease my ramblings.

I will beg advice upon one subject. As I believe I mentioned during our visit, Anne Darcy's mother still makes her home with us. It pains me to admit it, but Mrs de Bourgh despises me with all the vigour of her soul, and I am at my wit's end. I try to be understanding; she is grieving. It is natural that she should fail to appreciate, even resent, any sign that Mr Darcy's affections lie elsewhere, although his care for me has naught to

*do with her daughter. I am anxious for a happy home, but I
fear she can never be happy if I am. I simply do not understand how to help her, for she lives in a constant state of
misery, and eagerly seeks out company to join her in it.*

*I will stop complaining now, and, as Jane would no doubt
advise, instead count my blessings—of which you are one of
the dearest. Send me all your news, and please remind Ellen
that she owes me a sketch.*

Love&c.
Your Favourite Niece

After I finished her letter, I knew I ought to write to Jane.
My sister was too perceptive to be put off by commonplaces,
but I did not particularly relish explaining any of the difficulties of my marriage. How could she understand? She and Mr
Tilney were so devoted to each other and…I do not like to
complain, because it makes me sound worldly, but Jane
prefers proverbs when administering advice. If I had a guinea
for every occasion she has comforted me with 'To every thing
there is a season…'—well, I was not in the mood to hear it.
So, I sent her the commonplaces after all, and tried to
embellish them with lavish descriptions of Pemberley and its
surrounds. In so doing, I comforted myself. Pemberley
earned every bit of its extravagant praise. Presiding as its
mistress surpassed my wildest dreams. I would heed my
aunt's advice, and learn to practise patience.

CHAPTER TWELVE

A week passed, and I heard nothing from my husband. I tried not to dwell upon it, which was difficult. The weather turned nasty again, an icy sort of rain that managed to chill one to the bone without leaving any snow behind to beautify what it destroyed. I did some minor redecoration, changing the draperies in my rooms from dark velvet to a set of brighter green ones that were tucked away in one of the attics; Mrs Reynolds was a veritable treasure trove of information on Pemberley's vast stores of linens. I also found a number of beautifully stitched pillows in a trunk, apparently created by Mr Darcy's mother. They were whimsical and pretty and suited me perfectly. Come spring, I planned to repaint and repaper, but for now I was satisfied with my little changes. To further counter boredom and distress, I retreated to the library whenever possible, for an endless supply of entertainment, education, and edification.

My aunt replied to my letter, and, although she mentioned nothing of hearing any rumours, she reiterated that my husband's family was a fine one, and that I could trust my own judgment in these matters—that *she* trusted my judgment in these matters. About Mrs de Bourgh, she was inclined to advise patience, but in no case should I tolerate abuse, and should report anything of the sort to Mr Darcy— who she believed would support me in any demand for respect. *If he were here, perhaps,* I thought morosely.

Happily, the day came that Miss Bickford, Lucy in tow, made the trek up the mountain in an ancient black coach, not trusting, evidently, that she could indeed request one from Pemberley. Mrs Reynolds told me of their arrival, and I greeted them with enthusiasm and brought them to my rooms. Lucy peered around expectantly, probably imagining masked assailants rising up from the shadows. I think she was a bit disappointed by the elegance of Pemberley, with nary a gothic horror to be found.

Miss Bickford brought five dresses completed—or nearly so, for Lucy pinned and hemmed, while Clara was ready to apply any other finishing touches. We both looked with great interest at the new trims she had obtained for the remaining dresses as I made my final selections. There was another surprise, for Mrs Dale—of haberdashery fame—had made so bold as to send along some excellent examples from her stores for my viewing pleasure. I bought them all.

I cared not at all for her earlier snub, for it was as I had hoped—the villagers had been predisposed to view Anne Darcy with approval, at least in part because she contributed to their livelihoods. Pemberley was in many ways self-sufficient, never relying solely on nearby merchants. Hopewell had no doubt suffered by her death, and those who suffered would be Mr Darcy's loudest detractors. By giving a large order to Miss Bickford, I had sent a signal that my approval was worth earning. I ought to have had Mr Davis pull down half his store to show me his wares; only my surprise and shock had prevented me.

As Miss Bickford took her leave, she unexpectedly clasped my hand. "It is good to see you looking so well, Mrs Darcy," she said, peering at me significantly. "A dressmaker knows."

I was unsure just what she thought she knew, but I thanked her nonetheless.

The next day, I discovered how appearing in one of my new dresses improved my mood. A deep green velvet with ethereal gauze trims, it was warm, pretty, and suited me well —and I was shallow enough to find solace in it.

For I found Pemberley, though beautiful, a lonely place to live.

Perhaps a bit of my confidence had disappeared with Mr Darcy. I tried not to show it. I met at least twice daily with Mrs Reynolds, and felt I was earning her respect. But now that I understood the opinion of the villagers, I began understanding how it might not trickle down to the rest of the household very quickly.

The first Mrs Darcy had been much esteemed. Amongst the upper servants—those who had served during his parents' time—respect for my husband remained strong. The hostility of the villagers had not infected those whom he paid, and paid well. Nevertheless, even these servants were not all predisposed to look kindly upon the replacement mistress. They did not show it except in the stiff formality of their obedience, the slight questioning of some of my requests. I told myself it would simply take time to achieve full acceptance.

But amongst many of the lower servants, those who perhaps had not been here long, or who had close ties to villagers, there were more difficulties. Mrs Reynolds ran an impeccable establishment, but she could not control every sidelong glance, every smirk, every slight show of reluctance disguised as confusion or failure to hear.

As I turned a corner, I overheard one maid whisper to the other, "They say as 'ow she were from some fam'ly as 'adn't a sixpence to scratch with, an' she tricked the master inta weddin' 'er."

"Don't see's how she could've done so," the other replied in equally low tones. "She hasn't a button on the ol' mistress fer looks. O'course, there weren't many as fine looking as Mrs Darcy were. I always thought her an angel fallen from the sky. And now she's in heaven, too fair for earth, Lord rest her soul."

"My uncle says as 'ow 'e beat 'er for jealousy's sake, but I never saw 'im in a temper," the first whispered, a bit uncertainly.

"He never would!" the second hissed vehemently. "And don't ye let Reynolds hear ye even *think* such a thing, or ye'll be in the basket and out on yer ear. It were grief what fooled him, never doubt it. But he's made his bed, and now must lie in it."

"With 'er, poor man," replied the first, and they both burst out in laughter.

My first thought was to interrupt them with a scold, but I changed my mind and turned back the way I had come. What point was there? If Mrs Reynolds heard of it, she might turn them both off. I was hardly ugly, and cared nothing for their opinions of my looks. Still, some of my pleasure in my new dress faded.

I knew that even in smaller households, a mistress must earn her place, however much one might pretend it was the other way around. But with every day that Mr Darcy was absent, I could feel the undercurrents of distrust building.

It was not only a matter of winning over the servants.

After all, I had, actually, *been* a servant—or treated as one, at Rosings. I would never allow myself to forget the immense amount of labour these people expended to keep Pemberley in fine fettle. I would ensure their welfare and take care with their feelings and, eventually, they would be happy enough with my stewardship. No, a greater issue was that the opinion of many villagers was shared by at least some of the finer families in the neighbourhood, and gossip, as Mrs Reynolds had hinted in the beginning, was rife. Mr Darcy had neglected to litter the neighbours with calling cards announcing his new bride, as a gentleman ought. Now I understood why. By way of half-hearted explanation, he had mentioned that his greater acquaintance was in London for the Season. Only a few of those who remained had bothered leaving cards, which, of course, I had promptly returned—to little effect. Obviously, my new surname would help me as little with my neighbours as it had in Hopewell.

Still, I determined to maintain an optimistic attitude. Perhaps Easter would bring those more amicable home to Derbyshire. Perhaps we would visit London later, and expand our circle by that means. I would not borrow trouble, and assume a life devoid of friends—I was not formed for solitude.

A day later, when Mrs Reynolds informed me I had a caller, how pleased I was for the distraction. It was one of those whose cards I had returned, a tall, heavy-looking woman, perhaps ten years my senior; her card identified her as Mrs Isabella Longthorpe. I am afraid I nearly gaped at her appearance—she was dressed all in gold, golden feathers fluttering from her golden hat, golden rings twinkling on every finger. She reminded me of a great house we had once toured in Kent, every inch of its décor gilded, decorated, draped, and uselessly fine.

After the usual niceties, Mrs Longthorpe came right to her purposes in visiting.

"Tell me about your father's estate, I beg you. I have heard it was a grand place, but entailed upon a distant relation and unhappily lost."

Ah. She played the part of Collectoress of Information for the neighbourhood. As my mother had once fulfilled that particular calling, I understood its importance—to her, at least—and tried to exercise patience.

"Longbourn is still in the family, ma'am. Indeed, my younger sister yet resides there, and one of my dearest friends is its mistress."

Perhaps Charlotte and I were no longer close, but that did not mean I had no affection for her. And truly, she capably managed Longbourn, as well as her awful husband. But this answer was somewhat displeasing to my visitor, since it betrayed no particular grievance or sorrow.

"Ah, yes, I heard you were one of several girls. Of course, it cannot much matter to Mr Darcy, as he can do with Pemberley as he will. An entail is such an old-fashioned notion, I have always believed. You are the eldest?"

A dig upon my ancient birth. "No, ma'am. My sister Jane, wife to the rector of Matlock, holds that honour."

The lady nodded, and I managed to get in a question or two of my own regarding the area and its inhabitants, but she was a dog with a bone between her teeth, and unlikely to be diverted elsewhere.

"Matlock, yes—the earl is a relation of Mr Darcy's, I know. Is that how you met? Through your sister's auspices?"

"No, indeed. We have been acquainted for many years." Not a lie, though I felt I knew him less today than on our wedding day.

"He certainly wasted no time, I own. We all thought he

might look a bit closer to home. My dear daughter, only eighteen years and such a darling, biddable girl, might have filled his nursery. But men are impatient, and do not think out these matters. Dear Mrs Darcy is hardly cold in her grave, but I suppose he could not afford to wait *too* long, since choosing a bride of an, er, particular age. No offence meant, of course."

"Of course." I was mindful that my every word would be repeated—and embellished—throughout the neighbourhood, so I could not toss her out upon her ear. I did not order refreshments, however, and she could not introduce a topic that would encourage me to lengthen the visit. It drew to a thankful close shortly thereafter.

I laughed to myself as her gilded backside swished out the door, but I was not completely unaffected. When, within a few minutes, Mrs de Bourgh informed me that I had yet another caller in yet another parlour, I neglected to wonder why *she* had fetched me rather than a servant. In mentally arming myself for another, possibly difficult interview, I stupidly assumed Mrs de Bourgh and I would greet our visitor together, that she would perform introductions to another matron of the community, picking up where Mrs Longthorpe left off.

But incredibly, it was a man who stood in that elegant, refined parlour. And when he turned to face me, I nearly swooned in shock and dismay.

I had not seen Lieutenant George Wickham in many years, but I would never forget him. He had aged well. I could see the lines of dissipation within his handsome features, but only because I looked for them—one did not live a life such as his without leaving some sign of it. Still, his natural beauty was great. *Perhaps in ten more years*, I thought, *his aspect will better match his character*. He ought to be a loathsome figure of disgusting appearance, a monster, the stuff of night terrors.

"You," I said, my voice low and accusing.

"Mrs Darcy!" he cried, as if we were meeting at a ball or the theatre. "How lovely it is to see you again!"

I whirled upon Mrs de Bourgh, meaning to demand an explanation, but she only smiled malevolently and left the room, shutting the door firmly behind her.

"She is a cousin of my mother's," Wickham explained, as I gaped in shock at this extraordinary behaviour. "Darcy did not know it, of course, when he married our beautiful Anne. He neglected to inspect the blood of the blacker sheep in her family tree, because the flock in front of him was so very blue. Anne and I remained close all her too-short life. Very, very *dear* friends, we were. I grieve her, exceedingly."

"You should leave," I ordered, disgust filling me at his implication. Although I was angry at my husband, a wave of sorrow nearly overwhelmed me. I knew that many marriages were unhappy, and—especially it seemed, amongst the higher circles—disloyalty was almost expected. But my father, despite his great differences with my mother in so many areas, had never been unfaithful. He had made her a promise, and kept it. Wickham ignored my demand.

"Now, now, *mon cœur*," he said. "You needn't look so appalled. Darcy, of course, was horrified to learn he had obtained a connexion with me, but he has always been stuffy. Can *you* truly cast the first stone? Had you the inclination to reveal to him the fate of *your* youngest sister? The last I heard, she was selling her wares in a brothel in the East End. Not one *I* would patronise, of course. Too seedy, too many diseases." He grinned. "You *did* explain it all, did you not?"

I realised that if I suddenly found a pistol in my hand, I would be tempted to shoot him dead and never look back.

Had Mr Darcy's first wife been as evil? Lydia's sins had been ones of stupidity and misplaced affections. This man, whom she had trusted, had abandoned her and left her to die most miserably. If Anne Darcy was cut from the same cloth, Mr Darcy had suffered much provocation—perhaps beyond what any mortal *could* bear. Especially a man of his pride and standing.

"Dear Lydia used her last bit of coin to return home, did you know that?" he continued casually, as if remarking upon the weather. "Unfortunately for her, the new master of Longbourn was there to greet her. Of course, *he* thought death too good for her. *Such* a shame! Put her on the next post returning to London and thought himself charitable for paying her fare. Of course, if your parents hadn't been so foolish as to get themselves killed attempting her rescue, I might have found her more useful. But who knows, really, if they could have raised the blunt it would have required to keep me? I *am* expensive, and weddings are not cheap."

"You are revolting," I snarled, hatred choking me.

He only smiled more broadly. "She did try to keep our love alive, you know. I remember her begging me quite prettily to take her back. I did...for a night or two." He sighed affectedly. "Alas, she could not amuse me longer than that."

I could not restrain myself; I grabbed a nearby candlestick and tried to brain him with it. Unfortunately, I had little strength compared to his. He only laughed, catching the candlestick and wrenching it from my hand, then tossing it aside as he grabbed me, holding me closely before him with his arms wrapped around me.

"Oh, now, this *is* more amusing," he murmured in my ear. "I remember Lydia as a spirited little thing. Perhaps it is in your blood."

"Unhand me," I cried, struggling futilely. "Go away and

leave me alone!" I managed a kick, but my slippers were ill-suited to combat, and I only hurt my toes.

He laughed and arranged his grip more tightly to free one of his hands. It was infuriating how helpless, how frustrating it felt to be entrapped so easily, with his one arm exceeding the strength of my whole body. I was not afraid, not then, for I was too angry. I kicked him again, despite the pain.

"But we have not yet discussed my terms," he replied directly into my ear, his breath hot and wet and disgusting. "I require a price for my silence regarding your tainted family tree," he continued, stroking my cheek as he spoke.

"I would rather die than pay you so much as a farthing," I hissed.

"A mistake," he said, coldly now, his grip still like iron. "However, perhaps you do not realise it. When Anne was alive, she hinted to *so* many of what she suffered at the hands of her husband. She never shared any details, naturally. Too much the lady. I thought it a game, I admit. We laughed together about her rumours. But still waters run deep. Now, I find myself wondering. Upstanding Darcy, virtuous Darcy, respectable Darcy—who really knows what evils he might hide beneath his proper, prim, conceit?"

"If he did not murder you long ago, he is a saint," I cried, and tried to shove my elbow into his gut. Again, I was not strong enough to cause any damage.

"Oh, you are a fiery one," he chuckled, nipping my ear. "Lucky, lucky Darcy. Not that he could possibly appreciate it."

"I will scream, and have you arrested!"

He only laughed harder. "Mrs de Bourgh will have taken care there are no witnesses. Scream to your heart's content. I enjoy the sound."

"My husband will see you gaoled for this assault," I

accused, but I was beginning to feel the helplessness—and hopelessness—of my situation.

"I wonder if you truly understand," he murmured into my ear. "I have numerous friends in this area, as you do not. Many of them share my curiosity as to how, exactly, Anne met her death. She wrote to me, you see, asking me to come to her immediately. Sadly, I was unable to arrive here quickly enough. By the time I could, she was dead, and your husband and the magistrate between them hushed it up. But it will not stay hushed. It will never go away. I promise you, Mrs Darcy, that unless you make it *very* worth my while, I will feed and fuel and fan the flames of those rumours. Your illustrious husband will *never* have a moment's peace. I *swear* it."

His grip was bruising, but it was not so violent as those words. His hatred for my husband permeated every single one. It might, even, surpass *mine* for *him*—he had clearly been nurturing it for much longer. Despair filled me, for I could see no alternative to meeting his demands. I knew the power of gossip. He would make us both bleed unless we paid. He might, regardless.

And then, as if this were some sort of poorly written act from a bad play, the door opened, and there stood Mr Darcy. His gaze met mine, and as if I was watching a scene from my past, I saw the exact same look upon his face as the first time I had seen him meet George Wickham on the streets of Meryton, so long ago.

The same anger, the same helpless sort of fury. And Wickham...was stroking my cheek, still.

CHAPTER THIRTEEN

It was all too much; I lost every bit of control, and suddenly the hand upon my cheek was nothing but a target for my attack.

I bit him as if I were a rabid animal, feeling bone in between my teeth; his glove prevented much, if any damage, but it did startle him into dropping his hold.

He recovered swiftly enough. "Oh, my darling wishes for rough play," he murmured, just under his breath but loud enough to be audible. "You needn't act the injured maiden, my dear. Darcy is used to sharing his wives with me."

I dove for the candlestick, coming up swinging. But Mr Darcy was a step ahead; a solid punch to the face put Wickham to the floor. The next moment, he was dragging the unconscious scoundrel by the neck of his coat out the door. Just like that, I was alone.

My knees gave way then, and I collapsed to the rug. I curled up, trying to make myself small. There were no tears. I only wanted to disappear, to crawl into a hole, or perhaps fade away. Wickham had ripped open my scars, humiliated me before my husband, and resurrected the worst of my mourning. I had never felt such hatred, such vitriol, and it was like poison in my blood.

A part of me urged myself to get up before de Bourgh arrived to gloat over my misery. Before Mr Darcy returned to enquire as to why I had been wrapped in the arms of his enemy. Before I had to speak of my sister.

And yet, there I sat. I ignored my inner voice, calling me to action. Everything felt...ruined.

It was a good half an hour before a pair of men's mud-splattered riding boots appeared before me; my husband had returned, and all I could think was how dismayed Mrs Reynolds would be when she saw the dirt he had tracked in. I did not *want* to think of anything beyond the inane. I did not *want* to see what was in his face, to defend myself from his accusations. I wanted to bury my face in my knees. In truth, I wanted him to go away. I forced myself to look up instead; I am certain my expression was defiant.

His was impassive; to my surprise, he handed me a glass of water. Until that moment, I had not realised how much I needed to drink, to cleanse my mouth of the ugly taste of dirty leather. I drank thirstily, then set the cup aside. "May I bring you another?" he asked, but I shook my head. To my further surprise, he sat down on the floor beside me, leaning his head back against the settee, examining the ceiling. I am not sure how long we sat together like that; it seemed like a long while. I mirrored his position, for some time simply staring at the ceiling's masterful paintings of miniature land-scapes and sleeping *putti*. But at last, I decided there was no sense in delaying the inevitable confessions; I pretended I was telling the *putti* my sad tale, rather than an estranged husband.

"I do not know if you remember Colonel Forster," I

began. "His name is engraved upon my mind, but had not circumstances unfolded as they did, I would likely have forgotten him. It has been many years, I am sure, since you met him."

"I remember," he said quietly.

I continued as if he had not spoken. "His wife, Harriet, was much younger than her husband, and enjoyed my sister Lydia's lively company. When the encampment moved from Meryton to Brighton, she invited Lydia to go with them. I begged Papa not to send her, but Mama…" How to explain? How to defend my poor, dead mother? I certainly had felt anger enough at the time.

I sighed. "After Mama's death, I found three much-read letters she kept, tied with a satin ribbon. They were from an old lover, an impoverished officer who was completely inappropriate and wrote her bad poetry. I think she…relived her youth through Lydia's. Lydia was so pretty, so vivacious, and all the officers made much of her in Meryton. It is so easy to believe that life would be a certain way, a much more desirable way, if only this or that had happened, is it not? Mama gave Papa no peace until he agreed to the Forsters' invitation. Papa ought to have known Lydia was not ready for such independence. *I* certainly knew it. But perhaps he saw Mama in her, too, the pretty girl he once loved and took away from a life that might have suited her better. Who can know?"

I was glad my husband had nothing to say to this. If he remembered my parents at all, it would not be with admiration, and I forgave them years ago for their mistakes. They had both died too young, and I had plenty of better memories to dwell upon instead.

"I remember, you know, how you hated Wickham. He gave out some trumpery story about you cheating him of his inheritance, telling it to everyone in the neighbourhood. We all believed him at first. However, he owed so many, so much, upon his departure, I gave leave to doubt that he was quite as much the victim as he had explained."

There followed a long silence, while I struggled to find words to explain the next, most bitter part of the story. I was almost startled when Mr Darcy spoke instead.

"George Wickham is the son of a very respectable man, who had for many years the management of all the Pemberley estates and whose good conduct in the discharge of this trust naturally inclined my father to be of service to him. My father, also George's godfather, supported him at school and afterwards at Cambridge, a most important assistance, as his own father—always poor from the extravagance of his wife—would have been unable to give him a gentleman's education. Father was not only fond of George's society, but had also the highest opinion of him. He hoped the church would be his profession, always intending to provide for him in it. As for myself, it is many, many years since I first began to think of him in a very different manner. His vicious propensities and the want of principle, which he was careful to guard from the knowledge of my father, could not escape my own observations. Father died in 1806, and in his will, he particularly recommended to me to promote Wickham's advancement in the best manner that his profession might allow, and, if he took orders, desired that a valuable family living might be his as soon as it became vacant. There was also a legacy of one thousand pounds. Wickham's father did not long survive mine. Within half a year from these events, George wrote to inform me that, having finally resolved against taking orders, he hoped I should not think it unreasonable for him to expect some more immediate pecuniary advantage in lieu of the preferment. He pretended some intention of studying the law. I rather wished than believed him to be sincere, but, at any rate, was perfectly ready to accede to his proposal. I knew that he ought not to be a clergyman."

I made a contemptuous noise.

"Yes. Well. The business was therefore soon settled. He resigned all claim to assistance in the church, were it possible that he could ever be in a situation to receive it, accepting in return three thousand pounds. All connexion between us seemed now dissolved. I thought too ill of him to invite him to Pemberley or admit his society in town. For about three years I heard little of him, but on the decease of the incumbent of the living which had once been designed for him, he applied to me again by letter for the presentation."

"The blackguard," I muttered. "I hope you told him to stubble it."

"I did. However, many are the times since when I have wondered if, for the price of another three thousand, much sorrow and trouble might have been avoided."

I turned my head to peer at him, but he continued to watch the ceiling. "You cannot believe that. He only would have demanded more."

He shrugged. "My sister, not many months later, went to Ramsgate for the summer with her companion, a Mrs Younge. Thither also went Mr Wickham, undoubtedly by design—there proved to have been a prior acquaintance between him and Mrs Younge, in whose character I was most unhappily deceived. By her connivance and aid he so far recommended himself to Georgiana that she was persuaded to believe herself in love, and to consent to an elopement. She was then but fifteen. I arrived in Ramsgate unexpectedly a day or two before the intended event. Georgiana, unable to support the idea of grieving and offending me, acknowledged the whole. Wickham's chief object was unquestionably my sister's fortune, which was thirty thousand pounds; but I cannot help supposing that the hope of revenging himself on me was a strong inducement."

"Poor Georgiana," I breathed.

"I stayed with her in Ramsgate for a month, finding a very good companion for her. It was while there that I was introduced to Anne de Bourgh, through some mutual acquaintance. She was very beautiful, very charming, and of good fortune and family. I also knew she was interested in me. The near ruin of my sister underscored the importance of finding a bride and settling down. But I did not love her. I told myself that Georgiana had learnt caution, and threw myself instead into the project of helping Bingley find an estate."

It was odd to consider; if he had not prevented Georgiana from making a disastrous elopement, my sister's life might have been saved. His unpleasant demeanour during his time in Meryton was also much explained, what with all he had recently endured. Odder still to think of the deviousness of it all—that his marriage to Anne de Bourgh might only have been a continuation of the plots against his family, if any of what Wickham revealed was truth.

"You were betrothed to her when you were in Meryton? I thought I heard rumours of something like it."

"I was not. As I said, I did not love her, though my family all pushed for the match."

"Do you believe Wickham followed you to Meryton?"

"I did not think so, then. How could he have known his regiment would be thus assigned? Perhaps it was simply an awful fate. Did Miss Lydia follow him to Brighton, do you believe?"

"I did not think so. None of us thought any particular attachment was manifested in Meryton." I made myself look at him. "You have guessed, I see, that she put herself into his power."

He finally left off his study of the ceiling. "Yes," he replied soberly.

"I had been looking forward to a tour of the Lakes with my aunt and uncle, but business delayed it, so I was at home when the express came from Colonel Forster saying she was gone. Kitty, it turned out, knew of their affair in Brighton from hints Lydia put in her letters, but she thought Wickham meant to marry her. I do not see how either of them could have believed it, since she had neither money nor connexions to tempt him. We did hope, of course, but in vain. The colonel followed them, checking every inn, but he lost them in Clapham and could never pick up the trail again. She was only sixteen when Wickham took her."

"Too young," he murmured.

The rest was difficult to say aloud, and so I returned to addressing the *putti*. And if I spoke in a whisper, it was because whispers were all that could emerge from behind the lump in my throat. "My father decided to go to London to see if he could discover them. My mother insisted upon accompanying him. I thought he would refuse her, but he seemed to have lost all conviction of his authority in the shock of it. And I..."

He reached over and took my cold hand in his warm one. I hardly felt the action. "I rang a peal over him, accusing him of foolishness at best, and negligence at worst. I lost my temper utterly. My last words to my papa were ones of blame and denunciation."

That was the worst of it. The rest was only epilogue. "For some days we heard nothing, and then my uncle came to us. There had been an accident, when they were nearly to Gracechurch Street—the carriage overturned. Mama was killed instantly. My father lived for a few days in excruciating pain. I think he tried...I will always believe he tried his best to cling to life, for us. For Longbourn. And at least they never had to know for certain of Lydia's fate."

The tears, the futile, useless tears wanted release. I tried pressing my fists against my eyes, shuddering in an effort to restrain their force.

And then a pair of strong arms came around me, pulling me into a broad chest; his coat smelled of horse and wind and rain. I lost the battle for control then. With a sob, I let them free.

I soaked my husband's chest until the tears spent themselves. I felt, afterwards, the numbness that comes when all emotion has been exhausted. He had gathered me onto his lap; I vaguely noticed he rocked me, back and forth like a small child. I ought to have been embarrassed, but I could not summon the strength. When I spoke again, my voice croaked.

"He—Wickham—taunted me with it. About Lydia." I felt his arms tighten in response. "I knew it already—that she had tried to come home, and Mr Collins sent her away, putting her on the post to London without a penny to her name. Both Mary and Kitty wrote to me of it. Mary was inclined to think him justified, while Kitty was horribly upset but without the–the wherewithal to defy him. I *would* have. I would not have allowed Mr Collins to put her on that carriage! Or perhaps I could not have stopped him. But at the very least, I would have gone with her, taken her to my uncle's home in London. My uncle tried to find her, again and again. He never could, and finally we accepted that she was probably dead. I wish she had come to us there, but Kitty told me Collins expelled her from the family, ordering her to never see any of us again. I hate him more, I think, than Wickham. Wickham, at least, boldly declares his own iniquity. Collins pretends to righteousness, without an ounce of charity within his cold soul."

I felt his slight nod against my head, and looked up at him. "You knew of my parents' deaths though—you told Bingley."

"My aunt informed me of it at my wedding. Well, she told me of losing her vicar, and the reason for it. I made enquiries."

"Why?" I asked, my voice only a whisper.

For long moments he was silent. Then he said, "I knew you all thought well of him. I ought to have said something, let at least your father know that he was not to be trusted. Instead, I said nothing, perhaps for fear Wickham would start whispers about Georgiana, or perhaps because I thought him too far beneath my notice. Perhaps because I had not taken the time to consider how he might take his revenge. He saw my interest in you, I know he did. I cannot help but believe that he chose Miss Lydia, at least in part, as a sort of backhanded stab at me."

"How could he have seen it? *I* certainly did not, and he must have known that whatever interest you once had…well, you learnt of his wickedness on your wedding day, after you wed a *different* woman—he cannot have believed you were *still* interested in me?"

"He saw it, and that was all it required," was his stubborn answer.

I shook my head against his coat. It seemed preposterous.

"I have not even written to Mary or Kitty, much less Charlotte, to tell them of my marriage. I asked Jane to say nothing yet. I remember, you see, how my cousin importuned you at Netherfield. I can only imagine what he would do if he knew the connexion. He will never be ashamed of his brash, self-advancing ways. He always believes himself to be right."

He lifted my chin. "I can deal with him. He shall not bother you, no matter what he knows or does not know. You need not put off writing any longer." He paused, seeming to struggle with his words.

"You may, if you wish, write to your youngest sister as well. Lydia...she is not dead," he said at last.

CHAPTER FOURTEEN

S*he is not dead.* I looked up so sharply, I banged my head on his chin. He rubbed it absently.

"I found her. It took longer than it might have, had I been able to come to London sooner, because Wickham had already abandoned her by the time I discovered her…situation. She–she was not in good circumstances. I asked her what I could do to help, and she told me that she and another woman in the—" he broke off abruptly.

"The brothel," I finished for him. "Wickham told me she was in a brothel. I know what that is. He probably sold her to them," I said, my voice harsh, but with a trembling that began deep within. "What did she say?"

"She said that she and this other woman who was her friend dreamt of going to America and beginning their lives over again. I questioned her enough to believe her determined, and I arranged passage for them. She lives in Boston now and, with her husband, runs a mercantile."

I could only blink up at him, staring, my mouth open in shock. "Can it be so?" I asked shakily. "She is truly well?"

"I have a business acquaintance there who provides news of her and her family every so often. She married a Mr Brackett, a prosperous merchant, in 1815. They have two children, a boy and a girl. By all accounts, she is flourishing."

I dropped my head to his chest, unable to control my trembling. Of all the awful consequences of that terrible time, Lydia's death had seemed the most tragic. I knew her choices had been poor ones; yet, she had not deserved to die for them, even though my parents had—at least indirectly. She had been a silly young girl with too much freedom and too little sense. We had tried so hard to discover her; my uncle had expended a good deal of coin in the search. My husband's arms tightened around me, as if he could stop the shaking.

I tried to make my mouth form words. "I have thought, so often...if only, if only. If only Papa had refused her permission to go to Brighton. If only the Forsters had been better chaperons. If only I had remained at Longbourn, at least until she sought asylum there. If only she had come to Gracechurch Street instead."

"It is my understanding that she was unaware of the deaths of your parents until Mr Collins informed her. It came as quite a shock. I did encourage her to write—I promised to see that any letter was delivered. But she said she was dead to her family, and it was just as well she stay that way."

"That is what he told her," I whispered.

"I apologise for not informing you sooner," he said gravely. "I did not understand any news would be welcome. I ought to have realised you would never—"

I shot bolt upright. "Never apologise," I ordered fiercely, taking his face within my hands. "Nothing could exceed what is owed you for your unexampled kindness to my poor sister. Let me thank you again and again, in the name of all my family, for that generous compassion which induced you to take so much trouble, undoubtedly bearing excessive mortification, for the sake of discovering her."

He looked down upon me with affection and sadness in his gaze. His hands were in my hair, withdrawing pins, letting it down. "No," he said.

"No?"

"I am happy if I was able to ease some little fragment of the great pain you have endured. I feel, and always will, that Wickham chose her as his victim at least in part because of me. I did what I could for her because it was the right thing to do, and because, had I made known his character to the citizens of Meryton, it all might have been avoided. I could have ruined him in the neighbourhood and in his regiment. Georgiana *could* have weathered the word of a known scoundrel. I can see it now, but at the time I was too conscious of status and reputation and…my pride."

My hair was falling down over my shoulders like a curtain now. It was so heavy that wearing it up ached a little, a pain I was well-used to bearing. In fact, it was only its cessation that brought it to my consciousness. The news of Lydia's survival was like that. I had become so accustomed to the sorrow, I had not realised its weight until it was lifted. I smiled, feeling almost buoyant. Mr Darcy's hand went to my lips, tracing them, and I wondered if he could see something new in me.

"I received your letter," he said. "I returned home as soon as I read it. I did not mean to hurt you with my absence, I promise. I have been alone for so long, I fear I am not in the habit of explaining myself or my reasons for doing as I do."

There it was again—a reference to his essential loneliness. It spoke to my own.

"I suppose I am not, either. For instance, I ought to have

begun with an explanation. I did not know, when I entered this parlour, that Mr Wickham would be waiting for me within. When I attempted hitting him with a candlestick, he restrained me. You did not intrude upon a lover's embrace."

He gave me his sad smile. "I admit I was shocked to see you thus, but it only took a moment for me to see that he was imposing himself. I do not believe a word he utters. He could not speak the truth if a pistol were pointed at his head."

I nodded, and then said that which I most feared saying, for if he would not take my distress seriously, it would indeed be difficult—especially now that I knew what I owed him. And regardless of his rejection of my gratitude, he was owed a great deal.

"Mrs de Bourgh brought me to him, without warning, leaving me here alone with him. Obviously, he has informed her of my family's history with him, and doubtless she will use it to hurt me if she can. She hates me, sir. I can understand it. I understand grief. It would be better, far better, for her to live elsewhere—for both of us."

He opened his mouth to speak before dropping his head back to the settee. It was his turn to talk to the *putti*. "I made her a promise that would I watch over her mother."

He did not have to tell me who the 'her' was. Anne Darcy had extracted a vow from him—perhaps on her deathbed?—and his personal code insisted upon its fulfilment. Controlling him from the grave, to my mind, but he would likely not see it as such. I could go elsewhere—he would never stop me—but I would not be driven from my home by a bitter woman obsessed with the past. I had lost too many homes as it was, and I loved Pemberley already. I said the only thing I could, my own vow, made from the best part of myself.

"I will not leave you because of her. If this is how it must be, I will make the best of it."

And suddenly, I was in his arms, and he was kissing me wildly, passionately. A month ago, his intensity might have frightened me; now, I only returned it, my eagerness matching his. I lost awareness of where we were, even *who* we were. A thousand troubles seemed to be amassing against us, trying to keep us from an ever-elusive happiness. But in this, we were equals. There was joy here, each time we met like this—man and woman, two halves of a whole. The edges of our lives flared out from this point, separate, uncontrollable, at fate's mercy—but I could let those edges go, when we were one.

Some time later, I came back to myself, sprawled across my husband, breathless, and slightly awed by what had just happened. My hair was at its most untamed, and I reached up to gather it back—but Mr Darcy stopped me with a gentle hand upon my wrist, pushing it back down upon his chest where his heart thundered still.

"You will suffocate beneath it," I said, my voice muffled in his cravat.

"My preferred manner of dying," he replied, sounding completely serious.

I could not help but smile. "What if someone enters?"

"Then *they* die," he answered. "A murderous reputation must be worth something." But he heaved a sigh, and carefully helped me up. There were several moments of straightening and rearranging of clothing. His neckcloth was wrecked, as was my aforementioned hair—and most of our mutual dignity. Nevertheless, neither of us could summon much embarrassment. I glanced at his great coat, flung carelessly onto the floor in a way certain to give his valet an apoplexy.

"May I throw your coat over my head to return to my rooms?"

He ceased trying to make something of his cravat, turning to look at me. After examining me for a long moment, he moved to stand before me, tilting my chin up. "Have I told you how exquisitely beautiful you are, Mrs Darcy?"

I laughed. "As much as I appreciate the sentiment, and know I am a degree better than 'tolerable', perhaps your compliment is motivated more by gratitude than truth."

"It is many years since I have considered you as one of the handsomest women of my acquaintance."

I found this an affectionate exaggeration, but asked the question it prompted. "Did you know I was at Rosings? Did you come there...for me, specifically?"

"Of course," he replied, as if this were the most obvious answer ever.

"But this is unbelievable! How did you even know I was there?"

"I do try to keep in touch with Lord Matlock," he said.

His expression shuttered, I was certain of it, but I smiled, wagging a finger at him. "It would have served you right if I had increased by five stone and two chins," I teased.

He dropped his forehead to mine. "My dear, there is very little you could have done to avoid a proposal from me, if you were at all the same here." He put his large hand upon my chest, where my heart beat strongly beneath his fingers.

And it was to find us in that intimate attitude, that Mrs de Bourgh entered. Her disapproval was immediate and cold.

"Well! Is the reputation of Pemberley to be thus polluted by cavorting and excess? You ought to be ashamed, both—"

"Not another word," Mr Darcy said, his voice low, but with an inherent authority impossible to ignore. "As you are well aware, your own daughter cared very little for a moral code you now espouse. This is my home, and this is my wife. We shall do as we see fit. If you cannot respect us, another home will be provided for you."

"Why *should* she have cared?" de Bourgh hissed, as if she did not hear him. "You were fortunate to ever have obtained her notice! A spirited girl, always the prettiest in the room, always the centre of attention. To look at her was to fall in love. She was too good for any man!"

I glanced at my husband during this tirade, expecting to see his ire ignite; instead, he merely looked fatigued. "Perhaps you believe so, but you digress from the point. You allowed Mr Wickham here, and exposed my wife to him. You know he is not welcome at Pemberley and have disobeyed my express wishes. Give me your word that you shall never do so again, else pack your things."

"He *loved* her! Which is more than you can ever say!" she accused. The words poured out of her, vicious and mean-spirited. "He worshipped her, while you were the poorest husband to ever wed a woman. She deserved so much better than you! She *hated* you!" My husband did not interrupt, bearing her charges stoically. I was not so restrained.

"Wickham is a vile, disgusting worm! How can you defend him?" I cried.

"You only say that because he cannot be controlled by the likes of you! He is not bound by the decrees of others so wholly unimportant to him. He is brave and free, and you fear him—as well you should! He does as he likes, and he will punish my daughter's murderer. He has sworn it." Hatred blazed from her eyes, but it was self-righteousness burning in her voice.

My fury was choking me. I looked at my husband, but he maintained an impassivity I found frustrating. I wanted him to return her vicious words with his own, but he only sighed.

"You shall be removed to the Ramsgate property," was all he said.

"No!" she screamed. "*She* is here! *She* will not allow it! *She stays* and so do I!" She began to cry—noisy, racking sobs, so the opposite of my own conditioned restraint, I was taken aback. I think I took a step towards her, but she ran. Not *towards* me or Mr Darcy but—to my horror and disbelief —*past* us, with all speed, directly into the large windows behind us.

I flung up my arms, thinking she aimed for us, but still saw what happened next with perfect clarity. Longbourn's windows were made up of such small, thick panes as to require an axe, at least, to even chip at them. This, however, was Pemberley, and Anne Darcy had redesigned this parlour by adding tall sash windows to what had been a too-dark room; thinner crown 'lights' had been employed within them to avoid paying excessive glass tax. The panel lights were, unfortunately, large enough for de Bourgh's momentum and the impact of her body to impel her head and hand through it, shattered glass and blood spraying.

The next moments remain a blur in my mind. I screamed and suddenly the parlour began filling with servants, followed by Mrs Reynolds, Morton, and a half-dozen others. A young footman fainted. A maidservant was ill. Mr Darcy, splattered in a gruesome red, called for both physician and surgeon. Mr Williams entered from somewhere, helping my husband staunch the blood which seemed to be everywhere, coating everything.

I regained control of my own horror when Nancy, an upstairs maid, began to sob hysterically. "He's done it, he's done it again. We'll all be killed in our beds!" she moaned. Everyone who was not working over de Bourgh turned to stare.

I looked at her with a steely expression worthy of Grandmother Bennet. "Mr Darcy never laid a hand on her, and as long as you avoid dashing yourself against the windows, you need not fear a like fate. You will take yourself to your rooms, please, until you can be sensible." She shut her mouth, but I saw that some—especially the younger servants—looked fearfully in the direction of the fallen woman. An icy gust blew through the broken panes at that moment, chilling us all.

Nora prevented any further outbreak of hysteria, quickly going to Nancy's side. "Come, Nan—you know the old lady is dicked in the nob since the mistress died. Don't you be joinin' her in Bedlam," she said, leading her from the room. Mrs Reynolds took charge then, herding the rest of them away. Two footmen were assigned to carry Mrs de Bourgh up to her chamber to await medical assistance; others were charged with boarding up the broken panes until a glazier could be called. I escaped to my rooms, where I could pace and fret without an audience.

I could hardly credit the events of the afternoon. Wickham's horrible threats, his wicked revelations, and extortion demands. Mr Darcy's incredible report of Lydia's salvation, and even his confession of attraction to me, so long ago. He had referenced it before, briefly. It seemed just as incredible then as it did now. And as if all that were not enough, there were Mrs de Bourgh's furious words and insane conduct.

Except—I did not agree with Nora's conclusion. I had seen de Bourgh's face as she flung herself against the window. There had been determination, cunning, and hatred —but a loss of mind, the absence of reason? No. If she was mad, it was a devious sort of madness, perhaps motivated by her grief, but not consumed by it.

I would be willing to wager that before confronting us,

she had ensured many in the house knew of Wickham's visit, as well as my husband's subsequent expulsion of him. I was certain she embellished the encounter—making much of wondering whether I was 'safe' alone with Mr Darcy afterwards. And now, of course, she would lie to anyone who would listen as to exactly how her injury had occurred.

That is, if she lived to tell the story to anyone at all.

CHAPTER FIFTEEN

It was late before Mr Darcy retired for the evening. He had departed Pemberley in the company of Mr Williams, Clara said, after the doctor told him Mrs de Bourgh, though alive, would be hideously scarred for life. The young maid was obviously agog with the excitement and drama, hoping I would speculate. She was, of course, disappointed. I took a tray in my room rather than eat alone downstairs.

I waited in his chamber, in his bed, unwilling to take a chance that I would fall asleep in mine, and he fail to wake me. But I was restless, and the book I brought failed to engage my attention. Seeing miniatures upon the chest beside his bed, I moved in closer to examine them. I recognised his father and mother from their portraits in the gallery, though they were both much younger in these images. There was another of Georgiana, painted when she was very young, but still resembling her enough that I was certain of her identity. I certainly never expected to see anything of interest when I opened the chest's top drawer; I was merely bored, curious, and idly wondering whether he perhaps kept a book in there more appealing than my own.

I saw a ring of keys, but I did not pay any real attention to them. For there in the drawer was my handkerchief, the one I had given him when he'd departed Rosings. I touched it gently; the lock of hair was still within its folds.

I had been so certain that it had been a foolish notion on my part; it touched me that he kept it still, and kept it here, near miniatures of his family. I knew he cared for and about me, but this gesture seemed like something...well, something a true lover might do. One who wanted more than just a convenient bride.

Of course, by the time he entered the room at last, I was the furthest thing from sleepy, my thoughts chaotic and even anxious. I wanted a chance for us, peace for us, even, perhaps, love between us. I wondered if de Bourgh's machinations would keep us from ever achieving it.

I waited to speak until he blew out the candles and climbed into the large bed. For a long while, we lay upon our separate sides, neither saying anything. I wanted him to take the lead, to reach for me, to turn to me, to *talk* to me—and began to feel, even, some annoyance when he made no effort to do so.

I reined in my impatience. As I considered his feelings, I realised it had only been several hours since his dead wife's lover—the man who had taken ruthless advantage of his young sister and who had ruined mine—taunted him with her disloyalty. His marriage to Anne de Bourgh had been unhappy; my suspicions of his essential aloneness had been validated beyond reason. What had he done, those many years, trapped in a hideously dishonourable wedlock, when his problems and difficulties seemed insurmountable? The thought of him lying here just like this, isolated and friend-less, pierced me.

I scooted over to his side of the bed, somewhat gratified when he immediately put his arm out to wrap around my shoulders, pulling me in close. He was still silent, so for a time, I simply listened to his heartbeat, wondering what he was thinking and how to encourage him to tell me.

And at last, he did. "I am certain you find me pathetic."

I propped myself up upon his chest, trying to see his eyes in the firelight. "Of all the many adjectives I could use to describe you, dear husband, 'pathetic' is the last one which comes to mind."

I could almost feel his rejection of my sentiments; if he found *himself* pathetic, nothing I could say would convince him otherwise. I had no experience with such enormous betrayal as this. All I knew to do was be here for him now, touching him, reminding him he was no longer alone. I dropped a kiss to his chest, and he sighed.

"There was some truth in her accusations," he said at last. "I never did love Anne. I almost believe that lack of feeling was what attracted her to me in the first place, beyond my family and fortune—my fundamental disinterest, when she was accustomed to conquering men so easily. I want you, of all people, to know that I did try, however. Before I knew it was hopeless, I did everything in my power to earn her respect and affection."

He spoke tonelessly, some of that remembered hopeless-ness filtering through his words. "When did you come to know it was doomed?" I asked softly.

He sighed, looking unutterably weary in the fire's dim glow. "It was doomed before the marriage was a day old, but I did not learn that until much later. I have never much enjoyed the Season, and once married, I managed to cut my time in London more each year, while she loved it and stayed for every invitation. I knew I was dull. I knew she loved the glittering excitement of the *ton*. I knew we had different ideas on almost every aspect of life. I did not realise we had different ideas on fidelity, however."

"She had other lovers, besides Wickham then?"

"Her first was at our wedding breakfast, or so she said. I remained oblivious for far too long. She managed, oddly enough, to be both discreet and debauched. Her other affairs, by and large, took place in town with men of stellar reputation who had nearly as much to lose as she did if they were caught. When she had the idea for that blasted cottage I stupidly thought..."

"Thorncroft?" I asked.

He glanced at me sharply, but did not ask how I knew of it. "Yes. I thought it a retreat for us. I thought she was trying, as I was. She knew it was what I believed, and encouraged me to believe it. But it was merely a new place for her trysts, though I did not understand it then. I...I was too proud to acknowledge what was happening—that our marriage was an utter and complete disaster, and that I was repulsed by my own wife in every possible sense. Ignoring her was my quiet revenge, for she loved drama and attention above all things."

"I am surprised you did not repudiate her."

"I considered it, many times. For pride's sake, I never did. The world would have blamed *me*. She was the charming one with a thousand friends, invited everywhere, with a gift for saying exactly the right thing at the right time. And then there were the rumours that I beat her."

"Wickham divulged that. She started those rumours."

"I was certain she had, which is ironic because...well, it does not matter. The truth was, she was adored by almost everyone—I could just hear the gossip. I would be thought the jealous gudgeon and cruel abandoner, while she would have dined out on the scandal for years as its innocent victim. To be quite honest, I did not wish to give her the victory. Of course, some of my reasoning had to do with my sister. Georgie adored her, and after all, I had brought myself to marry her in part for Georgie's sake."

I did not comment upon what seemed to me to be bizarre logic—to tie oneself to someone for life, solely so that one's nearly grown sister might be a greater social success? When said sister was an heiress of immense fortune? But his revelations were not finished.

"One summer, as the Bingleys visited, Anne took it into her head that Georgiana ought to marry Bingley. It was an idea I had cherished myself, in the past, and one which his sisters wholeheartedly promoted. However, I had never seen any sign that Georgie held an affection for him beyond a friendly acquaintance. I thought it unlikely to succeed."

"Obviously she proved you wrong."

"Yes. She was a genius at persuasion, and of course, my sister wanted to marry. She was very shy, and Anne very convincing. Soon Georgie was determined to marry him, and probably thought it all her own idea."

"I assume she had your approval for the match."

"Yes. I still thought Bingley would be a good husband to her. I was the only one on earth who could have talked her out of it, but I did not try. I allowed Anne to use her wiles and machinations to arrange it, because I thought I knew best."

I was amazed at the intensity of bitterness in his expression. "Perhaps, in this case, you did," I said.

He sighed, a hopeless sound. "Once Georgiana was safely wed to Bingley, Anne seduced him."

I reared up in shock. "What? No!"

"I met them returning from the direction of Thorncroft, Bingley looking as guilty as the devil and Anne grinning at me, as if she were a naughty child who had stolen a sweet. I simply knew. Beyond any doubt. And from that point, there was nothing left but hatred between us, and she had an unmatched weapon at her disposal—the threat to destroy my sister."

"Poor Georgiana," I whispered. "Does she know of it?"

"I certainly did not tell her, and I doubt Anne did either— it was such a fine means of restraining me. But of course, you can see she is not happy. Bingley regretted it, I think, immediately. But he tries to pretend, to me and to himself, that it never actually happened."

"You must despise him! Such betrayal!"

"No, not really. Anne was a very capable seductress. She had the intelligence to run an empire, and yet used it only for petty manipulations and sordidness. He is not a complex man; he was putty in her hands."

"You cannot hold him blameless?"

"Not precisely, no, and yet, I judge him faithful to Georgiana now. He was never profligate, and I believe he was completely unprepared for Anne's seduction. He is just so easily *led*. I have unwittingly encouraged his dependence upon others for too long, and practically handed Anne a subject vulnerable to her schemes."

"I think you are too kind," I said. "He is a man grown, and ought to be able to tell right from wrong by now."

He hesitated, and then rolled onto his side, rolling me off his chest so that he could see my eyes in the reflected firelight. "When we were all together at Netherfield... I observed Bingley's behaviour attentively, and I perceived his partiality for your sister went beyond what I had ever before witnessed in him. Your sister I also watched. Her look and manners were open and engaging, but, I believed, without any symptom of particular regard. I came to the conclusion that though she received his attentions with pleasure, she did not invite them by any participation of sentiment. I shared my conclusions with Bingley and, since he had already drawn too much attention to his preference for her, I encouraged him to leave immediately. Later, I knew that she was in London, and I hid the knowledge from him as I knew he was still partial to her. Had I encouraged him to be open and honest, or better still, stayed out of it entirely, he could have learnt whatever he needed to know." He brushed a stray lock out of my eyes. "I misjudged your sister. At the time, I thought her willing to accept any marriage encouraged by your mother, whether or not she held any feeling for him. I have known her many years now, through Tilney, and I consider him the most fortunate of men. I apologise to you, because I never can say it to her. She is all that is good. I ought never to have interfered so profoundly."

A flash of the decade-old anger sparked, but without fuel it quickly died. Had I not decided that Mr Tilney was the better match, even before knowing of Mr Bingley's perfidy?

Before I could speak, however, he continued. "I wish to know how grave an injustice I inflicted. *Was* her heart touched? Did I hurt her, as well as my friend, with my officious meddling?"

I opened my mouth to speak the truth, but it was a different truth than my twenty-year-old self could ever have uttered. "It was wrong of you to meddle, and it is unfortunate that Mr Bingley did not have the confidence to make his own decisions," I said. "But I can safely say that Jane loves Mr Tilney with a fervent affection that Mr Bingley never could have inspired. Please do not add this regret to any others you have, dearest."

174

He smoothed the furrow in my forehead with his thumb. "You are very good."

"I am very angry at Mr Bingley," I said. "You did tell him of my parents' death, and he could have intervened, had his attachment been a strong one. And if it is wrong to speak ill of the dead, brand me a sinner. Anne de Bourgh was despicable. I understand why she was drawn to Mr Wickham—they share a common depraved character."

"I learned, after my marriage, of their connexion. It is not a close one—their mothers are second cousins. But they were intimate friends. He stayed with Anne's family while he was attempting to force Georgiana's elopement. Mrs Younge, Georgiana's companion at the time, was another maternal cousin. The clues were there, had I investigated. Sadly, I did not look at anything beyond her parents and her fortune, both of which had the world's respect."

The bitterness was back in his speech, but I could not really blame him. "Do you believe she purposely pushed Bingley and Georgiana together as some sort of chess move, to further entrap you?"

I felt his shrug. "My pride has been the worst of my weaknesses. I expected a…a role of her, and she performed it. I do not believe she truly feared reprisal for many years, so confident was she in her performance, and then, later, of my willingness to protect the Darcy name at all costs. Georgiana's situation was an added safeguard. Her hatred of me knew no bounds."

"But *why?*"

He sighed. "At times, I tell myself Anne would have hated whomever she married. She sought to do whatever she wished, whenever she wished it, and could never submit to the authority of a husband. However, it seemed the less I attempted to influence her, the more outrageous and harmful her behaviour. It was as if she craved discipline yet despised it. She collected people, as though they were artwork or chess sets, and admired or promoted them...then purged them from her life when no longer useful to her. I finally came to the conclusion that, to her, other people were not truly...real. They did not exist the way you and I exist to each other; her centre of attention was always fixed upon herself."

"What of her mother, then? She must have loved her."

"Her mother was endlessly useful to her, so she was never likely to be rejected. What is more, Mrs de Bourgh yearned for Anne's approval, and knew all the best ways to earn it. I feared she would be distraught at her daughter's death. I feared she would try to–to harm herself. I could not have predicted today's actions, but I am unsurprised she did *something*."

I wondered whether he would believe me if I shared my conviction that the events of today only proved Mrs de Bourgh's utter commitment to *his* destruction. "I say she must still be moved to Ramsgate, as you informed her before she launched herself into the glass," I said. "This bizarre...er, accident, is proof that her health is adversely affected by living at Pemberley, the site of her daughter's death."

It was his turn to present a furrowed brow. "I shudder to think of her next actions," was his reply.

I said nothing of my fears of her deeper plotting. He was accustomed to thinking of Mrs de Bourgh as a harmless appendage to her daughter—since that had been her role most all the years he had known her. He might think her noisy, and he already thought her maddened. However, I would not hesitate to remind him of what she had already done. "She brought George Wickham into this house and abandoned me alone with him."

His jaw tensed. "How could I have underestimated her

instability? The moment I arrived, Mrs Reynolds informed me of Wickham's presence at Pemberley. She said that Mrs de Bourgh told *her* only moments before, and with seemingly great apprehension."

"She saw you arrive, no doubt. Which means *she* could just have easily sent a maid in, except that she knew he was there to threaten me. She *knew* I thought it was one of the neighbours calling. She *knew* I was horrified to see him instead. She *smiled* at my distress." I would not yield on this point. If he were going to allow her to remain here, he must at least admit my right to feel troubled by it.

But he was swift to agree. "No, no, I did not mean to suggest that she could live with us any longer. As soon as she is healed enough to travel, she must leave," he said firmly. "I was only wondering *why* she revealed his presence to Reynolds, rather than allowing Wickham to proceed unhindered. Mrs Reynolds told me this afternoon that others have witnessed her speaking to you disrespectfully, treating you ill. I would have confronted and removed her sooner had I known, my darling. I am so sorry."

"My guess is that she hoped Wickham would act in a compromising manner, with or without my permission." Something eased within me at this evidence that he would take my distress seriously, that he would even take responsibility for something he could not have known. "I did not want to tell you how bad things were. I did not want to begin our marriage with contention. Mrs de Bourgh *is* grieving, and to eject her from Pemberley over a few mild confrontations would have made me—and you with me—appear cruel to the neighbourhood."

He shrugged. "I have lived for years attempting to appear the ideal, and I have given it up. The list of names whose opinions truly matter is very short, and yours is at the top of it." He touched my cheek, tenderly stroking. "Promise you will tell me if *anyone* abuses or insults you. It is not to be borne. All the footmen have been given instructions to eject Wickham from the premises on sight. Richard and I hired more men today, to keep watch. I do not want him stealing onto the grounds again."

I only nodded. I thought of asking him, then, how Anne had died, or even his reasons for going to London. I believed he would answer me truthfully. But the fact was, she had abused *him* throughout their married life. While I had determined he was incapable of murder, I had also discovered that I *might* be. And most of all, I no longer felt like discussing her, or any other conflict, especially within the bed we shared together.

"Do you know what I wish?" I asked him.

He appeared slightly wary in the firelight. "What do you wish? If it is within my power, I will see it done."

"It is very much in your power," I replied. "I wish you to kiss me now, and hold me, and make this day...go away."

Something in his expression changed, his intensity sharpening, his weariness fleeing. "I can do that," he said, and it sounded like a promise.

A frisson of answering excitement shivered through me. Our earlier encounter was a flaring conflagration. This was a slow, simmering burn that heated as it built, a spark he nourished and nurtured until it kindled into a blaze.

And, as promised, the trials of the day were consumed by its flame.

CHAPTER SIXTEEN

In the morning, I learned that Mrs de Bourgh now suffered from a terrible fever as a result of her injuries. I told Clara the details of what occurred in the gold parlour, deciding that, in this case, countering the potential of false gossip with the truth was a better plan than maintaining strict discretion. And then I sought out Mrs Reynolds privately.

"What have you heard about what happened yesterday?" I asked directly. "You need not varnish the truth. It is best we know exactly how bad the gossip."

If she was surprised by my question, she did not show it. "Most of it is nonsense," she said. "As if you would be taken in by the likes of Mr Wickham, in your own home. The old master cared for him, 'tis true, but he has turned out very wild. And the idea of Mr Darcy losing his temper, even touching the old lady in anger! Balderdash!"

"You are sensible, of course," I replied, seeing that I had correctly interpreted the reception of yesterday's events. "Mrs de Bourgh has allowed grief to consume her mind."

"A terrible truth," she nodded. "Of course, everyone knows Mr Wickham is not welcome here. Mr Darcy made it very clear after his treatment of poor Sally—a housemaid, you understand—that he was not to return." She furrowed her brows. "It was one of the few times the master and mistress openly disagreed. Mrs Darcy did not believe Wickham had done, er, what he was accused of, but of course, he was her cousin. We none of us like to believe the worst about our relations. Still, Sally told me and she was no liar, and I told the master, and he stood for her. Had Wickham run out of Hopewell, he did, or at least away from the few who still received him. Helped Sally resettle elsewhere, as well. Gave her a new start."

To my relief, it was evident that Mrs Reynolds would never believe anything Wickham said, and I blessed poor Sally for naming her despoiler. If the village was of a like mind, his assertion of 'numerous friends' and threats of ominously influencing public opinion were empty ones. "Mr Wickham claimed that the first Mrs Darcy hinted to others that she was mistreated by Mr Darcy, and that is why talk of his culpability in her death will not fade. I hope you will do your part to dispel any such malicious gossip. Mr Darcy is the very best of men, as I am sure you would agree."

"I certainly never heard the mistress speak of Mr Darcy with anything except respect." She hesitated. "Perhaps they had their troubles. Many marriages do. You may believe that I will not tolerate any scandalmongers in this house."

"Thank you, Mrs Reynolds. And, perhaps grief has disordered Mr Wickham's mind as well, that he would say such things. Mrs de Bourgh threw herself against the windows right before our eyes. There was not a thing either of us could have done to stop her, we were so shocked. Mr Darcy and I believe that living here, where she and her daughter were so happy together, is increasing her grief rather than diminishing it. We hope a drastic change of scenery will help her recover more completely. Mr Darcy will remove her to her old home in Ramsgate as soon as she is well enough to travel."

I did not mistake the look of relief upon the housekeeper's face. "Very good ma'am," she said.

"Feel free to repeat this information to the household, in order to quell speculation. I was alarmed by Nancy's fear of Mr Darcy yesterday, and remain appalled by the treatment I received by certain tradesmen in Hopewell. It is all ridiculous. I have known Mr Darcy for many years. My sister is married to the vicar who holds the living at Matlock Court; my husband is well respected by all, from the Earl of Matlock and his countess to the lowliest servant. The very idea of fearing him is preposterous."

It was, perhaps, a bit of hyperbole; Jane had never mentioned Mr Darcy at Matlock Court. I had, personally, spoken to the earl perhaps four times in my life, and I believe our conversations had more to do with the weather than his relations. But one could assume.

"Of course, Mrs Darcy. Pemberley is loyal to Mr Darcy, and always will be. I have spoken to young Nancy. It will not happen again."

"I do not wish her to be disciplined. I only say this because I cannot abide the idea of anyone here living in fear," I said, nodding. "There is no reason for it."

After leaving the housekeeper, I took my letter case to the green parlour; it was another of my favourite rooms, for it looked out onto Pemberley Woods. It took me some time to compose myself enough to begin writing. I wondered whether I ought to offer to bring Mary to Pemberley—an unappealing thought—and what Kitty, never an admirer of

Mr Darcy, would have to say about my marriage to him. Most of all, I wondered why Mr Darcy sought me out at Rosings after all these years, how he could possibly have remembered me, despite his claim of a long-ago attraction. Had it to do with his rescue of Lydia? It seemed more likely. Since he took responsibility for Wickham's seduction and *her* subsequent difficulties, he might also assume obligation for other consequences of it, such as my parents' deaths, perhaps even my lack of marriage prospects, though sacrificing himself on that altar was quite a stretch. He had indicated that if I was at all the same person he had known eight years previous, he was determined to propose marriage. But what had he really known of me then? That he liked my hair?

I had not even *liked* him in those days; I had thought him arrogant and unkind. I had believed every disparaging word Lieutenant Wickham uttered. Later, when Wickham's many unpaid debts to my neighbours became well known, I entertained doubts that the story of his lost inheritance was truthful. And then, when the true extent of Wickham's depravity was revealed, I even hoped the unlikely story *was* true, and that someone—even the callous and arrogant Mr Darcy—had gotten the better of the cur.

But mostly, I had forgotten him. It seemed wrong, somehow, now that I loved him so.

February 1, 1820
My dearest Jane,

I hope this letter finds you in the best of health, and that you are devoting several hours each day to rest and ease. But I know you will not, and I shall be required to write to Mr

Tilney to ensure you are taking good care. I received your letter requesting reassurances that all is well at Pemberley. If I have failed to convey this in previous letters, please understand from this one: I am happy, very happy, to be married to Mr Darcy. I know we did not like him, so very long ago. We were young, and we did not realise his character was of the finest. He has shared some private reminiscences that explain why his temper was not perfectly calm during the months he was in Meryton— but truly, I misjudged him.

I have realised that you must have encountered him over the years at Matlock, though you have never mentioned it— perhaps not wishing to recall to my mind any past unpleasantness. My husband is never comfortable with people who are less known to him, but I hope you have seen his essential good nature, regardless. I feel confident that you, with your kind heart, have long ago forgiven him for any misunderstandings.

And now I must share something that, however difficult the memories, is sure to reveal to you his goodness. Prepare yourself for something very wonderful: our sister Lydia lives! Yes, it is true. You know, of course, that we were sadly deceived in the character of Lieutenant Wickham. It seems that Mr Darcy has had dealings with that scoundrel going back many years. (You are not to believe the stories W. shared with us regarding him and his inheritance, which are all lies—if you ever did believe them. As I recall, you were the only one who gave leave to doubt from the beginning.) Mr Darcy discovered what had happened to poor Lydia through his aunt's connexion to Mr Collins. Oh, Jane, he sought her out! I quail to think of the indignities he must have borne in order to discover her. She was in the most vile and desperate of situations, but he arranged her passage to America, where she very much desired to go. He did not admit this, but I believe he must have given her something to live upon once she arrived, because she seems to have prospered most ideally. She is married to a successful man named Brackett and they have two children. We may write to her through a business associate of Mr Darcy's, although she may not acknowledge us, considering Mr Collins's edicts and the deleterious effect they had upon her. Nevertheless, if you wish to enclose a letter to her in your next missive to me, Mr Darcy has promised to ensure she will, eventually, receive our correspondence.

I finished with assurances of our coming visit in the summer, and said nothing of Bingley, of course. She must already know—must have discovered through her connexions to the earl—of his marriage to Georgiana. How very like Jane, that she had never mentioned a word of it to me. Had I heard of it in 1817, in my ignorance, I might have been bitter indeed. No, she had kept it all to herself. How astonished she must have been when she received word of my hasty engagement to Mr Darcy, with what she knew of my long ago and too-oft expressed opinions of him! No wonder she had required Mr Tilney to do his best to delay our wedding!

I wrote a similar letter explaining Lydia's circumstances to my aunt, which I knew would be most heartening to her. To Kitty, I wrote a rather longer missive, announcing my marriage to Mr Darcy and giving the details of Lydia's life. Kitty had suffered Lydia's loss most deeply, and, I think, felt somewhat responsible. Although she had not known the extent of Lydia's plans, I knew she felt a good deal of guilt and sorrow over the affair. She had married the first young man to ask her, a nephew of my Uncle Philips acting as his clerk, and while it was not an auspicious connexion—my father would never have approved it—I believed she was happy. As the Philipses had never had any progeny, and as my Uncle Philips is prosperous enough, and intends to provide for his clerk and eventually turn over his practise to him, her prospects are good. Her guilt, I felt, had kept us from having a closer connexion. She has something of my father's intelligence, and a surprisingly sly wit—my Aunt Philips often bearing the brunt of it, all unknowing. Still, in the last few years, her letters had been...softer, full of news of her son and the daily doings of Meryton, which I had found comforting. I believed this letter would bring her a good deal of comfort in return, as well as astonishment.

I struggled with what to say to Mary—and hence, to Charlotte. In the end, I simply announced my marriage and my new direction, with no explanations whatsoever. If Kitty wished to reveal Lydia's fate, she was free to do so; I, however, would not invite any of her opinions, conjecture, or judgments—or, worse still, Mr Collins's, expressed through her letters. Mary would always be...Mary. She would likely be happiest living out her days at Longbourn, which she loves.

Mrs de Bourgh's fever continued to rage. I would never be the sort of person who would hope for another's death, but I did not precisely miss her and her criticism and hatefulness. I still longed for the day when she was healed and on her way to Ramsgate.

I went into the village again and again; my husband insisted upon accompanying me. I was not sure his attendance did any good, for he mostly glowered like a very large, grouchy bear, ready to growl at anyone who might dare disrespect me. No one did, of course, while in his presence. I did my best to demonstrate such warmth and affection as I felt appropriate in public, counting it a victory when I managed to get a smile from him.

Georgiana and her husband arrived for another visit. I

was very glad to see her, for Mr Darcy was preoccupied with a great deal of estate business and I was hardly overwhelmed by visitors or invitations. At least Miss Bickford had now managed the awful drive up and down the mountain three different times, and my wardrobe was nearly sufficient for Mrs Darcy.

"I am so glad you are here," I greeted Georgiana with real pleasure.

"Oh, I had to come as soon as I received your letter," she replied. Within a few moments, as we were walking alone together, she asked, "How is Mrs de Bourgh?"

"Not yet recovered," I replied. "She lost the sight in one eye and is in a great deal of pain. The fevers come and go. The doctor says she must not yet travel."

Georgiana nodded soberly. "How horrible a thing to witness! I cannot imagine her behaving in such a manner. She has always been so dignified."

We had been walking towards my favourite parlour, but on impulse I said, "Oh, come with me." She followed me, incurious but willing, as we went to my sitting room—but we did not stop there. I went directly through my rooms and into my husband's bedchamber.

"I saw keys here once," I explained as I opened the drawer of the bed-chest, "and I wonder whether any of them fit the doors leading into the upper floor of the cliffside wing."

I looked at her as I said this to see her reaction. Her eyes widened. "Oh, dear…Fitzwilliam would not like that. He wants no one up there."

"I know. But I wish to show you something."

She said nothing further, and I grabbed the ring of keys. I wondered whether she would even follow me, but she did, keeping up as I strode purposefully to the nearest stair, our half-boots echoing loudly upon the steps leading upwards.

The door, as expected, was locked. The second key I tried, however, opened it, and we quickly found ourselves in the corridor nearest the mistress's chambers.

"It feels strange to be in here again," Georgiana said, almost whispering. "It all seems so...lifeless now."

She was correct. While it did not smell especially musty, one could tell that this floor no longer gleamed with precision spotlessness. The niches no longer contained empty vases and dust had collected in some of them; the rugs had vanished and the floors no longer shone.

"The last time I was here, it was pristine," I replied. "But Mrs Reynolds has since made it clear that none of the servants will be directed up here by other than herself or me. Let us see whether there are any other changes."

"You were up here before?"

"Oh, yes. It was...disturbing. I am almost happy to see it growing dusty with disuse," I said absently, counting doors. I did not enter my husband's former rooms, instead going directly to Anne's bedchamber.

This time when I entered, I was more prepared for the sight, but the changes were eerie ones.

"Oh my," Georgiana said.

Vases of flowers were still in place, but they were all dead and drooping. The rose petals scattered over the bed were blackened. A négligée was still draped across the foot of the bed, a different one this time, black, instead of pink, and matching the dead flowers. A silver brush set lay on the dressing table, as before, but the various cosmetics had all been tidied, their lids closed. The brush contained several golden hairs, as if its owner had just laid it down. I shuddered. I was certain that brush had been clean the last time I'd seen it.

"I wanted to show you this," I said soberly. "Mrs de Bourgh kept it all as it was when Anne was alive. She replaced the flowers daily, but of course, she has been ill so they have since died. I know Mr Darcy took her key from her, but plainly she had another. She is unhealthily obsessed." I gestured to the dressing table, telling Georgiana how it had appeared the last time I was here with its open cosmetic pots. I told her about breaking the figurine, and how Mrs de Bourgh had tried to embarrass me with its absence. And lastly, I told her about the unhappy surprise of George Wickham's appearance in the parlour to taunt me, though mentioning nothing of his affair with her brother's wife.

She turned white, and I thought she might swoon.

I shepherded her out of doors onto the terrace. Once again, the view struck me, and with it came the feeling, almost, of flying into the vast sky. There was no furniture out here, but I wished there had been a bench to sit upon and absorb the sight. On the other hand, it was chilly, and my companion looked quite pale.

"I am sorry to have mentioned him," I continued. "Your brother told me how he took advantage of you."

She appeared shocked, and then hurt at this betrayal of her secret. I placed my hand upon her shoulder. "I only wanted you to know that I understand, and why he shared with me your distressing experience." Then I told her of Lydia, and what her association with Wickham, ultimately, had cost her. And me.

"I am so very sorry, my sister," she said, immediately casting aside her own embarrassment. "Do you believe Mrs de Bourgh knows everything? But of course, she must, or else she would not have known to bring you to him. I wonder how she knows him?"

I admit to having been surprised by this question, although I should not have been. Possibly because of the way Wickham had spoken so boldly of his affair with Anne, and how plainly my husband had admitted their longstanding history, I had somewhat blithely assumed that Georgiana had at least suspected Wickham's involvement.

"They are distant cousins," I explained. "Wickham stayed with them in Ramsgate when he was, er, courting you. Mrs Younge is another cousin, and they set her up to deceive you and Mr Darcy."

Georgiana shivered, and I did not think it was entirely due to the cold. "But he had rooms in Ramsgate," she said in weak protest. "My brother wrote to him there."

"As I understand it, they disguised the connexion until much later. Your brother did not know until after the wedding."

Georgiana stepped slightly closer to the low wall, looking out over the valley floor, and I moved beside her. "All that time. This explains many things," she murmured. She glanced over at me, then back out at the peaks. There followed a long silence, broken only by a hawk's echoing cry.

When she spoke again, there was a definite bitterness to her tone. "Did Fitzwilliam also tell you that my husband is —was—in love with his wife?"

CHAPTER SEVENTEEN

In love? Mr Bingley, with Anne de Bourgh? I looked at Georgiana sharply. "No," I said. "That is not at all what he told me."

She resumed staring out over the wild scenery. Her voice, when it resumed, was as hard and dry as Mr Darcy's had once been. "We had only been married six months when I discovered it. I was very happy at first, and imagined myself in love. And then, during our Christmas visit of 1817, Mr Bingley began acting strangely. I was upset, and unsure what to do. I went to Anne for advice, and she-she told me…"

My heart froze in my chest at the thought of what she might have said.

"She told me that my brother hated her and she did not understand why but that she loved him desperately and would do anything to make amends. That she had been so despairing and ready to-to harm herself, and Mr Bingley had come upon her, had comforted her, and it had gone too far. That he had always been in love with her, and that she had arranged for his marriage to me because she wanted him to be happy, to forget about her. That in her moment of desperation and weakness, she allowed him to l-love her as he had always wanted, but never been permitted. That afterwards she had felt so guilty and broke it off, swearing to me that she would never consent to it again, on her life. I held her as she sobbed in my arms, begging that if only I would say nothing, if I would forgive her, we could pretend it never happened, that all could be put right."

"What utter balderdash," I said, borrowing one of Mrs Reynolds's favourite phrases.

"Yes," she agreed. "It could never be put right. I tried pretending, for a long while. But every time we–we were together, I could not...I could only imagine that he...that Mr Bingley pretended also. That he pretended I am her. Eventually, I could not bear it. I have not allowed him in my bed for over a year."

"Oh, Georgiana," I said, feeling an overwhelming rage towards Anne de Bourgh. She had played this poor girl like a fiddle, and she—and Mr Bingley too, as likely as not—had been dancing to her tune for years.

"I never told Fitzwilliam. Even though I could not feel towards Anne as I once did, I could not wish her ill, and I hoped my brother would be able to restore his marriage. He has always been a fair man, but I knew if he discovered what Bingley had done, it would be impossible to recover it. Although I do not think he has been happy, not for a long while."

I could only shake my head in dismay. "My dear sister, of course he has not been happy. But if you believe that Mr Bingley was Anne Darcy's only affair, you have been naïve. Furthermore, I would lay money that *she* seduced *him*, and just so that she could ruin your marriage and hurt your brother with it. He has known of Mr Bingley's perfidy since it happened. Anne made *certain* he knew."

Georgiana stared at me in open-mouthed shock. "N-no," she stuttered. "It cannot be."

"She carried on an affair with Mr Wickham for their entire marriage," I continued ruthlessly. "I do not condone Mr Bingley's actions, but I am certain he regrets them, and that *love* is the last thing he feels or ever felt for that dreadful woman. She was a monster. You must *talk* to your husband. You have been ill used, but you must not continue to be her victim. Her vicious games must die with her."

I decided that I had said enough, and sat down on the low wall to give her time to absorb my words. I was beginning to grow truly chilled before she spoke again.

"Anne used to sit on this wall," she said quietly. "But she sat with her feet dangling over the edge. I always hated when she would do it. I had told her long ago, you see, of a time when my brother was a very young man, perhaps sixteen years. He played a trick upon me, a horrible trick. He pretended to drop off this terrace to his death. I was terrified, frantic. But he had found a ledge beneath one section where the drop was only eight feet or so, and he had strung a rope ladder so he could climb back up—assuming he did not break his neck in the process. Papa was so very angry with him! Of course he apologised, most profusely, and never did anything like it again. And now I think...I wonder if she sat balanced on this precipice to taunt me, to remind me of the horror of that long ago, stupid, childish, prank."

"I certainly would not put it past her," I said.

"Oh, my poor brother," she murmured.

How soft her heart! She had been subjected to that woman's evil for years, and she only thought of him. He had suffered more often, perhaps, but she had not suffered less.

"Your brother's happiness can be restored," I said. "Once he knows you are happier, he will be so much improved. Perhaps your marriage cannot be revived, and trust is not easily earned. But perhaps you and your husband could work at...a friendship. Or would that be too impossible? I know I would have difficulty forgiving such a betrayal."

"I am not sure," she said. "Nothing is as I thought. It does seem to me that, now I consider it, he has tried more diligently of late to earn my notice. Since Anne died, I suppose. Perhaps she did hold it over him, in whatever ways she could. And of course, it is certain that what I *have* been doing has not brought me anything but grief. I have been so lonely."

I stood and reached to press her hand. "You have a different sister now. I promise you my friendship, whether or not you reconcile with Mr Bingley. Let us remove ourselves from these disturbing rooms and your unhappy memories, and ask Mrs Reynolds to bring us tea in the library. It is my favourite room in the house, to be sure."

"Fitzwilliam loves it too. Oh, I am so happy he married you, dear sister! I did not know...I never realised how he has—"

"He did not want you to know," I said softly. "He has a habit of deciding in favour of the happiness of others at all costs to himself." I remembered what he had said of Bingley's lack of confidence in himself, and taking her arm, led her back towards the stairs. "Just a thought, however—I believe your husband looks to *you* for guidance about how it shall be between you. Never wait for him to do or say or remember what you like—*tell* him. Men, I have learned, are seldom very good at guessing a woman's true feelings. Be bold."

I opened the door to the servants' stairs and locked it from the other side.

"Is that what you do?" she asked. "Are you…bold?"

"Only when it matters to me," I replied. "Which is, possibly, rather more often than your brother would wish." But I laughed, and, after a moment, she joined in.

At dinner that evening, I was pleased to notice a difference between Mr and Mrs Bingley. For one thing, he was much more attentive to her—and she, in turn, tried harder to be a part of the conversation. Of course, I saw that Mr Darcy observed them both carefully.

I suggested to Georgiana that we retire to the music room after the meal, as her brother claimed her most expert at the pianoforte—although in their previous visit, she had not touched it once. After only a slight hesitation, she agreed, and I asked for the tea tray to be brought there.

"I once loved to play," she murmured, after we had departed the gentlemen, "but I have not in ever so long. Years, I think."

"Why not?" I asked.

"I am not really sure," she replied, as we entered the music room. "Following…my um, experience with Wickham, I lost interest. Brother purchased this instrument for me soon afterwards, hoping to encourage me. I took it up again after my marriage but…"

It was a magnificent pianoforte, truly the loveliest I had ever seen. I imagined him having it made, giving his attention to the details of woodwork and ivory, longing for his young sister's spirits to heal, with no real way to make that happen. How hopeless he must have felt! No wonder he had not wished to dance and mingle with strangers in Meryton! Yet he had asked *me* to dance at Mr Bingley's ball. It seemed more meaningful now; he had not danced with anyone else beyond his own party. And what had I done? Taunted him with his supposed injuries to Wickham! He had hinted, of course, that I did not understand the whole situation, but I had not listened, believing my evening spoilt by Wickham's absence. Blaming *him* for it. How was it, I wondered, that he had remembered me with any fondness at all?

I was startled out of my reverie by Georgiana's playing. She had begun with the sheet music that was on the instrument, something that I—an indifferent musician—had been stumbling around in my usual lackadaisical fashion. She began slowly at first, and then with more confidence, until she was playing the difficult piece with beauty and power. The gentlemen re-joined us with gratifying speed, and Mr Bingley immediately went to his wife to turn her pages. Her music was joy, delight; happiness given substance. No wonder she could not play when she was miserable.

Mr Darcy seated himself beside me and took my hand in his strong, warm one. He appeared completely enraptured with his sister's playing but his thumb rubbed softly against the back of my hand, capturing almost as much of my attention as the lovely music.

When she finished the piece, Mr Bingley bent his head to murmur something in her ear. Georgiana blushed. Within the hour, the Bingleys had retired to their rooms, while Mr Darcy followed them with his eyes, a look of wonderment upon his face.

When they were gone and the servants dismissed, he turned to me. "Do you know what has changed between them?"

I hesitated, but only briefly; there had been far too many

secrets at Pemberley. I wished the truth would not hurt Mr Darcy so deeply, however. As surely it must.

I told him what lies Anne had administered to Georgiana, as well as what truths I had revealed to her. I knew he would not like her knowing he had been cuckolded, and I was prepared to defend my decision.

But he did not argue it, though he dropped my hand to run his through his hair, his own gesture of frustration. "I ought to have spoken to her long ago. I have only increased her suffering by hiding the truth. When will I learn that I know nothing?" Leaning forward, he buried his face within his hands.

I moved closer to him, rubbing his broad back with soothing strokes. "If it helps at all, I do not believe the truth would have done much good at the time. She was so terribly hurt, and it is likely..." I trailed off.

"Say what you think," he demanded. "You believe Anne would have twisted it into something still worse, even."

"She certainly was a master manipulator," I agreed. "It would have taken a concerted effort to break free of her machinations and likely she would have found many to believe her version of events if you had repudiated her, as you feared. Perhaps she would even have found a way to ruin Georgiana utterly."

"And perhaps I was a coward, and only feared she would," he said bitterly. "Why not confess to you the worst of it? Except for my sister, for whom my feelings were impossible to hide, I withdrew from every member of my family. I only saw my cousin, Matlock, on the most infrequent occasions, and then kept the knowledge from her. She demanded I accept the earl's invitations, but I always made my excuses, telling her I did not like any of them and could not be bothered. If I wrote to them, I wrote privately, and asked for any return letters to be sent in care of my man of business. I separated from all my friends, except for Bingley—and of course, there was already a rift between us."

"Cowardice? Is that what you call it when you strive to protect those whom you cherish most?"

"Do not forget—I protected myself, and my reputation, most of all," he retorted. "I have never been an amiable man. It was not too difficult to remove myself from amusements, clubs, and the people who frequent both."

I looked at him almost helplessly, certain that this disavowal of his family and friends had come about gradually. It was simply that he could see it all now, how she had increasingly isolated him from his peers and relations by playing upon his fears for himself and others. Until he was alone—utterly, mercilessly alone.

Again, I could have asked him then how she died, but in that moment, I did not care. I was, simply, glad she was gone.

I moved closer to him, placing my hand upon his cheek. "You must adopt my attitude—remember the past only as it gives you pleasure, and greater perception for the future. As you do, you will remember that you *did* protect them. You *were* successful. She was never able to make victims of other members of your family, correct?"

He nodded curtly.

"And even though you could not protect Georgiana to the extent you wished, neither do I believe the damage permanent. To at least some extent, Anne *was* held in check. She chose to preserve what hold she had, rather than causing more destruction."

He looked at me for a long moment. "Will you wait here for a few moments, my dear? I shall not be long."

I thought perhaps he was going to ask for the tea to be

freshened, since none of us had touched any of it, but instead of ringing for a servant, he left the room entirely. He was gone perhaps ten minutes, and when he returned, he again seated himself beside me. "I would like you to have this," he said, withdrawing a small velvet box.

Inside was a beautiful gold ring featuring a large rose-cut diamond surrounded by two rows of smaller diamonds with more on either side of the shank. I was so surprised, for a moment I could only stare. He misinterpreted my silence.

"This was my mother's betrothal ring. You need not wonder if Anne wore it first. She never even knew of its existence."

"It is beyond lovely," I breathed, slipping it onto my finger. It fit perfectly.

He took my hand and kissed it. "I hoped to give this to you on the perfect occasion, on a perfect day of nothing but perfect memory, but I find I cannot wait another moment to see my ring on your finger. I could not obtain it before the wedding as I wished, so I had my man of business retrieve it. I traced a ring of yours on paper so he could have it sized. When lately in London, I reclaimed it, and also brought back pieces for Georgiana. I dared not give them to her before—I figured Anne would, somehow, manage to manoeuvre them into her own possession."

I watched the reflected brilliance of the ring, admiring its sparkle upon my finger. "When Mrs de Bourgh leaves, I am going to have her daughter's things packed and removed to her Ramsgate property with her," I said at last. "In the normal course of events, I would suggest they be distributed to those who could use them, but her mother is obsessively attached to it all. Despite your demand that she stop—and until her recent, er, malady—Mrs de Bourgh continued to refresh the flowers in Anne's rooms daily and lay out a new négligée each evening. I went upstairs again, to see if it was so," I continued, hearing his sharp exhale, and shook my head in remembered disbelief. "She is taking hair from Anne's hairpieces to place in her brushes. I would not mind it, truly, if rearranging Anne's belongings brought her any peace. Plainly, it does not. If she is insane, it is the sort of madness that is most dangerous—an infatuation with her own hatred and grief. She is like a wilful child whose favourite toy has been taken away. I fear her tantrums might eventually be dangerous to someone other than herself."

"How did you enter?" he asked. "How did she?"

"I simply took the keys from the drawer beside your bed," I said, "and tried each one until I found one that fit. I expect Mrs de Bourgh has other copies. I wished to show Georgiana how cracked she is, and so I took her there this morning. She will tell Bingley. The servants already know it. Word will spread eventually, so that no one will believe a word she says in the future, at least hereabouts. In this instance, she over-played her hand."

He only shook his head at me, equal parts resignation and indulgence. "You are mistress here. Do what you like with Anne's things. I do not care. The worst moments of my life were spent in those rooms, and redecorating cannot fix all that I hate. Someday, you and I will decide together what is to be done with them. For now, I ask you to keep them locked, and to stay away from them. The servants may go in and clear them, and then stay out except for a monthly clean-ing. Am I unreasonable? Will that be acceptable, Mrs Darcy?"

"Of course. I trust Mrs Reynolds to supervise the clearing. However, I shall probably wish to review any jewellery with you. I imagine most would be locked away elsewhere, but I would not want to send off any Darcy heirlooms to Ramsgate."

"Most of the baubles up there are gifts from her lovers or things she bought for herself. Of heirlooms, she possesses none."

"Not the gold and diamond ring to match her costume at the last ball?"

He rolled his eyes. "Hardly."

"Truly? Not even from the early years?"

"I bought her a betrothal set, which was buried with her. I purchased her some jewellery in the beginning. It can all go. I…I could never bear to give her anything of my mother's. At first, I supposed parting with it was difficult due to excessive sentiment. But later, when I realised her character, I had to admit to myself it was exactly the opposite. A part of me had *always* rejected Anne's right to be Mrs Darcy, but since that part was a heart to which I coldly refused to listen, I deserved all consequences of the neglect."

"That seems excessively harsh. You could not have imagined how dreadful she would be. I cannot believe she failed to ask for the family jewels outright. It seems like something she would do."

He appeared a little embarrassed. "Oh, of course she did, eventually. I have always thought myself an honest man and yet I went to a great deal of trouble to conceal such valuables from her. She pressed me for them, and first I hesitated and then I resorted to deceit. I told her my father had sold all of it during a brief period of financial distress, except for a few pieces that were designed for Georgiana and of lesser value. Thus, their concealment far from Pemberley and London."

I was excessively weary of discussion of his first wife, but it was a poison he needed to exorcise. I judged that enough of it had been released for one evening, however.

"I believe that your sister will be thrilled to have the

pieces," I said. "And I would not be surprised if Mr Bingley does not add a diamond or two to the collection very soon."

He took my hand again in his, playing with the ring on my finger, and he spoke again almost absently. "When I asked you to marry me, I was fairly certain you would refuse. You looked so surprised, so alarmed even. There are more jewels for you," he added. "I would not like you to wear a style you do not care for. You may have any of it reset, if you wish. I-I know my mother would be happy for you to do with it as you will."

If I had not been fairly certain that I had his entire attention, however little he showed it, I might have believed him nonchalant. But I knew, somehow, he cared very much about my response.

"You may show me anything you wish, and I can safely promise to love it, if this ring is any indication." I kissed his cheek. "Tomorrow. Tomorrow, I shall love it all. Tonight, I wish to show you exactly how grateful I am for what I have already received. Shall we retire now?"

He stood so quickly I was almost startled. He held out his hand to help me up; I took it, and together we slowly walked up the stairs in silent anticipation.

Anne was, after all, a stupid woman. When she could have had *him* in her bed, *and* his love, *and* his jewels, I could not fathom why she had so deliberately ruined it. But then, she would always be a foreign creature to me, like some rare specimen at the London Zoo. So completely different from myself, a dull little country girl with a mostly undistinguished lineage.

My ring caught the light just then, with a blinding flash. And I smiled.

CHAPTER EIGHTEEN

The discovery of the dead body was really the fault of the fire, but I will admit to a share of the blame. A storm had blown in from the south, bringing no rain but dreadful winds and lightning. I was tempted to watch it rage over the peaks from the upper floor of the cliffside wing, but I knew my husband would not find that as entertaining as I.

Instead, we were enjoying our after-dinner tea with the Bingleys in the library. We had eaten early, as had become our habit; all of us, it seemed now, preferred to retire while the night was still young. Mr Bingley was the restless one that evening, staring out the window even though darkness had just fallen. In spite of Pemberley's thick-walled embrace, the wind made its presence known inside, shrieking down the chimney. Suddenly he cried out, "I say, the woods are ablaze!"

We all dashed to the window where he stood and sure enough, what appeared to be flames rose in the distance. Mr Darcy cursed.

Georgiana and I were left behind while our husbands tore

from the house, and though we watched diligently—even trying other windows for better views—we could not see much of anything. I worried for the trees—how it would hurt my heart if the woods were destroyed! But we saw no sign of the fire worsening or growing larger, and finally the flames disappeared completely. It was hours before they returned, wet, filthy, soot-streaked, and Mr Darcy looking grave.

"It was Thorncroft!" Mr Bingley announced excitedly, evidently energised by the whole experience. "We stopped the forest from catching, though. Would have been a wicked loss of timber, eh?"

"Lightning strike?" I asked.

"So it appears," Mr Darcy answered.

"Williams had fifty men there, but quick. Darcy had me ditch digging! I will have blisters tomorrow! Thorncroft was lost entirely, it was immediately apparent, but that wicked wind! It was a constant battle against sparks and cinders, but the forest is saved."

We all retired shortly thereafter. I gave my husband plenty of time to bathe and join me, as he always did. However, it finally became apparent that this evening would be an exception. I thought about leaving him to his brooding, but concluded that he could brood just as well with me as without me, and entered his chambers.

He was not there. I was puzzled for only a moment—and then, somehow, I knew.

I returned to my room for a shawl and candle. Then I made my way through darkened corridors to the nearest stair leading to the cliffside wing. As I suspected, the door to the upper landing was unlocked; a draughty blast of chilled air met me as I entered, nearly extinguishing my candle, the cold pinching at me.

His rooms were empty, but I walked directly through

them; I had not truly expected to find him within. The ghosts that haunted him were never to be found in his own spaces. Unsurprisingly, he stood staring out into the blackness from the huge, dramatic windows of the mistress's chamber. Jagged lightning streaks periodically punctured the night sky, putting on a show through the distorted glass panes, or so it seemed to me. Placing my candlestick on a nearby table, I moved beside him. He did not acknowledge me, which was unusual for him, in private at least. But I was cold, as, I suspected, was he, and stepped in front of him, wrapping my arms around him. After a moment, he returned the embrace, but a vital part of him remained far from me, lost again somewhere in the past.

The only sounds were the muffled shrieks of wind beyond the windows and the chandelier's prisms tinkling softly within. Patience, I must admit, is not one of my best virtues. I wanted to drag him from that awful room and its awful memories, whatever they might be. I was wondering how it might be accomplished, when I was almost startled to hear him speak. "If lightning struck Thorncroft, it struck the lower storey first," he said.

"You think the fire was set?"

"It would not surprise me."

"Perhaps village youths or even tenant sons, out upon a dare on such a night as this one? No one lived there, and it was becoming an eyesore. Such buildings, I believe, are often the victim of awful pranks."

He did not respond to this. I had grown accustomed to his affection; I hated his aloofness. Holding him was like holding a stone pillar. Stubbornly, I refused to let go.

"A wild night like this one would have amused her endlessly. She was like this terrible wind—unpredictable, randomly attacking and retreating, uncaring of whatever devastation was left in her wake, only pleased for the excitement of it. I felt her there at the fire, her presence as strong as if she were standing at Thorncroft, laughing at the flames. And I walked in here, half expecting to see her propped up in bed upon half a dozen pillows, wanting me to laugh with her."

I looked up at him. "Did she do that? Expect you to be amused at her...misbehaviour?"

"She had a very charming, attractive manner. When she shared an anecdote, her audience would be fascinated. There was a certain something about her that made one *want* to listen, to *want* her to continue talking, to *want* to be her friend. I was drawn in, too, at first. I liked the thought that my wife would be a sought-after companion, a leader in the first circles. The charm, however, did not last. I was repelled, but I wanted *not* to be. I wanted the appeal to return. And when it would not, I tried to at least *like* her still—even if I could not be attracted to her. After I discovered her betrayals, though, it was odd, the way she still wished to exert the same sort of allure upon me, although I no longer trusted her in any sense. Finally, I simply accepted my responsibility towards her as a gentleman and her husband, trying to prevent her from damaging others more vulnerable. I regretted that I could not manage much more than that. But it was as if she were a character in a play. I had been drawn to the character, but once I came to know the actor, I could no longer see her in the role. She resented my view even more than had I repudiated her utterly."

I did not much care for the odd, distant voice he used, as if he were a sleepwalker and the real Mr Darcy, only a dream.

"I do not think it unusual that you should have been attracted to your first wife. It would have been rather more peculiar if you had not been. And after you had committed to her body and soul, why not continue to search for the face of who you once thought she was? It is not human nature to admit to hopelessness easily."

He looked down at me for the first time, his eyes glittering in the reflected moonlight. "You are naïve," he said harshly.

"Perhaps I have not had a good deal of experience," I said, keeping my voice level with effort. "Would you rather I had more?"

He gave a humourless laugh. "I would rather *I* had a good deal less. You know so little of me, my dear." And then he kissed me, but it was not a kiss of affection—it was one of bitterness. Was it her he kissed? Or the Shadow Girl I had once been? Or, worse still, the Maiden Spinster who could not be expected to feel a man's passion or understand what forces might twist and pervert it?

I tore my lips from his, taking his face none-too-gently within my palms. "Perhaps *you* have experiences you would rather forget. But you have made all of *mine* memorable. I need not look further than what we do, how you are when it is only you and me, alone, to understand your character. When no one in the whole world would know—you could do *anything*. I would not even know how to fight it. But when you touch me, the sensation of it, it is as if you are underneath my own skin, knowing and understanding so much more than I do. The power you have when I am at my most vulnerable and yet, the control you have—of yourself, most of all. Yes, I must be naïve, for I have no words to describe those feelings. How you take me out of myself, pull me apart, send me flying...and somehow, some way, put me back together again before I hit the earth."

He seemed to return to himself with my words; the past released its grip, and when he kissed me again, it was me he kissed. He picked me up in one strong-armed swoop, making me gasp. In no time we were in his old room, and he tossed me on the bed, making me laugh. He kissed me, everywhere, until I cried out for him with impatience and greed. And when it was over, he did not insist we leave the wing, but rather drew the curtains round us and the blankets over us and fell asleep with his body spooned warmly against mine.

But my last conscious thought before sleep consumed me was a fanciful one: Anne's ghost would not much like the exorcism of this night; she would try and take her revenge.

And so she did.

My husband awakened me gently; he had opened the curtains surrounding the bed, but it was still dark—the windows were best for spectacular sunsets, not for dawn's morning glow.

"Darling, we should move to our rooms, before the servants mount a search for us," he said.

"Too cold," I muttered, unhappy with the loss of his body's heat.

"You may wear my banyan," he replied, and the thought of him strolling through Pemberley's corridors in his nightshirt, possibly startling the housemaids into dropping their buckets, tickled me into rising. He gathered my scattered night clothing and I hurriedly dressed—wearing only my own, and thus sparing the sensibilities of the maids. Hand in hand, we made our way downstairs, where he stopped and locked the door. Perhaps he had shed a few of his shadows, but some still claimed him.

We went to our rooms to find that the fires had already been tended; doubtless there would be talk of our absence in the servants' hall. I did not care, for the room was warm and I was chilled through. Mr Darcy was about to leave me to ring for his man, but I stopped him. "Come back to bed—it is still quite early."

"I shall never fall back to sleep," he complained.

"Let Pennywithers sleep for another half an hour," I said, taking his hand and tugging. I did not say it aloud, but I was not ready to be alone yet. He obliged, though I knew he was anxious to be about his day, and why.

When we were warmly ensconced within my bed, I brought up the subject I knew was pressing upon him. "What will you do about Thorncroft?"

"I shall have to ensure it is taken down completely, and immediately. There is a shell of a building left, quite dangerous."

"You shall want to do that as quickly as possible, of course. But what do you want in its place?"

He peered at me suspiciously. "I can see you have an idea of what *you* wish. I will warn you now, I am not fond of the idea of rebuilding it. Or of more silly hermitages dotting the landscape."

I sat up. "What about...trees?"

"Trees?"

"Of course, I realise it is a lovely piece of ground, but if you do not wish for another cottage, why not return the trees that were cut down to build Thorncroft in the first place? I love the idea of allowing Pemberley Woods to reclaim what was taken from her. Oak, sycamore and maple...to know that generations after we are gone, those trees will stand, fellow sojourners and silent sentinels to our future progeny. We had oaks and sycamores at Longbourn that had stood for more than a hundred years, and I used to think, 'My great-grandfather touched this very tree and rested beneath its shade, just as I am doing now."

"I expect that you were admonished often for climbing them," he said, the corner of his mouth tilting up in an almost-smile.

"I was, sir. I believed myself part bird, as I recall."

"One might suppose that Pemberley Woods are ample enough, and that *it* could not know the difference if it were shorted a few, er, fellow sojourners," he said, though smiling fully.

"Perhaps it would not," I said. "But I love the thought that it might feel the loss—or the addition."

He looked at me intently, and then he slowly nodded. "I believe I do, as well," he said. "I will meet with Williams and arrange the plantings. Perhaps we can relocate some more mature trees as well as seedlings, so it does not look quite so young."

I am not quite sure why his acceptance of my idea was so exhilarating; I do love trees, of course, and was happy to know that more of them soon would flourish in what had once been a sorry, sad space. But it was the quality of his attention to my wishes, I think, that delighted me the most. Which of course, led to an expression of my appreciation, and, what with one thing and another, we were late down to breakfast, after all.

I did not much care for the physician attending Mrs de Bourgh. Mr Donavan was a heavy young man in his mid-twenties with a servile conduct I found mildly offensive. Perhaps it was only that he reminded me, in both manner and appearance, of my cousin Mr Collins.

Mrs de Bourgh's fever sluggishly refused to mend, or so Mr Donavan claimed. I sometimes wondered, however, for Mr Donavan spent a good deal of time with his patient, recommending delicacies from the kitchen for her, which I suspected he ate himself. I would not have been at all surprised if he encouraged her illness simply so he could continue stuffing himself on Pemberley's excellent fare.

Mr Darcy had disclosed that old Mr Simpson—the doctor who had attended the Darcys for many years—had retired shortly after Anne's death to live with a son in Hampshire. I regretted Simpson's loss because of my dislike of Donavan, of course, but I could not help but remember the dress shop assistant's words about Mr Simpson being in Mr Darcy's 'pocket'.

Was there any connexion between his retirement and Anne's death? I could only feel relief for his absence, if so. Not only did I have no desire to question my husband regarding the means of her death, but I now feared anyone else doing it.

I frequently visited Mrs de Bourgh, and not only to determine whether she was mended enough to be moved. While I did not want to live with her and *could* not like her, I felt only pity for her aggravated grief. I wished her no ill whether or not she felt the same, feeling it my responsibility to ensure she received excellent care. The visits seldom went well.

I remember being surprised by the austerity of her chambers the first time I entered her small sitting room. In many homes, the higher the floor, the plainer the room, but such was not the case at Pemberley, since the upper floor of this wing had been designed as a setting for the spectacular cliff-side views. I had known, of course, that her rooms on this lower floor of the wing would not be as elaborate. Still, they had been hers from the beginning, and while they were only a staircase away from her daughter's former rooms, there was a world of difference in the décor. It was the furthest thing from lavish—dark and dreary even; the furnishings, while of good quality, unremarkable. Heavy curtains hid the room's one impressive feature, the view. There were no pictures, not even a miniature of her daughter, and no floral arrangements to brighten it.

I would walk through her sitting room, tapping on her bedchamber door before entering.

Mrs de Bourgh, deathly pale—nothing new there—would be propped up on a number of pillows, a bandage covering half her face. She would take one look at me and begin hissing like a snake disturbed in its nest.

"Have you come to mock my pain? Are my injuries not enough to satisfy you and the spawn of Lucifer you call a husband?" I can hear her voice in my memory still, a croaking sort of growl, weak and spiteful.

Her maid, the nurse, and the doctor would look on avidly, I noticed, no one doing anything to soothe their patient.

"I only wonder how you are feeling," I would say calmly, "and whether we can do anything else for your comfort."

"My comfort! As if you care for that! Let us have honesty between us at least! You were hoping to find me at death's doorstep, were you not? But I shall live through this, simply to spite you both!"

It made me sad, truly, to see that she would blame *us* for her injuries. She would never recover if she could not accept that she had caused them herself.

But I continued to visit, refusing to allow her to set the terms of my calls, and keeping my eye upon her, if nothing else.

After one such visit, Mr Donavan followed me out. "She is very ill," he said unnecessarily, standing too close while he spoke in his over-sympathetic, toadying sort of way. "It is likely best if you allow *me* to apprise you and Mr Darcy of her needs—I will certainly inform you when she is well enough for visitors again. But I encourage you not to take her words too much to heart."

I raised a brow. "I promise, I would not readily accept the word of anyone so feeble of mind as to throw herself through a window," I said acerbically. "I only hope you would not, either."

But, as it turned out, he did not heed my advice. When a dead body was found buried in a shallow grave near where Thorncroft once stood, and when that body was identified as Miss Caroline Bingley, he repeated every poisonous word she'd uttered, and to anyone who would listen. And there were many, many words, and many, many listeners, indeed.

CHAPTER NINETEEN

Derbyshire weather began growing warmer within a day of the windstorm, promising a temperate and early spring. Mr Williams helped me assemble a list of tenants who might be agreeable to a call, and Georgiana agreed to go along and make introductions—although once she'd looked over the names, she protested that some she knew best were gone. "I thought the Martins would live here forever," she said sadly.

"His wife died, and he couldn't stand the place without her," Mr Williams replied. "His son took a position as steward for one of Matlock's properties. Darcy has rented the home farm to Martin's nephew for now, but I know he worries. Too many sons are leaving."

It was a problem Mr Darcy and I had discussed before— how to retain more of the younger generation, who were beginning to find more prosperity labouring in the northern mills than they could in farming for their parents. The issues were complex, but I liked how he included me in his conversations about them. We were beginning to understand and rely upon each other, I thought, building a marriage and…a *love* I had once believed impossible. Though he never said the words, it was in his actions, his attention, his concern for my welfare, and his respect for my ideas.

Georgiana and I began visiting tenants, bringing baskets while she helped acquaint me with the wives and daughters. She was shy; this duty was manifestly not her favourite, and the tenants seemed a bit standoffish in return.

However, I had always enjoyed excellent relations with the tenants of Longbourn—not that Longbourn had nearly so many—and had grown up knowing well those upon whose labour we depended, understanding their families and needs and joys and sorrows. It was a connexion unlike any other. My father had been criticised for his liberality—often by my mother—but I shall never forget his opinions on the subject.

"We pretend to be masters of this place, Daughter," he would say while taking me along to visit the farms, bringing baskets of bounty from Mama's splendid kitchen. "But without men and their families to work the lands, tend the herds, and bring in the crops, Longbourn dies. Longbourn is the mother, and they are her children. What mother would allow her children to starve while she feasts? And if she does, why, soon she is a mother no more."

When he died, to a man, they came to me expressing a grief to nearly match my own.

I was determined to know these people of Pemberley and that they should know me—and, perhaps, to continue the legacy of care my father had demonstrated. Happily, by the end of each visit, I felt the goodness of new beginnings and new interests amongst our people, and their interest in me. Mr Darcy was a good master, it was plain—I saw no hunger or serious need. However, they seemed to hold him in some reverence. I was happy for respect, but found awe completely unnecessary. I thought it well that, through me, he should become more approachable to them.

Within two weeks of the fire, the site of Thorncroft was barren of any sign of the wreckage of the former cottage. Mr Williams seemed cheerful, even, as he supervised the work on the day that Georgiana and I walked up to view the progress. It had been decided that the soil was warm enough and the site protected enough to begin the plantings of saplings, along with several more mature trees that were to be replanted there as well.

Somewhat to my disappointment, Mr Darcy was nowhere about—I was wearing a pretty new dress, and was vain enough to look forward to his customary expressions of appropriate admiration. But one of the elderly gardeners, encircled by dozens of pots of delicate young trees, showed us which saplings were going where, fussing and clucking like a mother hen with her chicks. Amused, we listened to his botany lecture while crews of men—some moving pots, some digging holes in preparation for the replants—followed his commands.

Suddenly, one of the men cursed loudly. My head swivelled towards the sound, and the gardener, tutting disapprovingly, apologised and ambled over to where others were beginning to congregate beside the agitated man.

"I wonder what they have found?" I questioned idly.

Georgiana twirled the new parasol she had purchased at our last foray into Hopewell, bored. "Probably some Roman artifact. Every now and again, someone will find something ancient and unrecognisable and everyone makes a fuss. Shall we walk back down?"

Her supposition seemed unlikely to me, because our diggers today did not seem of the sort who would recognise unrecognisable artifacts, of any era. I watched Mr Williams stride over, looking impatient, the men making way for him as he crouched over something. And then he stood, speaking a few words to the men surrounding the site, one of whom immediately took off running. All work ceased. Men were milling about, talking amongst each other, but quietly, soberly.

I watched for several minutes, but work did not resume. "Something is the matter," I said at last, starting for Mr Williams. Georgiana followed me with some reluctance, which I could understand. The steward's expression was grim.

"What is happening?" I asked him.

If ever a man was the picture of reluctance, it was Mr Williams at my approach. His eyes darted from side to side, as if searching for any avenue of escape.

"There has been an, er, unusual discovery. I would, um, prefer for Mr Darcy to reveal any particulars at his discretion."

"Every single person here, with the exception of myself and Mrs Bingley, already possesses some knowledge of the matter," I retorted. "It is far too late for discretion."

At that moment, the sound of approaching horses caught our attention. Mr Williams appeared relieved as my husband and Mr Bingley dismounted. Tossing their reins to a man waiting to receive them, they strode towards us; Mr Darcy was hatless, which was unusual indeed. I wondered if he'd ridden here so quickly, it had blown off. I was to be disappointed in my quest for information, however. He nodded his head at me in an abbreviated gesture of acknowledgement and said but one word, addressed to Williams:

"Where?"

Mr Williams paced towards the spot where the men had been digging, Mr Darcy directly behind him. Georgiana had waylaid Mr Bingley, but he only shook his head, unwilling or unable to add anything more useful, and they trailed behind me as I followed him to the excavations.

I came up beside Mr Darcy, observing the ground before us. At first, I could only see what appeared to be scraps of rotting fabric. And then I noticed it.

Georgiana, peering over my shoulder, gasped. Mr Bingley, taller than both of us, cried, "Great gads!"

There amongst the mounds of dirt, protruding from the fabric's mouldering folds, were the skeletal remains of a human hand, golden rings resting upon the bones.

Before I could say a word of either wonder or horror, Mr Bingley fell to his knees. "No, no," he cried. "It cannot be. Darcy, why does it wear Caroline's rings? What can it mean? No! It must not be!"

And then, he retched upon the ground and began to cry.

Surprisingly, it was Georgiana who moved first. Her face had gone utterly pale and she looked nearly as green as Mr Bingley, but she went to her husband immediately, gently rubbing his back until he could stand again. Mr Darcy handed him his handkerchief, with which he wiped his sweating face; then did not seem to know what to do with it.

"Come, Mr Bingley. Let us return to the house," his wife said gently, and her words seemed to recall him to the present.

"I shall take you to my study," Mr Darcy said, but Georgiana objected.

"No. We shall retire to our rooms," she insisted.

"I will have the carriage brought up," I offered, but she shook her head.

"No. The walk back to the house will do us both good," she replied determinedly, taking his arm. "Brother, I am certain Mr Bingley will wish to speak with you…later. Preferably not until tomorrow."

Even amidst my dismay over the afternoon's discoveries, I recognised the new protectiveness in Georgiana for her husband. Evidently, she had indeed made great strides in overcoming the bitterness she had carried towards him for so long. He clung to her arm as if it were a lifeline as they made their slow way back to Pemberley.

Mr Williams cleared his throat. "Sir?" he addressed my husband, who stood frozen, his expression implacable. "Shall we…" he gestured towards the grisly remains.

Mr Darcy ignored him. "I will escort you back to the house," he said to me.

"It is not necessary," I said firmly. "I will speak to you later." Without waiting on his reply, I marched down the hillside after the Bingleys, not wanting him to see my trembling, or them to notice me.

I did not—or rather, had not *liked* Caroline Bingley. When I had known her, I believed her self-absorbed, petty, and unkind. But she was—*had been*—a human being, who loved her sister, pretty clothing, and dancing the cotillion. Had she been granted a longer life, who was to say that she would have remained small-minded and critical? Her opportunities for growth and self-improvement had been cut drastically short.

I remembered what Mr Darcy had said about her when I had asked him about the Bingleys, in Rosings's garden. Eloped, he had claimed. I had thought it extremely uncharacteristic at the time, but had not questioned it. I simply had not cared, then, if she had fallen off the face of the earth. She had wished for me to disappear, and her wish had come true.

218

Rather than dwell upon 'if onlys', I had shoved everyone from that old life out of my mind.

Poor, poor Miss Bingley.

Before I rounded the bend that would take me out of sight, I glanced back over my shoulder. My husband still stood in the same place, watching me go. His expression was as forbidding as I had ever seen it.

Mr Darcy did not follow me any time soon, and I suffered one of the longest afternoons of my life awaiting news. When Mrs Reynolds entered the gold parlour to inform me of a visitor, I was relieved to have some distraction. I ought to have known it would not be a pleasant one.

I well understood the neighbourhood's reluctance to welcome me into its bosom. The former Mrs Darcy had been a sought-after addition to their numbers, and her Pemberley entertainments were legendary, even in London. She had been popular, pretty, and added richly to the consequence of their little country society—whilst managing, through ill-natured gossip, to cast aspersions upon the husband to whom she pretended devotion. His lack of sociability made him an easy target for her machinations, but at least he held both wealth and power and thus, acceptance.

By contrast, I was a nobody from nowhere. According to widespread rumour, helpfully conveyed to me by Mrs de Bourgh—probably by way of the gossiping Mr Donavan and his nurse—I was regarded as either a scavenger who had taken advantage of the vulnerable, grieving Mr Darcy (and, it was to be presumed, unfairly snapping him up before their own daughters had even had an opportunity to try) or a weak-willed fool, stupid enough to marry an abusive husband.

Of course, it did not help that Mr Darcy had little interest in mending fences. I understood that he had been the subject of merciless gossip, and could not care for most of their opinions. I wished, however, that he could care more for mine. I wanted to make my own place in this community, judge for myself who should be my friends, and try to earn respect, however slow the progress.

Thus far, I had managed to become acquainted with only two women. Lady Harrington, a very elderly dowager, quite deaf, enjoyed my company greatly, though the visits were rather painful as I had to shout to be understood. The other was, of course, Mrs Longthorpe, though it was evident that she neither respected nor liked me. An inherent gossip, she pretended an attachment only because she could not resist imparting everything she had ever heard, clearly in the hopes that I would, in turn, spill something worth repeating. Still, I did not discourage the acquaintance. Instead, I used it, learning what was said and by whom.

Unsurprisingly, Mrs Longthorpe had immediately heard the terrible story of the recovered remains, and though I tried to subdue her wildest conjecture, she was impervious to my efforts.

"I was well acquainted with Miss Bingley, you know," she said, pretending shock and grief, even putting a handkerchief up to the corner of her eye to dab at an imaginary tear.

"We do not yet know the identity of the unfortunate person found on our property," I said quellingly, though, judging from Mr Bingley's reactions, the assumption would be easily proven.

"You would not have known," she replied, with false sympathy, "how very close we were. Of course, she was devoted to Mr Darcy. *Very* devoted, indeed." The rings on her fat fingers glittered as she spoke. "She often complained of Mrs Darcy's failures to be a proper wife to him. We tried, all of us, to help her realise just who was *improper* to whom. She would not listen. And now, it appears, she paid for her inattention with her life."

A wave of sorrow struck me. Caroline Bingley, whom I had once despised, had probably been the only person on earth who cared enough for—and who paid enough attention to—Mr Darcy to truly realise the sad state of his marriage. Unfortunately, she had addressed her criticisms to the wrong audience, all of whom were devoted to Anne de Bourgh.

"We have no idea how the unfortunate person discovered met his or her end. We shall leave it to Lord Cavendish and whomever else he cares to involve."

She smiled, all pretend apologies. "Of course, my dear, of course. I hear an express has been sent to him in London, although I wonder whether he will make haste to return. He has always shown such a prejudice in Mr Darcy's favour. It must be so unpleasant for you, being at the centre of such scandal. I find myself perplexed as to what *my* role ought to be. As your *sole* friend, I feel an obligation to inform you what is being said. But would you rather I did not? I would not hurt your feelings for worlds."

What a despicable woman! If I agreed, she had *carte blanche* to abuse me. If I did not, however, I would not learn what I wished to know. But it was hardly likely that Lady Harrington would be a ready source of information, was it?

"My feelings are not so delicate. *If* it is Miss Bingley, and I do not say it could be, my husband will do everything in his power to discover the villain."

She sighed, as if I were incredibly naïve. "Now, now, we are both women of the world, are we not? *Some* men, as I am sure you realise, Mrs Darcy, are not satisfied with what is easily available at home. A wife becomes less interesting. They require variety. *Some* women are weak, allowing a man to do as he will. It is an old story, if a sad one. I cannot imagine why anyone who had the first Mrs Darcy in his bed would look elsewhere, but of course, she never blamed him for it, did she?"

I had expected inferences, but not outright accusation. "I disagree wholeheartedly with your supposition," I said, forcing an evenness to my tone I did not feel. "My husband takes his wedding vows very seriously. He is a gentleman, and he keeps his promises. By all accounts, Miss Bingley was interested in another man entirely." After all, it was said she had eloped, and the family had believed it. There was another character in this tragedy, whether Mrs Longthorpe wished to mention him or not.

She waved this away, jewels glistening. "I do not judge. If Mrs Darcy did not care, why should I? Why, even, should he? But Miss Bingley was too demanding. It could not end well."

"What demands?" I asked sharply, the bile of her implications rising in my throat. "And to whom?"

She lowered her voice conspiratorially. "For a divorce, if you can believe it," she nearly whispered, her eyes gleaming like her rings. "She told me herself that she expected him to apply to Parliament for one. She hinted that she could say much more, and would, when the time was right."

I rolled my eyes and let her see my disbelief. "No one in their right mind would expect Mr Darcy to obtain a divorce, even if he set up tents for his mistresses on the front lawns. This is all nonsense, as you *must* have known then and *should* know now."

I could see I had made my point, for doubt showed in her expression. "Well, nooo," she drawled. "But she hinted at the most lurid of accusations. I am certain she embarrassed him deeply."

"And thus he *killed* her? Is this, then, your argument? Why should he subject his life, his reputation, and even the honour you suggest he defends, to such infamy? You contradict yourself madam. Either he cares so much for honour that he loses it entirely, or he had none in the first place. If the latter, why bother about the foolish imaginings of a foolish woman, who damaged only her own reputation with her foolish complaints? If we are making wild accusations without any evidence, we ought to at least include the other man whose interest she attracted."

"The German? But why should he do Miss Bingley any harm?"

Had Miss Bingley's lover been a foreigner, then? Of course, it mattered little now, and my frustration with Mrs Longthorpe's ridiculous assumptions mounted. "Exactly! Why should anyone? You have provided no sound reasoning to either accuse or suspect *any* person of a crime."

"Mr Darcy's reputation—" she began, but I interrupted.

"Has always been of the finest. Ask his servants. Ask his tenants. Ask his *wife*. He has no improper pride. He is perfectly amiable. You do not know what he really is; pray, do not pain me by speaking of him in such terms. You must search elsewhere for your villain."

She stood, insulted, and for no good reason I could see. "He is a proud, unpleasant sort of man, but I can see you are resolved on defending him. I fear, my dear, you are in the greatest danger in your marriage. I can only hope you will escape the discredit and misery—or worse—as I predict."

Turning on her heel, she flounced from the room. I sighed, rubbing at my temples, feeling the beginnings of a megrim.

Mr Darcy entered at that moment through the opposite door from the one Mrs Longthorpe exited. His face...oh, his face! It was frozen in an expression I hated. It was plain he had overheard every stupid, contemptible accusation.

"I am sending you to Darcy House in London," he said coldly. "I will send an express to Mrs Harris. She will have everything ready for your arrival. There will be no discussion. I will allow no further insult to either of us. Please ask Clara to pack your things. You will leave first thing in the morning." And, just like Mrs Longthorpe before him, he marched from the room without taking his leave of me.

I sighed again. It only wanted this.

CHAPTER TWENTY

I was angry at Mr Darcy, to be sure. My feelings were hurt at his abrupt dismissal of me, at his willingness, so easily, to send me away, as if I were some servant who displeased him. The worst part was his judgment of my fortitude, my ability to withstand the scandalmongering of a few—or even of many! Had he so ill an opinion of my character?

It had been an uphill struggle from the very start. Every time there were difficulties, he withdrew into himself, a stone-walled shell constructed over the course of his life with another woman. In some ways, she held him captive still, which was what I found most painful and least acceptable. I reminded myself of what I owed him—and patience was the least of it—as I attempted to compose a note to him while imagining his every rebuttal to my every argument. In the end, I only requested I be taken to my aunt's home in Lambton, rather than be banished to London. Three hours' distance was better than three days.

And then I sent another note with Clara, asking Georgiana whether she could spare a few moments to speak with me.

Georgiana came to my rooms at once in response; I was gratified to see that, though still pale, she appeared composed.

"How does Mr Bingley fare?" I asked, after we had exchanged a quick embrace.

"He is sleeping at the moment," she sighed, taking the seat across from mine.

"It must have been a dreadful shock. But surely, there is room for doubt as to her…identity?"

"Not really," she said sadly. "We both recognised its—*her* —jewellery. I feel so guilty."

I raised my brows, and she gave me a wan smile before continuing. "I assure you, I was as shocked as he was to realise Caroline is dead. I truly believed—we *both* believed— she had eloped."

"Mr Darcy told me she had. I found it very surprising, and very out of character."

She sighed again. "She was in love with my brother, did you know that?"

I grimaced. "I suspected it when I knew her all those years ago. He did not seem to encourage her, however. Surely, after he married…"

"Anne used to laugh about it, even needle her a very little bit," she continued slowly, as though she were seeing it in her mind's eye. "Although I could hardly blame her, when Caroline was so obvious! Such sheep's eyes as she made, and always agreeing with every word he said, even the ridiculous ones." She clapped a hand over her mouth—she was completely unused to teasing her brother—but I waved this off and smiled.

"Indeed. I once heard her wax eloquent upon his method of mending pens."

She returned my smile, though sadly. "Yes, that sounds very like her. She had offers, of course she did. But they were not the ones she wanted."

Ah, yes. She had aimed very high, indeed.

I stopped my train of thought immediately. If she had aimed too high, I had not aimed at all, expecting true love to swirl into my life like showers of dandelion clocks. When I knew her, we were both only twenty, and full of unrealistic views—of ourselves most of all.

"Surely, though, she gave up her infatuation? When it was hopeless?"

"I thought so. Eventually, she seemed to adjust, and even, finally, sought Anne's friendship, much to our relief. In the summer of 1818, Anne held a big house party, inviting Henry Krofford, along with his sister, Maria. They were the Austrian relations of a good family from Norfolk, a very sought-after pair during the season. And of course, she invited all of us. Both of Bingley's sisters loved Anne's house parties."

Henry Krofford, then, must be 'the German' referred to by Mrs Longthorpe.

"And Miss Bingley and Krofford...hit it off?"

"Yes! We were all so surprised, but then, he was hand-some and articulate. She was much livelier in his company, and seemingly welcomed his attentions. Mrs Hurst was displeased, of course, but only because his estate was not in England. Bingley and I were both very encouraging. She was not always the easiest person with whom to share a home, you see."

I could easily see *that*.

"But why did everyone believe she eloped?"

"Because she left a letter saying she would, and she and Mr Krofford—with his sister—disappeared at the same time. I have never been very certain of her reasons, but Bingley knew more than I. Something happened, something concerning my brother. Bingley said only that she and my brother had a falling out of immense proportions, and it had driven her to desperation. Bingley followed, of course, but never could catch them."

"Surely the Norfolk relations could help?"

"It turned out they were estranged, and not having participated in the Season that year, and having little to do with London life in general, simply did not know their relations had made so free with their consequence."

"Did you see the letter? From Miss Bingley, stating her intentions?"

"Oh, yes. It was most definitely her writing. There was not much to it, just that she was going away with Mr Krofford."

"Mr Bingley must have written—surely, the Kroffords' estate was not a fabrication?"

She appeared very troubled. "Yes, his Austrian estate is very real—and was much in need of Caroline's fortune, by all reports. But Krofford denied having eloped with my sister. Or anyone else."

"Why did he leave then? And where did you think Miss Bingley went?"

"There appeared evidence enough that she left with Mr Krofford. Just none that they married, afterward."

There was a silence as I digested this. It all seemed *very* unlike Miss Bingley. But then, she had never eloped at all, had she? There was something quite peculiar about the whole story, and that something had to do with my husband.

"Other than family, did anyone else know of the...alleged

elopement?" After all, Mrs Longthorpe had understood who I was speaking of, when I mentioned another man.

"There were whispers, but Anne did everything she could to distract her guests and..." she paused, and then continued in a low voice, "When Bingley left on his search for her, he put it about that he was taking her home to our estate for reasons of illness. The absence of the Kroffords was noted, of course, but Anne gave some excuse, and...well...that is... Caroline was not very interesting, to most people."

And there it was. No one had much cared what happened to her, beyond her immediate family—all of whom had the greatest interest in keeping her whereabouts quiet. *Poor, poor Miss Bingley.*

"I know that Bingley never stopped trying to make contact," Georgiana continued. "He wrote to Krofford several times, and each effort was upsetting to him. But he truly believed her away, living *some* kind of life in Austria. He is heartsick, now. I will take him home, where he can mourn her, and arrange for her burial."

In her immediate concern over her husband, Georgiana had as yet given little thought to other consequences of finding the body.

"Mr Darcy is sending me away," I said. "He wishes me to go to London."

She looked up sharply. "What? But why?"

It was my turn to sigh. "My dear, someone is responsible for Miss Bingley's untimely demise. The great opinion of the neighbourhood is that this person is my husband. He apparently finds me incapable of living amongst such conjecture."

I thought she would swoon, she turned so white with shock. "Oh," she choked. "This is so wrong! It is impossible! Will you go?"

"He has hardly given me a choice. However, I shall not go

all the way to London. I shall visit my aunt Gardiner, who lives but twenty miles away in Lambton."

"But why would he want you to leave? It makes no sense! I will speak to him."

But I held up my hand. "Please, do not. If he does not want me here, I hardly wish to force myself upon him. Still, you must tell me—do you think Mr Bingley will stand by him? Will he believe the gossip?"

I expected—and indeed, hoped—she would immediately sputter in indignation at the very idea. Yet, her subsequent thoughtfulness was a more realistic response. I understood then, that she was deciding whether *she* would believe the gossip, as well as Mr Bingley's reaction. I knew she would defend Mr Darcy publicly; she loved him dearly, and her own reputation had a stake in the scandal as well. But she had questions with no answers—or answers only he could give— and a husband with whom she had only recently reconciled.

"Bingley will stand by him," she pronounced at last, and I breathed more easily. Georgiana, at least, thought Mr Darcy had nothing to do with the death of Miss Bingley, and she believed her husband would be loyal. That was something, anyway.

After she departed, I called Clara to pack my things, my mind racing with urgent arguments protesting my eviction. Every part of my soul opposed the abandonment, for it felt like nothing less. I did have motive for acquiescing, however: a deep desire to seek advice and even solace from my aunt. I was in love with my husband, but—although I was certain he felt affection, at least at times—he, clearly, did not share the intensity of my own feelings.

It seemed to me that—after suddenly finding himself released from seven years of a miserable marriage—he had reflected upon the course of his life, remembered a girl he had once liked who was of good character, an orphan of small fortune, possessed of undistinguished family (or, in other words, the exact opposite of his first wife), and set out to marry me. Turning back time, so to speak, as a means of blotting out his past and the lost years. Living his life over again, our marriage nothing to do with the woman I *am* but rather who I am *not*. I shrank from these notions—there had been that kiss, after all, that first, perfect kiss, and all the ones thereafter. But kisses were not enough to build a life upon, as too many women learned to their regret.

As he was not well-respected by some of the neighbourhood, and since his first wife was both keenly social and traitorously immoral, he would not have wanted *too* young a wife—one who depended upon a vigorous society for her friendships and entertainment. He would want a quieter person, more bookish—the type who might love Pemberley as much for its trees as its place in the community. And of course, I had no parent to pester and vex him. He'd had more than enough of difficult family relations.

I hoped it was not so, and yet, if not...well, his reasons for marrying me remained as mysterious as those for his marriage to Anne de Bourgh.

I did not *regret* loving him. But I thought we had at least established a friendship, a mutual passion, a life's partnership. His habits of secrecy and retreat, however, were ingrained. Just as he had disappeared to London rather than speak to me about Hopewell's poor opinion of him, he was thrusting me from his sight rather than deliver any explanations regarding Caroline Bingley.

Well. He would not be able to forever retreat from those questions; the magistrate, Lord Cavendish, would, undoubtedly, demand answers. There would likely be an inquest, and my heart hurt at the thought of him facing it by himself.

But that was how he preferred to manage his troubles. Alone.

I wondered, the next morning, whether he would refuse to see me off. He had not come to me the night before, nor even sent a note responding to mine. I had been tempted to go to him, again and again, but was fairly certain I would cry, possibly followed by undignified begging, and I was determined to subject him to neither. The inequality in our feelings was not his fault, and yet I knew it would pain him if he knew how deeply I was hurt. I took a tray in my room rather than have to wonder whether he would join me for breakfast, barely managing to choke down tea.

But, ever the gentleman, he was waiting when I emerged from my rooms in my warmest carriage dress—for it looked like rain, yesterday's sunshine replaced by heavy clouds and a chill wind. Without a word or a touch, he walked beside me as we took the stairs, step by echoing step. He was the first to speak.

"I have instructed Mr Frost to take you to Lambton, as you wished."

I could only nod, my throat tight.

"I suspect that, had I refused, you would simply abandon him at the first posting inn of any size, and find your own conveyance to your preferred destination," he added.

I glanced at him, but there was no sign of humour—no sign of any emotion, really. Just a dry statement of his belief in my wilfulness, I supposed.

"I did not consider that you might refuse so reasonable a request, and thus made no plan for escape or otherwise," I said, my voice surprisingly strong considering my inner turmoil.

When we were nearly to the carriage, he asked, "Where is Clara?"

"I have given her a brief holiday; she will visit her family in Buxton. I will not require her services at my aunt's." In truth, I probably *would* miss her, for some of my new clothing would be challenging to manage by myself, and I had grown accustomed to her talents with my difficult hair—but it was not a great enough inconvenience to trade for the privacy I craved.

He nodded.

And that was all. No words of remorse, of course, much less any expression of regret at my absence. In my most optimistic moments, I had hoped he might say something like 'I will write' or even 'I will miss you'.

But no. He handed me in to the carriage, barely touching me and swiftly stepping away as if I were repellent. The footman closed the door and put up the steps. I gazed at him through the window, but he did not look at me, only nodded to Mr Frost. With a jerk, the vehicle leapt forward. Foolishly, I indulged myself, continuing to watch him through the rear glass. He stood against the backdrop of Pemberley, a solemn, lone palace guard, tall and straight, staring ahead and yet, seeing nothing. And then we rounded the bend, and for once I did not notice the cliff's edge or the road's curves, but only the distance between us as it grew and grew and grew.

My aunt was not as surprised to see me as I expected. Mr Darcy had sent a note with his courier, giving her advance warning of my arrival.

"What did it say?" I asked, curious.

She handed it to me. On elegant, hot-pressed paper, in bold and even handwriting, it said:

Dear Madam,

I hope it would not be too great an imposition if my wife were to join you for a time. I am certain Mrs Darcy will wish to explain in more detail. I apologise for the lack of notice; as matters stand now, she will arrive on the morrow. However, please do not hesitate to contact me if this is inconvenient, and it would be better to make different arrangements; my man will await your reply.

F Darcy

I sighed. If I had been hoping for insight into his reasoning for his actions, or a penned regret for sending me away, I would not find either here.

I did not ask where her mother or my niece and nephews were, as clearly she had arranged for privacy. We went into her cosy parlour, where a tea waited with all of my favourites. My appetite was lacking, my spirits were low, and I could not even think how to begin. Nevertheless, there was something about her sympathetic presence—and, perhaps, being surrounded by the pretty, familiar furnishings from Gracechurch Street—that calmed me. And, like a corset being gently unlaced, I gradually released the words, in fits and starts, to explain what had occurred.

I had, of course, written to her previously of Lydia's deliverance, but the worst parts of the story, I'd withheld; one could not always ensure a letter would reach its intended recipient, and Mr Darcy was far too well known in these parts to trust the mails. Only now could I reveal Wickham's appearance in my drawing room, his disgusting attempts at a blackmail, my fears that even now, he was finding sympathetic ears for his poison. This, of course, led to revelations about Mr Darcy's loveless first marriage, Anne's affair with the blackguard, and her own decimation of Mr Darcy's character, followed by Mrs de Bourgh's dashing herself through the window, the fire at Thorncroft, and, finally, the discovery of the body, with Mrs Longthorpe's subsequent unwelcome visit and my expulsion from Pemberley.

After I finished speaking, there was a long silence—but it was not an uncomfortable one. Although perhaps my tale was shocking, it was not easy to shock Margaret Gardiner. Instead, she only appeared thoughtful, as the fire crackled in the hearth and I realised that I had eaten everything on the plate she had set beside me.

"If your mama is watching all of this from Heaven, think what a commotion she is raising now," she said at last.

I had to laugh, an unexpected outburst. "It would explain why today's weather is vastly different than yesterday's. She would stir up every cloud in the sky." Inexplicably, my throat suddenly closed. I tried to cover the unpredictable emotion, looking up at the ceiling and down at my feet, but it was impossible to hide my true feelings from Aunt Gardiner.

"I wish I did not care for him so well, Auntie. Our feelings are...unequal."

At once, she moved next to me on the settee, drawing my head down upon her shoulder. And then, at long last, I released the tears locked inside me along with the confusion and the hurt, and I cried as if my heart would break.

CHAPTER TWENTY-ONE

Aunt Gardiner did not make suggestions, pronounce judgment, or attempt to organise my scattered emotions. Instead, she let me cry, then sent me to bed where, to my surprise, I slept for two hours. When I awakened, my niece and nephews were eagerly awaiting my appearance, and happily displayed recent achievements and related all of their own news.

I contrived to set aside my troubles and simply bask within the warmth of family. Mrs Spengler told stories of my aunt as a young girl; Ellen displayed for me a perfectly marvellous portrait of her younger brothers—although she did complain of their tendency to wander off while posing—and the boys vied with each other to entertain me with amusing anecdotes. I tried not to think of what it would be like to have my own children mussing the elegant formality of Pemberley.

The Gardiners had always had the children dine with them, once they were at the age where they might participate without disrupting dinner, and I looked forward to a lively meal when delicious smells began wafting through the parlour and Mrs Gardiner announced dinner should soon be served.

"But where is Mr Martin, Mummy?" Michael asked. "Shall I fetch him?"

"He will not join us tonight while we have company," she replied.

"Mr Martin? Is that not your hired man?" I asked, somewhat taken aback to hear he was, evidently, a regular guest at the dinner table.

But my aunt just smiled. "He joins us when he will," was her only comment. I was quickly distracted by the enthusiastic sounds, courtesy of Edward, of an old-fashioned dinner gong—another happily transplanted Gracechurch Street tradition. My appetite was restored by Mrs Spengler's excellent cook and my family's spirited conversations. Oh, it was good to be with them! How I wished that, someday, I might have the opportunity to bring my own children here, just as I had been taken to Gracechurch Street by my parents.

The next few days, the weather restored, I determinedly decided not to think nor speak of my troubles. I caught my aunt's thoughtful glances every so often, but she let me be. I was introduced to the hired man, however, and here I found something of a mystery.

He was perhaps in his mid-forties, large in stature, quiet in nature. Neither handsome nor ill-looking, his clothing was a good deal finer than that worn by any hired man I had ever before met. When I mentioned this later to my aunt, she blithely replied that he had donned his Sunday best in order to make a good impression upon me, and not to fear—while he repaired the roof, he wore fabrics more suited to the task. The sarcasm was quite unusual to her.

His manners were impeccable. While his speech was not, perhaps, that of a gentleman, he was obviously no simple villager. And yet, he performed the humblest of chores— repairs to the aforementioned roof, tilling the kitchen garden, fixing fenceposts, and everything in between. The stable, once derelict, was now sound; he stayed in the rooms above them, which he had refurbished himself. He had even arranged for a neighbour to rent a good portion of once-neglected land for grazing sheep, bringing income to Mrs Spengler.

I was deeply impressed but also slightly alarmed—mostly by my aunt's unapproachable manner when I hinted of my concerns. Perhaps he was some down-on-his-luck wanderer, of better birth than his circumstance now indicated, but my aunt—usually so sensible—ought to guard against being quite so familiar with him. A woman alone must be very careful. Certainly, there was nothing improper in the behaviour of either; on the contrary, he was a very interesting gentleman, almost scientific in his knowledge of botany—a favourite subject of my own—and my aunt was the furthest thing from flirtatious.

I considered myself more egalitarian than most. The world was changing, in many ways for the better. I believed a man could improve his lot in life, and heaven only knew, the blue blood of Lady Matlock had not influenced *her* character for the better. While my father might never have entertained the thought of a hired man at his table, I was inclined to believe Aunt Gardiner should dine with whomever she pleased. But her children? What would my uncle think of that? The servants my aunt brought with her would be loyal but if Mrs Spengler's servants gossiped about it in the village, her reputation could be ruined and her family's as well.

The day I saw Edward in the garden, chattering away about something while Mr Martin pruned rose bushes, it seemed to me that matters had gotten out of hand. To be sure, Edward was the one being a bother while the man performed his chores, but there was something...*affectionate* in the way Mr Martin smiled down upon him, making the occasional comment. And every night, Michael continued to ask why he would not join them for dinner. My aunt's fatherless sons were growing attached when, for all I knew, Mr Martin would be gone in the autumn; worse still, such familiarity could subject them all to gossip and scandal. I determined I must speak to her, however unpleasant I found the notion.

I waited until we were alone one afternoon, sitting together before the fire—Ellen and the boys at their lessons, Mrs Spengler napping—before I tried to put my fears into words. "About Mr Martin," I said, and my aunt put aside her sewing with a grimace.

"Yes?"

Her tone warned me to tread carefully, and I nearly winced.

"I am sure he is a good man," I began.

"Are you?"

I sighed. "It would be a great joke, would it not, if I were to volunteer romantic advice when my marriage of two short months is in shambles? I shall only remind you of some wise words you rendered me once, when *I* was indulging in an extremely foolish *tendre* for an extremely undeserving man. You advised me to be on my guard, and not to involve myself —or endeavour to involve him—in an affection which the want of fortune would make so very imprudent. I promise, I have nothing to say against Mr Martin; he is most fascinating. If he had the income I daresay he ought to have, or, as is likely, once had, I should think you could not do better. But as it is...my uncle Gardiner would depend upon your resolution and sense on behalf of the children. I believe you would not ever wish to disappoint him. And that is all I have to say about it."

"Lieutenant Wickham," she sighed, her posture relaxing. "I did advise you against him, but for none of the right reasons. I saw only what the rest of the world saw, and I believe I dredged up some memory of a slur against Mr Darcy in his childhood to repeat to you. Truly, it is difficult to know whether what the world sees is correct, or only popular."

What did she mean by that? Was she ready to flout the opinions of an unfair world? "Wickham was beautiful in appearance, and we thought his countenance and character matched," I replied. "I might have believed Mr Darcy a fine man too—I put such stock in physical appeal—except he had the audacity to ignore my charms when his friend attempted to push me on him. The world's opinion of Mr Martin does not trouble me, and except for the children's sake, I would not have mentioned it. If your good name is harmed, theirs is as well."

She smiled sadly, smoothing the fabric of the handkerchief she had been embroidering. "Oh, my dear niece. I will *always* love your uncle. Since losing him, I have welcomed the oblivion of sleep and forgetting each night, only to have memory flood me upon awakening—as if he died anew with every sunrise. It has only been in the last few months that I can open my eyes without sorrow in my first waking thought."

It broke my heart to hear the rawness of her grief, still. Who was I to pretend to know best, and what—or *who*—she needed in order to cope? "Oh, Auntie, I know you were the very best of wives, and *are* the very best of mothers. Forgive me for mentioning it, please. I am only just beginning to understand how much a wife might suffer in such situations."

She reached over and patted my hand. "I am by no means ready to part with my widowhood, dear, and I look upon Mr Martin as only a good friend. However, if I ever did decide to remarry, I can assure you that he is both eligible and respectable."

I raised my brows at this statement. How could this be?

"I told Mr Martin that you would quickly recognise that he is no common labourer—although, in my sorrowful straits when he first arrived, it took me much longer. I also told him that I would keep no secrets from you, but only if you brought up the subject would I reveal all. To understand the whole story, I need to go back in time. Perhaps even as much as eight years, though it is difficult to know for sure. It was a great secret, you see."

"Secrets, Auntie?"

"Yes, indeed. The revelation of them began with Mr Ferrars. He is honest as the day is long, and he has many influential connexions, but as you are aware, your uncle provided most of the financial aptitude in their partnership. Still, as you might recall, Mr Ferrars was often able to secure investors for Mr Gardiner's schemes, precisely because of his birth and trustworthiness. Most of the time, in fact, we knew these investors, and your uncle eventually developed his own connexions with them. On occasion, however, the investor preferred to remain anonymous."

"I remember Uncle explaining it," I agreed, wondering what all this had to do with Mr Martin. "He said that gentlemen might be criticised for participating in trade or appearing to work for their livelihood, but that he had a few silent partners of the gentry, at various times."

She nodded. "Yes. He seldom learnt the identity of those silent partners, for that was Mr Ferrars's realm. Now, as you remember, in Mr Gardiner's final venture—the largest, riskiest project he had ever undertaken—everything collapsed in disarray with his sudden death. The ship's cargo docked and was warehoused, but the ship's captain made false claims of ownership. Paperwork went missing. Mr Gardiner's partners were none of them silent, I promise you; they all contributed threats to see me ruined. I suspect at least one of them to have been in league with the dishonest captain. Mr Ferrars proved ineffectual. I knew coming to Lambton was our only hope, and I would have arrived here penniless except for receiving a generous eleventh-hour offer on the Gracechurch Street property."

It was my turn to nod, for I knew all of this.

"I informed you, at your last visit, that everything had come right. Mr Ferrars had managed the business after all, realising a profit far beyond what even your uncle antici-pated. That, it seems, was not quite true."

"It was less profitable?"

"No. But it was not Mr Ferrars who concluded the venture. He sent me some final papers not long ago, which included a signature I was not expecting. As it turned out, he had included the paper quite by accident, and was very embarrassed when I wrote to him, questioning about it. But at last he gave me the answers I sought."

I was still confused. "So...was Mr Martin a-a silent partner?"

She gave me a serious look. "No, he had naught to do with it. The signature was Fitzwilliam Darcy's."

I was absolutely flummoxed, and more confused than ever. I could only stare at her, mouth open.

"Mr Ferrars explained that Mr Darcy had often been a silent partner in their projects. I promise you, it was a complete surprise to me, and would have been to Mr Gardiner as well."

"It seems so unlikely," I said at last. "And...Mr Darcy was an unknown, silent partner in Uncle's final venture?"

"Not at all. Mr Darcy knew nothing about it, evidently, until he happened to learn of my need to sell our property on Gracechurch Street—and I have my suspicions about why he learned *that*—and, it transpired, was its purchaser, through his solicitor. At that point, he approached Mr Ferrars with questions regarding what had happened to my husband, and what investments he had been developing when he died. And then... he intervened. It was a dreadful tangle, and it took Mr Darcy some time to settle matters. But settle matters he did. Mr Ferrars tried to pay him from his own portion of the revenue, but Mr Darcy refused it, telling him that Mr Gardiner had helped his earnings with more than enough profit over the years, and if he wished to make things right, he ought to give the proceeds to his widow. Which was precisely what the very honourable Mr Ferrars did. It was an extremely large sum."

I sat in silence, trying to comprehend. *Mr Darcy* had purchased the Gracechurch Street home? But why? It could not have had *anything* to do with me—Anne was still alive then. Had it truly been a gesture of respect for a man who had earned him profits in the past? But my aunt was not finished with her explanations.

"I have gradually, over time, acquired the habit of divulging to Mr Martin a good deal more than lists of chores. He is articulate, sensible, and an excellent listener. And when

I poured out my confusion and astonishment over Mr Darcy's very welcome interference, he revealed more of his own identity."

"Who is he?" I almost whispered.

"He is, as you so astutely deduced, no mere labourer, but one of Mr Darcy's wealthiest tenants. He farms a large property held by Mr Darcy, but which he has leased for decades, and his father and grandfather before him."

This was both incredible, and made less sense than ever. "Why would Mr Darcy send him here? Why would he agree to such a request?"

"Mr Darcy did not send him, precisely. He only went to him for assistance with a recommendation. Mr Darcy had learnt, you see, of the state of the property here. He knew my financial situation at the time was bleak, and he intended to subsidise a hired man who could see to needed repairs at the miniscule rate I could afford. Mr Martin knows a goodly number of qualified men and could well advise him on the subject. However…"

Her voice softened, tears coming to her eyes. I remained silent until she could speak.

"Mr Martin lost his wife six months before I lost your uncle. He was in a state, he said, of near despair, missing her quite desperately. Upon hearing my story from Mr Darcy, he could picture it as if his wife had been left impoverished and alone with young ones, trying to start over again. Nothing would do for him except to see to everything himself. The servants not from Gracechurch Street, including our cook, are from his own home. Mr Darcy is his 'silent partner' in it all, I am certain, though I feel as if…as if Mr Gardiner himself arranged for my care. Likewise, Mr Martin feels as if his own dear Harriet brought us to him. I know it sounds odd, but we…we find much comfort in the situation. He needed a family, and I needed...a friend who could understand."

I was silent for long moments, but there really was only one thing to say. "Well, Auntie, I believe Mr Martin ought to begin joining us at the dinner table forthwith. Do not you?"

That night, as I lay upon my bed, I tried to think what it all meant. I could understand it at face value—Mr Ferrars was somehow known to Mr Darcy, and so he had invested in a few schemes, privately. He had never known either my uncle or aunt first-hand, though...so nothing else made sense. Why would he buy the Gracechurch Street home? What possible use could it be to him? If he were not affected by that final partnership's dissolution, why involve himself? And if it were only a matter of gratitude for the efforts of an infrequent former investment partner, why would he put himself to the trouble and expense of seeing to my aunt's immediate welfare, knowing, as he had, that it would all come right in the end?

My uncle had been dead for two years now. My aunt had struggled along on Mr Ferrars's reassurances for nearly a year before we deemed it hopeless and I went to Rosings, and she to Lambton. I had been at Rosings for a year before Mr Darcy's arrival. His wife had been dead only three months when he proposed. We had been married but two.

It meant that fourteen months ago, unbeknownst to me, Mr Darcy had saved my family yet again. I had accepted that he had felt some responsibility for Lydia's downfall, due to his silence on the matter of Wickham's character during his time at Netherfield. But there was no possible obligation this time. My uncle's heart had failed, not his character, nor anything to do with any possible connexion of Mr Darcy's.

I could not take it in. Finally, I arose again, lit a candle, and took out my letter case. I would not be able to sleep until I put pen to paper and asked my sister, Jane, a burning question: Just how did Mr Tilney gain the living at Matlock?

I had a feeling that I already knew.

CHAPTER TWENTY-TWO

I spent a great deal of time over the next week simply... walking. The area was a pretty one, the weather unseasonably dry, if cold. Mrs Spengler's property encompassed an apple orchard, as well as grazing grounds. I enjoyed walking in the long grass, envisioning how the place would appear when the trees were heavy with fruit.

My life felt quite purposeless when compared to my goals and dreams of only two weeks past. Then, my head had been full of plans for Pemberley and an estate school and learning how to be the best mistress possible. I expected to grow in love and connexion with my husband, and him towards me. Instead, I merely walked, meandering amongst dormant trees, dead grasses, and lifeless grey skies.

I had been reduced to waiting impatiently for the mail delivery, then feeling a new rejection with every absent letter. None arrived, from my husband, at least.

It was Georgiana who wrote first. Sadly, her news was most unwelcome. She said that public outcry was such that there would almost certainly be a coroner's inquest. She and

Bingley were doing their best to be supportive, but neither had much influence over the state of affairs—and her brother had booted *them* from Pemberley as well. The letter was not long, but included a caricature purchased in a London print shop, sent by some 'helpful' neighbour. In it, a man bearing an unmistakeable resemblance to Fitzwilliam Darcy stood in the middle of mounds of dirt littered with bones, attempting to shove an excessively tall beaver hat down over a monstrous pair of horns jutting from his head. The caption read, *'Nowhere to Hide'*.

I tried to understand his distance. He was a fiercely protective man—even, it seemed, towards near-strangers for whom he had somehow assumed responsibility. He would hate for me to be tarred with the same brush; I was certain he wanted me far enough away from Pemberley that I should not be mocked, scorned, or otherwise distressed by the encroaching scandal.

But I did not care about caricatures. If they drew one of me, I would frame it and put it on the wall—laughing all the while. If anyone *could* have goaded Mr Darcy to violence, Anne de Bourgh or Wickham ought to have driven him to it long ago, and yet he had never, it seemed, given way; the thought of him as a danger to Caroline Bingley was, simply, ludicrous. I wanted to be beside him in this adversity—but even more, I wanted him to *want* me beside him. I tried to conquer my hurt, yet it seemed he had put me completely from his mind.

The next day, the post arrived with a letter from Mr Tilney, informing us of the safe and happy arrival of our new niece. "A baby girl, at last!" my aunt cried. "Jane must be so pleased!"

I was ecstatic for her, and then overwhelmed by a sudden and horrifying wave of jealousy so strong, I was speechless with it. I turned without a word and fled the room, seeking the privacy of the empty parlour. There, I pushed my palms into my eyes, trying to halt the onslaught of stupid tears.

Of course, my aunt followed me immediately, sitting beside me and gently patting my shoulder whilst I regained control.

I *meant* to say that it was only my joy causing such emotion. I *meant* to find false words of cheer and happiness. Instead, I blurted bitterly, "I think I almost hate him. I will never have a marriage like Jane's. I will never have a family of my own! He sends not a word! Not even a short note to see if I am well! Nothing!"

My aunt looked at me sharply. "Forgive me, Niece. I have not seen any letters posted to him, from you, for him to answer."

I rolled my eyes. "He expelled me from his property, from his life. What am I to say to that? Plainly, he does not wish my affection. Should I express my anger and hurt, instead? Should I be as my poor mama, plaguing a husband who barely tolerated her?"

Her expression softened. "Your parents' marriage was often a difficult one. But my dear, you know that your mother seldom understood matters as they really were. Your father lacked the patience to explain. In this situation, there are other circumstances at work, having nothing to do with like or dislike. I am certain Mr Darcy would take seriously anything you wished to say."

After a moment, the bitterest truth tumbled from my mouth. "With nearly every difficulty, every time we are at odds, he retreats from me. It is up to *me* to make amends, to take *any* steps towards reconciliation." I told her of how, displeased with my disobedience in visiting Hopewell, he had withdrawn all the way to London, only returning when *I* wrote to *him*. And other disagreements, requiring me to venture into his rooms, his territory, so to speak, and aggressively demand understanding. "Just once, I would like him to make the first effort, however small. Especially in this situation, which *he* controls."

My aunt sighed while I seethed with resentment—tensing as I prepared to hear a lecture on my duty, and what I, what our entire family, owed him.

"What do you wish your last words to him to be?" she asked instead. "If today were your last day on earth, what would you say then?"

I looked at her askance. "I never did ring a peal over him the way I did Papa," I said stiffly. "I believe I have learned *some* self-governance, though I felt Mr Darcy's rejection most cruelly."

She took my hand and squeezed it. "I did not mean to imply you said or did *anything* wrong. It is only...once I, too, thought I had all the time in the world to say everything that matters most. My last words to your uncle were not ones of anger. As he was leaving for his warehouse, I asked him to see about getting Mr Baker to look at the porch rail. That is all. I did not add any expressions of affection or care, I am certain."

I squeezed her hand in return. "Uncle knew of your love for him."

"Yes. But all of our words are final, now. Nothing more can be added. I hope they were enough, but I wish there had been fewer exchanges over home repairs, and more of important things. You have every right to be angry, darling. I know you do not wish a marriage like your own parents had. You saw your mother begging for the crumbs of your father's attention, in all the ways least likely to result in getting it. But very often, it takes great strength to exercise humility. To let go of your sense of 'rightness', in exchange for something more important. I wish, now, I had done so more often. Of course, your uncle would never have taken too much advantage. He would not have seen my needs unmet, my wishes disrespected in favour of having things all his own way. Perhaps you cannot trust that Mr Darcy would feel the same." Squeezing my hand once more, she left me alone with the warmth of the fire and the cold reality of her sorrow.

'All of our words are final, now.' This struck me with a tragic sort of power. No, I did not fear that Mr Darcy would wish me to transform into a servile version of myself, such as his aunt, the dowager countess, had wanted. I would never be my mother, and Mr Darcy would never be my father. If I, or my husband died today, our last words to each other would be...nothing. Was that what I wanted? It somehow seemed almost worse than had they been words of anger, the silence a sort of ultimate indifference.

And so I fetched pen and paper, and stared for a long time at the sheet, picking through and discarding every word that occurred to me. Most of them were too angry to put to paper, for I had not learnt to conquer my resentment. Of course, resentment was not all I felt, either.

I missed him almost desperately. But if he did not wish for my affection, how was I to express it? Upon reflection, I realised I had erred in refusing to go to him that night after he had pronounced my expulsion. Only now could I see that my refusal came as much from fear as from any desire to avoid paining him with unrequited love. What if I begged to be allowed to stay, and was denied? My pride, hurt, and cowardice had combined to allow an acceptance of a fate with which I most heartily disagreed.

If there was one flaw I would never accept in my character, it was cowardice. It was always better to know than to wonder, and resentment hardly made for a comfortable alternative.

Dear Sir,

I wish you would come to see me, as soon as you can spare the time.

Sincerely,
Your Wife

I sent it by regular post. Mayhap it would take a day or two to reach Pemberley. Perhaps after all, he would not come. But he might write to tell me why he would not. I could be satisfied with that, I decided. It would be something.

But for six days, his silence stretched into its own ultimate indifference. I pretended not to grieve.

I was drawing in the orchard, though the air was chilly, and the clouds were thick and weighted with moisture. It mattered little, for I was there more for the solitude than the opportunity to practise my sketching. My paper remained as blank and empty as my mind. And then, a noise reached my ears, the sound of boots upon the dry grass, and I turned towards it.

And there he stood. Tall, stern, severe, as if dragged there against his will, his expression matching the forbidding sky. I rose and gave a small curtsey. He bowed slightly. And then he spoke.

"You have summoned me, madam. As you can see, I am here. How might I be of service?"

No greeting, none of the words I had both wished and yearned for, nothing of regret and longing. But then, life was not a Radcliffe novel, was it? Here I was, hurt and resentful and mystified by his manner, and there he was, impossible and arrogant and thick as Pemberley's walls. For all I knew, he might never stand before me like this again.

Anger and pride warred within me, begging for release, wanting to crush any pretensions he might cherish towards being a gentleman I could trust and respect.

And yet...would *those* be my final words?

His life bespoke a different story, one of silent, unacknowledged acts of kindness—of duty, of generosity, of caring. Towards Lydia, my aunt, possibly even Jane, over the course of years. Which man would I speak to, today?

"I-I have been most anxious to acknowledge to you how grateful I am for your intervention in the affairs of my aunt and my poor uncle," I managed.

These words, evidently, caught him by surprise, for his eyes widened and brow furrowed. "I am sorry, exceedingly sorry, that either of you ever learned of it. I did not think Mr Ferrars was so little to be trusted."

"It was an accident, I understand. A misdirected paper that hinted of your involvement. My aunt questioned him thoroughly and I am afraid he was no match for her. You must not blame him. She was determined to have the whole truth out of him."

He nodded once, crisply. And simply stood there.

I looked at him, begging him—in my mind—to take me in his arms, but the tender scene I craved apparently refused to enter his head.

"Is that all then? I must be getting back to Pemberley before the light fails."

I stared at him almost in disbelief. I had to force myself to speak. "Might I—that is, do you wish me to return to Pemberley with you?"

His face was as implacable as ever. "It would be better if you did not. No, I believe you ought to remain here." With unconscious motion, he smoothed his left brow with his left forefinger, appearing as if he were impatient to leave.

And somehow, in my shock and hurt at this new unkindness, I remembered something from what seemed ages past: as the Dowager Lady Matlock spewed nonsense, he had agreed with every foolish word she uttered whilst making that same unconscious motion.

My husband lied.

I took a step closer to him. His aspect was unyielding. But as I watched his eyes, those dark, expressive eyes, I thought I saw more. I hoped I saw more. I moved to within six inches of him. I could hear his breath's intake; my heart beat so hard, I was certain he could hear it. I set my hand upon his shoulder.

"What are you about?" he asked harshly.

"I do not know," I whispered, "but you are making a hash of our entire life together, and I cannot think how else to stop you. In a novel, a passionate kiss does the job. I simply haven't any better ideas, I fear." And I set my mouth to his.

For a moment he was immobile, a frozen statue beneath my lips. Then, with a groan, he was returning kisses wildly, desperately, his arms clutching me tightly to him. "I cannot stop this," he muttered. "I cannot do it."

"I do not wish you to stop. Do not ever stop."

He shrugged off his coat and threw it on the orchard floor, drawing me down with him onto it. I went so willingly, uncaring of propriety, of the setting, of the hardness of the ground or even of chill breezes in unusual places. I only cared to hold him as tightly as I could manage, to show him by every action and gesture that I was his wife, his helpmeet, his life's partner. And when we were as close as a man and woman could ever be, I looked into his eyes. "Never let me go," I begged, pride vanished. "Please, never let me go."

"I am not strong enough to do it," he said. "Heaven help you, but I am not man enough to keep away."

"The man I need is finally here," I disagreed most vehemently, and then there were no more words, only a man and his wife joined, bridging the long separation with connexion at last. And when the heavens wept gently upon us, we only laughed as my hair escaped from its pins and curled wildly around us both.

After we had finally quieted, he began to be anxious that I would take a chill from the damp—but, as it was hardly enough rain to moisten the ground, and as he was the one enduring any discomfort while I remained warmly wrapped within his arms, I told him to stubble it and to just hold me.

Thus, it was some time before my brain would actually engage enough to question him. When I did, I spoke into his shirtfront, the scent of his shaving soap comforting me, as he leant back against an elderly apple tree.

"You hardly took your leave of me," I whispered. "You might have talked to me about the situation, at least, before you sent me away."

"A man who felt less, might. I thought I was doing the right thing, keeping the vows I made on our wedding day to protect and honour you. I still think it. But never have I done something so abhorrent to my personal desires."

"How unlucky that you should have a reasonable answer to give, and that I should be so reasonable as to admit it. But what was your intention? To stay away indefinitely, had you been left to yourself?"

"I did not really plan it. I am still waiting for Lord Cavendish to return from London. As his daughter is marrying, he seems in no hurry to do so, although I expect he will by Easter. I wanted to see how it would be."

"Tell me why you prefer me to stay away," I demanded.

He briefly clasped me more tightly. "That is never my preference, darling. But I did not marry you only to drag you from one bad situation to a worse one. The talk, the gossip, will be merciless. I believe you better off in Lambton, where I have a few friends and you have many more."

"That might be true, if you were here as well. It can only cause more talk if we live apart. People will say I am afraid of you."

He sighed. "I do not care for myself. But come, it is growing dark and your aunt will be worried. We can discuss this in the warmth of her home."

I was certain I looked an utter wreck—my hair wild, my dress grass-stained. His hat was gone, his neckcloth ruined. I did not, could not care.

"I will not return until you give me your word that whatever we decide, we shall decide *together*."

He was silent for a long moment. "I suppose it matters not what I choose. If you call for me, I will always come."

"However unwillingly," I chided.

"*Too* willingly," he grumbled. "That is the problem. I exercised every bit of restraint I possess. I was as severe and harsh as I know how to be. And yet, you saw right through my guard to the man behind it, who was wishing to do nothing more than throw himself at your feet and beg forgiveness. I shall never know how you could tell." He set me on my feet and searched within the gathering gloom for his missing, probably wrecked hat.

I only smiled, glad he could not see it, and decided I would keep all my secrets at present. Men were so very contrary; a wife needed every clue she could get.

CHAPTER TWENTY-THREE

I ought to have been ashamed of my appearance as we crept back to the house and entered my chamber by a rear door and a servant's stair. I was too happy to feel much chagrin, I admit. However, I could also admit a longing for Clara when I saw myself in the looking glass. There was grass in my unmanageable hair to match the stains upon my gown—there would be no doubt in the mind of my aunt's maid as to what excesses we had been indulging. I must have made some noise of dismay, for my husband appeared behind me in the glass.

"I suppose I must assume all responsibility for such dishevelment," he said, smiling as he extracted a dead leaf from my hair.

"I ought to call Susan for help," I sighed. "My aunt's maid, that is. But she has known me since I was in the nursery, and she will not hesitate to say exactly what she suspects of the origins of such untidiness. Not that she would be so very far from the truth."

But he was not paying overmuch attention to my predicament. Instead, he began removing the remaining pins from my hair, plucking them one by one as he rifled through its masses, his strong fingers searching and his expression, reflected in the mirror, intent. When he'd found them all, he took up my brush.

He had played the lady's maid once before with my hair—although he'd mussed it far more than taming it. It reminded me of what he had said, then, of his attraction to me so long ago, at Netherfield Park. I had not known it, busy as I was hating him at the time—but in the newness of our marriage and intimacy, and the resolution of such an argument as we had been having prior to that moment, I had given little credence to his words.

But now, it seemed...important. I had tried to dismiss his reasons for seeking me out, for finding me at Rosings and then asking for my hand. Convenience, I had believed first. Responsibility, I had believed later. And perhaps it was those things, too. But not solely. Not only.

He wanted me again, though we had only just lost all sense and decorum in the orchard together. His passion for me, for what we had together, was as real as mine for him. It would be a long while before we were ready to make an appearance downstairs.

The children were somewhat in awe of Mr Darcy, for even in ruined neckcloth and wrinkled coat he was a figure of nearly overpowering distinction. His manners were of the most formal and grave sort, which was somewhat quelling to the natural exuberance of youth. However, my aunt—a superb hostess—was able to draw him out a bit, and an excellent meal further compelled the mood towards contentment. Mr Martin was my greatest surprise.

In my presence Mr Martin had always shown himself to be quiet, courteous in manner, and completely unruffled by any problem, no matter what it was. If the cow went off its feed or the well smelled sour or the boys were bickering, he simply…fixed things. My uncle had been a gregarious man, a handsome, generous and intelligent man. He was adored by all who knew him, and his family most of all. But he was not the person whom one might have called upon to restore an aging house to sturdiness, or to show a rambunctious eleven-year-old how to whittle a boat from a stick. I had grown much impressed by Mr Martin's calm, steady manner.

He was different in company with Mr Darcy. With twinkling eyes, he made much of my husband's presence at the table with a sort of exaggerated respect, mostly ruined by his occasional aside regarding the gentry's ability to misplace their wives. To my astonishment, Mr Darcy ignored this as if such teasing were a commonplace. The boys finally made so bold as to question Mr Darcy regarding his mount—evidently a horse with a distinguished lineage, about which Mr Martin and my husband found a great deal to say, and as if they had shared many such discussions over the years upon any number of similar topics.

After dinner, Ellen played for us quite prettily, and I told her of Mrs Bingley's prowess at the instrument and the duets we had been practising. We tried one of them for which Ellen possessed the music, and we laughed together over mistakes —usually mine—but were encored by our audience.

Finally, however, only the four adults remained in the cosy parlour and I grew aware of a tension building within my husband, a certain restlessness within his usual restraint. I was not left long to wonder at its meaning.

"Martin, what do you hear from your nephew? Regarding the current disposition of the villagers?"

Mr Martin sighed. "Better than it once was, but not as good as it should be. I do not think the mistress's absence is helping much. Folks think you chased her away."

"And so he did," I piped in. "And I still have questions as to why!"

Mr Darcy grimaced, but Mr Martin nodded. "In a word, 'Peterloo'," he said.

"Peterloo?" I questioned. "But...but what has that to do with poor Miss Bingley?" Last August, England's calvary had stormed into a crowd of sixty thousand citizens peacefully gathering in St Peter's Field near Manchester to demand political reform and representation in Parliament. Hundreds were injured and more than a dozen died. The papers referred to it as the 'Peterloo Massacre', while I called it horrific no matter its title.

Mr Martin glanced at my husband to see whether he would answer my question, but Mr Darcy's face had turned to stone. "Aye, 'twas a nasty business, and a shameful one as well. In trying to stifle rebellious voices, they only shouted their cause to the world. More than ever, folks want change."

"Change is all well and good," Mr Darcy spoke sternly at last, "but too many are too willing to tear down the old order without reason and stability, using violence to do it. Change takes time, lest more innocents suffer."

"Ah, but time is a luxury when the world is burning," Mr Martin replied. "Ye must convince more of those high and mighty grey heads to listen to ye."

Mr Darcy's grimace tightened. "More would listen, perhaps, if *their* properties were only fifty miles of good road from Manchester."

Mr Martin nodded. "The fact is, not all the owners of

great estates are as benevolent and virtuous as our Mr Darcy here."

"Perhaps I am thick-skulled, but I still do not understand how this relates to Miss Bingley's death," I put in.

"Nor I," my aunt murmured.

Mr Darcy remained silent.

"'Twas the first Mrs Darcy," Mr Martin snapped, showing an annoyance at complete odds with his usual calm demeanour. "Never did think much of her, despite her being so popular with all. That woman cared most about the face in the mirror. I thought it from the first time I saw her and never found any reason to change my mind. Then, just as the papers are full of this Peterloo madness and hatred towards anyone with a bit of blue blood—however benevolent—she up and decides to die, all mysterious-like. Folks are heaping flowers on her grave and crying and carrying on, blaming her husband for her death, even though they've known him all his life and he's never shown aught but kindness towards the lot of them. And Himself, here, refuses to tell a blessed soul how she managed it, instead breeding suspicion and resentment as if such were prized bulls."

Mr Darcy looked away from him, stubbornly, I thought, and Mr Martin sighed and stood. "But here, I'm naught but an old farmer, awake long past my bedtime. Thank you once again, Mrs Gardiner, for your excellent hospitality. Mrs Darcy, Mr Darcy." He bowed in a genteel manner that would have served well at court, and took himself off.

After he left, an awkward silence followed. Mr Darcy was either distracted or brooding, it was impossible to tell which. My aunt and I exchanged looks, and then she said, "I find I am rather tired myself. I shall see you both at breakfast tomorrow?"

Mr Darcy had not, precisely, promised to stay the night;

nor had he promised to take me with him. In fact, he had ridden from Pemberley, probably so there would be no carriage to convey me home. However, I was confident enough in my powers of persuasion to promise her that he would at least still be here in the morning. "You will, Auntie. Good night to you."

My husband stood as she did, bowed, and with perfect correctness, wished her a pleasant sleep; however, the greater part of his attention was not on this room or its occupants. What memories was he lost within? When we were alone once more, I determined not to dance around my questions, but ask them directly.

"The body—did it prove to be Miss Bingley's?"

This recalled him to the present, and he grimaced again. "Yes. I had no doubt of it, of course, for like Bingley, I recognised the rings she always wore. But the scraps of remaining fabric, and the hair colour…yes."

The gruesome vision appearing in my mind made me shudder. "Why would she leave a letter that she meant to elope? Georgiana explained that much, and her apparent *tendre* for the Austrian. I must say, I could hardly countenance her doing such a thing. Unless she had changed a great deal from when I knew her."

He grunted. "No, it was unlike Miss Bingley to behave in such a raggedy manner. But she had been recently humiliated, you see. By me."

I turned sharply towards him, but he did not look at me. Perhaps he could not, and still relive his bitter memories. There had been an argument of some sort, I remembered Georgiana explaining.

"Why?" I asked.

He did not answer, not immediately. Instead he stood,

taking himself to the hearth, grasping the mantel's marbled edge with both hands and staring into the flames.

"Anne knew what she had in me from the first," he said at last. "My pride, you see, would not permit me to allow anyone to know of my misery, or that I was a cuckold. I could not bear it. For many years, most all the years of my marriage, it seemed as though it was all I had—my love for Pemberley, my reputation as its master, my family's honour. It all must be shielded. I could never allow anyone to know of my foolish mistakes. Anne understood all this well before I ever did, understood that as long as she was discreet, I would pretend to the whole world that I was the happiest man in it. Even the servants were fooled. She was expert in deception. Every few days, she would retrieve something of mine—some personal item—and leave it lying in her bed chamber, so the household would believe I visited regularly. And part of me was disgusted by the deceit, but a greater part was relieved she took the trouble."

I did not, exactly, understand why he told me this, or what it had to do with Caroline Bingley's death. But there was such bitterness, such self-disgust in the telling, I did not interrupt, lest I disrupt the purge.

"She would throw magnificent house parties, inviting the crème de la crème of society so she could display her talent for entertaining. It was a dangerous game she played, for sprinkled amongst her illustrious guests might be a lover or two, or at least someone whom she had decided to seduce."

I was revolted, but he had mentioned Thorncroft and its uses to me before. He glanced over at me, his expression full of self-mockery.

"So blatant," I murmured.

"Not really. As I believe I have mentioned, she was clever, well-practised, and inherently deceitful. It took me a long while to figure it out, and some of it, only in retrospect. I knew she was not faithful, but I was dense and naïve about exactly *how* unfaithful she was. I knew about Wickham—whom she claimed to have loved since her youth—and he, of course, was barred from Pemberley. As well, I knew of her spiteful act with Bingley, purposely accomplished to wreck my peace and warn me to what depths she might willingly sink. But no, I formed most of my conclusions in hindsight, and the vast majority of them after Miss Bingley's elop...er, disappearance. That last year of her life, Anne made mistakes she would never have made previously. Mistakes of indiscretion, of recklessness. In the past I have spoken to you as though I understood what I had in her, but truthfully I am convinced I never will."

He had been married for seven years, and yet, he was saying, he had never really known his wife. Part of it, he had previously explained—she had driven him away, manipulated him, deceived him—but I was half convinced he had never really *wanted* to know her. He had made himself try, perhaps until she had fired a cannon into her marriage by means of her liaison with Bingley. The true mystery to me was why in the world he had ever married her in the first place, as I had often wondered.

"My sister told you of the Kroffords?" he asked, interrupting my thoughts.

"Yes. It surprised me, I will admit, to learn that Miss Bingley was still unwed two years ago. I had always believed her committed to the prospect of finding an acceptable partner."

"She did not take particularly well, but it was her own choice," he said grimly. "She had offers."

"Still, she had reached an age when one wishes for a home of one's own," I said. I certainly knew the longing.

"That was to be the purpose of this grand house party, 'the grandest party of 1818', Anne promised. She, who had never cared much for Miss Bingley, was suddenly obsessed with finding her a husband. And Miss Bingley, who had never cared much for Anne, was suddenly eager to spend every moment in her company and seemingly to accept her guidance in affairs of the heart."

"Was it because of Mr Krofford, do you think?"

"That is what I thought at the time. She had been introduced to him during the Season, and he was said to be a catch. Many other women certainly thought so, and I supposed she was competitive. For Anne's motives, I could not say. I distrusted them, but what was I to do? Krofford was accepted in all the best circles, and it was Bingley's duty to investigate him thoroughly." He ran a hand through his thick hair. "I had begun, by then, expecting more independence of Bingley. I *told* him he ought to look carefully into Krofford's concerns, and left it at that. A match seemed imminent."

He left the hearth and sat down beside me again. But his elbows were braced upon his knees, his head bent downwards, his posture, defeated.

"One afternoon, Miss Bingley entered my library when I was alone. Most of the guests were participating in a picnic of some sort, requiring half the household to serve them, so there were none to see her do it. Of course, I asked her why she was not with the others. By way of reply, she burst into tears."

"That…must have been awkward," I said.

He sighed and leant back again, staring at the ceiling. "She told me she loved me—had been *in* love with me for years. That she had no choice but to accept my marriage, and had wished me happy, but obviously I was not, because my wife was a cheat, a liar, a faithless harlot. She had proof, she said."

"Oh, my," I breathed. "How awful."

"Exactly. I told her it was none of her affair, and she ought to mind her own troubles and stay out of mine. I was humiliated, and rather harsh, I am afraid. And she..."

After a pause, he began speaking again very softly. "She offered to become my paramour. She said she did not *want* to love any other, that she had no care for her reputation. She asked for a house—she had picked one out, I believe—within ten miles of Pemberley, and another home in London. A horse and pair, an allowance, servants, and jewels. In return, she would see to my happiness in all...the most intimate of ways."

His cheeks flushed. Plainly, the memory embarrassed him, even now. And how like the Miss Bingley I remembered, to detail her pecuniary requirements along with her illicit proposal!

"And how did she expect you to explain it all to her brother? Her sisters? Your family? Did she really think you would care so little for your reputation as she evidently did for hers?"

He sighed. "I told her it was out of the question. I told her that her brother would kill me, that our sisters would be humiliated and neither would recover from the mortification. She responded that I need not worry about a thing—that Krofford had proposed an elopement, and she would pretend to take him up on it, but would simply escape him at the first busy inn and send word to me where she waited. The world and her family would think her scandalously connected abroad, but she was ready to start afresh. For love only, without rules."

"But with two homes, a carriage, servants, and jewels for comfort."

He smiled sadly. "I did not think of that, so much. She was offering to give up a great deal. It would be stupid not to demand comfort."

A silence stretched between us. I decided to ask what I wished to know. "Were you tempted?"

He looked at me fully, for the first time. "No. I *was* lonely, and I *did* wish for companionship, but she deluded herself in thinking that she would not be recognised ten miles from Pemberley, and gossiped over—as if the scandal would never escape her control—or even that she could be happy in such a situation. Besides myself, Mr and Mrs Bingley would be its victims, as well as the Hursts."

For all her wealth and education, had Miss Bingley clung to the same silly imaginings and unrealistic dreams as Lydia? A man like Wickham would only have taken advantage of such naivety, but I supposed it was unlikely that she had appreciated Mr Darcy's more honourable rejection.

He sighed again. "There were more tears, more pleas, more accusations against Anne, and more…offers. But I simply did not think of her as a lover and never would. It was a foolish dream, such as befitted a much younger, less intelligent, less well-bred female. In a word, it was stupid."

I winced. "I suppose you told her that?"

"Should I have allowed her to keep her silly fantasy alive? Perhaps wait until she chose to compromise herself in a way worse than simply appearing in my library unaccompanied? I thought to nip it in the bud."

I nodded, but it had been far too late for nipping—that bud had taken root over years and years and years.

CHAPTER TWENTY-FOUR

I could see it in his face now, his usual implacable reserve absent—naked guilt. He had picked through his last moments with Caroline Bingley and found much to criticise. It took me back to those hours after learning of the death of my father, the pain I felt at acknowledging the misery of our final conversation.

What I had said to my father had been honest, but it had not been kind. At least in Mr Darcy's case, no one could have expected him to behave otherwise—the *gentlemanly* thing to do was to disabuse Miss Bingley of notions of ruin. But she had boldly addressed his most sensitive concerns, deeply wounding his pride in the process, and he had lashed out in the one manner guaranteed to make her stop. I took his hand in mine.

"Would you like to retire for the night, sir? My aunt's servants are not accustomed to late hours, and I am certain they are standing about, hoping we will go upstairs soon."

Again, his wishes were clear to me—what he *wanted* was

to saddle his horse and ride for Pemberley. Anything to divert his thoughts and feelings away from a subject so painful.

"Please?" I added.

Nodding once, he stood, and helped me to my feet. Silently, we climbed the stairs and returned to my room. He became my lady's maid, and I valeted for him. There was something so intimate in this undressing by firelight; I saw his countenance lighten as he set aside his cares and fixed his attention upon me. I saw, too, how gently he untied every tape and extracted every pin, meticulously laying aside each piece as he removed it.

I had scraped my hair into the tidy bun that was all I could manage on my own, but I knew better than to expect he would leave it be. I decided that I did not much care what Susan had to say about it in the morning, and let him take it down.

Pennywithers would have still more to say to him when he saw the state of Mr Darcy's clothing, but I did my best to lay it out upon the clothespress so it would not wrinkle further, and hang his coat upon the chairback to try and reshape it.

And then we were in each other's embrace as if it had been days instead of hours, caught up in the passion so easily sparked and so carefully nurtured by both. I was a bit sore from our earlier antics, but it was all forgotten in the worshipful attentions of a worshipful husband. Afterwards, I rested in his arms, listening to him breathe.

My bed was small, but neither of us had considered he would sleep elsewhere. I expected him to fall asleep quickly, but I did not wish to slip away from consciousness so easily. I had taken for granted the very great pleasure of lying within the arms of the man I loved. I still did not know what he would yet do, but at least I understood more of why he had made the decisions he had, and that we were more equal in our affections than I had previously believed. It was not all I wished for, but I was content enough nestled up against him, staring into the dying flames. I had nearly dozed off, however, when he spoke again, his voice deep, soft, and tired.

"I truly believed she eloped with Krofford. I swear it to you, I had no notion of any other possibility."

I turned in the circle of his arms to face him in the firelight. Perhaps Georgiana had needed time to consider his innocence, but I never had. "I promise you, sir, I am not one of the Hopewellians, believing the worst of you. That you might have injured Miss Bingley, even by accident, *never* crossed my mind."

"You are one of very few," he said. "But she left a letter stating her intentions to go away with Krofford, and the man and his sister were gone in the morning. Of course, I immediately decided she was trying her plan of pretended elopement, that she had not believed me after all—perhaps that she even expected *me* to chase her down. And so I told Bingley what had occurred between us in every particular. He was horrified and made haste to follow quickly, questioning everyone he could, but they changed hackneys too often and at the busier inns. The postilions had little to say of use, but he did learn there were three who travelled, and the third matched Miss Bingley's description. It was thought that Miss Krofford put her maid on a post. After London, there was nothing. The three of them disappeared without a trace."

"Mr Bingley wrote, your sister said."

"Yes. He obtained their direction in Austria, and Krofford wrote back disclaiming any knowledge of Miss Bingley's whereabouts, denying all accusations. I made enquiries, which took a good deal of time. The most I learned was that Krofford currently keeps a mistress whose description *could* be said to match Miss Bingley's, although she goes by a different name. Bingley sent more letters, begging Krofford to tell his sister to write and assure him she was well. I saw the latest of his letters before he sent it—he informed Krofford that if he wanted her settlement, he must bring her back to England to be wed. He heard nothing else, but...we still had hope that, eventually, he would want her fortune enough to see it done. He never replied. I ought to have known the blackguard would have married her if he could have." He rolled onto his back, and I followed, propping myself upon his chest. "I ought to have done more. I ought to have prevented it. I ought to have *known.*"

I was not quite certain how he expected this. Murder would have been the last thing upon his mind, especially after the sordid scene he had been subjected to from her the day before. "Do you believe...do you believe he killed her?" I asked softly.

He shook his head in the darkness. "No," he said, his voice full of guilt and anguish. "I believe Anne did."

I was shocked. "What? No. Surely she would not!" I gasped.

"It would hardly be surprising," he replied, his voice hard. "After all, she tried to kill me."

There followed several moments of absolute silence while I simply stared at him, shocked speechless.

Why, I am still not certain; it was not as if females were incapable of violence. I had found it within myself, even. Wickham had goaded me sufficiently to visualise a moment of fury and yes, *satisfaction* at the thought of forever ending his ability to cause hurt and pain. I could, as well, envision a lover's quarrel ending tragically, of betrayal and passion culminating in death.

And yet, the thought of poor Miss Bingley involved in any such torrid episode was unimaginable. Even her proposal to Mr Darcy offering a forbidden liaison had been somewhat off-putting, with her list of practical requirements for property and wealth. No, it appeared she had been cold-bloodedly murdered, buried in a shallow grave, and—as if that were not horrible enough—her reputation mercilessly destroyed at the same time. And he believed his *wife* had been perfectly capable of perpetrating both.

"How? Why?" I asked incredulously, still unable to manage a coherent sentence.

But instead of answering me, he looked away. "I should not have mentioned it. Needless to say, she was unsuccessful in her attempt, and I have no proof, regardless. If it *was* she who harmed Miss Bingley, no one will believe it upon my say so."

I did not much care for either his vague reply or bleak conclusion; it was as if Anne held a pitiless power over him, even in death. I wished that speaking openly of her was not so difficult for him, that he was not so accustomed to keeping her secrets that he recoiled from revealing them even now. Still, I understood it. The deepest hurts seldom lend themselves to easy speech; they are wounds that bite and sting when poked.

Even so, I might have protested his response, except next he did an odd thing: suddenly, he clutched me to him, so tightly, I almost could not breathe. His heart pounded wildly beneath my ear, his own breath coming unevenly. Startled, I nevertheless moulded myself against him, holding him just as tightly in return, trying to think what I could say; the urge to comfort bested the yearning to prod.

He had suffered more than any man ought to have endured, in the darkness of that marriage. I tried to remember Anne de Bourgh's appearance from my brief view of the miniature in Lady Matlock's possession, but it had receded into hazy memory. An impression of beauty, of golden hair, and pale, perfect skin was all that remained. Knowing what I now did, would I still see loveliness of countenance? Would there be any hint of madness or murderous impulse? And why was it, the thought occurred to me, that I had not noticed her portrait when I had visited the cliffside wing's upper floor? Mrs Reynolds had indicated it had been put in one of the closed rooms, but I had been through them all now without ever noticing it. It had not been removed to Mrs de Bourgh's chamber. I certainly could not have missed it *there*.

Well, I would solve the mystery when I returned home—hopefully soon. *Hopefully* tomorrow, for I was certain Mr Martin could procure a vehicle. And it was time that I redid those upper rooms of the cliffside wing, repurposed them entirely. I was not certain yet for what, but it would come to me. They must be cleared of everything—every stick of furniture, every vase, every candlestick—and completely refurbished. If I could not erase those unhappy years for him, I could at least destroy the monument that upper floor had become to their memory.

"When we return home, I shall need the keys to the upper floor of the cliffside wing," I began to explain, but he interrupted me, rearing back so abruptly that I toppled off his chest.

"I know you understand my preference that you keep away from it," he said, in a rough tone which raised my hackles.

"You *are* an unlucky husband," I snapped, struggling to a

sitting position. "Your first wife was a sordid murderess, and your second—why, 'tis even worse! *She* insists upon entering any room in her home, at any time she wishes!"

The moment the words left my mouth, I regretted how quickly I had turned from patience and comfort to snappish vexation. But before I could apologise, he flopped back down onto the mattress and drew me into his arms, sighing, his large hand smoothing up and down my stiff spine, his hold comforting instead of his previous frantic embrace.

"I am a great trial to you, am I not?" he asked.

"For as long as we both shall live," I agreed acerbically.

"I am sorry, my darling," he said. "Even now, I have not yet accommodated Miss Bingley's death in my mind. I knew my marriage was a bad one. I knew we were in every way unsuited. I thought I understood all the mistakes for which I was responsible. And yet, it appears I have barely scratched the surface."

I wanted to tell him to let it go, let *her* go. But of course, the past could no more stay buried than poor Miss Bingley. It all must be resolved. Somehow.

I tucked my head beneath his chin, feeling his fingers stroking through my hair, revelling in his return to my side. I would not lose him to my impatience, or to Anne's sins. "This is the proper moment for me to offer just the right words of solace and relief. If you could, perhaps, pretend to have heard them?"

He brushed his thumb along my cheek. "Your very presence does it," he said. "I know I am the most fortunate of men in my second marriage. You...you understand I realise it, do you not?"

It was hardly a burning declaration of love, but its simple, awkward sentiment touched me regardless.

"I want to go home," I whispered. "And I want it to be *our* home. I...I hate feeling as if she owns part of it, even still."

And part of your soul, I thought but did not say.

"You heard Martin. There is talk. Talk about Miss Bingley now, as well as Anne. In Hopewell I was labelled abusive before, but I am henceforth to be branded the murderous Darcy. If you support me, if you stay beside me, you shall be dragged into it. The cartoonists in London have already begun to sell their work. When Lord Cavendish returns, he will not be able to avoid a public inquest, much as he would rather not. He is delaying, I am certain, hoping if he misses addressing it at the next quarter-day, it will fade away. It will not, and all my wealth will not protect me. Or you."

I felt the tension in him as he tried, with all his gentleman's heart, to convince me of my greater comfort and safety if I stayed in Lambton. As he pleaded with me to do the very opposite of what *I knew* he wanted, I smoothed my hand across the hard planes of his chest. "I am your wife," I said at last. "I wish to go home."

There was a long silence. He did not answer. I thought he had fallen asleep, and I nearly had.

"I know the rooms on that floor must be redone," he said into the night's darkness. "I would rather not live in them again, though. I do not believe its terrace to be safe, and hope you would stay off of it. If it would not ruin its architectural beauty, I would wall it off entirely. But I will give you every key I have. Tomorrow. When we arrive...home. Together."

And somehow, despite murderous mysteries, refused revelations, and a foggy future, I found a sleepy smile as I dropped quickly into dreams.

Late the next morning, I bid my aunt, my niece and nephews, and Mr Martin a fond farewell and boarded a comfortable carriage the latter had somehow produced. My husband said little, and I wondered if he regretted his decision allowing my return to Pemberley. I refused to think of it.

"This carriage is unusually fine," I remarked into the silence, only the sound of wheels against road and the horses' hooves between us.

He glanced around as if only just noticing it. "'Tis Martin's own," he muttered.

"Ah," I said. "He certainly prospers, if he can afford such a vehicle."

For the first time that morning, he unbent a little. "I did not think Mrs Gardiner would be long in guessing his ruse, but he wrote to me when she did. It lasted longer than I thought it would. He said you guessed immediately he was no pockets-to-let."

"My aunt was grieving and distracted. And I only guessed in part. I did not expect such a person to patch roofs. Is he in love with her, do you think?"

He looked mildly alarmed, and I laughed. "Very well, I shall not question you. I would not blame him if he is, for she is the very best of women. I hope he is prepared for patience if so, however, for she is hardly done grieving. If you had ever seen my uncle and aunt together…" A wave of the sorrow which at times so easily beset me stopped my words.

Reaching over, he took my gloved hand in his. "I never met your uncle in person, but by all accounts, he was a fine man, and he was certainly a wise and gifted businessman. I do not know Martin's feelings, but he is a much more cheerful fellow than the man I approached a year ago for advice upon hiring workers in Lambton. I could not have dreamt his solution, but I was pleased to see him take an interest in anything at all. He was so lost when his wife died."

"I hope neither is hurt, but I shall not worry overmuch. They are both of them happier together than they were alone. But will his lands suffer without him?"

Mr Darcy told me of Martin's very competent bachelor nephew, who had been entrusted with the extensive farming operations while his twenty-year-old son continued to expand his knowledge and experience with Matlock's stewards. He also spoke of the other tenants, some of whom were newer but many of whom had been with him for generations. They were not all as prosperous as the Martins, who were educated and affluent, but his goal was that all those who desired to prosper, might.

Unfortunately, as we began the twists and turns that marked the mountain road to Pemberley, I felt the change in atmosphere between us. Distraction would not work, I knew. It was better to broach the subject directly.

"When Lord Cavendish returns, what do you expect him to do? Will he take your part?"

"He will wish to, but he, too, understands what Peterloo meant. Gone are the days when a man with wealth enough might do as he pleases without repercussion, whatever my learned friends in the House of Lords believe. Especially as far north as we are, one cannot make enemies of everyone simply because one wishes to protect a friend."

I was not quite certain this was correct—certainly Matlock existed as it ever had and seemed always would. But perhaps change was in the air. And he believed it enough for both of us.

"Lord Cavendish will hold an inquest," I said, making it a statement rather than a question.

"I suppose he must," he replied. "In the matter of Miss Bingley, certainly, but perhaps for Anne, as well."

"You fear that everyone will learn how Anne died?" I asked, trying to understand.

"Hardly," he said, making a disgusted noise. "I fear all will learn how she lived."

I still could not comprehend it; I could not care less if the world learnt of her iniquities.

"Is...is Lord Cavendish a good man? Is he a friend?"

"A very good man. Has known me all of my life." He turned and looked at me directly for the first time in a while. "I went to fetch him, you know. When I left you so abruptly and went to London. I wished him to-to vouch for my integrity when you learned of Hopewell's opinion of it. But he was not in London, he was at some house party or another. And before he returned, you wrote to me and so I returned home."

This astonished me—that he had felt the need to bring in *a witness* to his character. To me, his own wife. That he had travelled all the way to London to seek out one of Derbyshire's most respected residents, hoping the man would assure me of his worthiness—as if he *required* a reference. As if believing his own word would not be good enough for me. What a humiliation that would have been for him! I could hardly credit it.

"I am glad he was not in London, then," I said. "I do not believe it is possible to hide one's true self, not without creating a good deal of real distance. At least not for long. And I trust my own judgment of your honour."

His expression remained solemn. "I could not bear for you to be afraid of me, not for one minute. I only thought to bring you reassurance."

I should not have been so surprised; such actions were

the essence of who he was. As we approached the house, I was overwhelmed by memories—some that had not crossed my mind in almost a decade, but now which I could never forget.

I pictured the ball at Netherfield, so many years ago, as if it were yesterday; the grandeur, the elegance, even the dress worn by Miss Bingley, a fashionable ensemble I had deeply envied, though I hoped I did not show it. It was also the peak of my stupid infatuation with Wickham, and I had believed my evening spoilt by his absence. I blamed Mr Darcy for it, resented having to dance with him—might even have taken the ruinous step of refusal but for Charlotte's reproof when she saw what was in my face; she warned me not to be a simpleton. I spent the entirety of the set subtly castigating him, taunting him about Wickham, and accusing him of aloofness, prejudice, and inconsideration.

"It is particularly incumbent on those who never change their opinion, to be secure of judging properly at first."

"May I ask to what these questions tend?"

"Merely to the illustration of your character," said I. "I am trying to make it out."

Of course, I had judged wrongly then, as had most of the county. As did most of the countryside now. It was no wonder he should expect a similar mistake. A wave of sadness surged through me, that such an ill performance should have been the only dance we had ever shared. The carriage drew to a halt, and as he moved to exit, I caught his hand.

"I could never fear you, and never will. In the future, I only ask that you talk to me first, before you decide upon any action either taking you from me, or taking me from you. Please."

He did not answer me, only squeezing my hand in what

was meant, I suppose, as reassurance. It frightened me, almost; the next time, he might destroy our marriage, if he truly thought it best for me. Well, I would not let him, I vowed. Whatever power I held with him, I would use it to *keep* him.

CHAPTER TWENTY-FIVE

E state business almost immediately called Mr Darcy away. Mr Williams greeted me in his usual kindly, shy manner, but it was the response of the servants which pleased me most. Almost every one of them managed to take time to greet me during the day, and Mrs Reynolds was nearly beside herself with what seemed like gladness. Nothing would do but that she send someone to fetch Clara, change the menu to my favourites, and continually ask what else she could do for my comfort.

Clara, too, once she arrived, was nearly as gleeful to be returned.

"I apologise for the lack of notice," I said to her. "I told Mrs Reynolds tomorrow or the next day would be soon enough."

"Don't mind it a bit," Clara replied firmly. "I like my family, but I was beginning to worry you might never return, and then what would I do? This is the best place I've ever had." And then she took great pains over my hair, until it looked better than it had in weeks.

"I have missed you, Clara," I said, peering at my reflection with a happy sigh.

One person, of course, was not part of my welcoming committee. Steeling myself, I tapped on the door of Mrs de Bourgh's sitting room. Mr Donavan, thankfully, was not there, but instead the solemn, pinched-face nurse; she looked as displeased at the interruption as he ever had.

"Mrs de Bourgh is having a bad spell today," she said. "It is not advisable that she be disturbed."

Especially by you, her look seemed to add. I did not take it for cowardice that I merely shrugged and left. I was too happy to be home to allow anyone's hatefulness to intrude.

The keys Mr Darcy had given me before he departed with Mr Williams demanded my attention. After leaving Mrs de Bourgh's rooms, I made my way to the nearest staircase leading to the cliffside wing's upper floor.

On my first visit to these 'hallowed halls', it had appeared as though Anne de Bourgh Darcy was only away, and all was kept in readiness for her return. On my next, the dead flowers and eerie draughtiness made it seem the perfect rooms for a ghost.

This time, it was merely empty. Mrs Reynolds and her workers had cleared everything from the former Mrs Darcy's rooms; not a stick of furniture remained, neither console nor clothespress. The hand-wrought crystals of the massive chandelier at its centre still tinkled softly upon an invisible breeze, but the mirrors had all been removed.

While they had not touched Mr Darcy's furnishings, I decided I would have those removed as well. Perhaps he would like to retain the picture of the dog, but I could not imagine him wishing for any of the rest of it. How had she felt, stealing into these rooms, leaving behind one of her handkerchiefs or a ribbon in the game of pretend she had maintained for so long? Taunting and triumphant, or despairing and depressed? What perceptions had driven her upon such a course? I wondered, even, if her love for Wickham had been at the root of it all, if he had taught her, too young, to tread such a miserable path.

No, there were too many terrible memories contained within these rooms, and they all required a completely new purpose. I returned to Anne's bedchamber, shivering a little at the chill, trying to see it with new eyes. The drapes were closed, preventing any of the March sun from reaching within, and cloaking the room in gloom. I pulled them back and sunlight flooded in.

That was when I noticed a set of gold velvet draperies covering one wall, against which the enormous carved wooden bedstead had once been positioned. Walking forward, I pulled them aside.

A set of three outsized portraits in expensive gilded frames hung behind them. In one, a pretty girl of perhaps twelve years stood beside an impressive-looking stallion. Her eyes were bright, her expression intelligent. The second was a much larger version of the miniature I had seen in Lady Matlock's possession, a ravishingly beautiful woman with golden hair and adorned in diamonds, wearing wedding clothes. The third must have been painted not long before her death. Still beautiful, even stunningly so, the artist had captured her sultry expression, a certain knowledge of her own feminine powers. Nothing in any of the portraits revealed a hint of the character Mr Darcy had sketched. With a sigh, I walked out onto the terrace that my husband hated.

The view was beautiful, even on this grey and gloomy day. The magnificent sky above, the sprawling valley below, all that was pleasing to the eye and heart dwelt here in one breath-taking prospect. Giving way to temptation, I moved closer to the low wall, where the bold Anne de Bourgh had loved to sit perched over its edge, heedless of peril. Or was she courting danger, the thrill of it, the only way her cold heart could feel alive?

To this day, I do not know what instinct made me suddenly turn. But there was Mrs de Bourgh, closer than I could have imagined; although leaning heavily upon a stout cane, she had made no noise in her approach.

"You were looking at her, were you not? Pretending you were her. *Wishing* you were her. I cannot blame you for that. She was the envy of every woman."

She had lost at least three stone, and a bandage covered one side of her face; what skin was visible was pinched and sallow. The nurse had not been lying to me—her patient looked very ill indeed.

"Mrs de Bourgh! You ought to be abed," I said, surprised. "You are ill."

"I am well enough. I have come to a decision. You are not to be blamed for attempting to take her place. You did not know, when you wed, the impossibility," she rasped regally. "I am too old to change easily. I shall live out my days at Pemberley, as few as they are likely to be. It is where I am closest to her. I must remain and mourn her, here."

Well. This 'offer' was somewhat astonishing. Her version of an olive branch, I supposed. Looking at her, scarred and sickly, my heart filled with pity. The part of my soul that was wearied to death of conflict wanted to accept it.

"I am sorry for you, and for your sorrow," I said, knowing my sympathy was unwanted. I walked past her and back through the door I had left open, into Anne's former bedchamber, hoping it would encourage her to come in out of the cold. "I hope you will understand that I bear you no ill will when I say that I feel your departure is best for your welfare as well as ours. I also hope you will take your daughter's portraits with you when you are well enough to travel, that they might always bring you comfort."

Her one good eye narrowed as she followed me. "You believe you can erase her from Pemberley just as you removed her belongings, her pretty things, her slippers and her dresses. But she is still here! She made Pemberley the grand home it ought to be, and it needs her, yearns for her! Though every servant in the place calls you by her name, you will never be Mrs Darcy!"

I sighed. "Mrs de Bourgh, you have admitted her unhappiness in her marriage to Mr Darcy. Why would you wish her to remain here, the scenes of such despair? If she hated him, why do you not take her back? Return her to her childhood home, where she was once happy and free."

"Pemberley was *hers*," she hissed. "Pemberley was everything. Even Mr Darcy understood it before he grew so foolish and weak. *Pemberley* was the prize, and it belonged to her! It belongs to her, still! She made it what it is, and she *is* Pemberley!"

I swallowed another sigh. "I am Mrs Darcy at the moment, but a century from now, God willing, there will be a different Mrs Darcy caring for it. We are none of us Pemberley, and Pemberley is not us. We Mrs Darcys must stand upon our own lives and loves, our own aspirations and accomplishments, just as Pemberley stands upon its foundations. Without those things, I am as empty as these rooms. I hope, most sincerely, that your daughter will be remembered fully by those who loved her, and not merely as the mistress of a house, however grand."

For a moment, uncertainty crossed her expression, as if a part of her mind could see the sense in what I said. But it was quickly gone. And swiftly, before I could step away, she spat at me, a glob of spittle just missing my boot.

I rolled my eyes. "A childish display that changes nothing. I will call for someone to assist you in returning to your rooms. You should not be out of bed." Matching words to action, I tugged on a nearby bell rope.

She just stood there, staring at me, breathing hard. I wondered, in fact, whether I should do something more, for she looked as if she might topple over. However, even in her present state of distress, she would probably prefer dropping to the floor rather than accepting my assistance.

A maid and a footman, both a bit out of breath, appeared from doorways at the opposite ends of the room.

"Mrs de Bourgh requires assistance returning to her room," I said, nodding at the footman.

"She forced me to come up here," she croaked, wailing. "I told her it was too much, I was too ill. But she insisted. And then, all she cared to do was taunt me with my poor, dear dead daughter's portraits. She threatens to burn them. My poor, poor, pretty girl." Great tears dripped from her chin. "And then she spat at me. I will never call her 'Mrs Darcy'. Never!"

"Please help Mrs de Bourgh," I repeated calmly. "And do give her nurse a message from me—she must keep a closer eye upon her charge. She ought not to have been allowed to climb the stairs alone."

The footman, John, tentatively approached the elderly lady, holding out his arm. For a moment she drew back, and I thought she would refuse it. Then, remembering she was supposed to be an injured party, she took it and slowly limped from the room. I turned to the maid, whose mouth was gaping.

"Martha, please clean up Mrs de Bourgh's, er, emanation

upon the floor," I said, pointing to the mess at my foot with a raised brow.

I saw her face clear as she realised just who had spat upon whom. Mrs de Bourgh had overplayed her hand. Again. "And ask Mrs Reynolds to come upstairs when you have finished, please."

Upon her departure, I took a somewhat shaky breath. Had she truly believed I could allow her to remain at Pemberley? Or was Mrs de Bourgh not quite so much the invalid as her appearance indicated? Had she slipped away from her attendants to recommence her visits to her daughter's rooms? Had seeing them stripped bare set off even darker impulses?

Sighing, I abandoned contemplation of the problem of Mrs de Bourgh in favour of a different matter entirely. Walking the length of the room, the dressing room, the sitting room, then through the same set of rooms on Mr Darcy's side, I considered them all carefully. I also looked in on all the rooms on the wing's other side, to which I had paid little attention in the past. By the time Mrs Reynolds joined me, I had the beginnings of an idea.

"Mistress, Martha told me what has happened here. I am so sorry. I had no idea the old lady was strong enough to dress, even. Her nurse says she only dozed off for a few minutes and her patient was gone when she awakened."

"Hmm. Did she ring for assistance in finding her patient?"

"She did not, ma'am." I could tell by her tone that she, like me, was not overly impressed with the nurse's performance. "I have stationed John in her corridor and will ensure, henceforth, someone is always there."

"Very good. I was looking at her daughter's portraits

before she entered," I said, gesturing at the pictures. "I am afraid the sight of them reminded her of all she has lost."

"Perhaps, but it is kind of you to say so, mistress, after her treatment of you."

"She is elderly and ill," I replied, which was true—but I was also fairly certain her grief had evolved to the worst kind of bitterness, and well before she had injured herself. "I cannot decide whether these portraits are better hung in Mrs de Bourgh's rooms, or if it would only exacerbate her, er, condition."

Mrs Reynolds looked pained. "I asked the master, ma'am, when you were away, what he would like me to do with them when we cleared these rooms." She hesitated.

"What did he reply?" I asked, curious.

"He said to put them anywhere I liked, as long as he never had to see them again. I am afraid the attics are too damp. I know they were painted by masters, costing ever so."

I came to a decision then. Normally, I would not share any such personal details, but the housekeeper had long since proven her devotion to Mr Darcy. "Mrs Reynolds, I tell you something now in the strictest confidence, something I am not sure Mr Darcy would care for you to know. His first marriage was terribly unhappy, for him at least. I suppose that the reasons for that no longer matter but you advised me once of your opinion that Mr Darcy is a good man. I would say he is the *best* of men, and has borne much while attempting to…"

I stumbled to an awkward halt, my throat closing at the thought of the pain he had endured for so long. She placed a gentle hand upon my arm.

"I understand," she said. "The master had been so… quiet, for so long, I simply grew to think it was his way. I always thought him content, until he brought you home and

I saw what happiness looked like on him. And then, while you were gone visiting your aunt, he grew sombre again so quickly, and I knew, somehow, you took his happiness with you."

I smiled at her, for it seemed to me he was always a quiet man—how much more silent could he have been? "He did not want me to be affected by the gossip," I explained. "He thought removing me to my aunt's would protect me from it. I insisted upon returning, but he worries, still. Lord Cavendish will be home within a few weeks, and I believe he fears a siege once the coroner's inquisition begins."

"I cannot believe it. I have heard the silly rumours, but surely not an inquest? They would not dare question Mr Darcy of Pemberley!"

"An inquest would reveal nothing," I said, "because he has done nothing wrong. He is no murderer. There is no evidence. He cannot be held accountable simply because no one has any better idea of who harmed poor Miss Bingley." I took a deep breath. I had not called the woman upstairs to alarm her but rather because I wished to speak of my ideas to someone who loved Pemberley as Mr Darcy did, and as I was beginning to.

"I will not fret about the future. I wanted to speak to you of a different matter entirely, regarding refurbishing these rooms. I have a design in mind, but we will need architectural assistance and a good builder in order to make some major alterations here. It is long past time, I think, for change."

As I revealed my ideas for this wing, and as I saw her dawning excitement at my account of them, I was encouraged to be excited as well. Perhaps Mr Darcy would also approve, and the work of change and renewal could transform even this hated scene of too many awful memories.

But to this day, a small, superstitious part of my nature wonders whether the very act of speaking of such plans and future hopes within the self-same spaces once presided over by Anne de Bourgh Darcy caused more trouble, after all.

Lady Day came and went, with no Lord Cavendish—sending a clear signal, I hoped, that he was in no hurry to act on the matter of poor Miss Bingley. Nevertheless, the reprieve could not be extended indefinitely, and he presented himself at Pemberley shortly after Easter. It was a surprise to find myself a participant in the conversation between he and Mr Darcy. I had been writing letters in the library, my favoured room, while my husband worked quietly at his desk. We often spent afternoons thus occupied, after he and his secretary or Mr Williams were finished for the day. Once every so often, Mr Darcy would say, "Listen to this," and proceed to read me a portion of some treatise or article he found interesting—be it agricultural, trade, or politics. He never assumed I would not understand, nor hesitated to answer my questions if I did not. It was my favourite time of day, and I resented the interruption when Morton brought a visitor's card to Mr Darcy.

His face lost all expression, returning to its most implacable. I realised, then, who the visitor must be. I stood, meaning to excuse myself.

But Mr Darcy came to stand beside me. "Please stay," he said, as Morton announced Lord Cavendish.

He looked nothing like my imagination had painted him: grey-bearded, portly, elderly and dignified. Rather, he was a short, wiry, restless, soft-voiced man not yet fifty, with a peculiarly penetrating stare. Introductions were performed and he scrutinised me with fixed intensity for a longish moment; I fought the urge to look away.

"Mrs Darcy," he said at last, "how do you find Pemberley? Are you settling in? I heard you have been away, visiting, an aunt, is it? But of course, we are more remote here, so close to the Peaks. Not everyone can be happy without convivial society."

"I would be a foolish woman indeed if I could not be happy at Pemberley," I replied. "But of course, the wife of Mr Darcy must have such extraordinary sources of happiness necessarily attached to her situation, that she could, regardless of any lack of welcome from her neighbours, have no cause to repine."

He looked a bit startled at this rejoinder, and I was surprised to feel my husband's touch at my waist—he was so seldom publicly demonstrative.

"Yes," he nodded. "Well put. I see, Darcy, that you have chosen more wisely this time."

My brows rose at this obvious disparagement of Anne; perhaps her legendary charm had failed her, for once?

"Have you told her yet what you had in the first one?" Cavendish asked.

"She knows," he answered stiffly.

"'Tis a fine mess you have landed in this time. Unlucky man! The Scriptures declare you reap what you sow! *You* sow nothing but trouble! Why is that?" He glared at my husband as if he expected an answer, which irked me.

"'Naked came I out of my mother's womb, and naked shall I return thither: the Lord gave, and the Lord hath taken away; blessed be the name of the Lord'," I quoted mildly. If he was here to accuse with Scripture, I would be happy to argue with him in a language he could understand.

It was his turn to be taken aback, before giving a sharp

bark of laughter. "Very well, very well," he grumbled. "I know you do not deserve it. But Darcy, I cannot stop it. Too many untamed tongues, and what with the latest foolishness from the House of Lords, well..."

"Why should we care if there *is* an inquest?" I demanded. "Mr Darcy surely has nothing to fear, for he has done nothing wrong!"

He only looked at me sadly. "Of course he has not," he said. "But what does it matter? I shall hold an inquisition. Evidence shall be presented that a blade, presumably the murder weapon, was found with the body. The blade is engraved with your husband's initials. It is, by his own admission to me, a blade he once kept in the desk of this very room."

I froze, not having understood that there was *any* evidence implicating Mr Darcy. But Lord Cavendish continued speaking, pacing back and forth across the library.

"You, Darcy, will testify that it has been missing for two years, and that you have no idea who took it from your library. Conjecture and rumour shall be presented. I will mention the names of all of the numerous persons, including every single individual who attended the house party during the summer of 1818, the last time Miss Bingley was seen, and who had access to this library, which is kept unlocked. I will call attention to the fact that though the blade was found with the body, due to the state of the corpse, there is no actual evidence proving it to be the murder weapon. I shall point out that it would be a stupid man, indeed, who would bury such incriminating evidence with the body on his own property, when a shrewder one could just as easily have replaced it in his desk drawer. I will emphasise that you were the one who gave orders for your steward, Mr Williams, to dig in the very area where the body was buried. I shall declare a verdict of death by unlawful killing, by a person or persons unknown."

He stopped pacing and looked at us both. "And it will not matter. You will be beset by conjecture and rumour and innuendo for the rest of your life. Worse, your pretty wife will endure it, and your future children as well. I ask you, Darcy, to tell the truth. Cease protecting a woman who is dead and buried. Sadly, no one truly cares about Miss Caroline Bingley. No one liked her, no one missed her, and that is the hard truth of the matter. They *cared* for Anne Darcy, and they wonder how she died. Tell them the truth, *all* of it. Give the world something else to talk about."

He stared hard at my husband. Mr Darcy's face had not changed, wearing that same rigid expression he'd worn when putting me in a carriage, sending me away from him against every softer feeling he possessed. *Obstinate, headstrong, man.*

Lord Cavendish saw it too. He stalked from the room.

CHAPTER TWENTY-SIX

I stood silent in my surprise, and turned to Mr Darcy.

His jaw firmed, the only movement in his otherwise rigid posture. But something in what Lord Cavendish had said struck me as significant: "Cease protecting a woman who is dead and buried."

Why in heaven's name would he protect Anne de Bourgh at the expense of his current wife and future children's happiness? I did not understand; but then, he would not allow me to. A wave of what might have been despair—and what was certainly anger—threatened my peace of mind. I wanted to storm out of the room like Lord Cavendish, perhaps throw things in my fury. I wanted to rage at him for all those secrets he held so dear. Somehow, I forced myself to calm.

Instead, sighing, I went to the settee nearest the hearth, sitting in front of the fire and staring into the flames. I did not know what he would do—leave, or go back to his desk and his letters and papers and pretend the conversation had not happened? Or, perhaps, was this why he had wanted me to stay for Lord Cavendish's call—so that I would be fore-warned how it would be? So that I would more willingly leave him? It was most disheartening.

However, he did none of those things. After several silent moments, he took a seat close beside me. Even, he took my hand in his own much larger one. It was so unexpected—and I was so relieved, after my dreary thoughts—that I scooted nearer to him, laying my head upon his shoulder.

"You have questions, I am certain, about Anne's death. Because you have never asked them, I once thought you did not care to know the answers. Or, perhaps, you were afraid of the answers. I want you to know that I no longer believe either of those suppositions to be true. I rather believe you have patiently granted me my privacy until such time as I would more readily tell you the truth."

"Not always patiently," I admitted.

He let go of my hand to reach his arm around me, drawing me more firmly into his embrace. I could hear his heart thundering beneath my ear, the only sign of his distress. "In order to explain what I know of it, I must now mention circumstances which I would wish to forget myself, and which no obligation less than my duty to you should induce me to unfold to any human being. Having said this much, I feel no doubt of your secrecy."

I nodded, feeling his lips brush briefly against the side of my head. His phrasing puzzled me—'what I know of it'? Did he not know all? Some moments passed as he seemed to struggle to put his thoughts into words.

"The end began, I suppose, the afternoon she marched into my chambers and announced that she was ready to bear my child."

I blinked up at him, and he grimaced. "She was expert at impediments to pregnancy, and had made it clear on our wedding night that she did not mean to have children any time soon."

"Oh," I said. "I was not aware there were ways to prevent it."

"They are not always effective, but if one is cautious enough, they might be. I suppose I ought to have told you of them, in case you wished to delay. I am afraid I have been selfish, hoping to make a family with you."

"I have no wish for delay," I replied, looking away. "But... perhaps you are disappointed that I have not yet conceived."

He tipped my chin up and bent to kiss me, a deep tenderness within the motion. "Of course not," he said at last. "If it is to be only you and me, I will still be the happiest of men. There is nothing you could do to displease me, except to lose all patience with me."

A weight lifted, a worry I had never acknowledged slipping away. I took a deep breath, and let it go. "So, she proclaimed her readiness for motherhood," I said. "Did that cause so great a disgust within you? As you had not repudiated her, she could have become with child in any of her, er, liaisons, bringing you another man's offspring."

He let out a long sigh. "I suppose I should start even further back in time—when I learned exactly what pleasing her in the bedchamber required. I hope you will forgive me for being so coarse, but I fear you will not understand unless I am exceedingly blunt. She had a-a disgust of tenderness. She wished...she wished for pain."

"What?" I looked up at him with some confusion; I did not understand. He explained further, though trying for delicacy. I had never in my life heard of such doings, and I confessed my revulsion.

"I admit, I do not truly understand either. I have known some, however, who have predilections that are unusual, and it does not render them evil, if both partners are willing. I will also acknowledge that I tried to-to more gently administer the punishments she demanded. It only infuriated her. I could not do it. What she needed in order to be, er, satiated, ruined every part of the union for me. We were as unsuited to be man and wife as two people could possibly be. I believed it was why she was unfaithful, you see. That she sought out partners who possessed similar...preferences."

I shook my head, not in disbelief, but incredulity. It was too strange. And then an awful thought occurred to me. "Both Wickham and Mrs de Bourgh claimed to have hinted to the neighbourhood of your supposed abuse of Mrs Darcy. Could it be that she *encouraged* such abuse, and then blamed *you* for it?"

"For most of our marriage, she was extremely discreet, but that last year, well...yes, it became something of a game to her, hinting to others at the reasons for her bruises. My reputation was being slowly shattered."

"You sound defensive of her choices, but she harmed you," I shuddered. "However... *titillating,* I cannot believe violence, especially intimate violence, to be healthy or natural."

"No, no, I do not mean to sound as though I endorsed her preferences; I only wish to make you understand that it was not her predilections upon which my dislike was founded. Long before I discovered her first affair, my opinion of her was decided. It was her insensitivity, her manipulations, her disloyalty and arrogance, her conceit and selfish disdain for the feelings of others, which were such as to form that groundwork of disapprobation, on which succeeding events built to an immoveable dislike. I found nothing, utterly nothing, I could respect in her, and her sexual preferences were the least of it."

There was little I could say to this. I felt awful for what he had endured, and continued to endure, at her hands. I could only tuck myself in closer within his sheltering arms, and hope he could feel relief within that simple connexion. After several moments of silence, he spoke again.

"But as I told you, she approached me in my chambers boldly demanding a child. I am still dumbfounded by her tactic, as she usually showed great skill in conversation, especially in manipulation of a person from whom she wanted something. Upon reflection, I am convinced that by that point, she no longer truly even saw me as a man, only as an object controlling something she wished to be hers."

"What did she say to you?"

"'In vain have I struggled. It will not do. My feelings will not be repressed. You must allow me to tell you how ardently I wish my child to be a Darcy,'" he repeated woodenly.

I flinched at her tastelessness.

"I was beyond expression. I stared, coloured, doubted, and was silent. This she considered sufficient encouragement, and then was not more eloquent on the subject of my suitability for fatherhood than of her deeply rooted dislike. She hated me, my judgmental attitudes, my inability to allow her the freedoms she required. In one sentence, she expressed how much she wished her children to be handsome, intelligent, responsible, and constant, as she admitted my virtues; in the next, how she had struggled to conquer any such consideration. She had nearly allowed Wickham to get her with child a dozen times, she said, wholly for the delicious irony of it. But his birth was not high enough, and she demanded better blood in any child of hers."

I felt sickened, his tone impassive as he continued his revelations, and could only stroke his broad chest in a small attempt at comfort.

"I was disgusted, as you might imagine. I attempted, at first, to simply end the conversation, but she was determined to press on, until I was roused to such resentment as I could hardly bear. Incredibly enough, I could easily see that she had no doubt of a favourable answer. She spoke of wishing forgiveness for her past indiscretions—and anxiety lest I could not give it—but her countenance expressed real security, so certain was she that I longed for a child of my own. She did not understand that I had discarded any such dreams years before."

"How did you respond?"

He sighed again. "I thought it most likely that she was already with child. Believe me, I had considered the possibility a thousand times. And despite her denunciation of his birth and station, I thought it even odds it *was* Wickham's get—I had heard rumours he was in the area, and I had no doubt she had been with him. But one cannot possess a faithless wife and fail to plan for such an outcome. I had already determined what I would do years before. To tell you the truth, it was almost a relief that the day had finally come, I had dreaded it for so long. And it was not so bad, truly, as I had once believed it would be. My feelings towards her had ceased to be full of hurt or hatred—mostly indifference."

"What had you decided?" I asked, curious. "There are probably not a dozen men in the kingdom who could greet such news with apathy."

"Not apathy, not really. Only a sort of fatalistic acceptance. I told her that I would welcome a child, but it would never be my own. I had already made my will. Pemberley would go to Georgiana and her heirs, if any, but I promised I would not *openly* repudiate any children she brought to me, that I would see to their education and careers, and if female, their settlements. That I would protect them from her choices and lack of character to the extent that I could, that she could live at Pemberley, or any other Darcy property, for my lifetime only—and never in the same home as they would live. That she would be left with everything she brought to the marriage, less those settlements, but nothing more. I could not think it right that either she or her children inherit the Darcy fortune. I still had some hope, you see, that Georgiana's marriage could, eventually, be salvaged, that perhaps this legacy might even motivate them to resolve their difficulties."

This was all very astonishing to me, for while ruining *her*, it also would completely ruin the discretion he had hitherto fought so hard to maintain. How it must have infuriated her, to have the tables turned and to find herself a victim of her own scheming! I hardly knew how to respond. "Her settlement allowed for that outcome?"

"Her settlement was poorly written and my attorneys, whom I trusted, took advantage. I did not mean for it to be so, but by the time I was searching for possibilities, I saw them easily enough."

"She was angry, I take it."

"Oh, quite. I had believed, when I planned for this very conversation, that I would feel revenged at best, satisfaction at least. But I felt nothing at all. Resignation, I suppose, while she railed at me. I told her that if I could feel gratitude for a single word she uttered, I would thank her for her opinion of my character—but that I had long since ceased to care. I succeeded only in enraging her. Sometimes I hear her furious words echoing in my dreams.

"'This, then, is your opinion of me!' she said. 'This is the estimation in which you hold your own wife! I thank you for explaining it so fully. My faults, according to your calculation, are heavy indeed! However, my offences might have been overlooked, had not your pride been hurt by my honest confessions. These bitter accusations might have been suppressed, had I with greater policy concealed my desires, my *needs*, instead flattering you into the belief of my being impelled by unqualified, unalloyed inclination—by reason, by reflection, by everything. But I am unashamed of my feelings, when *you* threaten to rob me of my future. They are natural and just.'"

His voice, even in the retelling, rang with her remembered passion.

"I do not understand her expectations," I admitted. "Most men would have thrown her out."

"Why should she have expected anything *except* my compliance? Our history together had proven to her that she would have her way, no matter the provocation. What did I do when she lay with my own sister's husband? Nothing. Nothing at all. Had I expelled her in the past, she might not have grown so vain and heedless. I was completely emasculated in her eyes. I cannot even blame her for her conclusions. It is only with time that I have been able to see it all."

Protests rose to my tongue—she had manipulated him and abused him. Perhaps, legally, he held all the power, yet emotionally she had managed to entangle and entrap him until he was under her thumb. But he would not like for me to point out how he had been vulnerable and maltreated. "You did what you thought was best at the time, and tried to honour your vows and your moral code irrespective of hers. Did you tell her to leave then?"

"No. Only that she could not have made me the offer of bearing a child in any possible way that would have tempted me to give her one of my own. Even then, I reassured her that I would certainly do my best to care well for any children were she to bear someone else's. Even then."

There was so much self-reproach in his words. I lifted my head again to look at him, but he would not meet my eyes, so I raised my hand to his cheek and moved him so he would have to. "Listen to me: at one of the worst times of your life, your thoughts were of innocent children for whom you would be legally responsible. Why do you castigate yourself for it?"

He only sighed again. "It all sounds so impossible now, to say these words aloud. Impossible and shameful. I ought not to have burdened you with them, when they are like poisonous water in my belly. It makes me ill to remember."

"Then I shall ask Mr Donavan for a poultice. They do not render *me* ill. I am as fit as I ever was, except for knowing that your first wife was an even greater dunderhead than I first thought."

He shook his head at my impertinence, for it was nothing less, but something lightened in his expression as he told me the rest of it. "At last she played her final card. If I would not give her the Darcy child she required, there would be a scandal to end all scandals. I would be known as an impotent weakling before the world. She would destroy my sister's marriage, finish her work of destroying my reputation. She threatened everything I had feared since first beginning to learn of her character. She promised complete and utter humiliation, for me, for Georgiana and Bingley, for the earl and his family."

I did not interrupt; his words were coming faster now, as those poisonous betrayals slipped from his soul.

"But she had waited too long. Of what had I to be proud? My life was a lie. Pemberley and its happiness, its advantages, were lies. I truly *was* a weakling. Too many already believed me to be an abuser. The earl would still be an earl, and could weather any storm. Georgiana's marriage was in ruins regardless. I, to whom disguise of every sort was an abhorrence, had participated in, even encouraged, one of massive proportions. I would no longer." He took a deep breath, and slowly exhaled.

"I told her that I would take Georgiana travelling for a time. We would do our own Grand Tour, and if Anne wished to ruin herself, her name, her reputation and standing amongst the *ton* while we were away, it was entirely up to her."

I nodded. In my opinion, he had hardly exercised an eighth of the authority he had over her, but it simply was not in his nature. He did not understand her, had never loved her, had grieved that he could not make her happy to the point of allowing great personal mistreatment, and, finally, allowed her to become irrelevant—leaving her to her own destruction, while attending to the sister he believed to be hurt by his mistakes.

"It sounds like an excellent plan," I agreed. "I can hardly imagine a different solution, truthfully. Her lies, obviously, had taken on some peculiar sort of reality—she appears to have learnt to believe them. I suppose she did not care for your decision, though."

"An understatement. She erupted in fury—that is when she told me that she had first betrayed our marriage vows on our wedding day, and gave me multiple particulars regarding her proclivities and many paramours that I wish I did not know. But something happened within me, as she spewed her threats and filth. Instead of alarming or destroying me, she only became more weak and wretched in my eyes."

"She was pitiful," I agreed. "I suppose it proves the old adage, 'Wickedness never was happiness'."

"Indeed," he concurred. "I once saw her as a force to be reckoned with, as a woman of great charisma and talents. I do not understand why she tossed away those gifts, but they had become illusory. I advised her that she was growing too old to maintain the sham by outward appearances alone, and if she did not take great care, all her charms would vanish with her youth and beauty." He appeared thoughtful for a moment. "You know, I believed myself perfectly calm and cool at the time, but I revealed a dreadful bitterness of spirit."

"I hardly think anyone could be blamed for a *little* bitterness, in such a situation," I offered.

"Perhaps not. But at any rate, that was when she turned, picked up a sharpened fire-iron, and attempted to run me through with it."

CHAPTER TWENTY-SEVEN

I t was an ugly story, and I understood perfectly now why he had not wished to share any of it. How terrible and vicious it had all become, what scenes of violence he endured, and I embraced him more tightly as I realised that he might have met his own early demise, just as Miss Bingley had. It was no wonder he believed Anne had killed her.

But he still had not explained how she had met her death.

While we had been talking, the late afternoon sun weakened into nightfall; the servants, probably noting Lord Cavendish's hasty departure and the fact we had remained closeted in the library, had not disturbed us. We were accustomed to eating early and rising early, country hours which appealed to both of us and our servants as well. Now we sat quietly by the light of the fire, simply holding each other. Mr Darcy seemed calmer now, his body peaceful against mine. That awful rigidity possessing him at Lord Cavendish's departure was gone. For the first time in our marriage, instead of walling me off from his pain, he had drawn me to him. His instincts were to protect me from ugliness. His experience had taught him that he was unacceptable and unlovable. He had overcome both instinct and experience in order to reach for *me*. And so, despite the dreadful topic of conversation, I felt closer to him, and more content, than I ever had. A part of me feared that if we did not complete this discussion now, we never would, so horrible was its subject. But a greater part of me simply trusted him. He would tell me what I asked, when I asked it. He was *trying*.

"Cook will have dinner ready by now, and Mrs Reynolds will be fretting about whether to risk her temper or yours by interrupting us," I said. "I know there is more to this story, and I very much need to hear it. Perhaps we should have our evening meal, and talk more when we are refreshed?"

He bent to kiss me, lightly, tenderly, a gesture of appreciation as well as affection. "Thank you," he said, "for listening to so much. Yes, let us take a respite from the past to enjoy what is here and now." Standing, he helped me rise and kept my hand in his as we left the library.

We were mostly quiet in our evening meal; I had much to contemplate, while Mr Darcy was never talkative. How had it been, at all those meals he had shared with the late Anne de Bourgh? Granted, by his own admission, he had been ignorant of the lion's share of her disloyalty. Still, he had known enough, had he not? He had known her disgust of him; he had felt his disgust of her. The violent rows, the huge betrayals, the parts of his marriage he had hitherto shared—these, perhaps, would not have been the worst part of such an unequal alliance. No, it would be the hours, day in, day out, of loneliness and isolation. The endless dinners while the servants looked on and she, maintaining her charade of perfection, chattered about the parties she organised, the shopping she'd done, the redecorations she planned—her mother her fascinated audience of one—while he simply ate, endured, and waited for the meal to be finished.

What had Mrs Reynolds said? The master had 'gone quiet' until she'd believed it was simply his way. I had wondered, when she said it, how much different he could possibly have been from his usual manner.

But though he was a quiet man, he was not a dull and solemn one. He thought before he spoke, and preferred to listen over speaking; he asked questions—how had my recent tenant visits gone to the Allen and Henshaw families? What news from the Bingleys in Georgiana's latest letter? Had I read of the recent unrest in the papers resulting from the Cato Street conspiracy? What were my thoughts upon the matter? And always, always, he gave my answers his complete undivided attention, as if I were the most interesting person he had ever met.

How could she not have loved him?

He came to me before Clara was finished braiding my hair, simply standing in the doorway, waiting. She quickly completed her work and wished us a good night, for there was something in his demeanour expressing impatience, though he said not a word to indicate it.

Could it be, I wondered, that he actually *wished* to speak of it all? That he found some sort of relief in unburdening himself thus? He took my hand, leading me back to his own rooms. He had candles lit, his fire built up, and the leather settee drawn before it. There was even, I noticed, a covered tray on the table beside it, a sign of refreshments available if we wanted them. He removed his banyan and tossed it onto his bed, taking a seat before the fire. I sat beside him and he drew his arm around me, but once we were settled, he made no move to begin speaking. Rather, he seemed content to just *be*.

The unburdening required completion, however, and so I asked my questions.

"Were you injured? When she came at you with the poker?"

In answer, he shifted away to pull his nightshirt off one side, exposing his middle and twisting around to present his back. "Is the light enough to see it? Right there."

I examined his skin where he pointed, immediately noticing a scar that I had previously attributed to some childhood injury. It was fairly thick, as if from a deep puncture, on the left side of his back. But as I scrutinised, I noticed other ones, not so obvious, as if she had stabbed at him again and again more shallowly while he twisted and turned away from her, and I shuddered. Even a non-mortal wound was dangerous, the risk of infection great.

I placed a kiss upon it, foolishly, as if that could heal the old wound, and he drew me up to stop me. "You had not better," he said, "or my thoughts will stray far from the past, to the perfect present, here alone with my beautiful wife, and nothing to prevent me from doing with you whatever I will."

The look in his eyes was an intent one I had seen many times before, and I admit I was dearly tempted. But it was time to put the past away, cut it off like deadwood, understand it, learn from it if we could—but press forward, regardless. I smiled back at him, but helped him replace the nightshirt.

"Thankfully, she was unsuccessful in her attempt," I said.

"She struck me from behind, as you can see, or her attack would not have amounted to much. Fortunately, my coat material was a dense wool, which protected me somewhat, though it hurt like the very devil. I suppose, had it been a normal day, the servants would have rushed in, as I yelled loudly enough—but it was a harvest feast day, most were away, and Pemberley operated with a skeleton crew. As soon as I got the weapon away from her, I asked her what she thought she was doing and told her I would have her committed to Bedlam."

"A fair consequence," I said.

He sighed. "She was completely lost to rage, cursing me, then threatening to do herself harm and running out onto the terrace. She had always loved sitting on the edge of the balustrade with her feet dangling over the edge, though I often warned her it was foolish. She did it again, threatening to drop, but this time, you will forgive me if I was not overly concerned for her health and safety."

"Of course," I murmured, remembering what Georgiana had told me regarding the prank he had once played, of pretending to drop from the balustrade while she watched, in reality landing upon a ledge beneath it. "You do not mean because of your wounds. She threatened to fall from the one place it was safe to do so?"

"Not by any means safe, but less perilous," he agreed. "How did you know?"

"Your sister told me of your hoax," I replied. "When you were a boy."

"Ah," he nodded. "I was a stupid, thoughtless gudgeon, and I ought to have been horsewhipped for terrifying her so cruelly. And perhaps my grandfather ought to have been as well, for creating so dangerous a terrace in the first place. Yes, Anne was in the exact spot it was safest to execute such a deception."

"But she knew you pulled the same trick in the past, that you would be aware of the ledge below."

He shrugged. "My guess is, she had always wanted to try it herself, and was angry enough to do it—to at least get *some* response from me after all my past warnings and to attempt to penetrate my current indifference. But once she let herself fall, I did not even glance over the edge to see whether she was safe. Instead, I returned to my rooms to clean myself up —I was covered in my own blood. I had at least *planned* my foolish, inconsiderate boyhood prank out beforehand, equipping the terrace with rope to enable a climb back up to safety. Hers was an impulsive, dramatic performance. I thought to let her stew and bandage my wounds before I rescued her. It was, perhaps, a quarter-hour before I went to fetch a rope ladder to haul her back up. It might have been a half an hour before I returned to her."

"Did she...had she broken her neck in the fall?"

"She had broken something. I saw she was lying at an awkward, unnatural angle on the ground beneath the ledge."

I shuddered at the image. "An accident then. But definitely not your fault."

He sighed. "I secured the rope ladder, then climbed down to her as quickly as I could. She was still conscious. 'I made the landing,' she whispered. 'I tried to climb back up again, though, and slipped, missing the ledge. I cannot move my legs, or feel them. Please, if you have one ounce of pity in your soul, push me the rest of the way over the cliff and finish the job.' I noticed then, how she had raked the dirt, trying to gain traction enough to do it herself. But she was a good four feet from the edge, and she hadn't the strength."

I looked up at him. "Did you do it? Help her finish her suicide?"

"No," he said gravely. "I assured her I would get help. I climbed up the rope ladder as fast as I could, hurrying to the stables to have Frost fetch the doctor. I nearly ran headlong into Richard, and told him, very briefly, what had occurred, and sent him to wait with her. Then I searched the stables for more rope, and something that would work as a makeshift litter, and hurried back with Frost's son. When we reached the terrace, I looked over the edge. There was no sign of Richard. There was no sign of Anne. I swiftly climbed back down the rope, peered over the cliff's ledge, and saw her broken body below."

"You believe he ended her," I said, rather unnecessarily.

"One of the many sordid confessions she threw at me in that final row was how she abused poor Richard, exploiting his love for her to make his life a misery. He resisted her—he never did anything adulterous, she claimed—but he is shy and awkward with women, and she, apparently, would repeatedly express to him, with great longing, how much she wished she was married to him instead of me, how unhappy she was with me. She laughed at the tears he'd shed over her, telling me that his pain was nearly as good as a whipping for her enjoyment."

"Oh. That *is* sickening," I said.

"He did not return to Pemberley for over a week. I am certain he was quite helpless against her orders. I never told a soul he might have been there."

"What did you tell the doctor when he arrived?"

He shook his head. "Old Mr Simpson was quite elderly. He never climbed down the rope ladder to examine the grounds. As it was, I could easily see the slight indentations where she had fallen, and the scratches in the earth showing where she had futilely tried to move herself. There were no indications that she had been able to get any further, but some of the scrub was bent or broken, a sign perhaps she had been dragged."

I found that puzzling. "But, did you not just admit he was

wildly in love with her? He seems quite strong enough to have picked her up. I beg pardon if I sound harsh, but dragging her body to the edge and a solid push is hardly the romantic work of a lover."

"Perhaps he only moved her closer, and I am mistaken in how. Perhaps she found the strength to push herself the rest of the way, once he helped her gain the edge. Either way, I know it haunts him. I cannot think how to make it better for him—if he truly loved her, would he appreciate knowing she was unworthy of it? Or would he believe it jealousy on my part? Is it cruel to ruin his image of her?"

"How could it be? He could not have loved her, not truly. He did not *know* her, only the façade she presented to him. Perhaps it happened the way you believe—but you must *talk* to him. You said Wickham was in the area. Perhaps *he* was responsible, and Mr Williams arrived too late. He may have been infatuated with the idea of her, but I gained from him the distinct impression he believes *you* to be responsible for her death. I cannot be certain, of course."

"I *am* responsible for it. If I had taken two minutes to lean over the balustrade and tell her I would be back with a rope, she might never have taken the risk of attempting an ascent without one. She would be alive today. Even if I *had* managed to return with a litter and get her to the house, she was horribly injured. Her life, as she knew it, was over, if she could even survive. My fault."

"I fervently disagree. No one told her to purposely fall in the first place, or endeavour to climb back up alone. Those were *her* decisions, made in anger, as the most senseless choices always are. Did you hear her calling for you to help her? I would lay money you did not, or you *would* have."

"No. But cannot you think it better to let sleeping dogs lie?"

"As much as I hate to remind you, the dogs growl and bark now rather than nap. Did you tell Mr Simpson the whole truth?"

"Yes, excepting Richard's part. I told both Simpson and Cavendish that she somehow must have pushed herself the rest of the way. I swore them both to secrecy, for I did not want her death to be thought a suicide. I pleaded with them to regard the whole thing as a stupid accident, since there was no assurance she would have survived, even had she not fallen further. I begged them to say nothing regarding the details of her death. I wanted her to have a Christian burial."

My thoughts on what good a Christian burial would do for a woman who had lived an amoral life filled with hatred and destruction, I kept to myself.

"And now Lord Cavendish wishes to be released from his vow, and clear your reputation by revealing hers, up to and including her supposed 'accidental suicide'. Would that be so terrible?"

"Then she lives on," he said, arising to lean against the chimneypiece and stare into the flames. "Scandal and gossip will thrive on the new tales, growing to legendary proportions, as talk surrounding the too-early deaths of fascinating, wicked, and beautiful people always does. And even more of them will believe I killed her, only now they will assume they know why. I just want her to stay dead. Is it too much to ask, I wonder?"

"Perhaps, as long as her death is shrouded in mystery, it will continue to inspire as much talk as the truth ever could. Surely the inquest would necessitate the truth's revelation, vow or no vow."

He just stood there, his tension returning. I understood more now, why he had hoped for it all to remain in the past, why he had so stubbornly clung to his silence. I waited, letting him ponder the myriad lies, confusion, mystery, and horror of it all. It was a lot, I could admit. At last, he sat again, but hunched forward, elbows on knees, head in hands —a desolate pose.

"All, now, is exactly what she would have wanted," I said gently, coasting my fingers across the thin fabric of his night-shirt, tracing the little pucker of his scar. "People talking about her, wondering about her, remembering her. Perhaps they always will. But they also talk of you, still spreading her poison, and casting your honour into doubt. If Lord Cavendish can clear it, we ought to let him try, I think. But I will stand beside you, and proudly, whatever you decide."

Sighing, he again took me into his arms, leaning back against the settee. "I cannot bear for you to be hurt by my stupid mistakes. I promise you that I sincerely believed it would all just fade, with a bit of time. Perhaps, had I waited to remarry, it might have. But I was selfish."

"I am happy we married when we did. With all that has occurred since, you might have thought you never should pursue remarriage. That would be the true tragedy."

He leant down and kissed my forehead. "Pemberley's people stay loyal, because I pay them well. The rest? It is as though the first nine and twenty years of my life did not exist, for all the world trusts in my integrity since my first marriage. And now the countryside takes it out upon you, the one most deserving of their respect."

"Pemberley stays loyal because they have had the best and most opportunity to know you as the good man you are. Your tenants respect you, and treat both of us well. I realise we have a vocal few in Hopewell who have taken a dissenting opinion, and perhaps detractors amongst Anne's friends in the country and London. If you are not ready to release Lord Cavendish from his promise, will you, at least, speak with Mr

Williams? If he had a part in her death, perhaps he would benefit from your understanding."

For long moments, the only sound was the crackle of the fire.

"As I have benefited from yours," he said at last. "I will do it. I will speak to him."

CHAPTER TWENTY-EIGHT

I was uncertain when, exactly, Mr Darcy would see fit to speak with Mr Williams—but I was not overly surprised when it happened within a few days. When Mr Darcy decided to act, he seldom delayed.

I had received a letter from Jane—a thick one by the feel of it—and was anxious to read news of her and her little daughter, her boys, and Mr Tilney. I wished to savour it, however, so I forced myself to wait until after I attended to the daily duties, inspections, menus, and business of the mistress of Pemberley before finally retiring to the library to read it.

But the library proved occupied. Mr Darcy and Mr Williams stood as I paused in the doorway.

"Oh," I said. "I did not realise you were still busy in here. I will go elsewhere."

"No, please enter," my husband said. "Mr Williams wishes to speak to you."

"To me?" I asked, surprised. Mr Williams seldom had a direct word to say in my company.

"I wish to apologise," he said in his usual diffident voice.

Shutting the door behind me, I took a seat upon the leather couch. Mr Darcy sat down beside me, with Mr Williams in the chair across from us both.

"I am certain you have nothing to apologise for," I said, after an awkward moment.

"Oh, but I do," he said. "I have known Mr Darcy all my life. Never have I seen him behave in any manner except as a gentleman ought, and yet I was mistaken, sorely mistaken in his character. Oftentimes, I decided that she must be wrong, that she must misunderstand. It seemed impossible, the things she said."

I did not have to ask who 'she' was.

"Oh, she never accused him of anything outright. It was all subtleties and subterfuge, hints and then retractions. There was nothing to confront him about, really—and all of the time, I was ashamed of my feelings and what they were. I knew it was wrong, to covet another man's wife as I did." He looked up at his employer. "If I had understood you knew, I would have resigned my post. I thought I hid it. I tried to hide it. I tried *not* to feel it."

"That is one of the many reasons I said nothing," my husband explained. "She *wanted* you to leave me. Estranging me from those I cared for was her first object, always. I simply said nothing for…too long. It has become rather a habit with me."

I took his hand in mine, and squeezed.

Mr Williams cleared his throat before resuming. "Mrs Darcy, you spoke to me about a subject of some significance shortly after your arrival at Pemberley. At the time, I was grieving and resentful of Darcy's new marriage, angry at him for so quickly replacing Anne as mistress. I want you to know, before I say anything else, that by the time your husband spoke with me this morning upon those other painful subjects, I had already decided that I was mistaken. Not only are you better to our tenants than she ever was, but Darcy is so much improved in spirits. I wondered, you see, if he would treat you with the same disdain Anne accused him of—instead, I saw the difference in how *you* treated *him*. I did not want to see it, I suppose. I wanted to believe her perfect and perfectly justified." His soft voice was bitter.

"If there is any apology needed, please render it to my husband. I would hope, if ever a female at Pemberley were to come to you with tales of abuse, you would go to him immediately—even if he was the one thus accused."

Mr Darcy demurred. "You did not know her, darling. Her manipulations were masterfully performed."

But Mr Williams shook his head, firmly. "You are correct, Mrs Darcy. It was only complicated in my mind—with shame, fear of losing my place, fear of losing what little connexion I had with her. I have already apologised, and will continue to feel self-reproach over my part in such deceit. Mr Darcy has rejected my offer to resign, wishing me to stay on. However, if you desire me gone, he has promised me that he will not object."

"Me? Why would *I* wish you to leave?"

"The day when you asked me if I believed he killed his first wife, I turned away from you rather than answering. I ought to have reassured you of his fine character, which I *knew* to be true and honourable. Instead, in my bitterness and grief, I justified frightening you, when I knew you were safe—would *always* be safe with him."

Mr Darcy sighed. "Oh for heaven's sake, Richard, tell her what you saw. Tell her what happened on the day she died."

There was an uncomfortable pause while the steward collected his emotions. When he spoke, it was his feet he addressed. "Late one afternoon last September, Mr Darcy informed me there had been an accident, that Mrs Darcy had fallen from the balustrade and was hurt. I went as quickly as I could to her side; to say she was hurt was to put it mildly. She was pale as a ghost and more dead than alive, I thought. I-I wept, to see her so broken. She opened her eyes to look at me, and then begged me to push her the rest of the way off the cliff, saying she could not live thus injured, that she could not feel her-her limbs. I told her I couldn't, I couldn't, that I would love her as she was, that I would care for her myself, if Darcy wouldn't."

The man was not sparing himself in the slightest in this candid retelling. I could see the memories deeply embarrassed him, and confessing them all before his employer—and, I thought, dearest friend—was a penance for his pride.

"That was very kind of you," I said gently. Mr Darcy squeezed my hand.

"She did not want my kindness," he said, a little of acrimony in his tone. "She told me to go away, that she did not want me there, that Darcy had promised to finish what he'd started and she would hold him to it. Those were her very words, 'finish what he'd started'.

"'He did this to you?' I cried. 'Surely he never would!' But she screamed at me to go, to get away, and I was afraid of further distressing her, that she would exacerbate her injuries. I climbed back up the ropes, re-entering Darcy's chamber and this time I noticed what I had missed before."

He hesitated, and Mr Darcy said to me, "The blood."

"Ohh," I replied. "You saw the results of her attack upon him."

"Except I did not *ask* him," Mr Williams cried. "Instead, I imagined multiple scenarios of violence gone amiss, of her guilt and his, mutually."

"Anne once told him that it was *I* who had a taste for pain," Mr Darcy said wryly. "But she also told him I was teaching her to enjoy it."

"She liked to say things to embarrass me, though," Mr Williams interjected, his cheeks almost purple with mortification. "I never did really believe it, not of either of you. I supposed she was teasing."

"I called Pennywithers in," Mr Darcy said, obviously giving Mr Williams a few moments to recover his equanimity, "and asked him to explain to Mr Williams the wounds I suffered at the hands of the first Mrs Darcy. You know, 'tis odd, I do not remember all the blood and mess of it, but Pennywithers assured us that it was as Mr Williams remembered. He said he had a dreadful time removing it from the carpets, and then gave us a rather gruesome exposition on how he accomplished it. To prevent any in the house from knowing, he burned the clothing, believing that he was protecting both myself and Anne from embarrassment. The soul of discretion, is Pennywithers. Finish the tale, Richard."

"I took the footpath down the mountainside," the steward relayed, more quietly now. "I was distressed, grieving, and I had only made it about half of the way down when...when her body went rolling past me. I looked up, saw only a part of a black coat. Mr Darcy wore a black coat when he sent me to her. I thought he might have obeyed her orders, but I never believed he hurt her apurpose. I knew he would never hurt *anyone* apurpose. I *knew* it. I also knew she was more dead than living, that her odds of surviving her injury were slim. And at times I thought I hadn't seen anyone or anything, that it was just a terrible memory, my mind playing tricks. I went to London and stayed...er... inebriated for several days. When I returned, I decided it was simply better not to know, to grow past it." He hung his head, so obviously ashamed and upset, I forgave him instantly for any words he might have misspoken in the past. After all, he had almost always been kind, but for that one day, one moment alone in the woods at Thorncroft. And I blamed *her* for that.

"Richard and I climbed down that rope again and had a look around that ledge," Mr Darcy said. "There *is* a crevice where a man might hide, if someone truly did climb down the rope besides just the two of us. Neither of us even dreamt of anyone else being there, and certainly we were paying little attention to such details."

There was a long moment of silence, as we all contemplated the possibility of Wickham's involvement. And yet, he had claimed he had a note from her, calling him to Pemberley, and that it haunted him, his inability to ever learn what she had wanted. Still, the man lied whenever he opened his mouth. If it were anyone, it had to be him. Yet I could not discount the notion that she *might* have found the strength to push herself.

"Of course I do not wish you to leave Pemberley," I assured him. "I think there has been more than enough suffering here, do not you?"

"You are certain?" Mr Williams said, looking up from his feet. "I would not blame you for feeling otherwise."

"It is time to look to the future, I think. And now gentlemen, if you will excuse me, I have letters to attend to. Mr Williams, will you stay to dinner? Cook is serving her venison pie, which I know you enjoy." I stood, and both gentlemen rose. I curtseyed, and Mr Darcy caught my hand again, kissing it. Mr Williams bowed low.

"Thank you, Mrs Darcy. Yes, please. I would very much enjoy Cook's venison." He smiled and I thought how much more handsome he appeared when cheerful. Not anything to

Mr Darcy, but still. I grinned at my thoughts, and made haste to my rooms, eager to read Jane's letter. Such letters as I could write her in return! Though likely, I never would. Who would believe it? Mrs Radcliffe ought to hear such a plot!

My Dearest Sister,

I apologise for the extensive delay since I began this letter, as Recent Events have interfered in its response. Oh, how I long for your visit, to introduce you to our beautiful baby girl! You shall be here in the summer, as I hope you remember to have promised. Her brothers are so good and sweet and kind to her…

What followed was a protracted description of each of her children—in whom she had a well-deserved mother's pride. For the first time ever, however, I only skimmed her first several paragraphs, looking as I was for information on a different subject altogether. At last, I found it.

You cannot know how happy I am that you have finally written on a topic that has troubled me for many years and more especially since the surprising news of your marriage. When I first learned of it (which was not, I think, until after Harry was born), it was easy to put it from my mind, for as much as I appreciated Mr Darcy's solicitude towards my husband, I knew you were not fond of him, and our acquaintance with him had been of such brief duration and transpired during a period of time perhaps better forgotten.

I smiled at Jane's kindly, convoluted way of saying 'we hated him, we did not want to think of him'.

But over the years, and each time the subject has arisen, I have wanted to write to you, and tell you that the man who we, doubtless wrongly, blamed for my disappointed hopes was not the villain we thought.

Well, he *had* been somewhat to blame, but I would never share those details with her, unnecessary as they were for her to know at this point.

However, when you wrote to tell us of Lydia's rescue at his hand, my astonishment was so enormous, I nearly replied with everything I know then and there. Only a promise I made to Tilney stopped me—for my discovery of the purchaser of Matlock's benefice and to whom we owed the living, was quite by accident. The earl mentioned it, not remembering it was to be kept a secret from me. Yes, a secret! I really had never given it much thought before that moment, but if I had, I would have supposed that Tilney was known to the earl. They were certainly on the best of terms, then and now. But no, that is not what occurred.

Completely unexpectedly, Mr Darcy appeared in his rooms—do you remember, those rooms Tilney once had on Honey Lane?—and told him that his cousin needed a good man to fill his living, and Mr Darcy wished to recommend him for the post, if he was interested. My husband was, of course, most especially interested, having hoped that his curacy would lead to a living elsewhere paying enough for him to marry. But as you know, he had been in it for four years with nothing to show for it, and though his family are all that is good and respectable, they hadn't been able to do much beyond his schooling. Still, he could not simply agree without knowing all the particulars, and though Mr Darcy was reticent, Tilney eventually learned that he was paying the earl for the benefice, as his own was filled. I know not how Mr Darcy learnt of Tilney's need. They went to school together but had not had any contact in some years.

Hah! When Mr Darcy wished to know something, he would soon know it! I had no doubt of it being at his instigation, but of course, now that I knew he often partnered with my uncle, it was easier to fathom how he had come by the information. All he need do was persuade Mr Ferrars, in that listening way he had, to provide details. If my uncle had suspected Mr Tilney's hopes in Jane's direction (which, from the perspective of time, seem rather obvious to me now), it would not take much prodding for him to reveal his concerns to his partner.

It was several months after our marriage before Mr Darcy came to visit the earl—he has never come very often, and when he does, it is only to stay two or three nights at the most—and he finally told Tilney (and only because my husband pressed) of his regret over the death of our father. The motive professed was his conviction of it being his own fault that Wickham's reputation had not been so well known as to make it impossible for any young woman of character to love or confide in him. He generously imputed the whole to his mistaken pride, confessing that he had before thought it beneath him to lay his private actions open to the world. He called it, therefore, his duty to step forward and endeavour to remedy an evil which had been brought on by himself—the evil of course being our father's death while trying to rescue our poor sister. I did not know then—and neither did Tilney—that he had also rescued Lydia, until you surprised us with the news!

Mr Darcy begged Tilney swear not to reveal his benefactor, and he did not. But when I did learn it, and then later, when I grew to appreciate his many kindnesses to our family (as he was also responsible for the renovation of the rectory after Jack was born, for which information I likewise owe to the earl) and I felt to tell you of his goodness—as I knew you had long outgrown any derogatory feelings—but Tilney was adamant. He had promised Mr Darcy he would say nothing to us, and though I had discovered the truth by accident, no one else should know it. I said I would not, but if you ever asked me outright, I would not lie. Of course, there was no reason you ever would or should. And then came the astounding news of his proposal to you! I begged dear Tilney to do his best to bring you to us, so I could determine whether this was some sort of charitable instinct gone too far—though of course, any man would be fortunate to win your regard.

I tried not to be insulted by her first feelings of distrust—had not I, too, experienced them? By any standard, marrying me was quite the extra mile for a long-ago debt owed a man dead nearly a decade.

But dear Tilney said you were both determined to have the wedding at once, and he could not persuade you otherwise. Oh, did it test the limits of my fortitude to keep my promise! I have hoped and waited for your quick mind to realise it was quite the incredible coincidence, such a connexion between Tilney and the earl and Mr Darcy.

Not so very quick, after all, but then, Mr Darcy had

subverted any enquiries by emphasising his connexion with Mr Tilney right from the outset, yet distancing himself at the same time. The trickster! I remembered him asking my nephews' names—when he knew them all, doubtless!

I will say one other thing—I do not think your Mr Darcy has been happy in a long while. I have quizzed my dear Tilney on the subject, and he could provide no particulars, although he admitted once that the earl did not care overmuch for Mr Darcy's first wife. I do not know what sorrows he has borne, only that he has them. Perhaps he yearns for a child— although when I mentioned my notion to Tilney, he simply offered to give him Jack, the teasing man!

I smiled, for Jack's adventurous spirit had landed him in a scrape or two; and how very like dear, sympathetic Jane, to notice my husband's hidden sorrows!

Since your wedding, I have eagerly awaited your every letter, hoping that your happiness was assured, but also hoping you would ask whether there was more to learn. I cannot help wondering now, dear sister, whether there was always more to Tilney's placement than what Mr Darcy felt he owed to our father? I will say now how much I like him. His behaviour to us has been, in every respect, as agreeable as anyone's could be. His understanding and opinions all please me; he wants nothing but a little more liveliness, and that, since he has married so prudently, his wife may teach him.

I did not need to hear this further confirmation that he had watched over each of us all these years. It changed nothing. But it was sweet to know, all the same.

CHAPTER TWENTY-NINE

B efore I presented my ideas to Mr Darcy, I read
everything I could on architecture and building, even
on the soil of Derbyshire. Pemberley's library made the
research a pleasure. It was a worthy distraction from the
ever-present concerns of inquisitions and public opinions
and a nearby town simmering with unrest. I wrote exten-
sively to Mr Martin; though he was not a builder of grand
estates, there was little about the county and its resources
that he was unacquainted with, and he was a regular repository of facts regarding Pemberley and its history. I was
pleased that he seemed markedly enthusiastic about the
potential for my plan, and what it would mean for the neighbourhood.

As to Mrs de Bourgh, I dismissed Mr Donavan's nurse
and hired one of my own—much to the good doctor's
chagrin and irritation. Nurse Rook was a deal less impressed
with the doctor—though of course, she was too sensible to
give him or her patient anything to complain about. In little
asides to me, however, she gave it as her considered opinion

that nothing was the matter with Mrs de Bourgh that fresh air, charitable works, and mind-improving reading might not cure, and that Mr Donavan merely played to her weaknesses. I was not quite so sure—and thus 'in patience possessed my soul'.

Regardless, I was certain that Mrs de Bourgh would not slip away so easily from Nurse Rook, and a footman was permanently stationed in the corridor evenings and nights when she was not with her patient. It seemed to me that she was better off at Pemberley, where I at least knew that those to whom she spoke were loyal, and Mr Donavan was too aware of who paid him for his services to do more damage than his gossiping tongue had already managed.

The Easter holiday brought home more than simply Lord and Lady Cavendish. The Ringletons, the Smythe-Joneses, the Talbots, and the Howards—amongst others—were all in from town for the holiday, and either manners or curiosity or both led them to return my calls and subsequently host us for tea or dinner. The impetus behind such invitations did not offend me; I was equally curious about them. There were one or two probing remarks regarding our hasty marriage, which I managed to deflect, and a few comments on how greatly the first Mrs Darcy would be missed. Nevertheless, though the world, in general, had as little sense as Lady Matlock, a sudden change in Mr Darcy's activities made it much more difficult for them to ascribe the worst possible motivations to so dignified a member of their ranks. He began joining me in my calls, doing his best to appear inter-ested in the concerns of his neighbours—not always easy, when their interests were more in balls and entertainments than serious matters. He suffered it all for me, which touched my heart and made me love him even more, if such a thing were possible. I knew him so well now; his life had taught him to be serious and thoughtful, to make decisions with care, to be cautious and prudent. And yet, he had a dry wit and quick intelligence that made him interesting, and a generous heart and even temper that made him agreeable. The quality of his attention was remarkable. I believed that whatever the churning rumours, being in his presence reminded them all of who he really was, and who he had always been. It was simply impossible to consider him guilty of *any* crime, much less murder.

The visits went well, and I felt, for the first time, that I was beginning to plant roots. Though these neighbours were wealthier and more fashionably attired than the society to be had in Meryton, and certainly Cheapside, human nature was surprisingly the same. Mr Smythe-Jones was gregarious, complimentary, and not incredibly perceptive, much like Sir William Lucas; Lady Howard was an inveterate gossip such as Mrs Philips had ever aspired to become. The Ringletons both seemed sensible and agreeable as my aunt and uncle Gardiner, while the Talbots were pedantic and a bit tedious, like the Gouldings.

I quite liked Lady Cavendish; she was only ten years older than me, and though not handsome, very lively and clever. And she, like her husband, had no use whatsoever for the first Mrs Darcy.

"Oh, we liked her well enough in the beginning years," she explained, the second time in as many days she had me over to tea. "She was so spirited and energetic. Always planning some new event, always so friendly and welcoming. However, she was impossible to truly come to know—one could only go so far and no further. I did not care so much about that—I do not require everyone to be my boon companion. But I began to notice a disturbing pattern. At one ball, Lady Howard hired pan pipes and drummers, giving a sort of Turkish flavour to her entertainment, which was very well received. The next thing we knew, Mrs Darcy held a masquerade, appearing as a Maharana covered in veils and silks, with what seemed the whole of Pemberley upholstered in satin cushions."

"Exotic," I murmured.

"Oh, very. Most of us were used to donning domino cloaks for such affairs, while there she was in golden satins and brocades, bird of paradise plumes crowned by a tiara of exotic stones. No one talked of anything else for a fortnight, and Lady Howard's ball was of course compared unfavourably. And after that, ever so gradually, it seemed that if Mrs Darcy did not approve one's entertainment, one was sure to receive a comeuppance."

"How unfortunate," I remarked, for I was not about to be led down any sort of revelatory path, even by Lady Cavendish, and seldom volunteered much opinion about her disclosures. It did not stop her.

"I did not notice for years, of course, because I am not one to pay overmuch attention to the foibles of my neighbours and she knew better than to try her little tricks against me. Until, of course, she did not."

I raised a brow.

"Oh, yes—I think she decided that her popularity was such that she was ready to take me down a peg or two. But she attempted a more personal hit, and tried to seduce Cavendish," she said baldly.

It was all I could do not to gape. I clamped my mouth shut to avoid expression of my feelings on the matter; my estimation of Anne's intellect had taken a downward plunge after Mr Darcy reported the events leading up to her death, but this was mad, indeed.

Lady Cavendish's expression grew thoughtful. "Something was different about her those last several months of her life. She was harder—or, as is most likely, who she had always been grew more obvious. I have never been pretty. My marriage was an arranged one, strengthening blood and fortune. On the surface, I suppose one might assume Cavendish to be an easy mark. At least, with the right incentive."

"No one, ma'am, who has been in company with you both could mistake his respect and esteem for you," I protested.

Her smile grew sly. "Cavendish adores me, as well he should. But she did not see it. She saw a man of average appearance wed to a woman even less handsome. She began with flattery. Cavendish repeated to me a conversation he thought odd—her fawning over some horse or other he'd purchased, calling him a genius, remarking upon his riding style. Cavendish was not charmed, only suspecting that she wanted to breed the horse.

"'I believe, my dear, 'tis you she wishes to breed,' I told him. He did not believe me, of course. Thought I was jealous or some nonsense. Over what, I ask you? I have everything I could ever want. I told him to watch himself around her, and eventually she grew bolder. He nipped it in the bud. Called on Darcy, told him to restrain her. Don't know what all he said to him, but she never came near him again."

I stiffened, imagining the deep embarrassment my husband must have experienced. I had a fair idea what Lord Cavendish would have advised. Repudiation. Public shaming. Public ruin. I felt I must say *something*, and did my best not to resent the necessity.

"As you most unfortunately discovered, his first wife was not a person easy to respect. I am grieved, indeed, for her thoughtless actions towards your family, but she is dead now. I thank you both, again and again, for your discretion while she was alive—it was all that is kind. I hope we can look towards our future friendship, rather than dwell upon past sorrows."

"Hmpf. It was not kindness, as you must suspect. Cavendish told me to say nothing for Darcy's sake, and I did not and never will. The rumours flying, here and in London, are particularly annoying to me as everyone assumes Darcy paid Cavendish to sweep scandal under the rug. Cavendish does not mind it, but I find myself irked."

This reasoning softened my own annoyance—who could blame her? Certainly not me, and I came off my high ropes.

"My husband's greatest fear is that, should her reputation become too sensational, it would cause even more negative consequences," I explained. "The danger is that she will grow in the public eye from wicked to fascinating. She has hurt too many. They should not be required to hear of her with admiration *or* abhorrence, day in, day out, for the rest of their lives."

"Very sensible," she nodded with a measure of her own appreciation. "I suppose you must desire to begin launching house parties, to prove to the world that the new Mrs Darcy is every bit the equal of the former?"

I smiled with real humour. "I fail to see how the success of a house party, however magnificent, can take the measure of my character. I am inexperienced, of course, in my duty to Pemberley, but most of my attention has gone towards knowing and understanding the needs of our tenants, and what improvements might benefit us mutually. I was speaking to Mr Marley and he believes that what schooling we offer is insufficient and much in need of improvement. One of our oldest tenant families, the Martins, is willing to put up a new building for a school on their leasehold, and we intend to support its construction in every particular."

"Do you not worry that you are encouraging disaffected persons into dissatisfaction with their place in life, causing more of the unrest so bothersome to so many?"

I withheld a sigh of disappointment at her attitude. "Perhaps more exposure to the great writers, the Scriptures, and philosophers will foment peace rather than discord. Certainly, having little or no access is not helping."

But she grinned mischievously. "Do you know, Mrs Darcy, I like you. Marley likes you, and he is a fine judge of character, even if he is a vicar. Cavendish shall hold an envy-inspiring ball of the sort Marley disapproves of most, to welcome you to the neighbourhood. We shall invite some of your antagonists for spice, and as the weather is fine, do not be surprised if half of London attends."

I was surprised at this generosity. "My lady, I am honoured," I replied.

"I am Aurelia to you—we *shall* be good friends, shall we not? And we will make it a charity ball, and require large contributions to your school as the price of entry. I love to see my enemies pay, do not you?"

Mr Darcy demanded I acquire a new dress for the affair, even tried to insist I go to a London modiste—or have one brought to Pemberley.

"I have a number of beautiful dresses as yet unworn, including a ball gown or two, you have already purchased," I reminded him.

"Ah yes. I have heard of your fiercely loyal following amongst the villagers now, a louder set than the naysayers. Still, you would have to spend a good deal more frivolously than is in you to quiet them all."

"All that anyone really wishes for is prosperity. The more prosperous the town, the happier its residents. There are many hardworking, excellent people in Hopewell. Pemberley will help them in any way it can. You will see that I can be frivolous," I assured. "Perhaps you have not yet seen the latest bills from Miss Bickford."

He shook his head—for I was not fond of overspending, and he knew it—but laughed. "Miss Bickford's ambitions shall soon require you to have the bed removed from your chamber to make room for her creations."

"I know where another bed is." I shrugged insouciantly.

"You do indeed," he replied, his voice lowering a notch as he stepped closer. "Perhaps I shall be the one to require the furniture removal, so you shall only sleep with me."

I knew he was teasing, but I grew serious, looping my arms around his neck. "I have perhaps grown too casual in assuming you never need privacy at nights, simply because *I* seldom do, and you never enforce a separation. You must only tell me, you know. You are too kind and might worry, I think, that you will hurt my feelings if you wish to sleep alone. I have invaded your private spaces—*frivolously*, even carelessly. Clara is forever feuding with Pennywithers because he will see to the laundering and pressing of any little articles of mine he finds lying about—only not to her strict standards, she claims. Which is nonsense, I tell her, as they look full new if *he* returns them. 'Tis only professional jealousy, as he will not share his receipts."

He pulled me in more closely to him, laughing softly. "Last week Pennywithers passed by me with a stack of your things and a smirk, saying, 'Very nice to see your chambers brightening these days, sir'—and I suddenly knew, beyond any shadow of doubt, that he never was fooled by Anne's deceptions. I cannot imagine why I thought he would have been." He kissed my hair. "My darling, those few nights a month when you choose your privacy are the longest nights of my life. You must do what makes you most comfortable, of course. But know I am longing for your return, and care little for any inconvenience, no matter the night. I require no privacy from you."

And as he kissed me, I marvelled. *He mentioned her simply, easily, and only because he wonders at his current happiness. She has lost her power over him, I think.*

The Cavendish ballroom was not more majestic than Pemberley's, but it was larger, and, like its master and mistress, the height of elegance. We stood with Lord and Lady Cavendish in an informal receiving line of sorts; I tried to memorise names and faces while utterly distracted by Lady Cavendish's little asides.

"Ah, approaching is Lord Howard, one of your most vocal detractors. In a drunken rage, he challenged Mr Worthington to a duel and when he sobered up, realised Worthington is a crack shot. Failed to appear, he did."

She smiled broadly in welcome to the peer. "Lord Cowar —oh, pardon me, Howard—my tongue is tripping! And what news from your son?"

Lord Howard flushed an unbecoming shade of purple, but quickly launched into a travelogue of his eldest's Grand Tour, from which Lady Cavendish managed to expertly extract us to greet the next guest, the deaf, slightly doddering Lady Harrington, who shouted to the company at large that the tea cakes at Pemberley were much improved since 'that new girl took over the run of the kitchen'. Mr Darcy stiffened, but I had to hide a giggle.

"The first Mrs Darcy had distinct opinions on each meal or refreshment served, and most often chose appearance over every other attribute," Lady Cavendish whispered. "Word is, everyone is eating better now, above *and* belowstairs."

I had to admit, it was somewhat of a chore to summon a 'company smile' when Mrs Longthorpe presented herself. "We have already met," I muttered to my hostess, who glanced at me sharply.

Taking both her hands, Aurelia said, "My dear Isabella, I understand you have already made Mrs Darcy's acquaintance. I wanted to assure you that the punch tonight is *completely* safe for consumption." She turned to me. "At poor Isabella's last garden party, three mice were discovered having a bit of a swim in her punch bowl. One of them leapt out and dove down the front of Miss Longthorpe's gown— oh, I can hear her screams, still, as she slapped herself silly!" She chuckled, still clinging to the hands of a very red-faced Mrs Longthorpe. "Isabella finally captured it with her lace fichu. Did not Lord Dibley publish an epic poem of over thirty stanzas memorialising the event?"

"I am certain I could not say," Mrs Longthorpe mumbled.

"Oh, but you were the talk of the town!" Aurelia began reciting, not precisely shouting but speaking with definite force:

"'A Parent so Fearless Redeemed the Occasion'
"'Of the Determined Vermin Bosom Invasion!'"

She beamed at Mrs Longthorpe, while those nearby tittered. I covered a smile. "So nice to see you again," I called as she hurried away.

In this manner, I learned much more about my neighbours than I ever would have known after a year of formal invitations. Her aim, I was certain, was to help me see them as people, not as the *ton* sitting in judgment. Their foibles, flaws, and families, their ambitions and apathies were laid out before me in such a manner as to help me feel comfortable with mine.

"My father would have loved you," I said, during a pause in arrivals. "He was a grand spectator of human nature."

"He was," my husband added, taking my hand. "It was not always comfortable to be an object of his wit, but it was always memorable."

"Lady Cavendish seldom aspires to mediocrity in her observations," Lord Cavendish remarked drily, but I thought I saw him wink at her.

The musicians began their playing, and the line disbursed as sets formed. I opened the ball upon Lord Cavendish's arm, while Mr Darcy paired with Lady Cavendish. It was a lively country dance, and while not conducive to conversation, neither was Lord Cavendish silent.

"Aurelia has taken a liking to you, in case you could not tell," he said. "Nothing would do but a lot of falderol and fuss on your behalf. She believes talk will die down quickly. Usually is correct, my lady is."

"I am sorry her affection resulted in so much bother," I smiled at him, glancing around at the marvellous decorations.

"No apologies," he said gruffly. "Always liked Darcy. Been a good long while since we could do much for him."

It was a lesson to me, I considered, when I had time to think about it later. Even when we believe ourselves to be utterly alone, there is help waiting in the wings. A situation is never hopeless, unless we give up hope.

To my surprise, I was inundated with invitations to dance. Most, as I am certain, were simply curious. However, I loved talking to new people and did not mind the conversational jousting matches from the more hostile. I found myself laughing frequently, and even when a particular jibe hit home, Aurelia had prepared me with enough fodder to man my own defences. Soon, all except for the most confrontational were treating me with civility and respect—and, as later became apparent, the most confrontational were seldom the greatest intellects. My upbringing had well prepared me to laugh at my neighbours rather than weep.

It was not until the supper dance that I paired, finally, with my husband. It was one of only two waltzes for the evening, and he had claimed both. He was the ideal partner, superbly fit and graceful; I could simply let him lead, knowing always, always, my shoe roses were safe.

We would be as silent, it seemed, as our first dance lo those many years ago. I was thankful to rest in his arms, enjoying the respite from enquiries and examinations, knowing my partner to be the most handsome man in the ballroom—though this was the least of his many attractions.

"Have I told you how beautiful you look tonight?" he murmured, sweeping me into a turn.

"You may have mentioned it," I said, smiling up at him as we floated—or so it felt—across the ballroom floor. "It is difficult to feel anything *but* beautiful when decorated in the Darcy diamonds." Earlier in the day he had given me the diamond-studded tiara with matching necklace. They had been his grandmother's, and I wore them with love and pride.

Georgiana and Bingley swept past us, Georgiana sparkling with enjoyment, her face positively aglow. "She looks so happy," he murmured.

"Plainly, she *is*," I agreed. "And Bingley as well." He had lost that paunch at his waist and appeared healthy and fit, much more so than…was it only four months ago that I had met him again? What was more, he looked into his wife's eyes as he twirled her dizzyingly past, very roguish and delighted in his partner. "He is quite the showman, is he not?"

While Bingley was not the man I had once believed him to be, he was no villain. Although his wife had rather easily forgiven him, she had taken years to trust him again. He had loyally waited. I could not imagine wanting him for Jane, but I was very glad he was the good husband of my dear sister Georgiana.

Mr Darcy surprised me then, dipping me outrageously low as the music came to its climactic finish; his eyes bright with mirth, he dropped a kiss upon my lips and drew me up again to the sound of the gleeful, shocked laughter of those nearby. And I was perfectly, simply, happy.

CHAPTER THIRTY

L ord Cavendish announced 'a formal coroner's inquiry
into the death of Miss Caroline Bingley' would be held
the next quarter-day, the twenty-fourth of June, and hied
himself and Lady Cavendish back to London.

I shoved any worries about the situation to the back of
my mind. Not only was there a lack of hard evidence, but
neighbourhood opinion seemed to be tipping in our favour.
Old Mr Davis, the linen draper who had been so impolite
upon our first meeting, now treated me (and my purchases,
it should be noted) with great courtesy, and others followed
suit. I did not look upon it as bribery—Pemberley would
never pay more than she should have to pay for goods and
services. But she would pay fairly, and between a flourishing
trade with Hopewell, new connexions with leading citizens,
and London gossip having moved on to much newer scandals
—well, no one was particularly pressing to have my husband
hauled off to the stocks, so to speak. Seeing Mr Darcy at the
Cavendish ball had reminded everyone who he *really* was,

making print shop caricatures and anonymous broadsheets seem utterly ridiculous.

Bingley and Georgiana stayed for a month, and during that time, Georgiana shyly confided that they were fairly certain of 'a happy event' before Christmas. I was so delighted for her, and Bingley was over the moon with happiness. Mr Darcy was very pleased as well, of course, and did not seem to feel any anxiety because we had not yet been likewise blessed.

"I am quite happy to have you all to myself for the rest of my days," he assured me when I quizzed him on the subject again. "Or, it will happen when it happens. It took them three years, when we have not even had one yet."

I decided never to tell him of the long period of abstinence his friend had endured. His keen conscience would only feel somewhat to blame.

I received the bulky package by express, in the late afternoon approximately two weeks after the Cavendish ball. Since that event, I had been inundated with callers, invitations, and the accompanying duties of a hostess. Almost, I missed the quiet days of my first months at Pemberley, where most of my time was my own. However, I had made some promising friendships during these weeks, of both older and younger matrons of Derbyshire society, so I did not regret it. Still, neither did I regret that most would be following Lord and Lady Cavendish to London this week to finish the Season, for I required time for what I had privately named 'The Great Project'.

It was, of course, impossible that I proceed without Mr Darcy's full cooperation and authority, but I wished to at least have drawings done which faithfully represented the pictures in my mind's eye. This was made easier due to the school building which—thanks to Lady Cavendish—had expanded in size and scope, and, as Lord Cavendish would say, folderol.

Mr Darcy looked up from his desk as I accepted the package. "The final drawings of the school?" he asked.

"Unquestionably," I replied, walking to his desk. "And something else besides."

My husband believed that the distinguished architect Mr Jeffry Wyatt had agreed to design the school due to Lady Cavendish's influence, which was true, insofar as it went. But the allure of devising alterations to Pemberley was the true motive inspiring his charitable impulses, and when meeting with him, Lady Cavendish and I had managed to discreetly bring him through its cliffside wing and explain what was wanted.

Heart pounding, I untied the string and began to remove drawings. The first were of the school, a rather simple but elegant, classical building which would lie halfway between Hopewell and Pemberley and be accessible to both tenants and children from the village. To build such a large one was an almost unheard-of measure, certainly excessive by any standard, and not even entirely wanted, except by myself and Mr Marley. But we were convinced of its usefulness, its *rightness* even, and had managed to push the concept along. Following the ball, monies for its construction were amply secured.

And then I withdrew from the stack the drawings of Pemberley.

Mr Darcy's brows raised in surprise.

"I have an idea for the cliffside wing—and new purposes, if you will," I said, somewhat breathlessly. "I wanted you to see it as I can in my imagination, and Mr Wyatt kindly agreed to sketch out my proposal."

"Kindness. Sketches. Indeed." Mr Darcy murmured.

I understood his sarcasm. What lay before us were hardly 'sketches' such as I had envisioned, but exquisite renderings, an elegant vision merged with my own and added thereunto. But my heart soared to see them, for they were everything I had hoped for and more.

My proposal was to *move* the entire wing. Reconstruct it in the opposite direction, so it met up with the rest of the house and formed a more classical rectangular shape—with the end result resting far from the edge of the peak it was currently perched upon. Of course, Mr Wyatt had taken it all a good several steps further than ever I dreamed, with *his* end result nearly doubling the size of the house—adding an orangery, a theatre, a Turkish bath, a dairy, a new kitchen and numerous servants' rooms—in addition to my particular project. I saw Mr Darcy comprehend what the drawings meant, saw the surprise on his normally calm mien.

"Mr Wyatt agreed there was sufficient room to build, and it would be possible to do so without tearing down the rest of the house, he said, although of course there might be some disorder and disruption for a time. Yes, it would be expensive, but Mr Martin feels that there is ample skilled labour in the county, and the jobs it would create in the short term might help to further our community goodwill. We would preserve everything possible in the reconstruction. At the same time, we could add some modern amenities—Mr Wyatt spoke of rather alluring-sounding plumbing, improved heating, and even exterior gas lighting."

Mr Darcy continued to pore over the plans, brow furrowed, before finally coming to a large additional drawing.

"The Great Library of Pemberley," he read. It showed an interior view, with columns where walls had once stood, added spacious windows and, in between them, massive ebony shelving to house books.

"What is this? Another entrance?" he asked, pointing to a set of exterior doors in what once had been the mistress's bedchamber.

"That is part of my idea," I said, talking more quickly in my anxiety. The very private master of Pemberley might not care much for this part of it. "Since, if we adopt these plans, there would be room to add exterior staircases, I thought, what if we were to provide a separate library entrance and enough um, supervision, to allow the public in?"

"Turn Pemberley into a–a lending library?" he exclaimed incredulously.

"Oh, no. No, of course not. We would not lend; any books must be read here. I thought perhaps we could hire a librarian, who could organise the books and help those who needed to find specific information. Such a person would help all of us, for we have so many volumes I cannot identify them all, including very many that will not fit in our current library. I realise there would be expenses besides the librarian—the extra fireplaces to keep the place warm throughout the day and more servants to ensure its security, although I think we should limit public admission to daylight hours, perhaps not even every day. And see here, a private reading room for the family's use only, very comfortable and cosy."

The family's 'cosy private reading room'—a larger room than the library we currently occupied—also was windowed, adding opportunity for reading or drawing with beautiful views of sky and clouds. It was a softened effect, perhaps, with no four hundred-foot death-defying drops, but what it lacked in drama it added in elegance, several times the original amount of space, and simple human appeal.

The ballroom would have to be rebuilt, of course, but in much the same design, with the addition of a large courtyard extending out onto the majestic cliffs, and a wrought-iron fencing surround, so that those who wished spectacular views of the valley below might have them safely. With the gas lighting, we might even offer out-of-doors dancing within it, when weather cooperated.

He continued to study the renderings carefully, occasionally referring between them. Finally, he spread them out upon the surface of his large desk, as if he were trying to picture each in three dimensions.

"What do you think of it?" I asked hesitantly, after some minutes passed.

He blinked up at me, as if he'd forgotten, momentarily, my presence. "Oh. Why, it is brilliant, of course."

My eyes widened. "Does that mean you will consider the changes? We could handle the construction in stages, perhaps taking—"

He stepped away from the desk, turning to me fully, his eyes alight. "This…this is everything I never dreamed of, for Pemberley, for others. I have been *stuck*, for lack of a better word, mired in the past. Not simply my first marriage, but for so long looking backwards only, at the expectations and perceptions of people long dead." He gently grasped my chin. "You, my darling, can see it so clearly, as you do so much else. The house is in the wrong place. It always has been, has *always* traded the full use of this land for one dramatic view, beheld by almost no one. *Of course* it ought to be redone, and, as we have the means to do it, we ought to be the ones responsible." He held my face within his hands, his dark eyes looking deeply into mine. "Only you. Thank you."

One of the unexpected results of our decision to redesign Pemberley was the announcement from Mr Donavan. His patient, he said, reported an improvement in her health. He told us almost reluctantly.

"I am most concerned that it is only her deep grief at seeing the destruction of her daughter's life's work at Pemberley, urging her to risk changes at a most unfortunate and fragile time," he sighed. "She, naturally, wishes to be gone from here and in her own home before she must witness it."

"I find it highly unlikely her health is connected to remodelling," Mr Darcy retorted. "After all, Anne expended a great deal of effort refurbishing Throckmorton time and again, and it burnt to the ground. Mrs de Bourgh seems to have accepted its absence, and will surely adapt to this change as well."

I could see the doctor wished to offer a scathing reply, so I intervened.

"We destroy nothing," I said more gently. "Her greatest contribution, the ballroom, will be rebuilt in every particular, her design remaining intact. We will preserve the panelling, the flooring, the chandeliers. We only add the glassed doors she wished for at the time, now that it would be safe to do so. It will be as beautiful as it ever was."

He sniffed. "Perhaps, to you. I have noticed that many of the gentry hereabouts are uninterested in topics of a serious stamp, such as the destruction of great art and architecture, though Mrs Darcy created it for the benefit of generations."

"Oh for heaven's sake," Mr Darcy retorted, and I knew he was about to give the good doctor an earful that, however deserved, would be twisted into something far worse than a reprimand when repeated.

"Certainly we do not wish for Mrs de Bourgh's health to suffer," I interpolated. "Like you, we believe that the sea air of her home in Ramsgate will be truly restorative. I am certain you are concerned for her safety on the journey, and naturally we hope to retain your services until she is settled in those familiar surroundings. Unless, of course, your patients here cannot spare you?"

Obviously, he had not expected this sop to his pride, for his startled expression quickly reflected covetous interest, and his next words suggested a new, conciliatory spirit.

"I am in agreement, and I do not think it of light importance that Mrs de Bourgh should have inattentive companionship. And though it is possible that some might suffer in my absence, I cannot acquit myself of that duty, nor could I think well of the physician who should omit any occasion of showing his respect towards one so closely connected to the House of Darcy." He bowed low. "I shall contact Mr Tilbury, of Buxton, to whom I have lent my own skills in the past. I am certain he shall wish to make himself available to the good citizens of Hopewell." With that, he hurried away, a new lightness to his step as he contemplated a seaside holiday.

Mr Darcy gave me a look of some exasperation. "Does Donavan truly expect it all to remain unchanged forever? Anne, herself, redecorated her rooms at least three times, and would likely have done it three more, given the opportunity. She would have gone through three fortunes doing it, if permitted."

I went to him, putting my hand upon his cheek. "I fear the new Mrs Darcy is spending more than the old one ever did on builders' schemes."

He turned his face to my palm, kissing it, and pulling me

in closer. "The new Mrs Darcy thinks only of her husband and the future with her scheming. And now you and your arts and allurements are distracting me from my frustration with that gudgeon—and doing a splendid job of it, I might add."

"Arts and allurements!" I protested hotly. "I only—" but he stopped all words with a kiss having nothing to do with schemes or builders or doctors or ballrooms, unfairly winning his point.

Hence, the first week in June, a carriage—carrying only a veiled Mrs de Bourgh, her maid, and her solicitous physician —clattered down the Pemberley drive. Mr Darcy and I, along with Nurse Rook—who Mrs de Bourgh, unsurprisingly, hated and had not wished to bring—Morton, and Mrs Reynolds alone stood at the top of the curving steps to bid her farewell. She had looked at none of us, and though I wished her a pleasant journey, she ignored me. Mr Darcy said nothing at all, remaining stoic.

"And there departs one excessively disagreeable woman," Nurse Rook muttered.

"She has had a great loss," I offered aloud, though inwardly agreeing wholeheartedly.

But the nurse snorted. "Loss! I have seen loss! My last place, four children stricken with fever and three of them died. The grieving father hired me to help the mother convalesce, her who'd nearly died herself, and *she* bore up better than that woman! Putting herself through a window and losing an eye! And for what? Does she think the master will lose sleep at night over it?" She seemed to remember herself then, and flushed. "Beg pardon, sir, ma'am."

Mr Darcy only nodded, and the nurse and the other two servants departed, leaving us alone in the crisp, cool air. The sky was grey with clouds, but it did not feel, particularly, like rain, and I thought they would have an unremarkable, though lengthy journey.

"She refused to take Anne's portraits," I said into the silence. "Not even the one of her as a girl."

He turned to me. "I heard all about that tantrum, though not from you." He tapped my nose. "Which is why the carts of Anne's belongings left beforehand by a few days, and the portraits are in them regardless of her ill-delivered opinions. I sent word to her new housekeeper there and all should be stowed safely inside her Ramsgate home well before she arrives. Perhaps, one day, she will be able to remember the past only as it gives her pleasure and perception. A wise woman taught me that, once."

I looked up at him; I was heartened and relieved at how peaceful his expression.

"And perhaps we ought to add something to Nurse Rook's wages before she departs," he added.

I smiled. "'Tis already done."

Despite the massive disruption to routine and the noise and confusion of so many workmen, the mood of the house was a cheerful one when construction began the very next day.

They would not begin on the house itself, of course, but digging foundations for the new wing. Mrs Reynolds's workers busily toiled at clearing, storing, and packing away all the remaining furnishings in the cliffside wing. Other workmen would be occupied removing all that could be removed, including panelling, marble tiles, carvings, and other woodwork. Mr Wyatt had arrived this morning and hopped between crews of men and Mr Williams, who directed them.

I welcomed the disarray, for it kept my mind from dwelling on inquests and a future beyond my control, in favour of events I could. Ten days or so previous, Miss Bickford had offered a remark about the planned-for renovations, which led to a discussion, which led, somehow, to my agreement to lead a contingent of the villagers on a tour through the cliffside wing before it was utterly dismantled—a surprising number of them having heard of the majestic view from the upper floor and strongly desiring to see it.

Mr Darcy was not enthusiastic about the idea, as it was difficult for him to forgive the slights I had received in the past; he had no desire to share the part of the house he hated with people he resented. But he was also more than willing that I should do as seemed to me best, and to support me in whatsoever way he could, and so he welcomed them all to our home and spoke a word or two to each of the seven villagers, six women and one man—the dogmatic Mr Davis. It was all a bit stiff and awkward, but I sensed no hostility, only the discomfiture of people from different stations interacting. I thought it was good for all of us; we were neighbours, and ought to treat each other with courtesy and kindness, no matter our differences.

As Mrs Reynolds shepherded them from the parlour where they had gathered, Mr Davis turned back to Mr Darcy. He cleared his throat, reddened, and spoke. "Sir, a word, if you will—my brother, him as owns The Ox and Mouse—he says Wickham be back in town. I just thought as you ought to know." With that, he followed the rest of the ladies out before another word could be spoken.

We looked at each other in shared wonderment. Of course, the news of Wickham's return was disagreeable. But the fact that a citizen of Hopewell disclosed it directly was a clear sign, I thought. The public had taken sides on the rumours and gossip of the past. They sided with us.

I smiled at Mr Darcy, and followed the villagers and Mrs Reynolds.

CHAPTER THIRTY-ONE

Mrs Reynolds and I had made a plan for the showing; her workers would only labour in rooms we would not open while we took villagers through the wing. While much had been removed, certainly not every room had been stripped bare. There were some paintings—which Mrs Reynolds could speak of—and several of the smaller chambers and Georgiana's former rooms were intact. Of course, the *pièce de résistance* would be the majestic views from the master's terrace.

Somewhat to my surprise, the tour was very enjoyable. Mrs Reynolds, as usual, was a nearly endless repository of information, sharing amusing and informational anecdotes about Darcy forebears and Pemberley's history. While it was a bit noisy, as the sound of workmen removing panelling echoed throughout the wing, no one seemed to mind. The tour of the upstairs ended on the terrace. The day was much warmer than any previous, and the view of sky and valley was as magnificent as it ever was. As they peered over the low balustrade, I heard gasps of awe or fear.

"I don't blame them for moving the whole blessed wing away from this cliff," muttered Miss Bickford, backing away several steps.

After all had looked their fill, we trooped down the stairs and into the ballroom, the one room on the lower floor that had not, as yet, been touched. A footman, Bertie, lowered one of the three chandeliers so they could look closely at its crystal perfections. Then Mrs Reynolds demonstrated the lever system that opened the windows, and explained how, in the new ballroom, they would be floor length and open as doors out onto a courtyard. As she closed them, Bertie displayed Mr Wyatt's drawing so that everyone could see how the new Pemberley exterior would appear.

We were all gathered around Bertie when I was startled by the sound of slow, loud clapping. I turned.

Mr Wickham stood behind us, a mocking smile upon his face.

"You!" I cried. "What are you doing here?"

"My dear! So inhospitable a greeting for your old friend?"

Bertie, the dear lad, did not hesitate. Dropping the drawings, he launched himself at Mr Wickham.

Unfortunately, Wickham was no stranger to brawling. Without missing a beat, he delivered a solid punch to the poor young footman that laid him out cold.

I started forward.

"Oh, not so fast, pretty girl." From his pocket, he withdrew a pistol and trained it directly on me.

The villagers cried out and Mrs Reynolds gasped. "Are you mad?" I asked, trying to herd the crowd behind me. "You cannot possibly hurt us all with that, but *you* will see a noose!"

"Mad? You could say that," he replied, not quite so

nonchalantly as in his initial greeting. "I have no interest in hurting them, but you will come with me. Your husband will learn that his wealth cannot help him in this. Perhaps he has not paid for murdering Anne, but pay, he shall."

I stepped forward. Old Mr Davis put a shaky hand upon my arm, but I firmly shook my head at him and he subsided. "As well you know, Mr Darcy murdered no one. Frankly, he believes *you* did it," I said, my voice imbued with a calm I could not feel. "You have known him since he was a boy, when you needled him for refusing to join in your wild exploits. You carried on an affair for years with his wife, and he did nothing except deny you welcome at Pemberley. You stand before us, training a pistol upon an innocent woman. Of the two of you, who is most likely to be a murderer?" I cared not that these were confidences, secrets that everyone hoped would die with Anne. I would say *anything* if it might stop this man from violence.

"He did! He *must* have killed her!"

"Why would he?" I said caustically. "You must know he did not love her, that any affection he once had died with her disloyalty. He simply could not care enough to *feel* such passion."

"He wanted a child. She said he did, more than anything. She refused to give him one, and he killed her for it!"

I rolled my eyes. "If he was so desperate to be a parent, then why, pray tell, did he choose a woman of eight-and-twenty as his next bride? His sister is his heir, and he is content that she should remain so, should we never have progeny."

"Because he is a bloody fool! Perhaps she *was to* give him an heir—but a by-blow! Perhaps even *mine*! How he would despise the bloodlines of Pemberley to be thus polluted!"

I sighed. "Mr Darcy is many things, but never a fool. Of course he knew he would have no true heirs from her. It would be impossible, for the obvious reason that he would not touch her. Provision was made for any natural children she might bear, which his solicitors can verify, with Georgiana remaining his heir to Pemberley. Simply because he did not repudiate her publicly, do you think he had not *thought* of this? That he made *no* plans?"

"She sent me a note!" he cried, and for the first time I thought I heard real anguish. "She begged me to come to her, but I was drunk, and did not read it until too late. Too late! Why did she send for me? What need had she? I loved her! I would have saved her!" The pistol lowered an inch as he seemed to deflate. Tears streamed down his cheeks.

"Imbecile!"

From the rear of the ballroom stood a man, hat pulled low over his face. After thus announcing his presence, however, his next actions were strange: he pulled a spill from the jar on the hearth and lit a taper; its light did nothing to reveal his shadowed features.

Wickham was not startled by the stranger's presence. "It's no good," he tossed back over his shoulder. "She is right. Darcy hasn't the pluck; he is too chicken-hearted. It makes no sense."

"It is not for you to decide," the stranger hissed. "Take her and we go."

"I only want answers, not *her*," Wickham said. "If I thought she would give them to me, I would. If I thought Darcy would *trade* answers for her, I would. But he never does do anything he does not want to do, or say anything he does not want to say. Perhaps Cavendish can get answers from him, or perhaps she tells the truth, and he knows nothing. We are wasting our time. Let us leave now."

"No!" the stranger growled. "You have not done as you promised. She leaves with us."

With the exception of a gasp or two, the villagers had maintained a silence during the entire fantastical conversation. But Miss Bickford had clearly had enough. "We are *all* leaving," she called. "Everyone, come with me." She began walking to the opposite side of the ballroom towards the main entrance and its two large double doors.

I quickly saw the sense of her actions, and herded everyone with me, giving Wickham and the stranger my back. After all, if Wickham shot—which he seemed disinclined to do—he could hardly shoot all of us. For whatever reason, I felt the real threat came from the stranger.

Oddly enough, we reached the door without incident, even with two of the villagers dragging poor Bertie. I hastened to throw it open—to no avail. We immediately looked to Mrs Reynolds. She withdrew her ring of keys, and with only slightly shaking hands selected the correct one and inserted it, pulling the door at the same moment. The key turned, but nothing happened. Mr Davis leaned in, putting his weight into it, but the door remained shut. I ran to the two other servant's doors that were semi-hidden within the panelling. Neither would open.

From the other end of the ballroom, the stranger began laughing, a peculiar, echoing laughter. That was when I knew, and spun to face our captor.

"Mrs de Bourgh. How lovely of you to join us. It is an unusual costume, however, for a masquerade."

She tossed aside the beaver; her hair was scraped back into its usual harsh bun, and she wore the clothing of a middling sort of gentleman. Without the voluminous folds of her black mourning fabric, I saw that the weight she'd lost was to good effect—she appeared muscular, strong. There was, as Nurse Rook had long and often claimed, absolutely nothing of weakness, of illness, in her. She held the candle up close to her scarred face; I knew the action was to frighten us, because she did indeed look horrible, though I felt only pity. But Mrs Dale screamed.

"People see what they wish to see, what they think to see," she said, smiling a ghastly smile. "A little face powder, a bit of paint, a cane and a weak voice—it is easy enough. Those doors will not open. And now, you shall come with me. Wickham, take her."

Wickham stood uncertainly.

"Do it," she urged. "Remember your poor, beautiful Anne." She pulled the draperies aside, and there stood the three portraits of Anne, propped against the wall. She must have known Mr Darcy would try to send them away. Had Wickham helped her, removing them from the cart and placing them in here, the least-used room of the house, at her bequest? I gave a shudder, imagining him lurking at night within our home.

"Look at that creature! Look at what has replaced our dear Anne! Is this to be endured? But it must not, shall not be. Anne would never submit to any person's whims. Do it for her!"

And so, with renewed determination, he came for me. Everyone froze in place, uncertain of his pistol. Fortunately, he seemed to almost forget it was in his hand—striding towards me confidently, as if I would obediently, submissively toddle off with him.

"You have forgotten something," I said, as he neared. He smiled, the same old winning smile, as though we were at the Netherfield ball, and he was claiming that dance I had once hoped for, so long ago.

"What is that, dear lady?" he asked, reaching for me, not bothering at all with the aggressive stance he'd taken against poor Bertie.

"I am Elizabeth Bennet Darcy, and no Lydia," I replied, and, exactly as Mr Tilney had taught, I punched him in the soft cartilage of his nose. He shrieked, blood spurting, and drew back his fist, but old Mr Davis and even Miss Bickford fell upon him, and he was soon unconscious upon the floor, the pistol in Mr Davis's possession.

"It is over now," I said to Mrs de Bourgh when I looked to her again.

"He was an idiot," she snapped. "I am not. You will come with me now, or else."

The question 'Or else, what?' was to be unnecessary. For she held her candle dangerously close to the draperies nearest her.

Quickly, I calculated. Somehow, what with all the strange workmen about, they had managed to secure all doors except the one we had entered by—which she now guarded. Draperies lined the entire wall behind her; the fire would catch and quickly spread. The windows were tightly shut, so there was no hope that someone outdoors would notice the smoke; rather, it would be the choking death of all, maybe even before the flames could burn us. *But would she allow Anne's portraits to be destroyed in the conflagration? Yes*, I realised. *She would do anything.*

"Why do you do this?" I cried with unaffected astonishment. "I swear to you, Mr Darcy had *nothing* to do with your daughter's death!"

I expected her to rant or rave or hurl accusations at my husband's name, but she did not. Instead, she laughed again, a bitter, reproachful sound. "Of *course* he did not. He is too weak, too cowardly. Do you think it was easy?" she scolded. "Poor, sweet, courageous Anne, so beautiful, so broken, from a leap only *she* would have dared. 'Mama, please,' she begged me. 'Do not let me live this way. I cannot! I will not! You must finish it, as *he* would not!' Do not you see? If he had only done as she begged, *I* would not have had to. But he left it to me. Always the most difficult jobs, left only to me."

A chilling sensation crept along my spine as realisation struck. "And Caroline Bingley?" I asked. "Was that a 'difficult job' left to you?"

"Hardly difficult," she scoffed. "She threatened my daughter. It was not to be borne. As you do, now. I came here with the determined resolution of carrying my purpose, and I will not be dissuaded from it. I have not been in the habit of brooking disappointment."

"How," I asked, desperate to keep her talking, "could I possibly be a threat to Anne? She is dead."

"You," she said coldly, "are the worst threat of all. I know how to act. One of you idiots, remove Wickham's cravat, *instantly*, and tie her wrists and arms together. Do it!"

"She is mad," I murmured quietly. "Just do as she says."

"Mrs Darcy, you cannot go to her! You mustn't! She is a murderess!" whispered Miss Bickford as she made a show of —very slowly—unknotting the cravat. Wickham groaned as she removed it, but did not waken.

"Hurry!" de Bourgh screamed. "Do not deceive yourself into a belief that I will ever recede!" From her pocket, she removed a pot of something; expertly removing the lid— while not letting go of the taper—she dashed its contents upon the draperies and portraits nearest the door she guarded. I had no doubt it was a kind of terebinthine oil or something equally flammable. She had planned this.

"Do it," I urged.

Reluctantly, Miss Bickford obeyed, wrapping my arms together—in front of me, rather than behind me—and as slowly and loosely as she could. But it was a lengthy piece of cloth, and there was no way to secure it without creating far too much of a binding.

I met Mr Davis's eyes as he implored me without words to take the pistol; however, there was no way to do so without de Bourgh noticing. The frightening old woman waved her candle ever nearer the draperies, heedless of the danger to herself, but there were gasps from the villagers. The fear of fire was so ingrained, I doubted I could rally them in an attempt to overpower her; besides, she would set her blaze long before we could reach her.

I did not have a great deal of hope—whether she lit the draperies and shoved me out the door, locking them inside, or even simply set me afire to watch me burn...I could hardly stop her. I had little doubt but that she planned to burn the place regardless—she had been much too free with the truth to let anyone live, if she could prevent it. But if challenged, she could simply set the fire immediately. It seemed to me best to play for time.

"Stay here, all of you!" I demanded. I looked at Mr Davis. "Use that pistol to try and shoot the door bolt once I am taken. Perhaps it will open. Or perhaps someone will hear the report." The pistol looked old and I had no idea if it was even loaded. Mr Davis cursed and someone else whimpered, but Mrs Dale dropped to her knees and began to pray. Miss Bickford bravely started forward regardless, but I gave Mrs Reynolds a look, part pleading, part insistent, and she put her hand upon her arm to stop her.

"Don't interfere! She has her plan, can't you see?" the housekeeper implored, and she stilled.

Plan? I had no such thing. Only the design to walk as

slowly as I dared, and hope that the distance was great enough, that it took time enough, for some brilliant, miraculous intervention to present itself. She would not wish to give up her one means of control until I was close enough for her to keep it; as long as I inched forward, she would not light the drapes, though she goaded and shouted insults. "Do not imagine you can escape me! You only delay the inevitable! I *will* carry my point!"

I was very much afraid she would. And then I was only eight feet from her. Seven. Six. Five...

With a deafening crash the door nearest the villagers opened, and I whirled to see Mr Darcy—followed closely by Mr Williams—thunder in with a half-dozen others, knocking over poor old Mr Davis in the process. Mrs de Bourgh did not hesitate. She held the candle directly to the portraits. Whatever she had poured upon them caught instantly, and the velvet did the rest, the flames crawling up the drapes and leaping towards the ceiling faster than anything I ever imagined. I turned to run but she grabbed me with nearly inhuman strength, throwing me into the nearest portrait, trying to hold me close enough for any fabric upon me to catch—as if into Anne's fiery embrace.

But the scent of the oil she'd splashed was strong upon her, and in her attempts to shove my kicking, flailing, struggling person into the flames, she ignited. Still, she did not give up—even when her hair lit—only trying to use herself as a brimstone match to set me aflame. And then Mr Darcy was there, snatching me away from her, though my skirt and the cravat bindings had begun to burn, rolling away with me, over and over, to extinguish any flames. The ballroom was rapidly filling with smoke; he scooped me up and ran with me towards the open door.

Through watering eyes, I caught my final glimpse of Mrs de Bourgh. She made no move, not to escape the blaze, not to quench the flames encircling and encompassing her, not to cry out or reach for the door behind her.

She had lost, and she let herself burn.

"Oh, my darling. My darling Elizabeth. I am so sorry, so sorry," my husband said, over and over again.

He had run with me to a raised hill, far beyond the flames and smoke; I was dazed and coughing, but gradually, as the fresh air infused my lungs, began to make sense of my escape.

"You came," I rasped, for my throat felt sore as if I'd been screaming—although I was fairly certain I had held them in. "Please do not apologise. You came for me. I am safe."

"'Tis all my fault," he said, soothing my hair away from my face. "I cannot express—"

"It was not," I said, a little more strongly. "No one could have guessed she would be so diabolical."

But he held me tightly to him, murmuring words of affection and guilt. "You have not understood, you could not know. I brought this upon you, I did. Oh, my dearest, loveliest Elizabeth." A single tear tracked down his soot-stained cheeks.

Once I could not have fathomed this proud man in tears, but that was before I knew how soft and kind his heart. "No, no," I whispered, trying to put my hands up to press against his cheeks. But they were still bound.

With a muttered curse, he began tearing away at the filthy, singed cravat tying my arms together. It had protected them, for the most part, but I began to feel the effects of my close encounter with fire. My skirt, of a high-quality wool, had resisted burning through; however, a few small burns upon my upper arms stung a bit—nothing too serious, I was certain, but I could not prevent my hiss of pain.

"Oh, my love," he said, anguished, as he saw the angry red marks. "My dearest love."

At that moment, we were joined by a troupe of men from the estate, led by Mr Williams, as well as Mrs Reynolds—who thankfully appeared utterly untouched by smoke or soot or flame. Mr Darcy did not appear to notice them. I stroked his cheek and looked into his eyes.

"I am well, I promise. Please, go and rescue the rest of the house for me. Ensure all are safe and the fire does not spread. I have plans...remember?"

"I will take good care of her, sir," Mrs Reynolds promised.

"Take her to my home," Mr Williams offered. "It is close, but well away from the house and quite safe."

"That will do very nicely," I agreed. "And look, here is Miss Bickford and her party coming to meet us. Let us all go to Mr Williams's home, where we will be out of the way, while you and the others do the more dangerous labour of stopping the spread of the flames."

After a last agonised look at me, Mr Darcy took the men away with him to lead the fight against the fire. For a moment, we all stood together on that grassy hillock, watching the bustle of activity swarming the cliffside.

"They will try and choke it out," Mrs Reynolds said knowledgably, calmly. "Fire needs air to breathe. But Pemberley also has the latest in fire engines, to better apply water."

"Bertie...is he safe?"

"Oh, yes, mistress. They brought him 'round quickly and

nothing would do for him but that he immediately join the men fighting the fire."

I closed my eyes in relief, but other worries beset me. "What if she applied her oil earlier, to other draperies? We do not know how long she was there, lurking, or what they have done with the doctor or the coachman. Obviously, she was not ill, and has not been for some time."

"Ah, but we have had footmen stationed beyond her room's door these last weeks, and Nurse Rook was not the type to fall asleep while attending her patient. I do not think the old lady decided to harm Pemberley until she learned of the renovation, and by then, she was too closely watched. I do not believe she has been here for hours, even. There were too many about, and few places to hide. Now, mistress, let us go to Mr Williams's cottage. His housekeeper, Mrs Pruitt, will have something for those burns. Or shall we ask for a litter to carry you?"

At last, I heard it—the trembling in her voice. Cool, steady Mrs Reynolds was unmistakeably overwrought.

"I can walk without difficulty," I assured her as the party of villagers joined us—*sans* Mr Davis, who had stayed to help the other men. The women were chattering excitedly and, I was happy to say, more as if it had all been an adventure than any true ordeal. But then, I have always felt that these women, most of whom worked dawn to dusk in their trades, were far more resilient than many hothouse flowers amongst the *ton*.

"Mrs Darcy, you were heroic!" Miss Bickford exclaimed, to the enthusiastic agreement of her compatriots. "Such madness! You saved us, gaining time for our rescuers to discover our plight. We could not have imagined a better champion!"

"That she is," Mrs Reynolds agreed. "However, the

master will not be pleased if we keep her standing out here in the sun whilst she is injured."

The ladies immediately expressed their compassionate concern. While guests in my home, they had been assaulted and abused and subjected to great danger, and yet there was nothing of blame or outrage. It touched me deeply.

"I am so happy you are all safe. Now tell me: what have they done with Mr Wickham?"

As we walked towards Mr Williams's home, they told me of how the steward had personally dragged Wickham out of the burning ballroom, ordering him roped and bound over for justice. The scoundrel would sit in a gaol cell until the quarter-day, when *he* would be answering the magistrate's enquiries, rather than Mr Darcy.

And because they deserved to know the rest of the story, when they questioned what Mrs de Bourgh had meant by her words regarding Anne's 'leap', and of what she had 'had to do' because Mr Darcy would not, I explained most of it—at least the part about Anne's pretended suicidal drop off the terrace whilst angry at her husband, her foolhardy attempt to climb back up again, and the subsequent fall that had broken her. "She would, most likely have died regardless," I said. "She could not have lived long if her back was broken, I do not believe."

"So she begged Mr Darcy to finish the job?" Miss Bickford, ever bold, demanded.

"Mr Darcy could not commit such an act," I said. "As it was a festival day, with few servants about, Mr Darcy ran to the stables himself to have Mr Simpson fetched. When he returned with a litter and assistance, she was at the bottom of the cliff, already dead. Until today, we had no clue as to how she'd fallen the rest of the way." I saw no need to mention Mr Williams's presence.

Everyone was silent in contemplation, understanding, finally, the choices Mr Darcy had faced. To declare his wife a suicide, denying her a proper burial for what was, after all, an accident? To seek out another responsible for what had been meant, most likely, as a merciful act?

"It was a terrible thing," Miss Bickford said. "I would believe the old lady was driven mad with the guilt of it, but I heard her words. She as much as admitted to killing poor Miss Bingley, and without an ounce of regret. I cannot pretend to mourn her."

I was silent as we walked into the embracing warmth of Mr William's well-situated cottage. I accepted that we would never truly know who had killed Miss Bingley. Doubtlessly Mrs de Bourgh would have taken responsibility for the murder, whether or not it had been herself or Anne who accomplished it; I was certain the plan to have the Kroffords depart suddenly and suspiciously and thus obscure her disappearance was purely Mrs de Bourgh's idea. In my heart, I will always believe Anne the most likely perpetrator of an impulsive murder—as demonstrated by the shallow grave too close to the house and my knowledge of the two impetuous, temperamental, and spoilt women involved. Only Anne would have used Mr Darcy's blade and flaunted it, whereas the more devious Mrs de Bourgh, to my mind, might have preferred to carefully replace the blade in its accustomed spot as if it had never been removed. But this was all conjecture— for all I knew, they dug the grave together.

In all the ways that mattered, however, it was unimportant. In life they had acted as one; even if Anne *were* the murderess, her mother had hidden the truth and protected her from any consequences. They were two halves of a whole, and without Anne, Mrs de Bourgh was only half a person. I firmly believed her guilty of setting the Thorncroft fire, thinking to destroy whatever evidence might have been inside it of Anne's terrible life. She had come to Pemberley intending to die today; she had only hoped to bring me with her, and leave Mr Darcy without home or wife—alone, as she had been.

CHAPTER THIRTY-TWO

Mrs Reynolds returned to Pemberley after leaving me in the care of good Mrs Pruitt; while she had ensured that all her people were out of the house before joining me and Mr Darcy, she knew they were still frightened and in need of useful purpose. I would very much have liked to join her, but my burns had grown uncomfortable. Mrs Pruitt anointed each one with a pain-relieving unguent she swore was healing, dressed them, and then sent me to rest in a spare bedchamber. As I lay there in that bright, cosy room upon a hand-stitched quilt that might have been sewn by Mr Williams's mother, echoes of quiet chatter just beyond the door, I tried to comprehend all of what had occurred.

I had been brutally attacked; Mrs de Bourgh had wanted me dead, more than she wanted her own health or liberty or even life itself.

It made little sense to me. I did not like her, true. I had arranged for her care and visited her, but only out of duty. I had been thrilled at the announcement that she was returning to Ramsgate, ending that obligation. I had not planned, in fact, to think of her ever again, was only resolved to act in a manner which would, in my own opinion, constitute my happiness, without reference to her, or to *any* person so wholly unconnected with me.

Why could she not have felt the same? I believe I had heard of Anne de Bourgh, or rumours of Mr Darcy's attachment to such a person, years ago in Meryton, but I had quickly forgotten her. We had nothing whatsoever to do with each other. My existence meant nothing to the course of her life or her death. If I had believed de Bourgh's actions were a strike solely at Mr Darcy, some strange vindictiveness for his hasty remarriage, I could perhaps understand her better.

But this, too, was incomprehensible. Beyond the fact that she'd known Anne's marriage to be an unhappy one on *both* sides, Mrs de Bourgh had never seemed to show much interest in him. Her sentiments seemed exactly the same as Mr Darcy had described Anne's feelings—who, by the time she announced herself ready to bear his child, had looked upon him only as a chess piece to be moved about on her board. That her husband meant nothing to her had been proven by the absence of her apparently famous tact and charm when demanding he give her one. Likewise, those villagers in the ballroom had not existed to Mrs de Bourgh, except as obstructions to her one true goal—to kill me.

She enjoyed the thought of destroying his home and his marriage, but her real purpose was to ensure no other Mrs Darcy ever ruled Pemberley, I thought. *Anne de Bourgh was to be the last.*

It was late in the afternoon before Mr Williams entered the small parlour where Mrs Pruitt and I waited. Apologising for his filthy appearance, he explained that Mr Darcy had specially charged him to immediately give me the news that they had been able to extinguish the fire long before it reached the main house. For the most part, only the ball-room and the rooms directly above it were utterly ruined. Since they were to be demolished regardless, it mattered little beyond the loss of a few furnishings. Mr Darcy, he said, would be here to fetch me as soon as he had washed away the soot.

He came for me at the twilight hour, the fresh evening breezes blowing away the waning scents of smoke and soot. His hair was still damp from a recent bath, his features solemn and troubled. He bowed to Mrs Pruitt, thanked her for her ministrations, and together we departed.

Mr Darcy had brought a carriage, but I requested we walk the bare half-mile distance.

"You are hurt," Mr Darcy said with a sober frown, looking at my ruined gown and the bandages upon my arms. Mrs Pruitt and I were not at all of a size, so she had done her best to freshen the dress and I had donned it again after my own bath.

"Truly, I am well. Whatever Mrs Pruitt used to treat my small injuries has relieved any pain. I have wished to make the walk home for some time, but she was so hospitable, I did not wish to cause her worry by disappearing from her care."

"I owe her even more of my thanks if she bid you rest," he said before instructing the young man holding the reins to return the vehicle to the Pemberley stables.

We walked in silence for some minutes; he carefully matched his pace to mine, but made no move to touch me, to offer his arm. Of course, I knew him so well now—he had doubtlessly taken entire responsibility for the actions of the villains and for any tiny ache upon my person. So I tucked my arm in his, despite a little stinging, and as I expected, he seemed to ease a bit.

"How did you know?" I asked. "How did you know we were hostages?"

"I did not," he replied. "I only kept watching for you and your party to emerge from the ballroom. And when you did not, I was impatient, and thought to look in on your group. Then I found the door had been nailed shut and I was alarmed, as was Mr Williams, and so we burst in upon you. Which led, of course, to her setting the place afire."

"Oh, she meant to do that regardless. There was no good way to prevent it. What with all the workmen's hammers, we did not recognise the sound of nailing, I suppose. Do we have any idea what happened to Mr Donavan and Mr Frost?" I asked. "They were supposed to be delivering her to Ramsgate! Mr Frost most of all, of course." I grinned up at him, but he could not yet be teased.

"Mr Davis gave me a full accounting of the events in the ballroom. After speaking with him, I met with Wickham. He was...unusually cooperative. A veritable fountain of information," he replied gravely. "Mrs de Bourgh wrote to him about a week ago, asking him to meet her at The Bell, a coaching inn that was to be their first night's stop. There, she simply hired a woman to play her part on the journey to Ramsgate, instructing her maid to say nothing of the ruse."

"She was veiled," I remembered. "I suppose, if their actress is clever, they might make it all the way to Ramsgate. If she is sly, as well, they might never find out, and return home none the wiser. But if she is not, they might return to Pemberley speedily. It was a risk...she could not have held auditions for qualified actresses."

"She only needed to be a day ahead of them," he said

grimly. "She did not mean to return to Ramsgate, I am thinking, although Wickham denies that much."

Since I had drawn the same conclusions, I only nodded. "What did Wickham say *was* their intent?"

"Only to question us and insist upon real answers as to the cause of Anne's death."

"I believe that was *his* intention," I said slowly, working it out in my head. "However, he heard enough to realise, by the time she ordered him to collect me, that it was not hers. I do not believe he came to kill me, but I would be unsurprised if he was willing enough that she should."

His arm tensed beneath my hand, and I sighed. "I do not, I cannot understand it. Her hatred of me makes no sense at all, no matter how I puzzle it out."

"I do," he said, after a small hesitation. "She had worked out who you were, and I was too thick to realise she might have understood."

"Who *I* am?" I queried, half-smiling. "An orphan from Hertfordshire and Cheapside? An impoverished spinster? A relation of one-too-many vicars?"

He let out a heavy sigh, and said nothing for several more minutes. The moon rose, lighting our path well enough. In the distance, I could see the lights of Pemberley, and smell the bruised scent of burnt wood and singed stone. Somewhat to my surprise, however, Mr Darcy led me off the direct path to the house, instead guiding me into Pemberley's version of a hermitage—far more elaborate than the one at Rosings, perched upon a hilltop with wood and garden views from all sides. Of course, it was too dark to appreciate them, but he lit a taper and then seated himself upon the padded wood bench beside me. For a time, he simply sat there in contemplation. I could not have said why, but he appeared more fiercely alone than I had seen him since before our wedding. When he spoke, it was with a grim note of determination.

"I fell in love with you whilst still at Netherfield Park," he said at last.

I bit my lip. He had mentioned it before, a certain attraction he had held then; I liked that he had, at some point, remembered me fondly and even with desire. Love, however, seemed an exaggeration wrought by time and, perhaps, the unhappiness he had borne since. I felt my memories were closer to the truth. "You did not," I protested gently. "I recall those days fairly clearly. And it was not simply your refusal to dance with me at an assembly, although I believe you when you say you decided I was not so unattractive, after all. Still, I would put your feelings for me then rather closer to disgust than to love."

He sighed. "I am embarrassed to confess to you how meanly I considered the inferiority of your relations, although I am certain my arrogance comes as no surprise. Of course, you and Mrs Tilney avoided completely any like share of censure. I have already divulged the dishonour of my part in separating Bingley from your sister."

"And I have discovered your role in elevating Mr Tilney, to the point of buying Matlock's benefice so that you might see her happily wed."

"But towards you, I behaved more dishonourably still," he said, continuing as if I had not spoken. "I was in love with you, but felt your family an insult to my station. My uncle, the old earl, who knew of Georgiana's near escape from Wickham, believed her misjudgement entirely due to my bachelor state, and that what was needed was a maternal figure. I understood my aunt could not be that person for her. I say this not to excuse myself, but only to explain my rationalisations at the time. I knew you would be an excellent sister, but I imagined with abhorrence introducing the rest of your family to the earl, of listening to him rage at my lack of sense. I never wanted to admit this to you. I am ashamed of what my feelings once were."

It was not precisely easy—though hardly a surprise—to listen to his memories. But had *I* not listened to Wickham, allowing *his* perceptions to so easily rule my own feelings? Had not my family—especially my mother and younger sisters, but at times, even my father, embarrassed me?

"I understand," I said quietly.

He glanced over at me, the first time he'd really looked at me since entering the hermitage. "I doubt you do," he said acerbically. "Even after I brought Bingley away, I thought often of you by day and dreamt of you by night. I hoped somehow that you would leave Hertfordshire, visit someplace where I might see you again. At one point, I even considered buying Netherfield Park so that I would have some excuse to spend time in the neighbourhood. The only thing that kept me from it, I believe, was the thought of trying to come up with some excuse to keep Bingley out of it."

He shook his head at my open-mouthed astonishment. I had been to visit Charlotte in March of 1812, and thus he certainly could have seen me at Matlock Court. But of course, Lady Matlock had never had me to dine, and it is doubtful she would ever have mentioned such an undistinguished guest of her rector's wife.

"Meanwhile, there was Anne," he continued, "whom the earl had met and approved, and he was pushing mightily for the match. I extended myself to go out into society, accepting invitations as never before, hoping, I think, to find someone who was exactly like you and yet who could meet my family's expectations. Everywhere I was, there she was also, and as I *wanted* to like her, and repeatedly looked for ways we might suit...well, before I knew it, I had created expectations in her, in everyone."

I could see it all so clearly. Manipulative Anne de Bourgh, with her mother's assistance, and perhaps with the cooperation of the earl or some other spy learning which invitations he had accepted, ensuring she was always nearby—and then that the right ears heard fabrications about his intentions, creating enough talk, until an obligation had been formed in his mind. A subtle trap, indeed.

"And why should you not have?" I said, keeping my voice steady. "She had the approval of your family, the wealth to replace your sister's dowry, the beauty, and the birth."

He gave a bitter bark of laughter. "Because it was the *essence* of dishonour. To waken every morning longing to go back to sleep, to recapture the dream of you. To wish, in my heart of hearts, that the woman I had just given my body to was somebody else altogether—*every single time*—until I had to force myself to be a husband to her. It was almost a relief, really, when I found she was repeatedly unfaithful, and had an excuse to stop trying once and for all."

I took his hand, brought it to my lips, kissed his cold fingers. My heart swelled at these admissions, and I revelled in the constancy of his adoration. But I would not have him suffer needlessly.

"Dearest," I said, "I believe with all my heart that you tried to love her. It was only that she was so cold, so heartless herself, that you could not find any emotion to cling to, to build a foundation upon. Yes, you were mistaken in her character. But I do not believe for one moment that your affection for me could have withstood the test of time, had she been even slightly worthy of your efforts."

Meanwhile, I thought but did not say, *she manipulated and abused you and your loyalty and trust, separating you from nearly every person you cared for, until she finally could push you no further.*

He took my face within his hands. "Listen to me," he said. "If I had done as I ought and asked you to marry me in 1811, *none* of it might ever have happened! I could have explained Wickham's perfidies to your father and prevented the Brighton excursion that led to your parents' deaths and your sister's disgrace."

I smiled softly at him, placing my hands over his. "And yet, my darling, you forget an important impediment to our happiness. I did not *like* you then. I am certain I was perfectly capable of refusing your proposal of marriage, for all the stupidest reasons in the world."

He rested his forehead on mine. "What are the odds," he said with a hint of self-reproach, "that I might have proposed in so elegant and humble a manner so as to have changed your mind?"

"That might have been one of the labours of Hercules," I said, smiling. "And I cannot believe you said anything of your feelings for me to Anne, no matter how many times she disappointed you."

He looked into my eyes, his reflecting his deeply held regrets. "But I did. When she lay, broken and dying, as I thought, she said she was sorry, sorry for the pain she caused to me and mine. It was a deathbed repentance, but she did feel it in the moment, I was certain. And I apologised as well, for marrying her when my heart was engaged to another, and for any pain it might have brought her, however unknowingly done. I did not want her to die holding onto it all. I wanted to be free of it myself."

"I am happy she apologised at the last, for you were certainly owed one. I am happy if your confession gave you a bit of peace, for never has a man deserved it more. And if Mrs de Bourgh somehow overheard you saying it, well, perhaps the old lady *did* suspect your feelings for me. Nevertheless, I can safely state my belief that she would have despised me with every fibre of her being, with or without that information."

He pulled me into his arms, a bit more forcefully than was his wont, causing my gasp. "The best act of my entire life was begging you to marry me."

I grinned up at him, our faces so close, our breath intermingled. "I do not remember the begging, but perhaps my memory is faulty."

He did not smile back. "I knew you were going to say no," he said. "I was certain of it. I knew I had not the means of convincing you. And I thought, I must have one kiss, dear Lord, please, just one kiss, to last me the rest of my life."

And he kissed me again, taking away my breath, my mind, my reason, just as he had with the first one. This time, because I was not *quite* so astonished, I had enough sense to return it in full measure, over and over again.

When I finally caught my breath enough to speak, I whispered, "I do hope you would not have been so poor-spirited as all that, to concede defeat so easily had I been foolish enough to say no the first time you asked."

"I love you, Elizabeth," he said. "I thought I loved you then, but I had only scratched the surface of my emotion, at what I was capable of feeling for you. I want you to know that I did not bring you to Pemberley for my pleasure, though it has been everything I ever dreamed of and more. I brought you here to give you the life you ought to have had, as soon as I could give it, had I not been such a fool."

Everything felt new and bright within my soul. I was his, and he was mine; I felt younger than I had in years.

"Fitzwilliam," I said, and he kissed me again at the sound of his name upon my lips. "I *have* had, I think, the life I ought to have had. Perhaps it was not the life I would have chosen, but a valuable life. Precious years with my uncle, experiences in service that have built compassion within my soul and made of me a better mistress for Pemberley. Any wisdom I know of marriage or motherhood, I have learnt from living with my aunt Gardiner. And not simply me. If Lydia and Jane are happy, it is due to you. If you could not mend everything, you mended everything you could. It was—*is*—more than enough. I love you."

"You do?" he asked, almost as if he could not believe my words.

"*Of course* I do."

"I have been afraid to hope. When did you..." a tinge of pink touched his cheekbones, and he clamped his mouth shut.

I laughed. "When did I know I loved you? Was it the first time you came to me as a husband, and were so careful, so gentle, so...adoring, though I was so ignorant? Was it during long walks on that meandering journey home to Pemberley, tramping about the countryside so patiently whilst I explored? Was it the first time you admitted that I was in the right and you were so, so wrong?" I grinned. "I cannot fix on the hour, or the spot, or the look, or the words, which laid the foundation. It is too long ago and took hardly any time at all. I was in the middle before I knew that I had begun."

"I want you," he said, his thumbs stroking my cheeks. "I want you now."

"I will want you always," I said. "Let us go home, to our beautiful home, and to the beautiful life we have before us." I kissed him again, and grinned. "I believe there is also a beautiful bed somewhere therein."

"Not necessary," he said. And we did go home—much later—after expressing ourselves as only a couple most happily wed and violently in love could be supposed to do.

EPILOGUE

L ast night I dreamt of Pemberley again.

I woke, sitting up, heart pounding, to the lovely dawn views of Pemberley woods framed by a perfectly placed window in the bedchamber that had become 'ours' rather than 'his' long ago. Fitzwilliam smiled sleepily at me.

"Awake so early, darling?" he asked, reaching for me.

I snuggled in close beside him, waiting for the wisps of night terrors to utterly subside. I had not had the dream in many years, but it was no real surprise that it had come now. Our youngest son, Bennet, was leaving for school today, and though he was perfectly excited, with two older brothers having eagerly prepared the way, and with Richard's eldest son—Bennet's best friend—joining him in the adventure, my mother's heart *would* feel all the anxieties of this new season of life. For long minutes, Fitzwilliam and I lay facing each other while he expertly combed his fingers through my hair to ruin the braid restraining it.

"I wish tutors were adequate, and that little boys would remain little for much longer than they do," I said softly.

"We shall take great care and pay careful attention," he assured me. "The moment it appears Bennet is not thriving, we will bring him home, or find a different situation for him. I swear it."

I smiled. "You made the same promise with the other two, and I have yet to have a son returned to me."

"And you would not have it any other way," he added. "Nor I." I saw, then, his own little sorrow, joy, and pride, in perfect alignment with my own.

"Motherhood is difficult, at times," I whispered. "But you are the rock that strengthens me. I can do anything, bear anything, as long as you are beside me."

"You are my heart," he said simply. And when tenderness and affection slipped into something more passionate, I welcomed him eagerly. We would face this, as we had so much else, together.

When my husband's even breathing told me he had fallen back to sleep, I slipped out of bed and into my sitting room to watch the sun come up over the trees. On those rare occasions when the dream disturbed, I liked to be alone for a few moments to remember the past, to ensure I remained grateful for the present. Unbidden, my mind drifted to the memory of listening in on a tour of Pemberley some two or three weeks ago.

Mrs Reynolds lives on the estate and conducts the public tours on most Wednesdays for her niece, to whom she handed over the reins some years ago. Her knowledge of the place is unmatched, and though she might at times forget the day of the week, she always knows her Pemberley.

We all, of course, avoid the tours, and in a home as large as ours, it is easily done. But I was in a parlour off the gallery, deciding on paint colours for its refurbishment, and so I could hear her peroration on the portraiture, which I always enjoyed. And when she took questions, I heard them, and her answers. The first few were on provenance and worth, as usual. Every now and again, someone asked something more gossipy about the family. These enquiries were not unusual, and Mrs Reynolds had a repertoire of routine answers—all more complimentary than we, perhaps, deserved. But it had been years since Anne de Bourgh had merited one.

"Wasn't Mr Darcy married once before the current Mrs Darcy? Why isn't there a picture of her?"

The answer, of course, was that they had burned with her mother; the last time the question arose, I believe Mrs Reynolds had replied that the first Mrs Darcy's family had claimed all her portraits—truth, if not all of it. But this time there was a long pause...so lengthy, it grew awkward and I heard feet shuffling and throats clearing.

Then Mrs Reynolds said in her gentle, somewhat quavering voice, "I apologise...I am growing old. I do recollect Mr Darcy was married before the current Mrs Darcy. I remember hers was a portrait unfortunately destroyed when the old cliffside wing burned in 1820. According to her family's wishes, she was reinterred in her family cemetery in Ramsgate, beside her parents in 1821. But for the life of me, I cannot recall her name."

Another question was posed about an artist and the party moved on, but I was struck by the simplicity of her words. Mrs Reynolds is aging, doubtlessly so, but she remembers still, and in incredible detail, every fact and facet of her one true love—Pemberley. And there is nothing left of Anne de Bourgh at Pemberley. Nothing except the occasional bad dream.

Smiling, I raised the sash so that the scent of woods and

dewy morning breezes would freshen the chamber. And there Clara found me a few moments later.

"I knew you would be up early today, mistress," she murmured quietly, and I observed with appreciation the small tray she carried with a pot of chocolate upon it.

"You are a treasure," I sighed. "Will you have a cup with me?"

Clara had long since grown to be a dear friend; she was accustomed to my less formal ways, understanding that I would never forget the time I had spent in service to the Dowager Lady Matlock—now long since interred beside her husband at Matlock Court. Mr Darcy had seen to Dawson's pension. Clara would never be just a 'servant' to me.

"Not today, mistress, for I have much to occupy. Windsy is in a taking, bless her. I haven't seen her in such a state since Edward left for school. As soon as you are dressed, little Jane Elizabeth and I have much packing to do."

Mrs Lindsey—dubbed 'Windsy' many years ago by our oldest son, Fitzwilliam Thomas, until few remembered she had any other name—was the soft-hearted nurse who had charge of all the children. She was bound to be emotional today, even knowing, as she did, of Bennet's keenness to go and that Fitzwilliam and Edward impatiently awaited him. Fortunately, I had no doubts that cheerful little five-year-old Janey's disposition would ultimately prevail.

Jane Elizabeth, our surprise addition to the family, apple of her father's eye, and the beloved little ray of sunshine to everyone she met, adored 'helping', especially bestowing the favour of her talents upon Clara and Cook.

"Clara, you have the patience of Job. I will come and help you repack everything she arranges."

"No need, no need. I like to listen to her dear little thoughts—it's as good as a play, it is."

I had to smile at this. Janey had both my inquisitive nature and her father's introspective one. She noticed what few would notice, read like a child much older than her years, and had the vocabulary of one as well. My father would have adored her.

And so I dressed early, and by the time Janey stole into my sitting room—she was adept at evading nursemaids—I was ready for the day and at my desk making lists.

"Mummy!" she cried, running to me. "What are you doing?"

I lifted her onto my lap—she was my baby, after all—and cuddled her for a few precious moments. "Did you tell Susannah you were coming to visit Mummy?"

"Oh, but I don't need to! She always knows where to look first!"

I squeezed her. "And what is the rule, my sweetest lamb?"

She looked up at me with eyes identical to my own. "But Mummy, what if she says 'No'? And then I would *have* to be obedient, and I might miss you! Early mornings are the bestest times, before everyone begins asking you one million questions. And today will be worst of all because Bennet is leaving and I will miss him and Windsy was pretending to sneeze but she was crying, I know, and who will give me riding lessons and play hide and seek and pretend to let me win at chess? And everything just seems so, so terr'ble."

Janey's grief was genuine, but she was clever enough to point it out so that I would not immediately return her to the ever patient and longsuffering Susannah. Still, I snuggled her a bit more tightly.

"Do you remember what we are doing tomorrow?"

She immediately began bouncing on my lap with excitement. "Going to Auntie Tilney's!" she squealed. "And Uncle

Tilney's! Oh, oh, and I can ride with you and Auntie Bingley and Catherine Caroline sometimes!"

The Bingleys had never been close to the earl and his wife —primarily, I believe, due to Georgiana's dislike of travel and company. But once I had determined that my husband must reconnect with all his family, I dragged her and Bingley along as well. It was a *tiny* bit awkward, the first time that Jane and Bingley met at Matlock Court, but Tilney—obviously in the know—and Georgiana—obviously *not*—both contrived to put everyone at ease. And of course, the delight of the children— the Bingleys had three, two boys and a girl, with Catherine Caroline being Janey's favourite—smoothed over any little embarrassment in the beginning. It had never occurred to me, before that meeting, how much Georgiana and Jane had in common, and they quickly became the best of friends, all the scars of the past fully healed.

But little Janey was not finished with her enthusiasm. "Papa will be on Thunder and Uncle Bingley will be on Gallant and they will want me to ride with them sometimes, and Windsy and Susannah will want me with *them* some-times and Auntie and Uncle Martin will miss me if I don't ride with them, too!"

I had never become *entirely* accustomed to calling my aunt by her surname of Martin, rather than Gardiner, although I never stumbled over it aloud any longer. But just before Edward was born, Mrs Spengler had died, and in an action surprising everyone, Robert Martin and Margaret Gardiner wed. They sold the Lambton property and built another house on the Martin leasehold, Mr Martin having no interest in resuming the running of the farm. Mr Darcy arranged for another profitable lease for his nephew, as Mr Martin's son and new wife returned home to farm the Martin property. Mrs Martin the younger had a pretty sister, with whom

Richard Williams grew smitten, and in less time than I could ever have expected, the shy steward was married and beginning a family of his own. His eldest son and my Bennet were fast friends, and I was delighted they would have each other in this new adventure.

Watching Bennet and young Richard happily playing, I had often reflected on history repeating itself. Once again, the steward of Pemberley had a son who was godson to its master. But Emma Williams, Richard's wife, was nothing like old Mrs Wickham; an excellent and capable manager, she was a good mother and kept a happy home. Bennet had been as much a son to her, almost, as her own; Fitzwilliam and I felt likewise about young Richard. And of course, the boys had all grown up on stories of how a different Pemberley boy almost the same age as their papas had made all the wrong, mean, and selfish choices he could make, instead of helpful and kind ones, ultimately coming to a bad end, dying on a transport ship bound for Australia.

Pemberley, of course, was flourishing. Perhaps England had its troubles, but our little corner of it was idyllic. Our library was rather famous—nothing like the Bodleian in Oxford, certainly, but scholars from all over northern England took advantage of its vast wealth of knowledge.

Life was not perfect, of course, for no life ever was. The death of my sister, Mary, of a fever in '31, had struck me rather hard. I had never been close to her, but she was my sister, a part of my youth, and my only real connexion to Longbourn, which she had loved more than any of us. I do not believe that Charlotte, for all she had given Mary a home these many years, truly understood her either. But she had written to me very sweetly, of all the kindnesses Mary had extended in devoted service to her family, and of the sorrow of her children at her loss. And then she'd added a startling observation: "*Mr Collins is devastated. He loved her, you know, as she did him. Oh, neither of them ever admitted it, to themselves even, I am certain. And I have long been convinced I was put on this earth to keep them both sensible, for I seldom heard a practical thought from either. But with Mary gone, I suppose I shall have to listen to him much more than is my custom. I shall miss her every day for the rest of my life.*"

"Mummy, will I meet my Auntie Philips? I don't remember her."

Since Janey sounded a bit worried, I hastened to reassure her. "You will, my darling, but you are not to be anxious. She is very kind. She met you at your christening and thought you were the most beautiful baby girl in the world. And Auntie Duncan will be there too, of course. You know her."

Ellen Gardiner Duncan was her cousin, of course, but in Ellen's several visits to us accompanied by her husband and children, it had been easier for Janey to think of and address her as 'aunt'.

"Yes!" Janey said proudly. "And she will bring the twins! And she will paint us a big, beautiful picture!"

Ellen had married the son of her old drawing master, a Mr Ethan Duncan, himself an already-established portrait artist, and they worked together brilliantly. He and Ellen were meeting us at Matlock Court to begin work on my birthday gift from my husband—a portrait of Jane, Kitty, and I together, something I had grieved over not having done sooner, after losing Mary. Many examples of their exquisite work already hung in the Pemberley portrait gallery, as the Duncans had produced all of our family portraits for the last several years.

"Will Auntie Bingley be in the picture?"

"Not this one, darling. She is a Darcy sister, and this picture will have only Bennet sisters in it, and she says she needs all her attention to keep little Charles out of trouble. But your Uncle Bingley will have another commission for Ellen soon."

"Of Catherine Caroline! She told me when she is twelve years old, she will go up on the wall by Auntie Bingley's portrait when *she* was twelve! Yes! And we're going to send a small Bennet sister picture to Auntie Bracket in 'merica," Janey added.

I had written often to Lydia over the years, without any reply. For all I'd known, she had consigned them to flames, unread. But, since she gave no specific instruction for me to cease writing, I continued to do so, care of Mr Darcy's man of business in America. My first letter was full of apologies, I think, but as the years passed, I wrote to her of simple, family things, such as I often shared with my other sisters. I ensured that she would know each of her nieces and nephews, if she cared to, and of all the doings of the Gardiner offspring.

But it was my grieving letter regarding Mary's death to which she finally responded. My missive was one long letter of 'Do you remember?' anecdotes of Mary's life—a few shared by Charlotte over the years, but most of them from when we were young and silly girls at Longbourn. I had recorded some of Papa's sly witticisms at her expense— which she'd never understood—and Mama's hysteria the time when, at the tender age of six years, Mary gave her bonnet to the goat because it was too 'ostentatious' for Sundays, she felt.

Three months later, I received a letter from Lydia in a package which included a miniature likeness of herself with her husband.

She looks *exactly* like Mama. I had laughed and wept to see it.

"Mama, are you sad?" Janey said, her sensitive little heart immediately perceiving my feelings.

"I was just a little lost in memories," I replied. "But I am not at all sad. How could I be, when I have you, your brothers, your papa, your aunts and uncles and cousins and all of Pemberley, all to love, and a wonderful trip to Matlock Court to look forward to?"

"But why does Auntie Bracket have to live all the way to 'merica?"

"That is rather a long, sometimes sad and often happy story, in which there are several heroes and several fools," I replied. "And some are both, at the same time. Someday, when you are a quite a bit older, I shall tell it to you."

"Like Hans in 'The Poor Miller's Boy and The Cat'?" she asked, naming one of her favourite tales. "He was foolish, but it did not hurt him. Mummy, why do boys have to go to school? I will read every book in our library, and be smarter than them all!"

"And then you shall be cleverer than your old Papa, and *he* shall read while *you* take care of Pemberley," came a deep voice from the doorway.

"Papa!" Janey cried, running to him with her arms outstretched. He swung her high in the air, as she loved, his laughter and her squeals of delight filling Pemberley with joy, before finally bestowing the kisses she demanded.

He was the handsomest man of my acquaintance, still. Moments like these, watching his real and obvious affection for the child we had created together, my heart swelled with love for them both. We did not, either of us, take our happiness for granted.

"I believe Susannah is searching for you, young lady," he said, with mock severity. "How would it be if you allow her to help you dress and do your hair? The day is wasting."

"Bennet is leaving today," she said mournfully, in case this would delay morning ablutions. "Mama is sad, and I am helping her be happy."

"As I understand, Clara is in great need of assistance with packing for our journey. I will shoulder the burden of cheering Mama." Slyly, he winked at me.

I smiled at them both. "And I thank you for your kind help, sweetling. But let Papa take you to Susannah now, so that you do not disappoint Clara."

"Very well," she sighed, laying her head upon her father's shoulder.

He bent to kiss me before turning to leave, but Janey called out to me, and he paused in the doorway.

"Mama, you should write down your story of fools and heroes, so you do not forget it before I am old enough to hear. What is it called?"

"Oh, it does not have a name," I replied. "But I will not forget."

The End

The author and publisher thank you for reading this book. We hope you have enjoyed it. The favour of your review would be greatly appreciated.

Subscribers to the Quills & Quartos mailing list receive advance notice of new releases and sales, and exclusive bonus content and short stories. To join, visit us at www.QuillsandQuartos.com

ACKNOWLEDGMENTS

I mean this book as a tribute to the influence of beloved Jane Austen and Daphne DuMaurier, though it does not approach the genius of either. Also, it would never have been written except for the persuasive efforts of Sarah Cooper and Allyson Kuykendall, and their commitment to choosing Netflix over sleep. Ladies, you are an inspiration.

ABOUT THE AUTHOR

Julie Cooper, a California native, lives with her Mr Darcy (without the arrogance or the Pemberley) of nearly forty years, two dogs (one intelligent, one goofball), and Kevin the Cat (smarter than all of them.) They have four children and four grandchildren, all of whom are brilliant and adorable, and she has the pictures to prove it. She works as an executive at a gift basket company and her tombstone will read, 'Have your Christmas gifts delivered at least four days before the 25th.' Her hobbies include reading, giving other people good advice, and wondering why no one follows it.

In addition to *Nameless*, Julie is also the author of *Tempt Me* and its companion novella *Seek Me; The Perfect Gentleman;* and *Lost & Found*.

to attend to the business of producing heirs and keep out of all else. A girl easily moulded, incurious, indifferent, and demanding nothing beyond access to his fortune.

Fitzwilliam Darcy knows exactly who he needs. He can fix on the hour, the spot, the look, and the words which laid the foundation for an obsession he rejected. But ten years later, at an assembly in an obscure village in Hertfordshire, he finds himself in the middle once more.

His needs are unalterable. But can he resist the one woman he truly wants?

Seek Me: Georgiana's Story

...death cannot stop true love.

The happily-ever-after for the Vampyre world's most important couple goes on for centuries, but the daughter of Fitzwilliam and Elizabeth Darcy is seeking her own happiness. Dr Georgiana Darcy has spent two centuries pursuing a career dedicated to helping others, but has yet to find romantic love. That could change when the Darcys and their Vampyre family return to Pemberley for the first time since Georgiana was a young girl. Will history repeat itself, and another generation of Darcys fall in love with a mortal?

Seek Me is a companion novella to Julie Cooper's *Tempt Me* and tells the story of Dr Georgiana Darcy's quest for love.

Lost and Found

Sisters. Chaos at home. A father who isn't paying attention. A powerful hero, whose behaviour is anything but heroic. Sound familiar? Some of our favourite characters from *Pride & Prejudice* star in this story set in Fairy Tale England, where enchantments—of the magical and of the heart—meet.

Once upon a time, there lived two sisters. Jane was fair, with mild blue eyes and hair the colour of corn silk. Elizabeth had long, dark, thick curls and eyes the startling green of a spring glade. Soon after the arrival of an evil stepmother, the girls found themselves starving and alone in the woods.

Their fairy tale ending is not easy to accomplish as one sister disappears into the home of a witch and the other sister—the valiant Elizabeth—is set to work as her slave. Wickedness is all around, and only by working with, and trusting, the cursed master of Pemberley can she break free of her captor, and release her sister and her beloved Darcy from the spells cast by the witch.

Made in the USA
Columbia, SC
30 June 2021